M.A. Nichols

Copyright © 2024 by M.A. Nichols

All rights reserved. No part of this publication may be reproduced or transmitted, in any form or by any means, electronic, mechanical, photocopying, recording, or otherwise, without the prior permission of the copyright owner.

The characters and events portrayed in this book are fictitious. Any similarity to real persons, living or dead, is coincidental and not intended by the author.

Books by M.A. Nichols

Generations of Love Series

The Kingsleys

Flame and Ember
Hearts Entwined
A Stolen Kiss

The Ashbrooks

A True Gentleman
The Shameless Flirt
A Twist of Fate
The Honorable Choice
A Light in the Dark

The Finches

The Jack of All Trades
Tempest and Sunshine
The Christmas Wish

The Leighs

An Accidental Courtship
Love in Disguise
His Mystery Lady

A Debt of Honor

Christmas Courtships

A Holiday Engagement
Beneath the Mistletoe

Standalone Romances

Honor and Redemption
A Tender Soul
A Passing Fancy
To Have and to Hold

Fantasy Novels

The Villainy Consultant Series

Geoffrey P. Ward's Guide to Villainy
Geoffrey P. Ward's Guide to Questing
Magic Slippers: A Novella

The Shadow Army Trilogy

Smoke and Shadow
Blood Magic
A Dark Destiny

Table of Contents

Chapter 1 1
Chapter 2 11
Chapter 3 22
Chapter 4 27
Chapter 5 35
Chapter 6 42
Chapter 7 50
Chapter 8 58
Chapter 9 65
Chapter 10 71
Chapter 11 78
Chapter 12 85
Chapter 13 96
Chapter 14 103
Chapter 15 113
Chapter 16 121
Chapter 17 129
Chapter 18 138

Chapter 19	145
Chapter 20	155
Chapter 21	162
Chapter 22	168
Chapter 23	175
Chapter 24	186
Chapter 25	194
Chapter 26	202
Chapter 27	210
Chapter 28	217
Chapter 29	224
Chapter 30	231
Chapter 31	239
Chapter 32	246
Chapter 33	255
Chapter 34	263
Chapter 35	271
Chapter 36	278
Chapter 37	286
Chapter 38	293
Chapter 39	300
Epilogue	307

Chapter 1

Greater Edgerton, Lancashire
Spring 1831

"No."

A single word, yet it rang out like a booming cannon. Three sets of hard eyes turned, staring him down, and Benjamin forced his spine not to bow beneath the weighty silence.

Birthdays were a source of celebration. Or at least they had been in Benjamin Leigh's life. Though most eschewed such anniversaries, his had been met with parties, well-wishes, and presents aplenty. The day revolved entirely around his whims, and despite the twinge of guilt that dimmed the day when he compared the festivities to those afforded to his sisters (namely, none), Benjamin couldn't help but enjoy the grand jubilee surrounding the commemoration of when he'd entered this mortal coil.

Twenty birthdays gone, and each had built to this all-important twenty-first. Yet rather than participating in anything celebratory, Benjamin found himself spending his birthday in his father's study.

Father sat behind his desk, the joy leaching from his expression as he watched Benjamin with a narrowed gaze. Mother perched at Benjamin's right, her frilly handkerchief dabbing frantically at her cheeks. And Mr. Longman hedged in on the other side, his eyes darting amongst the trio as his fingers tapped a busy beat against his leather satchel.

A long silence stretched out as Mother's tears worsened and Father's expression darkened, and Benjamin tried to breathe. Finally, Mr. Longman broke the standoff.

"You do realize what this means to your family, Master Benjamin?" the solicitor asked. "The entail your grandfather placed on the estate prohibits your father from selling off any of the property—even unnecessary parcels. Your parents do not intend to split the fields and decimate the family's income. Quite the opposite, in fact. The money they can make from that venture will provide handsomely for the family and overcome any deficit they currently face. If you do not break the entail, Whitley Court will remain whole, but at great personal cost to your parents."

Meaning Mother couldn't expand the dining room, parlor, and drawing room to meet her high social aspirations, nor could Father build himself a library to rival the one in ancient Alexandria. Great personal cost, indeed.

Mr. Longman's fingers tapped along the satchel once more, as though beating to an unheard melody. "At present, they cannot even mortgage the property to pay for necessary improvements, as many—if not most—estates do from time to time. This leaves your parents in an inevitable position of living solely off the income generated from the current estate, which is far less than it ought to be after so many economic downturns our nation has faced over the past years. To say nothing of the vast modernizations and mechanizations required to compete in the farming industry, all of which cannot be adopted without funds."

Solicitors were renowned for their ability to twist logic to their own means, and Mr. Longman was a credit to his profession. For all that his pleadings were sound, they were naught but a thin rainbow veneer painted over a dark truth: the Leighs' motives had naught to do with necessary improvements to the estate, and breaking the entail would only bring grief upon the family.

Perhaps not to his parents, but to the future generations.

"As you are the heir and have now reached your majority, Master Benjamin," continued Mr. Longman, "you can overturn your grandfather's edict, break the entail, and allow your father to run the estate properly. Without your assistance, Whitley Court will flounder. Please do not allow your family's legacy to be ruined—"

"You know all this, Son," interrupted Father, his gaze growing stony as he stared his son down. "Now is not the time for missishness. You know your duty. Sign the agreement, and we will be done with the wretched thing."

"Do it now, Benjamin," added Mother with a sharp sob. "Do not hurt us so. We've given you so much, and we ask only for this little thing."

Drawing in a deep breath, Benjamin sorted through his words. What more could he say? The simple "no" had done no good—not that he had anticipated anything else. Of course, he'd known this conversation would be dreadful, but reality rarely matched anticipation, being either better or worse than those imaginings. Unfortunately for Benjamin, this situation seemed to be firmly stuck in the latter possibility.

Mother wept, and Father glared with enough heat that Benjamin was liable to burst into flames.

"I promised Grandmother Cora I wouldn't," he blurted.

If nothing else, being a Leigh taught one to act; when one's parents rejected reality, one must adopt fantasy, and Benjamin was trotting his talents out in force and keeping his cheeks from flaming. That statement wasn't a lie, but blaming it upon his grandmother was an act of cowardice.

"Don't be ridiculous," said Father with a scoff. "You were a child when she passed—"

"Yet I remember her clearly, and she made me promise never to break the entail. To sign that document would be to go back on my word. A gentleman's honor is paramount, after all," replied Benjamin, snatching old and familiar words his father was fond of saying.

"Don't be ludicrous!" Mother shot to her feet, drawing her son and Mr. Longmore up as well (though Father kept his seat). But it was more habit than conscious decision that spurred Benjamin to move, for he was too shocked at her tone to register the mannerly need to stand in the presence of a lady. "After everything we have done for you, how can you be so selfish?"

Selfish was a strange word. When turned inward, it was rarely warranted, for those with such self-awareness were generally too aware of others to be truly egotistical. No, it was the rallying cry of the hypocrite, for those lacking any charitable inclinations were quick to trot it out. His parents adored the word.

So, it was no surprise that she introduced that old friend, yet Benjamin couldn't help his brows from climbing at her tone. Mother was no demure flower incapable of raising her voice; the house rang with her demands and exclamations when she was distraught, and his sisters had often vexed her to no end.

But never Benjamin.

Her dear boy.

Despite her being far shorter than Benjamin, it felt as though Mother towered over him as she railed at him, unleashing vitriol he'd never received before.

"You ungrateful child! I demand you sign it now—"

"Gertrude!" snapped Father, cutting off her tirade. Whipping around to glare at her husband, Mother drew in a deep breath, straightening her spine and lifting her chin in the air before she turned away and stormed out of the study. The door slammed behind her, reverberating through the air.

Father nodded at their seats, and Benjamin slowly took his.

With a tight smile, the gentleman drew in a breath. "I applaud your sense of duty, but surely you have a duty to us as well. Your mother and I have done so much for you, and we are only asking this small favor in return. We fully plan to keep the majority of the estate intact and only trim the fat, so to speak. Every estate has unnecessary bits of land, and selling them off is no great loss to the property as a whole. But if that does not suit you, we can take out a minor mortgage on the property instead. Something manageable. My father wouldn't begrudge me that."

Benjamin held his tongue, giving himself a moment to gather his thoughts. Though he didn't believe Father was blatantly lying, the assertions that it would only be "minor mortgages" and "unnecessary bits of land" sold off in their pursuit of greater wealth were certainly shortsighted; once fostered, greed never remained within set bounds, and his parents had fed and coddled theirs until it was quite the ravenous beast. Small actions often led to large regrets.

An estate's income came from agriculture and husbandry, neither of which was possible without land, and masters never intended to hobble their fortune by selling off the majority of their property. They trimmed the edges here and there until the whole of it was eaten away, and his parents were certainly shortsighted enough to believe they wouldn't do such a thing while still doing it.

As Virgil once said, "The descent to hell is easy"—or rather, *"Facilis descensus Averno,"* but the translation had been close enough to suit his schoolmasters. And nothing would be easier than to sign the agreement. Just as it would be easy to justify larger mortgages and splitting up more of the property.

"I must do as my conscience dictates," said Benjamin, rising to his feet once more. Though he didn't scurry away, he moved with purpose toward the door, stepping through it before Father could stop him. Striding down the corridor, Benjamin couldn't outrun the feelings nipping at his heels.

People often spent their lives in search of a purpose and meaning and never understood the weight that came with such a curse. Benjamin's had been conceived before his birth, springing into being the moment Grandfather Edwin had placed the entail, and it had been a constant companion through his childhood.

Benjamin Leigh had a purpose, to be certain, and it only involved a signature.

That knowledge pressed down on him, squeezing his chest like a vise. Such a little thing, yet to give in would be to see the end of his ancestral home, and to remain firm would bring his parents' scorn. Cursing them and Grandfather Edwin, Benjamin scowled. Whatever he chose would cause pain, and though he was not the source of the trouble, he would be forced to bear the brunt of it.

He needed to get out of this house. Away from these people. With the front door in sight, his feet picked up their pace, drawing him toward the freedom beyond.

"Letter for you, sir," said Polly with a bob.

Impulse wanted to ignore her; he was in no mood for correspondence; he needed to move. But even as Benjamin's hand landed on the door handle, a familiar voice rang through his thoughts, chiding him for his cool treatment.

"True gentility isn't born of money. It is demonstrating kindness to everyone, regardless of their rank or status."

Though Benjamin couldn't attribute those words directly to Mr. Price, his conscience had taken the form of his schoolmaster's voice, and the sentiment aligned with the fellow's teachings, so Benjamin couldn't dismiss them.

"My thanks, Polly," he said, taking the letter from her as he continued on his way. A small kindness, something of which she received little with a demanding mistress and oblivious master.

Bright air enveloped him, soothing his heart in a way that only springtime could. The shifting of the seasons carried an extra vitality, filling one with all the possibilities the future could bring. Benjamin's feet moved faster, his shoes crunching against the gravel, and he filled his lungs again and again. Just being free of Whitley Court's confining walls lightened his spirits. As much as he longed to fetch his horse and gallop across the blooming countryside, his clothes weren't fit for the endeavor, and the thought of crossing back over the threshold made his stomach sour.

Visiting David was a possibility, though he dismissed that thought as readily as it appeared. Even before his marriage, David Archer had been a busy man, but now, happily situated with his bride, the fellow had little time for Benjamin anymore—despite being both a friend and now his brother-in-law. One might think marrying into the family would ensure the friends would see each other more often, but one would be wrong.

Letting out a sharp huff, Benjamin crossed the lawn and dropped to the ground beneath the great oak tree. Keeping it between him and the stables and house ensured him as much privacy as could be afforded in this wretched place.

The letter crunched in his hand, and, glancing at the inscription, he set it aside. As the handwriting wasn't familiar, it couldn't be important, and there were far more pressing matters that needed his attention at present.

However, Benjamin had spent most of his life considering these troubles. He couldn't recall a time when he hadn't known his role in the family and his value to his parents. He was the one to save them from the entail. And it had been some time since he'd decided where he stood on the issue. Unfortunately, it hadn't provided him with any clarity on how to manage it all.

Getting his sister married off to David had been a great victory on that front, for Katherine wouldn't be made to feel his parents' wrath for Benjamin's decision. And his promise to Grandmother Cora granted him a stay of execution. However, he knew his parents too well to think this was the end of it.

Thoughts swirled in his head like a whirlpool, dragging him downward. A happy birthday, indeed.

Benjamin glanced at the letter. With a sigh, he snatched it up. A distraction was just what he needed.

Breaking the seal, he found a second sealed letter inside the first—and he knew that handwriting very well—but his attention turned back to the open missive.

Dear Mr. Benjamin Leigh,

I regret to inform you that Mr. Irving Price passed away.

The air fled his lungs, and Benjamin stared at those little words that shattered the last remnants of happiness he possessed. The words blurred, and his ribs constricted. Mr. Price was dead?

After a prolonged battle with lung fever, he succumbed to the illness on the 7th of February. He wrote your letter on his deathbed, and as his vicar, he gave me charge to deliver it. I apologize for not sending it sooner, but I have been quite busy of late as I've assisted his daughter in planning his funeral, settling his affairs, and securing her a new situation.

Sincerely,
Mr. M. Gastrell

Such a small thing, yet those few lines struck Benjamin like an icepick to the heart. Mr. Price was gone. Though he hadn't seen his old schoolmaster since leaving Weathersby College, their letters back and forth had been a balm. And now, he didn't even have that connection.

Benjamin's eyes prickled, and despite the phantom voices of old school chums mocking such a display of weakness, he couldn't fight the emotion rising to the forefront. Mr. Price was dead. Lowering his head, he let the droplets fall, the world blurring as he embraced the moment, allowing himself to fully mourn the gentleman's absence. Leaning against the trunk, he clutched the letter as his mind flooded with memories of his time at school.

Despite the misery in his heart, the sun shone brightly above, trekking slowly across the azure expanse. The first truly glorious weather they'd had since winter had given way to spring. That it coincided with his birthday celebrations had seemed providential, but he'd been a fool to think such a thing.

Curiosity pressed him to break the seal and scour the dear man's final words, yet Benjamin couldn't bear to do so. There would be no other letter from Mr. Price. No more shared laughter. No more words of guidance. No more kind rebukes. To open that folded paper would be to confirm the wretched truth, making the loss real.

Yet Benjamin couldn't ignore it forever.

My dear Mr. Leigh,

I am sorry to say that the physician thinks I am unlikely to survive this illness, so I am writing to give you my final farewell. It has been a pleasure to watch you grow into the young man you've become, and I am very proud of all you have accomplished in your life. I have taught many over the years, and though they are all dear to me, you are like the son I always longed to have.

That sentiment, echoing from his own heart, brought forth another bout of tears, and Benjamin didn't bother to wipe them away. Tucked away as he was, there was no one to see him mourn the man who'd been more a father to him than Osmond Leigh.

As my adopted son, so to speak, I hope you will help me in my darkest hour. Though I pray for a miracle, I am happy with the life I have lived and feel at peace with whatever may come—except concerning my daughter, Ann. We have little money, and with my passing, she will lose her home as well. I have no other family to claim her. She will be left alone and at the mercy of an all too merciless world.

Benjamin stared at the words, his heart sinking even as his brain struggled to comprehend that which his instincts recognized was happening.

Please, Benjamin. I beg you with my dying breath that you will do for her what I cannot. I know what this will mean to you, and I do not ask it lightly. I have no one else who can do this for us. She needs protection and a home. Safety and family.

I give her into your care, my dear boy. Please watch over her.

Sincerely,
I. Price

Tears gone, Benjamin's eyes darted through the letter twice more before his hand fell away, dropping the paper to the ground whilst he leaned against the trunk, his eyes wide and unblinking as he stared at the horizon. This could not be true.

Yet Benjamin hadn't mistaken the meaning. Mr. Price wanted him to marry his daughter.

Chapter 2

Mr. Price may not have written the dreaded "M" word, but the meaning was rife in his pleadings. A bachelor, especially a young one, could not shelter or financially aid a grown woman without fundamentally destroying her reputation. Only lightskirts were treated thusly, and Mr. Price would never wish his daughter to join those ranks, even if only in public opinion.

For all that Mr. Price claimed him as a son, Benjamin wasn't one by blood, nor did he know Miss Price well enough to claim an emotional tie that might allay society's judgments and allow him to provide without being her husband. As the Prices lived away from the school, Benjamin's path hadn't crossed Miss Price's much in the decade he'd called Weathersby home, and he knew little of the girl.

A year or two older than him perhaps, but that could very well be a misperception, for she was tall enough to rival a man. And all elbows and knees, from what he could recall. But her porcelain complexion would've been the envy of his mother and sisters—if not for the fact that it was paired with silver-blond hair and gray-blue eyes, giving her an unnaturally monochromatic appearance. Rather like a specter come to life.

I give her into your care, my dear boy. Please watch over her.

The vise around his chest tightened its hold once more as he considered the breadth of Mr. Price's request. Marry a stranger? Such a thing to ask. It was impossible. Matrimony was not a small favor. It was a lifetime commitment. And what did he have to offer her? Heir he may be, but Benjamin Leigh was in a precarious position at present. No doubt their vicar could do more for Ann Price than he.

Lifting the first letter, Benjamin read Mr. Gastrell's words again. The conclusion caught Benjamin's attention as it hadn't before.

...I have been quite busy of late as I've assisted his daughter in planning his funeral, settling his affairs, and securing her a new situation.

That was significant, wasn't it? Whether or not Mr. Price had vast amounts of money, he'd owned a massive library worth no small sum. And the vicar was assisting Miss Price. Though Mr. Gastrell didn't disclose what the new "situation" entailed, it sounded promising. Surely a vicar wouldn't turn his back on one of his flock.

Miss Price had lived in Birmingham her entire life. She had friends and community. Would it be right to uproot her and transplant her into a war between him and his parents? Surely, after such upheaval, Miss Price wouldn't wish to marry some scruffy former student of her father's.

Clearly, Mr. Price had written without discussing it with the vicar, and though it spoke well of him that his final thoughts were of his daughter, a fever-addled mind didn't boast the soundest judgment. Benjamin wished to do right by Mr. Price, but surely, if the gentleman's wits had been intact, he would've realized how bizarre it was to ask this of anyone.

Or perhaps in his weakened state, Mr. Price's good sense had been eroded enough that he didn't understand the implications rife in his plea. Matrimony may not have been his intention. Perhaps Benjamin could simply send a bit of money to

Miss Price anonymously; he didn't have much ready cash at the moment, but a few pounds now and then might be all that was required.

Perhaps he could ask Mr. Gastrell to write if Miss Price required more assistance.

Yes.

Those thoughts settled into his heart with a rightness that lightened his spirits considerably. There was no need to be hasty, after all. Mr. Price, himself, had counseled against foolhardy actions and rushing into action before careful consideration, and over the passing days when doubts drew his attention once more, Benjamin merely needed to point back to his reasoning, and that discontent settled again and again.

Surely, matrimony wasn't what Mr. Price intended. Mr. Gastrell had settled Miss Price in a comfortable situation, so she surely didn't need some young man sweeping into her life, disrupting it once more when she had already suffered so much.

Yet when he placed the mourning band on his arm every morning and spied it in looking glasses, Benjamin was struck anew with those concerns. And when those days turned to weeks, those niggling doubts strengthened, forever haunting his thoughts as the justifications weakened.

Which was ridiculous! Miss Price was quite content. Settled with the assistance of the vicar. No doubt, she was surrounded by ladies of the parish and being looked after far better than any ridiculous bachelor, a year or two her junior, could do.

Surely Mr. Gastrell would've responded to his letter if there were a pressing need. Benjamin had been forthright in his correspondence to the vicar, and a man of the cloth wouldn't miss the meaning behind the inquiry, so if Miss Price required something more than the assistance she was already receiving, Mr. Gastrell would send word.

But then again, the vicar had been slow in forwarding on his parishioner's final words, and though Benjamin couldn't claim a close acquaintance with Mr. Gastrell (having never required the vicar's assistance during his time at school), the gentleman seemed a tad forgetful. Or had Mr. Gastrell's letter been waylaid? It wasn't commonplace, but neither was it unheard of for missives to go missing on their journey from sender to receiver.

That was simply creating trouble where there was none. The faint memory of some phrase or quote from some long-dead philosopher tickled his mind, though Benjamin couldn't recall who it was or the pearls of wisdom it bestowed. But surely it was better to let things lie than to rush off anticipating evils that may never befall.

Miss Price was happily situated. Mr. Gastrell hadn't bothered to write. Benjamin could send her a bit of money here and there. All would be well. The rightness of that settled into him once more, allowing him some peace, but as Benjamin leaned into an armchair, he found himself staring off at the wall opposite, his eyes not noticing the pattern of the curtains framing the window.

Sunlight filtered around the heavy fabric, warming the space, and Benjamin rather longed to stretch out on the rug in the golden glow, though that would draw odd looks from his hosts.

"You force your way into my study, and then you just sit there, silently stewing?" asked David in a dry tone as he scribbled a few notes in his ledger.

With raised brows, Benjamin turned his gaze to his sister, who lazed on the sofa beside him, her feet propped on a footstool and a thick blanket wrapped around her.

"Are you not going to defend me, Katherine?" he asked. When that elicited no response, Benjamin spoke her name louder, and she jerked her attention from the book. "You are reading while your brother has come to visit you?"

Katherine huffed. "You burst into our home, demanding our attention, and then grew quiet and sullen. I was bored of watching you."

Benjamin sighed and settled deeper into his chair. "And here I'd believed marriage had softened you."

Snapping the book shut, Katherine turned her full attention to him. "If you wish to visit, then speak."

"You are being unusually pensive," added David in a distracted tone, without looking up from his work. "What has you so preoccupied?"

"With Mother and Father in a frenzy over the entail? Is it any wonder?" he responded with a dry laugh.

Katherine straightened, her brows furrowing. "What have they been up to?"

"Nothing since my birthday, thank the heavens," said Benjamin. "I had expected them to lay siege, but they haven't mentioned a word about it since."

"That is only temporary," she replied with a frown. "With you in mourning, I doubt they wish to open themselves up to possible scrutiny and judgment by haranguing you."

Drawing in a deep breath, Benjamin considered that. "I've spent significant time reviewing the ledgers and household accounts in secret, and I've consulted the steward, and we are both confident that the estate is healthy, and Whitley Court will thrive without breaking the entail. No doubt Mother and Father will ask me again, but they've accepted my reason, and though they were angry at first, things have settled now."

He straightened and smiled, the memory of his victory playing through his thoughts again. "In fact, things are better than before. Mr. Turley recommends a few improvements, and as he's been the steward for a few decades now, I trust his assessment. Though Mother and Father refuse to curtail their spending in any manner, I discovered some wasted funds and diverted them into investments that should pay off handsomely with some patience. There's no reason we cannot afford the improvements in a year or two without a mortgage or selling off the property. As of now, the only threat to Whitley Court's future is breaking the entail and allowing our parents free rein, and unless that changes, I will not change my mind. And they cannot force me to sign it."

"Do not underestimate them, Benjamin," she murmured.

David's gaze lifted from his work and turned toward his wife. Then, setting down his quill, he added, "But there is more to your quiet than that. Something is clearly bothering you. Is it to do with your work on the estate? I thought Mr. Turley was keen to have the assistance—"

"All is well on that front. As you said, it has taken some time for him to grow comfortable with my taking on some of the responsibilities, but he's been left with far more to do than he has hours in the day, and he's starting to see I am in earnest." Benjamin huffed, a hint of a smirk on his lips. "I had thought it might be difficult to keep it from Father, but Mr. Turley speaks to him as little as possible, and as long as he's left to his books, Father is blind."

"Then out with it," said David with a frown. "What is the matter?"

Drawing in a deep breath, Benjamin firmly grasped his resolve and replied in a light tone, "My former schoolmaster asked me to marry his daughter."

That earned him the shocked reaction he'd desired; his sister and his friend sat there with twin expressions—eyes wide, they stared at him—and Benjamin forced a laugh.

"Not truly, but he did ask me to 'assist' the girl. However, the man wrote to me on his deathbed and his wits were addled, I do not believe he knew what he was asking. He simply wanted to ensure she had someone to watch over her. However, she is too old for a guardian, and I am not certain what to do for her or if I even ought to. It sounds as though she is quite happily settled, as their vicar found her a new situation. I wrote to the fellow, and he would've replied if something were amiss or I could do something for the girl. Surely, he would do so. He's a vicar, and it is his duty to see to his flock, after all."

The words came out in a rush, muddling all his carefully considered explanations into a jumbled mess. These thoughts had plagued him for a month now, and it was impossible to distill all that pondering into a few succinct sentences.

Katherine held up a staying hand, and Benjamin stopped his babbling.

"That is a lot to ask of a pupil..." she began.

"He wasn't simply a schoolmaster to me, and I was not merely a pupil to him." Benjamin drew in a deep breath and let it out in a long sigh. "When I left for school, I was very much on a path to be the spoiled 'darling' our parents groomed me to be. You girls and our grandmother attempted to keep my pride in check, but it was impossible not to believe myself so very much more important than everyone else. Mother and Father gave me anything I desired and praised me to no end."

Rising to his feet, David moved around his desk and sat beside his wife, grasping her hand in his.

"Then I went to school, and I was surrounded by other boys just as wealthy and connected as I was," continued Benjamin. "That provided me with a healthy dose of humility. However, it was Mr. Price who altered my path. He was wise and kind and took me under his wing, yet he didn't spare my feelings when I needed correction. He expected much of me, and to have someone who gave genuine praise and honest censure when needed was far more appealing than I would've believed before I left for school."

"And you grew to hate being at home more and more," said Katherine with a sad smile.

Benjamin's heart panged at the sentiment steeped in those few words. Only a few months ago, he had considered her irredeemably irritating, but with his eyes now opened to the depths lurking beneath her prickly exterior, he could honestly answer that statement.

"Not because of you, Katherine. But whenever I am around our parents, it is far too easy to slip into the role of pampered fool, which they wish me to be. Mr. Price was so good to me and helped me to become something better..."

The pain of that loss made itself known once more, though the strength had ebbed somewhat in the passing weeks. Strangely enough, it wasn't speaking of Mr. Price that had the power to fell him anymore. No, it was the strange, quiet little moments when he found himself thinking, "What would Mr. Price say?" Or when Benjamin longed to write to him of his new work on the estate or ask for advice on what to do about the conundrum in which he'd found himself.

"And he wrote to you on his deathbed to ask you to take care of his daughter," said David.

"He gave her into my care," Benjamin clarified.

His friend's brows rose. "That sounds like matrimony to me."

Shaking his head, Benjamin offered the words he'd clung to over the past weeks. "He never said a word about marriage. He just wished for someone to watch over her, and the vicar seems to be doing just that."

"Seems to?" asked Katherine with an arched brow.

But David spoke at the same time. "That is matrimony, and you know it, Benjamin. No matter how fever-addled you claim his mind to have been, he wouldn't have wished his daughter to be viewed as a lady with loose morals, and you are not her brother to take care of her without raising speculation. If he gave her into your care, I think it's clear that he wanted you to marry her. Begged you to, in fact—with his dying breath."

Benjamin's gaze jerked away from his friend, turning back to the curtains and the window, though he didn't see either. For all that the tightness in his chest had eased at times, that vise remained fixed around his ribs, making itself known at odd moments. Or perhaps it wasn't that the tightness eased as much as he'd grown so used to it that he didn't notice the pressure.

Rubbing at his sternum, he rose to his feet and paced the length of the room. "I am in no position to marry. I haven't an income beyond my allowance, and with all the unrest at home, how can I in good conscience bring another into that mess?"

"And you're more comfortable with ignoring the dying wish of a man whom you considered a father figure?" asked Katherine.

"Of course not! But marriage?" Throwing his arms wide as though pleading with the heavens, Benjamin launched into a detailed description of all his reasons that he'd settled on leaving Miss Ann Price be. Having given the idea much thought, Benjamin didn't want for strong excuses, however haphazard they were.

"Even if Mr. Price had intended for me to marry his daughter, surely he wouldn't have asked such a thing if he knew the full extent of my circumstances," said Benjamin. "Katherine, you keep saying that Mother and Father won't leave things be, so is it fair to bring her into such an uncomfortable situation? My allowance isn't enough to allow us to secure our own lodgings if they are beastly to her."

Katherine turned her gaze from her brother to her husband; though Benjamin couldn't surmise the meaning in that expression, David seemed to have no trouble discerning it, and he gave his wife a look in return.

Turning to Benjamin, David sighed. "In my experience, a desperate need to justify one's actions is the sign of a guilty conscience. If you felt secure in your chosen path, you wouldn't feel the need to do so. Peace and confidence don't require validation."

That drew Benjamin up short, and he turned to frown at the others. "You two may be my favorite people in the world, but I would like you better if you allowed me to simply enjoy my ignorant bliss once in a while."

"Isn't the fact that he challenged you the very reason you loved Mr. Price so?" retorted David with a smirk. "Besides, I know from personal experience that ignorance is not bliss, and my life is daily blessed because I opened my eyes to my own stupidity."

Katherine's eyes lit at that, and she slanted a warm look in her husband's direction. The pair gazed at each other in a manner that had Benjamin clearing his throat loudly, and his sister appeared to snap from her thoughts.

"Surely you ought to see the girl, at least," she added. "See for yourself that she is comfortably settled. If she is, then you can rest easy."

Rising from his seat, David crossed back to his desk and opened a few drawers. Snatching a coin purse, he pulled out a handful of coins and placed them in Benjamin's hand, who pushed the money back to his friend.

"I cannot take this," he said with a shake of his head. "I still have my allowance for the quarter, and I have some savings."

"You may have some ready cash, but we both know your savings are tied up in investments that aren't easily liquidated," said David, pushing it back. "Consider it an early wedding present. It should be enough to pay for the license and ceremony. Getting to and from Birmingham will cost a pretty penny, especially if you are bringing a wife home. And if you decide you do not require it, you may return it."

Benjamin shifted the coins in his palm, staring at the bits of silver. "I have spent the last four weeks avoiding Miss Price. What makes you believe I will know what to do when the time comes?"

"You are a good man, Benjamin Leigh," said David as he returned to his seat beside his wife. "If you weren't, you would've dismissed any guilt you felt in the first place. Go, appease your conscience and see if Miss Price needs rescuing."

Clutching the coins tight, Benjamin drew in a deep breath and nodded. The part of his heart and soul that were still that young, confused boy warmed at the compliment that reminded him all too well of Mr. Price. For him, if nothing else, Benjamin needed to do this.

He reached into his pocket and retrieved his pencil and notebook; turning beyond the pages filled with notes concerning his previous meeting with the steward, he quickly outlined what he ought to pack, what plans needed deciding, and any other pertinent information for the trip ahead.

Those thoughts were interrupted by Katherine. "But I wouldn't suggest telling our parents what you mean to do. They will do their utmost to convince you not to go."

Her advice was sensible, yet Benjamin couldn't help but shake his head. "If it could end with a wedding, surely I ought to give them some warning first. Simply appearing on their doorstep with a wife in tow is hardly appropriate."

David quirked a smile. "If you marry the girl, send word to me, and I will break the news to them."

Benjamin's brows rose. "You wish to?"

Threading his wife's arm through his, the gentleman huffed a laugh. "As long as it isn't directed at Katherine, there is nothing I love more than seeing them in a dither. Telling them that their precious Benjamin eloped with a schoolmaster's daughter will be most entertaining."

His wife's furrowed brow eased as David spoke, her eyes brightening as she considered that idea, which did nothing to settle the unease churning in Benjamin's stomach.

"Oh, yes. That will be quite entertaining, indeed," she said with a grin.

Chapter 3

It was said life moved quicker in the city, and though the sentiment was evident in the commerce and crowds choking the streets, it was just as apparent in the architecture. Cozy hamlets looked the same as they did one hundred years ago and would likely remain unaltered one hundred years from now; though surface decorations may change with fashion, it was merely plaster painted over timbered exteriors. The country changed little over the years, shifting so incrementally that it was nearly unnoticeable.

Permanence was as unlikely a thing in cities as changeability was in the villages, and Birmingham was no hamlet. Though it possessed a fraction of the population of London, it was one of the largest cities in England, and the growth was accelerating with remarkable speed. One couldn't expect to see the same sights and shops year in and year out, and as the stagecoach crept along the clogged streets, Benjamin couldn't help but gape at the alterations wrought during the two years since finishing his schooling.

Having ridden this path many times over the years, Benjamin knew the Dog & Duck well, and though the inn had been altered not a jot, the bank to its right was now a haberdashery, and the chemist's shop had been replaced by a grocer.

Shaking off the last of the rain from his greatcoat, he tossed a sixpence to the porter and left the servants to settle his things into his room; for all that the two days of travel had been exhausting and his bones were in dire need of thawing, he couldn't bear the thought of disappearing into the inn.

Better to get the business done with posthaste.

Benjamin slipped out of the courtyard and into the crowds drifting along the road. The energy was everything he remembered, but it was strange to see so many places transformed. His favorite pie shop was no longer there, replaced by a coffee shop (though the scent of baked goods wafting from the front door said that perhaps the change was not all bad).

But as much as Benjamin tried to focus on the scenery around him, it was his destination that held all his attention. No doubt Miss Price was content and happily situated. No doubt whatsoever. Once he verified that fact, he could enjoy a warm fire, a bit of mediocre stew, and a wretched night's sleep in a bed that hardly deserved to be called such. Just thinking that helped him to shake off the last of the lethargy from his trip.

The spire of the church peeked above the surrounding rooftops, and Benjamin gazed at the grand sight. Religious edifices weren't known for their variety and creativity (a church in Warwickshire looked the same as in Lancashire, Yorkshire, and any other shire in the country), yet still, the sight inspired awe. But then, that was the intent of their design, their grand lines sweeping heavenwards, drawing the attention away from the profane world around them.

Stepping through the church gate, Benjamin strode around to the adjacent rectory. A rap on the door, and he was ushered into the parlor by the vicar's housekeeper.

"Mr. Leigh," said Mr. Gastrell with wide eyes as he cast aside his newspaper and rose to greet him. "What an unexpected surprise. I hadn't expected to see you in our fair city now that your schooling is complete."

"I was hoping you could provide me with information concerning Miss Ann Price," said Benjamin.

The vicar straightened. "Is that so? I didn't realize you two were acquainted."

"She is like a sister to me," replied Benjamin. Even if it wasn't factually true, the sentiment was; Mr. Price had been like a father to him. And perhaps that might stem the curiosity stirring in Mr. Gastrell's gaze. "You said you helped settle her into a new situation, and you did not respond to my letters, I would like to see for myself."

The gentleman's brows jerked upward, and it was clear to see thoughts swirling in his head. Benjamin raised a hand to forestall them.

"I merely wish to ensure that my mentor's daughter is comfortable. You mailed his final words to me, and he made it clear that he wished me to ensure she was provided for," said Benjamin.

But the speculation in Mr. Gastrell's gaze didn't dim. "Is that so?"

"As a brother, of course," he hurried to add. Benjamin forced his jaw to relax, though it insisted on clenching quite tightly. It took so little to bruise a lady's reputation, and he wouldn't do any good by railing against it. All he could do was tread carefully.

Nodding at a chair, Mr. Gastrell returned to his own. "Would you like some tea or coffee?"

"No, thank you. I would simply like to know where Miss Price is."

With an absentminded touch of his fingers, the vicar fiddled with the newspaper he'd been reading. "I found her a position at a school. She hasn't the skills or connections to secure a position as a governess or companion, so I did what I could for her. Considering she has no teaching experience or formal education, it was a godsend."

"Her father was one of the greatest teachers at Weathersby—"

"That may be so, but from what I ascertained, his manner in educating her was unorthodox and rather haphazard. Not at all the sort of learning that recommends her for the position," replied Mr. Gastrell. "I was lucky enough to find a school willing to overlook such...deficiencies."

Drawing in a sharp breath, Benjamin's thoughts whirled at that implication, for it did not speak well of the institution. "Where is she?"

"Queensbury School," said Mr. Gastrell, waving another irritatingly airy hand. "It's on Haycock Lane."

Benjamin frowned, piecing together the geography, though the city was large enough that he didn't know every corner of it.

"It's near St. Barnabas," supplied Mr. Gastrell.

Shooting to his feet, Benjamin gaped at the fellow, and though he knew better, he couldn't help the exclamation that leapt from his lips. "What the blazes, man?"

Mr. Gastrell might be a man of the cloth, but even a vicar deserved a blistering exclamation when being so thoroughly dense. He might have two decades more than Benjamin's own two, but the fellow had no more sense than a child.

"You secured her a position in one of the most dangerous parts of the city!" said Benjamin, swinging a hand wide to point at the window as though it lay just outside. "She's a gentleman's daughter. A lady! She is alone and unprotected, and you throw her to the beasts?"

Straightening, Mr. Gastrell glowered. "I did what I could, young man."

"She lived in *your* parish her whole life, and the moment she is in need, the lot of you turn your backs on her?"

Mr. Gastrell rose to his feet. Though he likely thought he would meet Benjamin's eye, the fellow was noticeably shorter. "Miss Price is an odd creature, and she had few friends in the parish—none of whom could take on the expense of an additional member of the household—and besides having the same financial constraints, as a single man, I cannot keep her under my roof. We provided her lodging whilst I did my best to secure her a position. So tell me, Mr. Leigh, what else ought I to have done?"

The more he spoke, the more Benjamin was struck by the picture the vicar made, and he couldn't help but wonder if he had looked and sounded similar to David and Katherine when he'd listed all the reasons he hadn't done something about Miss Price. Benjamin's stomach soured, and the vise tightened around his ribs, making it hard to breathe.

"The position provides room and board as well as a modest income, and I assisted her in selling off her father's things, which paid for the burial costs and provided a little savings, though nowhere near enough to live upon once all his accounts were settled. If Miss Price is frugal, there is no reason she cannot be as comfortable as any impoverished young lady might expect." Mr. Gastrell shrugged. "And she is still young enough to marry. Perhaps she might find a grocer's son or a tailor's apprentice."

Yet the vicar's tone did not inspire confidence, for he clearly believed even that low connection was unlikely.

Shaking his head, Benjamin strode toward the door, but as much as he wished to be rid of the obtuse vicar, lessons from his youth prodded his conscience, pulling him to a stop on the parlor threshold. Benjamin couldn't bring himself to look at the man, but he couldn't leave without acknowledging what was right and proper. Though Mr. Gastrell hadn't done much, it was more than some would've done, and the anger burning in Benjamin's chest had as much to do with himself as it did the vicar.

"Thank you, Mr. Gastrell. I am grateful you sent Mr. Price's letter to me and that you did what you could for his daughter."

And with that, Benjamin strode from the parlor and out the front door, not pausing as urgency turned his feet toward Queensbury School. Things needn't be settled this very moment, but he knew he would find no peace until he saw for himself that Miss Price was safe.

Chapter 4

Rows of dark wooden desks stood in stoic alignment along one side of the room, each bearing the gentle marks of age and use, but the class had abandoned them, gathering around in a circle so the girls could enjoy the company as they worked, training their fingers to make even stitches and neat seams whilst the murmur of little voices broke the silence.

Having never attended proper school before, Nan Price couldn't say if her methods were good or bad, but the girls seemed to relish their time at school—though she wasn't certain if it was because it afforded them time away from their work at home or because of some magic she cast over them as the new schoolmistress. Regardless, she smiled to herself as she watched over their work.

Hands tucked behind her, Nan wandered among the girls, gazing over their shoulders to inspect their work. The girls were all circled around with various sheets and petticoats out, their little needles working quickly to mend them. In the fireplace, the pot bubbled with more of their work, filling the classroom with the scent of roasting vegetables. The timbered roof sat heavy overhead, making Nan feel as though she needed to stoop, though she was several inches shorter than the lowest beam.

A leftover bit of chalk sat on the ground, and though Nan wished to simply leave it alone, she'd received too many lectures about school expenses to ignore it. Reaching for it wasn't a horrendous endeavor. Yet as she crouched and straightened, her back and knees cracked like an octogenarian's. With a twist, she stretched her back.

"How is this, Miss Price?" asked little Betsy, nodding at the linens on her lap.

"Wonderful," she replied as she took the section in her hand and examined the work.

Betsy raised her brows as though questioning the truth of that statement, and Nan pointed out a section in which the stitches weren't quite as orderly. "That needs to be redone, but you are doing marvelously. I would say you can have a fine future as a seamstress."

With bright eyes, Betsy set herself to her work, and the others in the circle doubled their efforts. Whilst they worked away on their stitches, Nan circled the girls and called out multiplication tables; as such mending hardly required thought, it was easy enough to do both.

A shrill blast of a whistle signaled the close of the shift from a nearby button factory and the end of their school day. Though Nan had never met the former schoolmistress, it had taken the whole of a month to train the girls up properly for the end of the day, and she was pleased to see them quickly move about the room, putting things to rights for tomorrow rather than leaving it to her alone.

Once at the door, they each gave her a bob and a "Goodnight, Miss Price," before hurrying out into the streets to join their families for dinner or begin their shifts at the various factories and mills round about. Shutting the door, Nan sagged against it with a sigh, but her feet and back screamed for her to sit, forcing her to move once more.

A curtain hung in the far corner, partitioning off her private quarters, and she pulled it back before dropping onto her cot, not caring that some of the straw from the mattress poked her skin. It was a mistake to lie down, and she'd known it before she did so, but Nan needed a moment before she could clean the rest of the classroom. Even with the girls' assistance before they left, there was still so much to be done.

Rain last night meant great piles of mud had been tracked inside; no matter how well the children cleaned their shoes on the boot scraper before entering, it seemed like more was inside the school than on the doorstep. And she'd hoped to clean the windows, for they were quite grimy, and the children couldn't work without light.

Then there were her chores to be seen to and lessons that needed preparing. So much to do, but Nan longed to remain precisely where she was.

The faint tang of burned vegetables pulled her upright, forcing her to her feet, and she flew to the fireplace to rescue the bubbling pot. At least when they had cooking lessons she didn't need to attend to her dinner; though the girls had all tasted their feast, there was enough to feed Nan and save her from having to spend the next hour scraping together a soup or relying on the dodgy pie vendor next door.

Leaning over the pot, she breathed deeply and savored the aroma. Gillian's touches on the stew exceeded Nan's skills; the girl would be a talented cook, and if fostered properly, her skills would grant her a far better living than her parents. Nan made note to bring it to Mrs. Queensbury the next time their patroness visited.

As much as she wished to dig in, that way lay madness. With a full belly and her feet up, Nan knew she wouldn't wish to move again until morning. Best to wait until she could truly enjoy it. She placed the pot close enough to the fire to keep it warm without burning it any further and then turned to the task at hand. Fetching a cloth, she tied it around her hair, securing the many wisps that had broken free throughout the day.

The room was so very quiet. Though it rang with children's voices all the day long, the silence that followed was equally deafening. Striding to the window, Nan pushed against it, though the poorly made thing was stuck in place. With a few solid jerks, she was able to open it a crack, and though the room was bound to be covered in a layer of dust before the night was through, she couldn't bring herself to close it again. The sound of the horses and passersby filled the space with life once more.

Her ears didn't thank her for it, but her heart did.

Grabbing the bucket of sand and her weed broom, Nan set to work. Bending over, she took the bundle of sorghum and brushed at the dirt. The layer of sand she'd laid down the night before had done its job beautifully, causing the wet mess to clump enough that it could be easily swept up. With quick movements, she gathered it together and moved it toward the door, throwing it open as she flung the mess—onto the gentleman standing on her doorstep.

Shooting upright, Nan stared at the fellow as several of the clots clung to his jacket and waistcoat, hanging there for a silent moment before falling to his boots. The gentleman stared at the mess, and she forced herself to move.

"I do apologize, sir," she said, hurrying forward to brush off the remnant bits. Just as she brandished a rag to wipe at his boots, he stepped away.

"It was an honest mistake. Of no consequence," replied the gentleman. "I am covered with the usual mess and muck from wandering the streets. A little more won't hurt."

Despite knowing the truth of that statement, Nan felt her cheeks heat. There was a vast difference between mud one collected on oneself and having it flung at you when you were simply attempting to knock on a door. Even a glance at the gentleman made it clear he was a man of means with his finely cut jacket and supple leather gloves, either of which cost more than all her clothes combined.

With a flick of his hands, he brushed the last of it from his jacket and turned his attention to her. "May I speak to your mistress?"

"She isn't often at the school."

Something about the gentleman was familiar, though Nan couldn't say how she knew him. His dark hair curled around his ears and collar, framing a strong jaw, though his nose was a touch too large to match the rest of his features. Though not handsome enough to warrant that description, Nan thought him attractive. His eyes were remarkable. Brown was common enough, but his were such a rich shade as to almost be black. Warm and deep. The sort of eyes that drew one in.

And she had been staring into them for far too long.

"Pardon?" asked Nan, for she was certain she'd missed his response.

"I am looking for the schoolmistress, Miss Ann Price," he repeated.

Her toes curled inside her shoes, and Nan brushed a hand down her apron, seeing anew every smudge marring the linen. Thankfully, the fiber's natural color hid most; she didn't know why ladies employed white aprons when they were intended to safeguard from dirt. Then again, she suspected most were decorative. The ladies she'd seen wearing them certainly hadn't been engaged in any activity that warranted such protection.

And their gowns were worthy of preservation. Nan's work dress had seen better days, and those were long before she'd inherited it from her mother.

Yet she didn't think herself so very poorly put together that he would mistake her for a maid. Glancing down at the bucket of sand beside her, she put down her sorghum brush, and that was precisely when she recalled the linen tied rather hastily around her head. Smiling to herself, Nan brushed away the remnant embarrassment just as she had the dirt on her floor.

"I am Miss Price," she said, extending her hand.

The gentleman's brows rose as he stared at her limb, and just like that, her muscles tensed anew as a metaphorical gust of wind carried the dirt right back into her home, scattering it far and wide. A lady didn't shake hands, a fact that had been difficult to remember when she was living the life of the genteel, but all the more when such manners were only trotted out now on Sunday.

Yanking her hand back, she dropped a quick curtsy instead. "And you are?"

"Mr. Benjamin Leigh."

Instantly, the niggling familiarity of his features coalesced into true recognition. As Father didn't often entertain students at home, Nan had met the young man only a few times in passing over the years, but his was a name she knew well.

"My father spoke often of you," replied Nan, unable to stop her brows from furrowing.

Surely the gentleman knew about Father's passing. Women may be known for their inclination to gossip, but men were equally guilty, and word had spread quickly amongst his former pupils. Condolences aplenty had rolled in, leaving her postman quite busy in the first weeks, but only a few of the local boys had bothered to attend the funeral, and none of them paid a call on her.

Yet Mr. Leigh stood on her doorstep, shuffling from foot to foot whilst looking beyond her to her meager classroom. His brows drew together, and Nan straightened, refusing to let another ounce of discomfort past her defenses.

Lifting her chin in challenge, she added, "I apologize if you haven't heard the news, but I fear my father—"

"I received word of his passing," he said in clipped tones. With a furrowed brow, Mr. Leigh softened his tone and added, "It pains me to know he is gone, and I am sorry for your loss, Miss Price. Your father was a wonderful man. One of the best I have ever known. He will be missed."

Condolences weren't known for their creativity. Having received a wealth of them of late, it was easy for Nan to see the similarities between all the sentiments, and though it was clear Mr. Leigh meant every word, his was like all the rest. Yet the conviction with which he spoke brought a new wave of pain, and she clenched her jaw together to stave off the feelings swelling in her heart.

Nan couldn't trust herself to speak. For all that the ladies of her former parish believed her to be a hoyden of the highest order with no ability to curb her behavior, she was far more civilized than they believed. Being raised by an absentminded widower didn't mean she was wholly without refinement. And so, she kept her counsel. Her opinion didn't matter at that moment, so it was better to remain silent and allow Mr. Leigh to arrive at the point.

"I have something of importance to discuss with you," said Mr. Leigh.

A spring breeze swept through the doorway, and Nan stepped back, beckoning him to enter. "Would you please come in?"

But Mr. Leigh remained where he was, his brows furrowing so deeply that one could grow potatoes there. And though it took a moment for her to realize the issue holding him in place, Nan's dusty manners quickly dusted themselves off.

"I do apologize if that makes you uncomfortable, Mr. Leigh, but I assure you there is nothing untoward about you joining me inside," she said, motioning him in. "Benefactors of the school—many of whom are gentlemen—are known to observe my teaching or inspect the classroom. With windows facing the street, we are hardly without an audience."

She nodded toward the windows arraying the wall on either side of the entrance. Though there was still an ongoing debate about whether or not to brick them over to save on the window tax, for now, they remained where they were, and they were more than adequate to console genteel sensibilities.

"I would consider it a kindness," she added. "There is a bite to the air this afternoon, and it is difficult enough to keep the room heated without the door standing wide open."

Despite having only a maid-of-all-work in her father's home, Nan had been spoiled, living in ignorant bliss of the difficulties of keeping a space warm. It was little wonder that large households required so much staff, for keeping the fires maintained required constant stoking and tending; once one died, it took far too much time to build up another set of good coals.

Thankfully, Mr. Leigh did as told and stepped inside, allowing Nan to close the door once more. The damage was done, but thankfully, it was minimal.

As Mr. Leigh continued to stand mutely by the door, Nan moved to the fireplace and shifted the coals, letting out the deeper heat hidden below. It would take some time before the room returned to the previous temperature, so she fetched her shawl, draping it around her shoulders.

And still, Mr. Leigh stood there, shifting in place. Grief took many forms, and though Nan wished she could be more compassionate toward his, her stomach growled its protest and her chores remained unfinished, demanding her attention.

"Would you mind if I finish my chores while we speak?" she asked. "There is much to do before I can retire for the evening."

Nodding, he stepped out of the way as she moved to her bucket and began sprinkling a new layer of sand across the floor. Upon becoming the schoolmistress, Nan had quickly learned the importance of this daily chore. Mud was an inevitability, and without a good layer on the floor to soak it up, keeping the schoolhouse clean was a herculean feat. Scrubbing the boards was a miserable task—one Nan didn't wish to do every day.

"Now, what is it that you need to speak to me about?" she asked, as Mr. Leigh still seemed caught in his stupor.

"Your father wrote to me on his deathbed," he said in a low voice; Nan couldn't tell if it was for her sake or his. "He asked me to marry you."

Chapter 5

Nan snapped upright and spun around to stare at Mr. Leigh. "Pardon?"

"Your father was the best of men, and I owe him so very much," said the gentleman whilst shifting from foot to foot. "He asked me to ensure you were cared for and not left alone in this world, and I am here to do my duty to him, and by extension, you."

With brows raised, Nan stared at him. "Is that so?"

Mr. Leigh gave a sharp nod. "Mr. Price taught the importance of honor, and I will not dishonor all he has done for me by shirking a responsibility."

"One that was thrust upon you." Nan refrained from adding "unwillingly," which she thought particularly beneficent of her, for the gentleman's clipped tone and fidgeting made it clear his current course of action was not done of his own free will. Not that she could blame him. Nan was not particularly pleased with the thought of being an obligation, any more than he wished to fulfill it.

"Regardless, I owe your father a great debt of gratitude. One cannot pick and choose how to repay a debt, and I will not quibble about his request, Miss Price."

Nan couldn't help but chuckle to herself at that unintentional play on words, for a marriage of convenience to a Price was a high price indeed for a debt of gratitude. But Mr. Leigh simply stared at her, unaware of the turn her thoughts had taken or the slight amusement to be found in that instant.

Snatching her bucket, Nan wandered to the cupboard and tucked away those cleaning implements. "I appreciate your commitment to duty, sir, but I assure you it is unnecessary. I have found myself a position. It will never make me wealthy, but it provides for my needs. Whatever your debt, marrying a stranger is hardly fair compensation."

And before Mr. Leigh could respond, she hurried to add, "No doubt his mind was addled from the fever, or he wouldn't have asked such a thing. A young man cannot afford a wife, and that would leave both of us worse off than if I remain here."

"I may be young, Miss Price, but I am not without means. I am the heir to an estate that will provide amply for us. Money is not a concern," he said, and, shifting in place once more, he added, "And I do not believe your father's wits were addled. He was desperate to provide for you, but that does not mean that he didn't understand the implications."

No, but Nan could. For all that Mr. Leigh extolled her father for providing for her, surely Irving Price would've provided for his daughter himself if he cared about her future, rather than dropping the responsibility onto someone else's shoulders.

An old, familiar twinge made itself known, and Nan rubbed her hands across her apron and set herself to straightening the chairs.

"I appreciate your offer, Mr. Leigh, but do not concern yourself with my affairs," she said, dusting off one of the desks with a rag. "My father spent most of his time at the school, so I am quite accustomed to being on my own. My position provides room and board, and if I am frugal, I can set aside most of my income for my savings."

Of course, that assumed that she maintained the position indefinitely, which was never a guarantee, and then there was the matter of whether or not those savings would be enough to provide for her in her dotage, but those were troubles for her to sort out—not a stranger.

"I can manage," added Nan, holding fast to that certainty. One way or another, she would.

Though Mr. Leigh maintained an impassive expression, there was a tightness to his shoulders that eased unconsciously as she spoke, and if Nan had doubted her course of action before (which she hadn't), that small sign of relief confirmed it.

"Thank you, Mr. Leigh, but I assure you that your duty is fulfilled, and you can leave with a clear conscience."

Straightening, she nodded toward the door and turned back to her work. Footsteps sounded as he moved, and for all that Nan expected to feel relief, a heaviness settled into her limbs.

Frowning to herself, she forced her way through it, shoving aside that ridiculous reaction. Mr. Leigh didn't wish to marry her, which was no great surprise, and she certainly didn't wish to marry a stranger who didn't wish to marry her. Still, however fleeting, that feeling had been real, and Nan couldn't ignore the fact that some part of her was disappointed.

When was the last time she'd had any company in the school after the children left? That was an easy answer to give, for it was never. The school's patrons visited occasionally, but usually during classes, and it was never a social call. People of their status and wealth didn't socialize with lowly schoolmistresses anymore than the working class were willing to befriend a gentleman's daughter.

It was a silly thing to feel. Ridiculous, in fact. It wasn't as though Nan's life had been bursting with visitors in her father's home. Being raised by a widower was hardly suitable training to step into the world of young ladies, assemblies, and parties, and it was no secret that the ladies of her parish didn't know what to do with the decidedly odd Miss Nan Price who knew more about ancient philosophy than dancing.

Neither fish nor fowl, as they said, for Nan hadn't found her footing amongst them, nor amongst the young men, many of whom didn't care for Latin and history when they were forced to study it in school and didn't wish to discuss it now that they were free of their schoolmasters and tutors. Especially with a gangly young lady.

Nan was alone in the world. It wasn't as though that was altogether different when Papa was alive, but at least he'd been home for a few hours in the evening. Those visits may have been more about quizzing her on her studies, but it was a conversation of a sort.

Snapping out her rag, Nan scoffed at herself and turned her attention to the novel that eagerly awaited her once her chores were done.

No doubt Mrs. Queensbury would be shocked that her schoolmistress indulged in sweeping romantic adventures, but then, she had been shocked when Nan divulged that she read Greek philosophers in their native tongue. Apparently, being bookish or frivolous was equally shocking. But Nan's subscription to the lending library was her one indulgence, and she wasn't about to ignore her varied preferences simply because her employer disliked it. She simply hid the books when Mrs. Queensbury was around.

"No," said Mr. Leigh.

That single word snapped at Nan, quite literally jerking her out of her thoughts with a start as she turned to find Mr. Leigh still standing there. Hadn't he left? She couldn't say one way or another, but she supposed it didn't matter as he faced her down, his expression showing quite more fire and determination than he'd demonstrated so far.

"No, Miss Price. I will not leave. Not until you consent to be my wife."

Nan gaped at him. She couldn't help it. But before she could think to respond, Mr. Leigh snatched the hat from his head and knocked it against his thigh.

"I apologize. I didn't mean to sound so demanding. I am making a muck of this." For the first time since his appearance on her doorstep, life seeped into his words and actions, stripping away the stilted man from before.

"I know my offer is hardly flattering, Miss Price, and I cannot blame you for being offended by it. I cannot say I am any more happy than you to be put in this position, but it does no good to sit about and moan over one's lot."

Twisting his hat in his hand, he dropped it onto one of the small seats. "Your father meant the world to me. You say marrying you is too high a price, but he gave my life meaning by teaching me to give of myself rather than surrendering to the idleness and ennui that so many gentlemen embrace. I cannot return to my home knowing I am leaving you alone and in such dire straits."

"He wasn't in his right mind—"

"No." Mr. Leigh repeated that word with as much force as before. "As this letter is as much about your future as it is mine, you'd best read it. Though I do believe he and I shared a special bond, I was not his only student who viewed him like a father, and it is no coincidence that he asked this of me. As the heir to an estate, I can afford a wife where the others cannot. That alone proves Mr. Price was of sound mind when he wrote to me."

Pulling a bit of paper from his pocket, the gentleman handed the letter over, and she quickly scanned the lines. Though the words were not made explicit, even Nan's meager understanding of the intricacies of society caught her father's meaning.

Her legs grew weak, stealing away her strength, and Mr. Leigh was there with a chair at the ready, helping her to it.

"I am not going to faint," she said.

"Perhaps not, but if your shock is anything akin to my own, you need to sit," he replied.

With a huff, Nan shook her head. "Then you didn't expect your favorite schoolmaster to lob his daughter at you?"

"I wouldn't describe it as such, Miss Price. Your father was concerned and did what he could to secure your future."

Yet Nan couldn't help but feel that "lob" was the precise word to describe the letter. If Father had been truly concerned about her future, he would've set aside some money for her rather than spending it on himself and relying on the kindness of his former student to save her from penury.

"I appreciate your concern, Mr. Leigh, but I assure you I can manage on my own. I have spent most of my life looking after myself. My position may not pay well, but there is more to happiness than a healthy income. 'It is not what we have but what we enjoy that constitutes our abundance.'"

"Epicurus," said Mr. Leigh, supplying the originator of her quote. "I suppose I shouldn't be surprised that Irving Price's daughter would quote ancient Greek philosophers."

"And I can do so in Greek."

"I would expect nothing less," he replied with a laugh to his tone. It was a little moment, but that flicker of amusement lightened the air around them, and Nan found herself able to breathe once more.

Coming to squat before her chair, Mr. Leigh held her gaze. "I know neither of us expected this turn of events, and if I were to be honest, I came here fully hoping to find a way around it. Yet as I stand here, I know I cannot leave you here. If nothing else, this part of town is far too dangerous for anyone on her own. Do you think my conscience will allow me to leave you here?"

As much as Nan wished to argue the point, there was none to be had. There was a reason she never ventured forth from the school at night, and though she'd avoided any trouble, one's good fortune could last only so long. One day she would find herself robbed, attacked, or worse. As if to punctuate that, a bottle crashed in the alley outside, followed by bellowing shouts from some unknown source; the laborers, done with their work for the day, would pass their evening in the pubs, spending a significant portion of their meager income on drink, and it was not wise to be out and about when things grew rowdy.

Mr. Leigh's brows rose, his gaze pleading. "Please, Miss Price. I know this is far from ideal, but I feel deep in my soul this is the right thing to do."

When she did not answer immediately, his smile quirked, bringing a slight teasing tone to his voice. "I cannot bear the thought of abandoning you, and I am certain I will carry that guilt the rest of my life. Would you condemn me to such a terrible fate? Please marry me."

"Ah, so rather than you rescuing me, I am bestowing a mercy on you?" she asked, matching his grin.

"Absolutely," he responded with a solemn nod. "I am a shag-bag of a man, and you are getting a rum deal with this marriage."

Nan laughed. She couldn't help it. For all that this conversation had begun with stilted awkwardness, Mr. Leigh stripped it away and left her feeling far more lighthearted than she had in some time.

But the levity in his tone dropped away as he continued, "You don't know me from Adam, but I assure you that I have every intention of treating you well. I know I am young and bound to make many mistakes along the way, but I do not believe marrying you will be one of those."

"You are so certain, are you?" she asked with a frown.

Mr. Leigh drew in a deep breath, and though Nan anticipated a jest in response, he considered the question a while before answering. "I cannot describe it, but I feel this is the right decision. Whether it is peace at knowing I am doing my duty or direction from On High, I cannot say. But I am doing this of my own free will. Please, Miss Price. Will you marry me?"

Chapter 6

Now this proposal was a different beast altogether. It was easy to dismiss Mr. Leigh when he was begrudgingly doing his duty, but something had shifted in the man, and Nan could see he truly wished to marry her. Perhaps not for love, but such sensibilities were the providence of other ladies.

Though Nan thought herself perfectly average in appearance, others' appraisals were less complimentary. Perhaps they would not say she was "plain," but Nan Price couldn't dream of attracting the elusive "love at first sight." And though Papa's profession had left him a gentleman of sorts, that didn't mean he had money enough to entice young beaus.

From her earliest recollections, Nan had known herself to be odd. A child with her unusual upbringing couldn't help but find it difficult to blend with social expectations. Though she remembered her mother, illness had claimed Constance Price when Nan was only seven years old, leaving her without a maternal figure as she grew into womanhood. For all that Papa had thought social skills were the least important knowledge one could possess, Nan had never found a use for reciting Virgil's *Aeneid* whilst navigating society's unspoken rules.

A bluestocking with no dowry and average appearance was a potent (and deadly) combination.

Yet Nan had still dreamed of marriage, and Mr. Leigh's offer dredged forth all those lovely dreams once more. To have a family. A proper one. She had enough memories of her mother to remember what it had been like. Though Papa had always preferred "his boys," he'd spent more time at home. Meals together. Evenings of reading. Walks through town. Little, unremarkable moments that Nan had never realized were special until they were gone.

Considering all those things now, Nan couldn't even say love served as the driving motivation behind her matrimonial dreams. Romance was well and good, but there were far more valuable things in life. A companion with whom to pass the long hours. Someone with whom to share a meal and discuss the goings-on of her day. When was the last time anyone had engaged her in a proper conversation?

"As you haven't thrown me out on my ear, am I to assume you are considering it?" he asked.

Nan drew in a sharp breath. "Yes."

Giving that a considering nod, Mr. Leigh rose to his feet and shifted one of the seats around to face her. "I imagine it's a bit startling. I've had some weeks to consider things, but even I wasn't entirely sure what I would do until I met you."

"Somehow I find that comforting. Had you arrived with no fears or doubts, I wouldn't trust your good sense. Honor or not, it is best to assess a situation before making such a weighty decision."

Mr. Leigh huffed and nodded. "What can I do to assuage your fears? I suppose we needn't make this decision this very minute. Though I do have the money to purchase a license, we can have the banns read and take those weeks for you to acclimate."

"Though that is appealing, I'm not sure what a few extra weeks will tell me. It takes more time than that to know a person."

"True," he said with a considering look.

And then his expression shifted ever so slightly, though Nan couldn't say precisely what it was. A lightening of his eyes? Or a faint smile on his lips? All she could say was that there was something impish about it, and she expected his teasing before he spoke.

"But surely someone able to quote an ancient philosopher's discourse on inner contentment can manage to be happy in a marriage she didn't expect. Or would a life with me be far more tortuous than living in a one-room schoolhouse in the slums of Birmingham? Surely, if you can manage a few dozen children, you can keep one husband in line."

"Not if he is as impish as a few dozen children," she replied with an arched brow.

Mr. Leigh laughed and nodded. "My sisters would certainly say I am. But what say you?"

And though there were doubts aplenty, Nan couldn't say he was wrong on any count. Having lived this life for the past two months, she knew full well how difficult it was and would be.

And lonely.

"Yes," she said, forcing the word out.

"Yes?"

"Yes, I will marry you," said Nan. And despite how terrifying the prospect was, the tension twisting inside her eased a fraction as Mr. Leigh grinned. The expression was so genuinely pleased that she couldn't help but feel peaceful. No bounder or blackguard would be so content to marry such an unremarkable miss with only a few pounds to her name.

"Good," said Mr. Leigh with a sharp nod. "So, we are getting married."

Her husband-to-be. Not Mr. Leigh or some stranger—but the man she would marry. That thought stole away her words, leaving her mutely staring at him, and it was easy to see his thoughts had traveled down a similar path, for he gazed back as though expecting something more yet not knowing what that ought to be. Silence fell between them, and Nan couldn't put enough of a coherent thought together to break it.

Rising to his feet, Mr. Leigh pulled a small notebook from his pocket and began scribbling notes whilst murmuring to himself. "I suppose I ought to procure the marriage license and write to David... What else?"

Nan stood as well, her brows pulling together. "Would you care for some dinner? It isn't much, but the girls prepared soup and bread as part of their lessons today, and there is enough for two."

Mr. Leigh paused and turned his attention to her once more. Another long moment passed, though Nan couldn't trust her perspective, as there were no timepieces on hand to mark the minutes—just a thumping heartbeat, and it quickened as her invitation hung there for a long moment before Mr. Leigh smiled once more. It was quite a nice expression, for it was broad and filled him with a light that spoke of one comfortable with such joyful displays.

Nan couldn't help but respond in kind as she ushered him toward her makeshift dining table whilst he tucked away his notebook once more. She hardly had space enough for the pair of them, but she found enough dishes to suit their needs, and Nan puttered around, embracing the task at hand. It gave her something to do—other than think about the fact that the man bringing chairs over was the man she would wed.

Once everything was situated, they took their places and stared at each other over steaming bowls of stew. For all that a new wave of awkwardness descended, Nan couldn't help but feel lighter as his cutlery rattled. Whatever may come, someone was beside her, and surely that was something to celebrate.

As he took a bite, Mr. Leigh's brows rose. "Your students made this?"

"Yes..." Nan was about to tack on his name, but calling her husband-to-be something so formal seemed strange. Though married couples often referred to each other by their surnames in mixed company, it was only the two of them present. Yet to call him anything else felt too forward, whatever their present relationship.

The gentleman's brows rose even higher at the clear confusion coloring that simple answer, and that smile of his returned to cut through the strangeness of the moment. "I suppose, as we are to be married, we can dispense with formal address, Ann."

Wrinkling her nose, she shook her head. "Nan, please. No one of any consequence has ever addressed me by my given name."

"As I wish to be someone of consequence to you, I will make sure to use it, then," he said, and with a significant tone, he added, "Nan."

And then she did something entirely ridiculous. Nan laughed. But not some dainty, tittering thing. It wasn't even a proper guffaw. No, she snorted. Her hands flew to her nose, her eyes widening, but Benjamin merely joined in with her. As much as her cheeks heated at the embarrassing slip, Nan couldn't help but get lost in the unexpected merriment.

"Are you always such a flirt? Or have you decided to trot out your skills especially for me?" she asked.

Benjamin gaped in mock affront. "I would have you know that my flirtations have made many a young lady swoon."

"You cannot be that skilled, else you wouldn't brag about your conquests to the newly affianced bride-to-be," she teased, and that elicited more laughter, yet when it calmed once more, she was left staring at her soup, uncertain what to say. Such a strange situation in which she found herself, and as much as Nan wished to urge more conversation, she couldn't think of a single thing to ask at that moment—which was ridiculous, as she knew nothing about him, leaving a whole wealth of things she could ask him.

Thankfully, Benjamin seemed not to notice or struggle as she did, for he immediately asked, "You teach your students cooking?"

Clinging to that familiar topic, Nan nodded. "Among other things. During the days, I teach boys and girls arithmetic, reading, writing, grammar, and geography. Then in the afternoon, they split for more practical training. The boys learn shoemaking, carpentry, and even blacksmithing, depending on who in town is willing to train them. The girls remain with me, and I teach them cooking, laundry, sewing, and the like."

Dipping a bit of bread into the stew, Benjamin glanced at her. "You sound as though you enjoy it."

"I do." A smile crept across her face. "Though they test my patience often, I enjoy teaching."

With a big bite, he nodded. "It is in your blood. Your father was an excellent teacher. He could make even the driest subjects interesting, instilling his love of it into his students. It was like magic." Pausing, Benjamin considered that and gave her a considering look. "But then, I do not need to tell you that. No doubt you spent countless hours learning from him. Though I cannot imagine it was easy to have a parent as your teacher, for they often demand more of their children than their pupils."

Benjamin continued to wax poetic about the supposed blessings of being Irving Price's daughter, and Nan focused on her food, forcing the bread and stew into her mouth. She'd heard such sentiments before, as whenever her path crossed with one of his former students, she would hear tale after tale about Papa's kindness and skills.

Her stomach burned, though it had nothing to do with her dinner, and she tamped down the heat surging in her heart. It wasn't Benjamin's fault that her father had shown little interest in a daughter, and Benjamin didn't deserve a lick of resentment simply because he'd been worthy of her father's attention. It did no good to dwell on old wounds, and Nan wasn't willing to reopen them. But neither was she willing to feign interest in her father's grand exploits with those he deemed worthier of his time.

"If you are so very keen on teaching, I am certain there is a charity school or two back home in which you can volunteer," said Benjamin.

Nan paused with the spoon halfway to her mouth, and she stared at him. Perhaps she ought not to have been surprised, as the gentleman had traveled to Birmingham to propose, but like so many aspects of this evening, she hadn't considered that she might be relocating.

Eyes widening, she asked, "Where do you live?"

"An industrial town not far from Preston in Lancashire by the name of Greater Edgerton," he said.

For all that marriage itself was a shock, the thought of leaving Birmingham was a greater one. She'd lived in the same corner of England her entire life, and even moving to the other side of the city had been surprising enough. To leave the county and settle in a new town?

Lawks. What a thought.

When she focused on Benjamin once more, he was watching her with a wary expression. "Are you reconsidering?"

Nan shook her head. "Startled, that is all. I have never left Birmingham."

"Did your father never take you traveling?" asked Benjamin. "He adored geography so much that I thought he must've been a great traveler."

Nan smiled to herself, for though Benjamin was entirely correct concerning Papa's love of geography, Mr. Irving Price was the sort of scholar who enjoyed learning more than doing. And yes, he often ventured into Edinburgh and London, for those places boasted the sort of scholarly discussion and pursuits one cannot find in Birmingham, but one cannot enjoy such intellectual offerings with a child in tow. Better to leave little Nan at home with the maid-of-all-work to see to her.

"Coaches and inns didn't agree with him. Papa preferred books," she said.

Benjamin smiled. "I can well imagine that. I will forever picture him sitting in an armchair, surrounded by mountains of them. I do not think I ever saw him without one in his hand."

"And what of your family?" Nan snatched at the question, grateful that something of use came to mind when she needed it, for she was curious about the answer. Though any distraction from that previous subject was quite welcome. "You know so much about mine, but I fear I know nothing of yours. What of your parents? Do you have siblings? Are you the eldest, youngest, or somewhere in the middle?"

Nan forced herself to stop talking. One question was quite sufficient, and Benjamin's brows rose as each new one followed after it. Digging into her stew once more, she silenced her words with a bite.

"I have four siblings—all girls—and I am the youngest. Francis is just older than me, and she married some years ago. She settled in Yorkshire and rarely returns home, so it may be some time before you meet her, but the rest all live nearby with their husbands and children." He paused and amended, "Rosanna, the second eldest, splits her time between London, Greater Edgerton, and her husband's family estate in Kent, so you shan't meet her until the autumn, but I am certain you will love her when you do. They are the dearest of ladies."

With little prodding, Benjamin expounded on his siblings and their children, weaving together the sorts of tales Nan had read in books, filled with the picturesque sweetness rife in families. As he spoke, she imagined it all and embraced the warmth that spread through her at the thought that soon, they would be her family, too.

Chapter 7

One's twenty-first birthday was a significant milestone. It was the age of one's majority, when one became a free agent unto himself. In theory, at least. Most still required assistance from their families, and whether or not they had a legal right to do so, few went against their parents' wishes; yet still, that all-important year remained a rite of passage of sorts.

Benjamin had always known his twenty-first year would be especially poignant—but because of the entail and not because it was the age he would bind himself in holy matrimony. Had anyone suggested five weeks ago that he would be standing before a vicar, exchanging vows with Miss Nan Price, Benjamin would never have believed it. How could one predict such a strange shift in circumstances?

Yet for all the uncertainty and fear he'd felt upon receiving Mr. Price's plea from beyond the grave, Benjamin felt peace whilst facing the marriage altar. The feeling wove through him, imbuing him with such clarity and confidence that he felt not a jot of the infamous nerves that plagued so many brides and grooms. Benjamin couldn't explain why that was; he ought to be terrified.

But then, any other gentleman likely would've seized the escape Nan had presented when she'd rejected his marriage proposal so thoroughly the first time. Benjamin had attempted to do just that, but his feet had refused to cross the school's threshold. The sight of her scrubbing the floors with sorghum and sand was burned into his mind and heart, making it impossible to flee.

There was nothing wrong with hard work, but what sort of gentleman would he be if he abandoned her to grueling labor for the rest of her days? Despite Nan's assurances that she'd manage on her own, so little stood between her and the gutter.

Nan's willowy frame was too thin to be hauling buckets about, and there was a sickly edge to her complexion that had plagued Benjamin's nightmares since that day; one rough winter in that poorly heated schoolroom would've been enough to steal away her life. Nan needed to be protected, and surprisingly enough, Benjamin rather liked the thought of taking on that role.

The vicar droned through the marriage ceremony, rattling off the words with so little inflection that Benjamin wondered why the fellow insisted on all the pomp and circumstance. To his thinking, it was better to simply get to the heart of the ceremony and have the thing over and done with.

Such a strange turn of events. A mere sennight ago he'd embraced any excuse to avoid this very moment. Now, he wished to hurry the marriage along and avoid returning to Greater Edgerton. Just the thought of arriving at Whitley Court with his wife in tow sent prickles down Benjamin's spine.

Nan did not fit Mother's definition of a lady of quality. There was no point in denying that fact as not one of the ladies he'd attempted to court had met with Mother's approval. None were good enough for her dear boy. And he'd be a fool to believe she'd be pleased for him to bring home a young lady with no dowry or social standing. Benjamin's stomach was making certain he did not forget that.

But all would be well. No doubt it might be a tad strained at first, but surely Mother's disappointment would settle in time. The deed was done (or nearly so if the vicar would speak faster), and there was no undoing it once the vows were exchanged, so it was pointless for her to fuss and fret over it once the initial shock wore away.

That niggling feeling skittered down Benjamin's spine, and he wondered if he ought to warn Nan. But what good would come from poisoning that well? Mother might be perfectly cordial to his wife, and Nan need never know that she wasn't the bride Gertrude Leigh had expected Benjamin to find.

That bit of logic settled his thoughts once more, allowing him to embrace his newfound peace anew. Yes, this was the right course of action.

What was she thinking? Nan drew in a sharp breath and paused as the wreath on her head slipped. As kind as it was for Benjamin to gift her the flowers—and the azaleas were a beautiful mix of purple and pink—she couldn't help but feel ridiculous. They may be a common adornment for brides on their wedding day, but most brides wore their finest gown. Not one nearly two decades out of fashion.

At least she was free of her mourning. Purchasing or converting her wardrobe into mourning clothes had been impractical and financially impossible; thankfully, a few lengths of black ribbon were enough to give the appearance of propriety. But even those hollow signs of sorrow were unnecessary on one's wedding day. A bride mustn't wear such dour things.

Yet being freed of that guilt didn't allow her heart to settle.

Benjamin had chosen this path. Had begged her to accept. He was doing this of his own free will and volition. Nan hadn't forced the issue. Quite the opposite, in fact.

And it wasn't as though she'd misrepresented herself, hiding her shabby wardrobe and poor manners. From the very first, Nan had behaved as she always did, so there was no reason for the growing pressure in her chest as the vicar worked his way through the ceremony. Benjamin knew she was no refined lady, yet he'd chosen to marry her. Perhaps a vast knowledge of party etiquette, embroidery, and flower arranging wasn't of high importance to him.

But he was only doing this to appease her father.

Having spent a lifetime believing herself kind and thoughtful, it was startling to realize just how selfish a creature she was. Despite bringing Benjamin some pleasure by fulfilling his duty (if the broad smile on his face were any indication), this arrangement benefitted Nan first and foremost.

Their marriage was ridiculous. Benjamin Leigh was an heir, and if not overtly handsome, his features were arresting, to say nothing of the fact that he was congenial and honorable. He didn't need to stoop to a marriage of convenience to secure a wife—especially not one who was both older and as tall as him. The difference hadn't been noticeable before, but as she stood beside him, it was clear that she matched his height. Such surface things were hardly important, for they did not mark the quality of a man, but Nan felt like a gangly old spinster beside him, despite being undeserving of any of those descriptors.

Benjamin Leigh could do better.

Yet Nan couldn't stop him as he recited the vows, echoing Mr. Livingston's prompts as he bound himself to her, body and soul. And when it came to her turn, she proved just as weak as before, for she hesitated only a heartbeat before speaking the vows herself. Time sped forward as they exchanged rings and the vicar pronounced his blessing on those symbols of their commitment and on the marriage itself. And with grand solemnity, they were pronounced man and wife. Unbreakable and irrevocable.

Facing her, Benjamin smiled with far more joy than Nan thought the moment warranted. Once more, her tongue tied itself in knots as she tried to think what to say to her husband. In other circumstances, they might sweep back down the aisle to greet the friends and family in the congregation, but the pews sat empty.

"If you will come this way to sign the wedding registry," said Mr. Livingston, shepherding them toward the vestry with their enlisted witnesses trailing behind them. In short order, Nan and Benjamin placed their signatures on the document whilst the vicar's wife and the parish clerk added theirs. With a flourish, the marriage certificate was presented to Nan for safekeeping, and the newly married couple was ushered back down the nave with all the care of one shooing away a fly.

Standing in the church vestibule with their luggage gathered round, Nan held the paper close while husband and wife stared at one another. Though the exchanging of vows and rings seemed formal enough a binding, it felt as though this momentous occasion deserved something more. No doubt, other couples would take the moment of privacy to share their first kiss as husband and wife, but that hardly seemed fitting for an arrangement born of necessity.

And so, they stood there, staring at each other for a long moment.

Benjamin laughed, the sound echoing back into the nave as the church was utterly silent. "I suppose I am not alone in thinking this is extraordinarily strange. I feel as though there ought to be something more substantial to end such an important moment, yet we were just brushed onto the church steps."

And in an instant, the strain eased, evaporating as it always did when faced with Benjamin's mirth.

Then he held out his hand, offering it to her. "Mrs. Leigh."

Taking hold of it, she shook it with a slight smile. "Mr. Leigh."

Before Nan knew what he was about, Ben shifted his grip and bowed low over their hands, pressing a kiss to her knuckles. Despite the paper in her hand testifying that such tokens were not only acceptable but a required part of her life now, Nan couldn't help her brows climbing upward. Or the heat suffusing her cheeks.

Peeking a look at her, Ben gave her a rascally smile, and Nan jerked her hand away.

"That is enough of that, sir," she said.

"As you wish, dear wife of mine," he replied with a waggle of his brows. Nan huffed, though any feigned irritation melted away when her cheeks heated to untenable levels. She'd married a rascal. But as her lips kept tipping into a smile, she couldn't say that was a bad thing.

"We'd best get a move on if we wish to make it to the stagecoach in time," said Nan, reaching for the basket sitting atop her trunk.

"What is that?" asked Benjamin, leaning closer. "It smells heavenly."

Pulling back the linen covering it, Nan displayed an array of buns and pies. "My students wanted to give us a wedding present, so the girls prepared us a picnic basket to take on the journey home."

Every bit of the gift, from the container to the food and the carefully monogrammed linen, had been lovingly prepared by their dear little hands, and Nan's heart swelled at the sight. She may have known them for a short time, but perhaps she'd done some good in their young lives. And some part of her couldn't help but wonder why it was that she was blessed with an escape from poverty whilst they would likely spend their entire lives mired in it.

"That is so kind of them. I wish I could thank them myself," said Benjamin.

Nan drew a finger across the white stitches that formed the simple monogram. Embroidery had never been her forte nor had it been featured in their lessons, but the girls had made a valiant attempt, and Nan loved it all the more for the crooked lines and oddly sized stitches.

The church bell rang, snapping Nan from her thoughts. "We ought to be on our way."

Reaching for the floral wreath, she tucked it and the marriage certificate into the basket, shifting the burden into the crook of her arm before reaching for the handle of her trunk. Before she could grab it, Benjamin was there, hefting it up onto his shoulder. Nan blinked at him, for he did it with far more ease than she would've expected; she may not own much in this world, but it still weighed a substantial amount.

"Perhaps I can..." she began, reaching to help, but Benjamin turned to give her a warning look. No words followed it, but Nan felt his meaning well enough. So, she moved to fetch his portmanteau, but once more, she was stymied when Benjamin snatched it up and tucked it under his other arm.

"That is too much for you to carry," said Nan with a frown. "I am quite capable of managing a bag."

"And forgo an opportunity to display my great strength?" he asked with another of his impish winks. "Let it be. If you will carry my satchel and greatcoat, that will be assistance enough, Mrs. Leigh."

Doing as bidden, Nan hurried to the church door to open it for him before he insisted on managing that as well. Yet as she did so, she couldn't help but marvel at the oddity that was her new name.

"Mrs. Nan Leigh," she murmured as Benjamin stepped around her and out onto the church steps. But when the name came to her lips, she stopped and stared off with wide eyes.

Benjamin paused and looked back at her. "What is it?"

"Nan Leigh," she repeated. And when he only stared back at her with raised brows, Nan said the name again quickly, blurring the names together. With a startled little squeak, she shook her head. "My name sounds like 'manly.'"

Dropping the trunk down on the steps, Benjamin met her gaze with a barely controlled laugh. Covering her mouth, Nan shook her head as chuckles took hold, and the pair dissolved into snickers.

"Nan Leigh!" she blurted. "And going by my given name wouldn't be any better."

"I do apologize."

But with another huffing laugh and a shake of her head, Nan took up her bags again. "There is nothing to do about it now."

"True, my good sir," he said, following suit and taking up the trunk once more. "Let us be on our way now, *Mr. Leigh.*"

Nan gaped at him, though the fellow looked entirely unrepentant. Stepping around him, she marched down the street with her head held high, and when he fell into step beside her, Nan couldn't help but feel that this unforeseen shift in her life might just be a great blessing in disguise.

Regardless of how ludicrous her name was now.

Chapter 8

"We're full," called the guard before turning around to bellow at the porters as they hefted the luggage up top, but Benjamin moved after him, following on his heels.

"What do you mean, you're full? Surely there is a seat available—"

"Full means full," barked the guard, waving him away. "If you wanted a seat inside, you ought to have arrived sooner or secured your place earlier."

Benjamin's jaw ached as he forced it to relax, though he couldn't ease the tightness in his chest. The skies overhead were dark and gray, the clouds promising a truly miserable ride for anyone unfortunate enough to be trapped up top.

"Please, sir," said Benjamin, following the man as he settled the other passengers. "Is there anything I can do to change your mind?"

"Magic me a new carriage that can fit more than six inside," came the brusque reply.

Gritting his teeth, Benjamin rubbed at his forehead whilst cursing his stupidity. He turned around and peered inside to find four of the occupants were ladies, leaving him no recourse there, but as the final two approached, Benjamin forced a broad smile as he approached the gentlemen.

"Dear sirs, might I throw myself upon your mercy?" he asked, drawing closer whilst holding his hands up in supplication.

The first gave him an arched brow. "I am not trading seats."

"Not for me, but my wife," replied Benjamin, motioning toward where Nan stood, holding their picnic basket. "Surely one of you is willing to allow the lady the comfort of sitting inside. I will repay the cost of the ticket."

The pair glanced in her direction, their eyes sweeping over her before returning to Benjamin, and if he'd hoped for some sign of sympathy, he found none. They stepped around him and moved to enter the carriage. With a quick tally of his coins, Benjamin shoved a hand into his pocket and retrieved the only ones he could spare.

"Two guineas will amply cover the cost of your ticket, and you can have my wife's seat up top for free. Surely that is worth a little discomfort."

The first gentleman ignored him and climbed inside, but the second paused with his foot on the carriage step.

"Please, sir," added Benjamin. "This is our wedding journey home. We married not an hour ago."

The look in the fellow's softened, and just as Benjamin felt ready to celebrate his victory, a drop fell from the heavens, drawing their gazes upward. With a shake of his head, the fellow stepped inside, and the guard nudged Benjamin away so he could close the door.

He strode quickly over to Nan, who watched him with furrowed brows.

"What is the matter?" she asked.

"You married a fool," grumbled Benjamin, but he stopped short when Nan grabbed his arm.

"It is rather early in our marriage to deem yourself a failure," she replied with a slight smile.

That lightened Benjamin's heart the tiniest bit, but he shook his head. "I made many plans for our wedding and trip, but I fear that I didn't take into consideration that securing seats inside might be difficult. I never bother with purchasing tickets ahead of time because I don't mind sitting up top."

"Then we shall sit up top."

Drawing in a deep breath, Benjamin sighed. "The weather will likely be poor the entire journey, making for a very miserable two days."

He ran through quick tallies again. The travel here, plus staying a full sennight in Birmingham, plus the marriage license and wedding costs had eaten through most of his ready funds. Even with David's assistance on that front, Benjamin was left with a small sum of money to aid their journey home. If they slept rough tonight, they could save some money on a room at the inn, and he could put that money toward a larger bribe.

"Let me try again," he said, turning back toward the carriage, but Nan grabbed his arm, holding him in place.

"Let it be, Benjamin," she said.

"It looks like rain, which means you will be drenched and frozen to the bone," he said with a shake of his head. "And if I cannot get him to budge, perhaps we can secure seats on a later coach."

Yet even as he said that he knew the chances of success on either front were minimal. With how terrible the weather had been of late, it would be near impossible to find an empty seat today. They'd need to wait a day. Maybe two. And that brought Benjamin back to the issue of their limited funds.

Travel was an expensive prospect, and not only because of the obvious reasons. Beyond the ticket and price of the inn, every servant who crossed their path in the next two days would expect at least a sixpence to attend them. Chambermaids, barmaids, innkeepers, porters, the guard, and even the coachman held their hands out for that honorarium before they did a lick of work. Every added day of the journey tacked on more and more, eating away at the meager funds he had on hand.

For all that he'd written down every step he'd needed to take and subsequently checked each off in turn, his notebook did no good if he didn't note an item in the first place. Benjamin may have taken the journey to and from Greater Edgerton many times, but he hadn't considered just how different it would be with a lady. His wife.

There had to be some way to reconcile his coin purse with his husbandly duties, but just as Benjamin turned back to do something (though he didn't know what), the lady in question stopped him.

"It is not worth the price," said Nan with a shake of her head.

"Yes, it is," he said. "I want you to be dry and cozy."

So many young ladies dreamt of heartfelt declarations, bouquets, and stolen kisses, but Nan couldn't think of anything greater than Benjamin's words. Granted, he hadn't meant them as a token of affection, but that made them all the more meaningful. He wasn't madly in love with her, yet still, he took pains to see to her comfort. Nan's heart burned in her chest, ensuring that she was unlikely to feel the nip of cold Benjamin predicted.

Love was well and grand, but consideration was far more meaningful.

Papa had loved her in a fashion, yet how often had he stirred himself on her behalf? He'd not considered it worthy of his time to secure her a governess or schooling, choosing instead to check in with her studies when it suited him in the evenings. He hadn't thought twice about her wardrobe being older than herself. He hadn't provided for her future, leaving her at the mercy of strangers.

Taking Benjamin by the arm, Nan held him fast. "I would much rather sit with you up top."

"That is kind of you to say, but you do not know how miserable it will be—"

"I have been cold and wet plenty of times," she said with a faint smile, a phantom shiver running down her spine as she contemplated just how many evenings she'd struggled to keep her quarters warm during this frigid spring. "I would much rather keep company with you. I was able to borrow a copy of the latest *Blackwood's Magazine*—"

"*Blackwood's*? How scandalous!" he replied with a mock gasp.

Nan leveled a narrowed look at him. "You—"

"Are you taking your seat, or are we leaving you behind?" shouted the guard as the coachman rose to his box up front.

"And I prefer the view from up top, anyway," she said with a bright smile.

Benjamin's brows pulled low, and he frowned as he looked at the carriage interior again, but Nan pulled him toward the steps built into the exterior. Other passengers were seated on the roof behind the driver and guard's box, leaving Nan and Benjamin the boot. Reaching for the hand holds, she hefted herself up, and when her shoes slipped, hands circled her waist, holding her steady; no doubt Benjamin thought he was helping, but the feeling was so strange that Nan could hardly climb the makeshift ladder.

Settling into the seat hanging off the back, Nan felt a slight flutter of unease, as there was nothing to keep them from bouncing back off the bench. And for all that she'd hoped for a fine view, the mountain of luggage strapped to the roof effectively blocked off much of it, which was likely why these were the last unoccupied seats. The carriage rocked as Benjamin rose beside her and took his place.

With only two of them on the seat, there was space aplenty to spread out a touch, but Benjamin drew close, his arm coming around her back as the guard blasted the trumpet, announcing to all and sundry that the stagecoach was leaving. And though that little tenderness was quite welcome when they jolted forward and she was nearly knocked backward, Nan couldn't help but be keenly aware that a man's arm was circled about her.

Not just any man's, but her husband's.

Heavens. What to feel?

Despite the loss of her parents, Nan's life had plodded along in a rather unremarkable fashion. Even if she'd longed to mix more with others, she hadn't a natural talent for collecting people, leaving most of her three and twenty years filled with quiet and solitude. Yet now she was seated atop a stagecoach, rolling away from the only home she knew, with her husband seated cozily next to her.

Benjamin loosened his hold as they rose to speed but kept her still anchored in place as the carriage pitched about with each bump of the road. Though she found her gaze straying to his profile on more than one occasion, Nan couldn't help but stare at the passing buildings as Birmingham drifted past her, quickly fading into the distance. The carriage swayed, and Nan's stomach dropped a time or two as she spied the very far drop, but whenever her gaze drifted toward that unpleasant view, Benjamin's arm tightened around her, grounding her.

For all that the air had been pleasant at first and the wall of luggage provided some protection, Nan couldn't help the sudden shiver that took hold of her. But then Benjamin was holding her tighter, bringing with him his warmth, which, though it did little to stave off the outward chill, sent a flush of heat through her.

"Now, *Mr. Leigh*, what was this about you reading the latest issue of that scandalous *Blackwood's Magazine*?" he asked when the noise of the city faded and the horses settled into a steady pace as the English countryside stretched around them.

"It is hardly scandalous."

"Few young ladies would deign to read such a subversive publication, let alone be eager to discuss it with me."

"That speaks poorly of the ladies you spend your time with, not the publication," she replied in a dry tone that drew a smile from Benjamin.

The stagecoach jumped, no doubt having hit some dip in the road, but the arm around her kept Nan in her seat whilst her heart leapt from her chest.

"In truth, my sister Katherine would likely enjoy the magazine, though I do not believe she has ever read it." Benjamin paused and considered that. "Prudence might as well, though ever since she married Parker, she is more keen on scientific publications."

Turning his attention back to the subject at hand, Benjamin asked, "What were you reading in the perfectly respectable and entirely ordinary *Blackwood's Magazine*?"

Though there was a rather entertaining and scandalous satire concerning the goings-on in Parliament, Nan chose to ignore the fellow's teasing tone. "There was a fascinating commentary about the French Revolution."

"*Vraiment*?" he asked, the French word rolling off his tongue.

"*Oui, vraiment.*"

"*Dites-moi,*" he prodded.

But as Nan's skill in speaking the language was not all it ought to be, she switched to English as she set about describing what she recalled of the article—and he listened, giving her his full attention. It was wonderful and heady all at the same time, and though they were practically trapped in place, she kept expecting him to grow bored of her conversation and withdraw.

At times, she didn't even know what she was saying, as the surprise of having another's undivided attention left her feeling a bit out of sorts. But in the best way possible.

Chapter 9

Wind nipped at Nan's cheeks, tugging relentlessly at her cloak as the stagecoach bumped and swayed along the country lane, but the scent of rain-soaked earth and ripening barley filled her nose, a far better perfume than the soot and coal dust that choked the cityscape. The storm clouds, with their swirling mists of gray, were a marvel as flashes of sunlight lightened the edges with their golden hues. A patchwork of green stretched in either direction as though continuing forever, broken only by the hedgerows, their branches shuddering as the wind ran its fingers through the leaves.

Despite being just beyond the edge of the city, Nan had never witnessed the untamed beauty of the English countryside; paintings attempted to capture that beauty, but they couldn't quite convey the spark of vitality thrumming through every blade of grass. She could only imagine what a sight it would make on a clear day with the heavens a stark blue.

A drop struck Nan's cheek, and she glanced at the darkening sky as Benjamin let out a heavy sigh. The coach barrelled toward the storm, and she tucked her cloak tighter around her, though the wool hardly protected from the chill. Shifting in his seat, Benjamin quickly shrugged off his greatcoat, whipping it around to cover her.

"You need it," she said, pushing it away just as the carriage drove into the curtain of rain.

But Benjamin pulled it tight around her. "Not as much as you do."

"Don't be silly!"

"Keep it, Nan."

And though she wanted to protest, his tone was unflinching and hard, refusing to give way, and Nan knew she would not win this argument. Tucking her arms into the sleeves, she drew close to him, hoping that her warmth might give him some relief. But soon, even his sacrifice meant little as water soaked through the greatcoat.

Together, they huddled close behind the pile of luggage, and that provided some protection against the wind. But with each passing mile, Nan grew colder.

"I am sorry," murmured Benjamin.

Nan turned to glance at him. "For what?"

"A husband's duty is to care for his wife, and only a few hours into this marriage, I have already failed on that score."

"That is ridiculous," she said with a frown, though she couldn't keep her teeth from chattering ever so slightly.

"I had plenty of time to secure you a seat inside if I had bothered to think of it beforehand—"

"Either situation would've been uncomfortable, though for entirely different reasons, and I would much rather suffer a little rain and wind with you than be dry and crushed inside with five strangers," she said as rain dripped from the rim of her bonnet. "None of them would debate the finer points of philosophy or history with me."

"Or I might've ensured that we'd left your winter gloves and cloak out," he added. "If I bribe him handsomely enough, the guard might bring down your trunk when we arrive at the inn, but none of our stops before tonight is long enough to get it down, even if he could be bothered to do so."

"You underestimate all you have done."

Benjamin gave no response, though she could practically hear his dismissive grunt.

"In truth, you've done more to care for me than anyone else," she said. "You've shown more concern for my comfort and well-being than I've received in my entire life."

Though the statement sounded like hyperbole, Nan sifted through her memory and found not a single one to dismiss her assertion, however overinflated it may seem. Perhaps her mother had shown her many kindnesses, but Nan didn't recall any offhand, and though Papa had never been cruel or purposefully neglectful, he'd never exerted any effort in securing her happiness. Except to write a single letter on his deathbed.

Even Mr. Gastrell, who'd aided her after Papa's passing, had expended only the barest of efforts. In a cruel light, one could even say that his securing her a position at the school had been done to rid himself of a troublesome parishioner. Once she was outside of his realm of influence, her former vicar had shown no interest in assisting her further.

Yet Benjamin seemed genuinely interested in securing her happiness. That kindness was enough to make Nan's eyes sting, and the rain was not helping matters, though it masked the brightness in her eyes as she considered the man at her side. Stripped of his heavy coat, he was still attempting to shield her from the worst of the wind and the rain with his body.

"That is kind of you to say," he replied, and Nan could say nothing more to dispel him of that notion. So, leaning closer to him, she gave him her weight, showing with her touch how much she trusted and appreciated him.

Her muscles strained as she fought to keep them from trembling, but when a slight grumble from Benjamin's stomach warned of other troubles, Nan set to work alleviating the one discomfort she could. Careful to keep most of the basket at her feet, protected beneath the edge of her skirt and cloak, Nan snuck out a few buns and handed them to Benjamin.

Looking like bedraggled street urchins, they nibbled on their bounty, and Nan set to distracting him with more questions about his sisters and childhood as she hid the tremors in her limbs. As miserable as the adventure seemed from an outside perspective (and it truly could be deemed a misery), Nan couldn't help but enjoy the wretched business.

With the wheels struggling in the mud, they made terrible time, and the sun sank low before they approached the inn for the night. A call of the carriage horn had them straining to see around the luggage, and they spied the outcropping of buildings growing closer.

But the moment they crossed into the inn's courtyard, Benjamin pulled free of Nan and leapt from the carriage, dropping to the ground before it came to a stop. Nan gasped and sent up a prayer of gratitude that he didn't break his neck, for it seemed a near thing, but he sprinted away without a backward glance. Perched on her seat, she stared as he disappeared inside the inn.

The behavior was odd, to be sure, but she was certain there was an explanation, and Nan left him to his business. Perhaps he needed a chamber pot. But then, Nan knew enough of men to know that they didn't bother with such niceties; she'd quickly given up scrubbing the messes left by the pub patrons along the side of the school.

Having spent most of the day tucked in one position, her legs didn't wish to bend as she rose. The passengers inside moved stiffly as they disentangled themselves with more than a few grumbles about the smell of one particularly pungent passenger. A waft of the breeze carried a hint of it, and Nan shuddered. Yes, a chill was far preferable.

Benjamin's greatcoat slipped from her shoulders, but she held fast to it as she stepped to the edge of the carriage. Though she saw the steps clearly enough, Nan couldn't quite imagine how to twist about and reach them without falling, and it was a high enough perch that she didn't wish to risk it. The people in front used their ladder, and it seemed easy enough as the gentlemen climbed down, but they didn't have to manage it in skirts, and hers kept twisting about her ankles as the wet edges tangled in her feet.

"Might I have a hand?" she called to the porter below. The young man's gaze drifted down the length of her before turning back to his work, assisting the higher-paying customers inside the carriage.

Nan's cheeks heated; yet again she'd been weighed, judged, and dismissed in turn. For all that she was a gently bred lady married to a proper gentleman, Mrs. Nan Leigh looked like a laborer's wife, bedraggled and hard used. Her gowns weren't fine at the best of times, let alone after hours atop a carriage. No doubt, if she were handsome and dressed as finely as the other ladies inside, the fellows this morning would've considered it a gentlemanly duty to see to her comfort.

And Benjamin was nowhere to be seen.

Nan's chin trembled, and at that slight tremor, she shook her head and drew in a deep breath. Fustian! She had managed well on her own for most of her life, and a few hours of Benjamin's tender care shouldn't erase that ability. But she was cold and tired, and the man who had seemed so very intent on taking care of her had disappeared without a word.

Sucking in a deep breath, she straightened her shoulders; she simply needed to ignore just how high up she was, and how far a fall it would be if she slipped. Turning in place, she gripped the top handles and edged her foot downward. With her skirts in the way, it was impossible to see where the step was, and though her toes caught hold of something, the moment she put her weight on it, her foot slipped. Her stomach fell to the ground, and the pull of gravity threatened to throw her off balance, but clinging to the rail, Nan felt for the step again and put her weight on it.

Slowly, she moved to the next one—

"Nan, wait!" called Benjamin, and a moment later, his hands were there, guiding her feet to where she could not see, helping her down with far more speed and peace of mind than she could manage on her own. When she stood on solid ground, she turned to find him frowning at her.

"Why didn't you wait for me?" he asked.

"You disappeared without a word. I didn't know when you were coming back." Or if he was coming back, rather, though that was a silly thought, for Nan couldn't imagine him abandoning her after doing so much. Yet she couldn't deny the conclusion to which her mind had leapt.

His brows climbed upward, and he winced. "I apologize. When we arrived, I knew I needed to act fast if I was going to secure us a proper room before everyone alighted. There was only one left, and it is ours."

"Truly?" Nan didn't think such a little thing could make her so happy, but the thought of a proper bed and fire sounded heavenly, and she'd read enough books on travel to know such things were not always available on the road.

"After such a miserable day, you ought to have a proper rest," he said, motioning her forward with a hand at the small of her back. "Tomorrow is likely to be just as uncomfortable."

Yet Nan didn't think it was possible for her to ever feel truly miserable with such an attentive husband. Even if their journey the next day proved as frigid as this one, there were far worse things in the world.

Chapter 10

Being so caught up in happy thoughts, Nan almost missed the maid ignoring them as Benjamin led her into the inn proper. Others were being relieved of wet things and waited on as though they were the grandest of visitors to ever grace the Fox & Hound. Benjamin called to one of the girls, but no one bothered to acknowledge the pair.

No doubt, those sitting in the more frugal seats up top weren't high-quality guests, but that was quickly remedied when Benjamin tossed one of the girls a sixpence and instructed her to show them to the Red Fox Room.

That earned him a bob and a wide-eyed, "Yes, sir."

And just like that, their invisibility lifted, making them the focus of the servants' attention. Soon, they were bundled up the stairs and tucked into a chamber. Despite the flames dancing in the fireplace, a chill in the air testified that it had only recently been lit, but it felt heavenly all the same as Nan stripped off the greatcoat and her outer things.

"I wanted to have a bath drawn for you, as that would do wonders to warm you up, but the innkeeper wanted more than I could afford," said Benjamin with a tone that said he thought it another failing on his part.

Turning toward him, Nan put her arms around him and held him close. "You've done so much already. All I need is some dry clothes, and I will be right in a trice."

Benjamin stiffened and stepped away. "The portmanteau. Of course—"

And though Nan hadn't meant to chase him away, he turned on his heel and strode toward the door with such purpose that she knew he wouldn't be swayed. But she stopped him long enough to help him put the greatcoat on once more.

"It's soaking wet, but it will do you some good to have another layer," she said, tugging on his lapels to pull it close around him.

"My thanks," he said, drawing Nan's gaze to his.

For a long, silent moment, they stood there with her skirts twisting about their legs; he was so close that if she drew a deep breath, she would bump him. Yet Nan couldn't breathe. Not properly, at any rate.

"It is you who deserves the thanks. You've done everything you can to see to my comfort today," she whispered.

"It is my honor."

Though that was a trite phrase tossed about with careless abandon, the manner in which Benjamin spoke those words was anything but meaningless. As though he meant every syllable.

The air felt heavy in the room, and Nan wasn't certain what to say or do at that moment; she felt a tug toward him, as though she ought to draw closer, and she rather missed the feel of his arm around her as she snuggled close to him. That was something to look forward to tomorrow.

"The portmanteau," he said, jolting Nan out of her thoughts.

With blazing cheeks, she stepped back from him, and Benjamin strode out the door.

...

With hurried steps, Benjamin climbed back up the stairs. As they'd covered the luggage with a tarpaulin, their things had been spared the worst of the weather, though he couldn't know for certain if the clothes were entirely unscathed. There was nothing to be done about it at this point but hope.

Opening the door to their room, Benjamin halted on the threshold as he found his new wife crouched beside the bed with a small looking glass held next to the mattress.

"What are you doing?" he asked with a frown.

Nan straightened and cast a glance at him. "I read that sheets in inns can be damp, and it's best to check them before you retire for the night. You can see condensation on the glass if they are."

Benjamin cocked his head to the side and stared at her. "Would it do any good to know if they were? We are already soaked to the bone, so damp bedding isn't likely to do much more damage to our health. Besides, it is not as though we have sheets to replace them, and assuming the innkeeper has any on hand, he'll charge us a small fortune to replace them."

Placing her hands on her hips, she considered that. "I suppose."

Lifting the portmanteau, he offered it to Nan, and her face lit with a smile.

"You are a dear," she said, pulling it open, and Benjamin found himself staring at the nightdress sitting inside.

As having an easily accessible bag was necessary for overnight travel, they'd decided on packing the majority of his things in her trunk and leaving his portmanteau free to carry their essentials, but it was an odd sight to see his old, familiar bag stuffed with feminine unmentionables. Benjamin's throat tightened, and his eyes darted to the lady holding the bag, who stood there, staring back at him as she clutched her night things to her chest.

"You ought to change out of your wet clothes..." he began, but his words drifted off when his attention dropped to the nightdress in her arms. Benjamin's gaze snapped back to her eyes, finding her staring back at him with raised brows.

They were married. Man and wife. Thus, there was nothing untoward about seeing his wife's undergarments. But the flush of his skin couldn't seem to recall that fact.

"I'll fetch us some dinner," he said, spinning on his heel and leaving the way he'd come. If Nan said anything at his retreat, Benjamin didn't hear it.

Confound it! He was a grown man, and the lady was his wife; both things ought to ensure a bit of decorum when facing a woman holding a nightdress. No doubt many of the lads he'd attended school with would mock him mercilessly for such cowardice, but though he'd spent many an hour flirting with the fairer sex, that had been innocent fun. Beyond a few stolen kisses, Benjamin hadn't wished to venture any further.

Whatever the world may think, a true gentleman treated women with respect, and thus, true intimacy was to be shared after he'd promised his fidelity and protection at the wedding altar. Those were words Mr. Price had echoed many times when he'd caught the schoolboys gossiping about their conquests, however innocent they might've been, and Benjamin couldn't shake those teachings from his thoughts.

Of course, the lady in his bedchamber was his wife, but Benjamin felt no different than a few hours ago when he'd made those very pledges. And matters weren't helped by the fact that the lady in question was Mr. Price's daughter. And practically a stranger.

He shook aside those thoughts and focused on the task at hand. Coming down the stairs, he called to the barmaid and ordered a tray of dinner to be prepared, then took a seat in the corner of the public house. With a stagecoach in for the night, and the laborers done with their work for the day, the room was filled with patrons all vying for attention, and though Benjamin wished to get Nan some proper food, he was quite content to have a few minutes alone before returning to their chamber.

Unfortunately, it allowed his thoughts to travel back to his previous worries.

Their wedding night. Benjamin was not so naive that he didn't know what that entailed. A young man couldn't reach his majority without crossing paths with some worldly gentleman who felt it his duty to educate others on such things, yet it was an odd thing to be faced with an experience that was taboo one moment and acceptable the next.

More than acceptable. A requirement. One's marriage wasn't fully formalized until the deed was done, after all. Yet Benjamin couldn't shake the discomfort that accompanied such a thought. He and Nan hadn't even kissed yet, and if that still felt like taking a liberty, surely sharing anything more would be unnerving for them both. Hardly an auspicious beginning to their marriage.

Yet he couldn't help but reflect on the weighty moment that had passed between them when they'd stood so close to one another. For all that it was a touch odd that his wife's height matched his own, Benjamin couldn't help but appreciate the straightforward manner with which she met his gaze. So many young ladies demurred, but Nan met him without pretension or coyness, her eyes alight with the glow of the fireplace.

And then he'd retreated.

"Here you are, sir," said the maid, plunking down the tray with two bowls of stew that smelled edible enough, though the bits of beef and vegetables floating in the broth left much to be desired. At least the bread was free of any pests, as Benjamin had been unfortunate enough to eat quite a few weevils at obliging inns.

The barmaid stood before him, not moving until he dropped a couple of farthings into her palm, and Benjamin rose to his feet, carrying the tray before him. A penny might've gotten the girl to deliver the tray, but doing so himself allowed Benjamin to slow his return to their chamber.

Standing at the door once more, he stared at the wood. It had taken far less time than he'd hoped to fetch dinner, though at least a quarter of an hour had passed. Surely that was enough time for her to change. His mother and sisters had taught him how much time it could take for a lady to ready herself, but surely it was quicker to divest oneself of the trappings of the day than to put them on. That was true for gentlemen, at least.

Benjamin stood there for several long moments before he shifted the tray in his hands to allow him a free one to knock on the wood.

No answer.

Was that good or bad? Inn walls were notoriously thin, and Benjamin had never visited one that didn't allow people to easily hear what was happening inside, so if there was no answer, Nan must not have responded. Yet Benjamin couldn't say for certain. Shaking his head, he pushed open the door and focused his attention on the tray (just in case), but he saw no sign of Nan in his periphery. Raising his gaze, he spied her in the bed. Sound asleep.

Her gown hung over the back of a rickety-looking chair, positioned toward the fire for it to dry, but Nan huddled in a ball beneath the blanket. Thankfully, the maids had taken his tips to heart and given them a proper counterpane, rather than the threadbare rags usually provided. To secure the room had cost him a king's ransom, but it was worth every penny to see Nan cozily situated.

A small table provided a place to put the tray, and though Benjamin hated to wake her, she needed something substantial after the day they'd had. But when he called her name, she didn't stir.

Coming to the side of the bed, Benjamin crouched beside it. Her hair was still bound up in its chignon, a fact that she would likely regret later, but with the color finally gathering in her cheeks once more, he couldn't bear to disturb her. Though paleness was a coveted quality in a complexion, Benjamin preferred to see the pink. Nan seemed a hearty and hale sort of creature, but her coloring too often made her look the opposite—especially when drenched to the bone.

Nan's lips puckered, her brow creasing as though something disturbed her sleep, but still, she didn't respond when he whispered her name.

His wife. Such an odd thought, yet Benjamin couldn't help but smile. Which was even stranger. Nan was quite the surprise. Certainly not what he had anticipated finding at the end of this journey, but once more, that feeling of rightness settled into him, strengthening with every passing mile and every hour spent in her company.

"I would much rather keep company with you..." Nan's voice rose from his memory, ringing in his mind. Had she truly meant it? Or had it simply been a kindness meant to assuage his guilt for her poor seating?

Benjamin couldn't deny that the journey—however uncomfortable—had been far more enjoyable with her beside him. Having ridden up top many a time before, he'd never considered just how much more desirable a situation it was when one had a comely lass cuddled up close, her face turned toward him as she spoke animatedly about such a strange array of topics.

His wife. Benjamin grinned.

Chapter 11

Disorientation was a common feeling when stirring from sleep, though it didn't usually plague Nan. She didn't know why it was the case, but from the moment her consciousness stirred to waking, she was aware of her surroundings. Nightmares might linger a moment or two, depending on how disturbing the images were, but she still knew precisely where she was and what was happening.

But then, Nan usually did not drift off into sleep quickly, either.

Despite having only closed her eyes for a moment, the world around her jumped, and when her eyes crept open once more, she jerked at the unfamiliar sight around her. A fire flickered, casting dancing light across the walls in strange patterns, and for a brief moment, Nan couldn't say what was up or down, or how she'd come to this foreign land.

Her marriage. The carriage ride. The inn. All swept into her mind in a flash, but still, Nan couldn't say how she'd fallen asleep. The allure of the bed had been far too great to forgo once she'd rid herself of her wet gown, and somehow sleep had taken hold. Papa had always been able to sleep the moment his eyes closed, but Nan always struggled to calm her thoughts enough to rest.

Movement outside the window testified that the hour was not so very late, for people still stirred within the inn's courtyard, though Nan suspected there would likely be someone about at all hours of the night. And the hum of voices from down below hinted that some patrons were still enjoying their tankards of ale.

As it was turned away from the fireplace, her backside was a touch chilly, but heat pumped through the room, loosening her tight grip of the bedclothes. The chair she'd placed beside the fire as a makeshift drying rack had gained more articles since she'd spied it last; a tailcoat was slung over the arms and a waistcoat was draped across the seat. On the other side was the chair's pair, and her new husband slept there, a blanket slung over him.

"Benjamin?" she whispered, but only a nasally breath met that. Nan considered the situation for just a moment before she raised her voice.

"Nan?" The blurry edge to his tone testified that Benjamin was not as quick a riser as she, but only a moment later, he straightened from his chair. "What is it? Is something the matter? Do you want something to eat?"

Beside him sat a small table with a tray holding a set of dishes, one of which was empty. For all that she ought to be hungry, she had no interest in the food.

With a wry smile, she replied, "You decided to sleep in a cold and uncomfortable chair—that is the matter."

Rubbing at his eyes, Benjamin groaned and stretched. "I didn't wish to crowd you."

Nan sat upright. "This bed is far larger than any I've ever had. Far larger than my cot at the school. There is room enough for us both." Silence met that, and Nan added, "We are married, Benjamin. It's natural to share a bed."

How she managed to say it in a steady tone was a bit of a miracle, but if his sudden departure from their chamber earlier was any indication, any sign of jitters might cause him to flee again. He silently considered it, but before he could voice any objection (as he seemed ready to do), Nan hurried on.

"You were just as soaked and cold as I was today, and you deserve to have a proper sleep," she said, pulling back the covers and patting the mattress beside her.

Holding up his hands in surrender, he grimaced. "I appreciate your concern, but we needn't...press the issue...or..."

With the shadows darkening his cheeks, it was impossible to tell for certain, but the manner in which he tripped over his words made her think Benjamin was blushing, and his meaning brought a flush of heat to her own skin. Nan supposed it was natural for there to be more than a degree of awkwardness between them given the significance of tonight, but she'd hoped they could simply ignore it.

"I had thought we could avoid speaking directly about the matter, but I suppose it is better to be upfront," he added with a frown.

Nan's brows rose, for yet again, it seemed as though his thoughts aligned with hers.

"I have no interest in rushing matters," he said. "We are married in every way that matters to me at present, and though I would like...that...in the near future...of course...I do wish this to be a true marriage..."

Lawks, her face was about to alight with flames. Nan cut off his rambling with a smile. "I grasp your meaning, Benjamin, and I agree. We needn't torture ourselves any further. However, there is no reason we cannot share a bed. Besides, you staved off much of the chill throughout our journey, and I need help keeping warm."

Dropping his head with a chuckle, Benjamin paused a moment before rising from his seat. Nan shivered on poor Benjamin's behalf when it was clear all he had beneath the blanket was his shirt and his trousers. The fabric top billowed like the sails of a ship as he hurried to the other side of the bed and toed off his shoes. Stretching his blanket atop the quilt, he slipped into bed beside her.

"Good gracious!" she gasped, not able to stop the exclamation when the icy digits he called toes brushed against hers. Even with his stockings on, they were shocking. His feet jerked away, but Nan threw back the covers and went to the portmanteau. Digging to the bottom, she found her extra pair of woolen socks and brought them back to the bed.

"Here," she said, helping to get them on with quick movements. "You'll lose a toe if you don't warm your feet."

Despite being almost thawed, the air was chill enough that Nan worked quickly and hurried back into bed, throwing the blankets back over her as they burrowed into the bed.

For all that she knew she ought to feel awkward at having a man beside her, having spent the better part of a day plastered to his side helped to ease away some of that discomfort. Side by side, there was just room enough for the two of them, so she turned to her side and came face to face with Benjamin.

Pulling the blankets around her, she kicked back and forth.

"What are you doing?" asked Benjamin with a frown.

"Warming the bed again."

"Is that so?"

Nan smiled. "I do it every night. How else do you warm up the bed but with a 'warming up the bed' dance?"

"Remind me never to stand up with you, if that is your idea of a dance," he said with a smirk.

Silence followed, and she lay there, holding his gaze. Doing so before had never bothered her, but then, Nan had never done so whilst lying in bed with him. Her heartbeat slowed as they stared at one another, and she struggled for something to say. Or to feign sleep, but for all that her exhaustion drove her to fall under so quickly, the nap had granted her another burst of energy.

Turning over, she stared at the dying flames of the fire, and though she wished to offer him the closer position, she knew he wouldn't accept it.

A tiny jolt of surprise burst through her when their feet tangled together once more, yet it somehow felt familiar. The heat at her back begged her to draw closer, and though some rational part of her knew it was forward to do so, Nan couldn't help but lean into him as she had so many times today. Benjamin stilled, and she followed suit, her eyes widening as she stared at the flickering flames.

For all that she had the monstrous ill-fortune of matching her husband's height, that fact seemed unimportant in this position. The way the two of them fitted together was both delightful and startling all at the same time. The strain in his muscles relaxed, and Nan felt like breathing once more as they nestled into bed.

A laugh cut through the silence in their room, and her brows knitted. Together, they looked out at the darkness, their ears trained for the sound again. A masculine chuckle was quickly followed by another feminine giggle, which devolved into murmurs as the fellow hummed with pleasure.

Mouth agape, Nan looked over her shoulder at Benjamin, whose eyes widened as well.

"The walls are notoriously thin in inns," he whispered, his voice rising slightly to cover the low sounds coming from the next room.

Holding hands over her mouth, Nan shook her head, but she couldn't keep the laugh inside as they both dissolved into mirth. Especially as she considered the blessing that Benjamin was content to leave things be at present, for she couldn't imagine facing the other travelers tomorrow if they were to overhear something they ought not.

His chuckles dying into a sigh, Benjamin whispered, "I do apologize for everything. For all that today was your wedding day, it has been far from ideal."

Nan glanced over her shoulder with a frown. "*Our* wedding day, Benjamin. And frankly, I think it has been wonderful. I am very happy."

"Do you promise?"

The question was quiet, and though she didn't think Benjamin meant to imply so much with that one word, she felt the unease and doubt in which it was steeped. For all that he was new to being a husband, Nan couldn't imagine anyone taking the role more seriously than he was. As words didn't seem to reassure, she cast aside whatever reservations she'd felt and let her weight lean fully into him.

"I promise. You've done everything in your power to see to my comfort and contentment. How could I not be happy?" That was met with silence, and she hoped that Benjamin was taking her words to heart. Nan didn't know why he doubted the truth when she spoke it, but she hoped he would grow to accept it.

"I am sorry I didn't come for you sooner. I don't think I said so, and I want to say it now."

"But you came, Benjamin. Many wouldn't have done so, or they would've taken the escape I offered. You are a much better man than you give yourself credit for, and I am grateful you are my husband." Nan wished there was something more to say, for those little words felt so small in return for everything he'd done for her. How could she be anything but happy when he was so good to her?

Benjamin's arm draped over her waist, curling around her, and Nan smiled as she held fast to it. For all that she ought to feel uncomfortable at such an intimate gesture, she reveled in the feel of him pressed close, almost surrounding her.

A little thing, yet combined with all those tiny kindnesses he'd bestowed today, Nan couldn't help but feel protected. Here she was safe. Wanted, even. Her throat closed, and a sheen of tears filled her eyes. Nan didn't bother to shoo them away, for they bubbled up from a heart so full, and she couldn't remember the last time she'd felt so content.

Then their neighbors grew a bit more animated, and Benjamin coughed to smother another laugh and quickly added, in a voice loud enough to cover the sounds, "Tomorrow is bound to be just as miserable."

"I told you, today wasn't miserable. Who else will listen to me prattle on for hours?" replied Nan.

"I was a captive audience. Quite literally," he replied in a dry tone, but even as he teased, his hand found hers, wrapping warm fingers around hers, and Nan's heart skipped a beat.

"Such a blessing, indeed. I can trot out my most boring subjects with which to torment you," she said. "Perhaps we can discuss the nuances of Golding's translation of *Metamorphoses*. His artistic choices for some of Ovid's turns of phrase—"

"Please no," he groaned. "I have had enough of Latin to last a lifetime."

"*In nova fert animus mutatas dicere formas...*" she began, borrowing the first line of that work.

Benjamin sighed, and she felt him shaking his head as she dissolved into laughter.

"Have no fear, husband of mine. I only know that much because my father was so enamored with the ancients," she replied. "He tested me for hours on the subject."

"I can imagine."

"But as to your original assertion," she said, circling back to her point, "I had a grand time today, all things considered, and I am certain tomorrow will be equally enjoyable as long as we are together."

Except then she would meet her new family, the thought of which set her heart fluttering uncomfortably. She had so little experience with such things. Nan could hardly believe they would embrace the lady their son felt obligated to marry. To say nothing of the fact that the majority of Benjamin's relatives were female, which boded especially ill for Nan.

But those thoughts faded as her heartbeat redoubled when Benjamin's arm squeezed her, holding her firm to him.

"If you say so, *Mr. Leigh*," he whispered, his breath tickling her neck. For all that the pet name ought to embarrass her, Nan couldn't help but grin at the growing blackness.

"I do, Mr. Leigh," she replied.

Chapter 12

The road from Birmingham and Greater Edgerton was familiar, and Benjamin knew each bend and crest. Each passing landmark. And his stomach sank with each one—which was yet another familiar part of the journey. However, this was accompanied by something (and someone) new, and that added uncertainty left his insides twisted into knots no sailor could untie.

Mother and Father had sent a carriage to meet them. Surely that was a good sign. They weren't ones to hide their disappointment, and Benjamin couldn't imagine they'd show such preferential treatment if they did not wish to welcome their new daughter-in-law. Mother certainly didn't bother to hide her irritation with Katherine or the other girls when they did not meet with her approval.

Of course, there was a chance that David and Katherine hadn't told them; despite their apparent eagerness before, it wasn't a pleasant task to complete, after all. Yet Benjamin couldn't imagine his friend and sister shirking the responsibility once they'd taken it on, so Mother and Father must know the circumstance in which Benjamin was returning to Greater Edgerton.

Which just left him to ponder the chaise's meaning once more.

"It is so nice to be in a proper carriage," said Benjamin, slanting a look at Nan. Her gaze was fixed to the window, and though he might believe her to be studying the buildings of her new home, her brows were pulled tight together, and her fingers worried the edge of her cloak.

"Yes, of course," she murmured absently.

Resting his hand atop hers in a manner that was becoming quickly familiar, Benjamin squeezed it with a smile, drawing her attention to him.

"They are going to adore you," he said.

Nan's lips pulled into a tight smile, and though Benjamin wished for something more to say, there was little he could do to assure her; as long as Mother and Father weren't openly rude to her, he would count it a success. He forced a smile and shifted in his seat. His conscience dictated that he tell her the truth of what was likely to happen, but if he were wrong, it would only cause Nan more strain, and she already looked too pale for his liking.

In quick succession, Benjamin weighed the possibilities once more. At worst, Mother would pitch a fit, which was quite the sight to behold. For all that she was a lady of breeding, who expected the utmost decorum from her daughters, Gertrude Leigh's voice could shake the rafters. If the lady spoke even a single word against Nan, they would simply have to decamp to one of his sisters' homes. Benjamin had witnessed far too much of that vitriol pointed toward his sister, Katherine, and he wouldn't repeat the mistakes of the past and allow Nan to bear the brunt of Mother's scorn.

But in truth, Benjamin suspected she would likely be cold and dismissive of the lady, which had been her favorite method of dealing with the other ladies he'd deigned to pursue. Mother had been far more keen to turn her attention toward convincing her son to choose better, and though he disliked the lectures, that was an easy burden to bear if Nan were spared.

And it wasn't as though Mother could do much now that the wedding had been performed. It was legal and binding, and she could rail against it all she liked, and it wouldn't alter the truth. Benjamin and Nan were husband and wife. That allowed him to settle into the squabs once more, his muscles relaxing.

The carriage slowed, and Benjamin leaned forward to peer through the window as they turned onto a drive. Whitley Court was not one of the finer homes in the area, for it was naught but a squat rectangle like so many other structures. The red bricks common to the area had been painted over with white stucco, giving the bland facade a breath of brightness, which he knew Mother expended a fair amount of funds to keep pristine. The ivy that had attempted to artfully climb up one side had been beaten into submission, and Benjamin rather thought the house the lesser for it; though there were practical reasons to clear it away, the green highlight was so picturesque, especially when the garden was in full bloom.

With the wet and cold spring, the blossoms were late in arriving, and with the gray skies overhead, the visage was far from impressive. Benjamin frowned at the sight.

"It is lovely," said Nan, her tone so full of genuine awe that his gaze snapped to hers. A smile lit her face, easing away the tension that had tightened her muscles as she gazed at the house and the greenery around it. "I cannot wait to explore the grounds. The area around my school had no gardens or greenery of any kind, and I've missed seeing trees and flowers."

The pressure in his chest eased at that pronouncement, and Nan released her grip on her cloak, turning her hand to wind her fingers through his. Benjamin's pulse slowed to a tenable speed.

"Then, you like it?" he asked.

"Very much," she said with a nod.

When the carriage pulled to a stop, Benjamin emerged with an easy step, holding his hand out to his bride as she climbed down and stood before the building. She threaded her arm through his, and they strode toward the front door, which opened before Benjamin touched the handle.

"My dear boy!" cried Mother as she threw her arms around Benjamin's neck, which pulled him out of Nan's hold. "I was worried you'd been waylaid. You are hours later than we expected. It is nearly full dark, and I was afraid you were stranded somewhere."

But before Benjamin could respond, she released him and turned to her new daughter-in-law. The moment seemed to stretch on as he held his breath, hoping and praying.

"And you must be our newest Leigh!" she said with a beaming smile before throwing her arms around Nan as readily as she had her son, and Benjamin couldn't help but beam when she released her new daughter-in-law, only to take her by the arm and drag her along to the parlor. The tightness in his chest released, filling him with such relief that his strength ebbed, leaving him quite lightheaded.

Bless the stars. Mother had chosen the path of acceptance.

"Oh, my dear girl, you must be exhausted. You look so ghastly pale and worn to threads, and your clothes are a mess, but it is no wonder when you've traveled so far. It is only natural to look a fright after such a journey," said Mother in rapid succession before calling out for Polly to fetch some refreshment.

Pausing just inside the parlor, Mother took Nan by the hands and stepped back to study her, and with a bright tone, she said, "My, but you are quite tall. Lofty, even."

"Yes, isn't she regal?" asked Benjamin, which drew his wife's attention, her brows pulled together. As Mother's attention didn't turn away from her examination, he tried to mouth to Nan, "I was right. She adores you!"

But his wife merely stared back at him, though that attention was pulled away when Mother took Nan by the chin, turning her face this way and that. "And you have the palest complexion. I must know your secret. Is it your cold cream? Perhaps an extra dash of almond oil? Or rose water?"

"I fear I do not use cold creams, Mrs. Leigh—"

"Oh, do call me Mother, my dear," she said, taking hold of Nan's hands with another beaming smile. "I already have four daughters, but with them all gone and married, it has been so very lonely here of late, so I am very happy to have yet another lady about the house. And with such unique features, my dear. Quite extraordinary. Certainly, not like other ladies."

Nan glanced in his direction, and Benjamin grinned at her. He knew all too well how discomforting Mother's effusiveness could be; it was like being smothered by a pillow stuffed with eagerness and praise, and though he knew it was not good for his pride, he hoped Nan basked in the warmth of that attention.

With what he hoped was a silent show of support, he nodded, but Nan's expression didn't relax. Releasing her hold on her daughter-in-law, Mother ushered them toward the seats, placing Nan in an armchair whilst nudging Benjamin toward the sofa and taking the place between them.

"Oh, when I heard the news from Katherine, I was simply flummoxed," said Mother, her brows pulling together as she shook her head. "Such a tragedy, my dear. I cannot imagine how painful it must've been to lose your father."

"Yes," replied Nan, her hands clasped tight together in her lap.

"But how very lucky of you to find such a savior as my darling boy," said Mother, threading her arm through Benjamin's and pulling him close. "Such a dear, dear boy. So very handsome and intelligent. Quite the catch for any young lady. And I cannot imagine it was easy for you to make your way all alone in the world. So very fortunate that Benjamin is a man of honor and fulfilled your father's final wish."

Mother continued to fill the air with praises for her son, speaking as though his actions were the height of goodness that everyone ought to aspire to, and Benjamin couldn't help but fidget in his seat now that his mother's effusion was turned in his direction. Wincing at Nan, he tried to share a silent laugh, but the lady wasn't looking at him.

The parlor door opened, and Polly swept in with a tea service. Mother directed the girl to lay it all out, and quickly the hostess went about preparing a heaping tray of goodies for Nan.

"Oh, you are such a thin creature. We must put some meat on your bones or you're liable to blow away in a stiff breeze. After such clearly strenuous travel, I would hate for you to fall ill," said Mother.

"My thanks," replied Nan in a flat tone, and Benjamin frowned, but the lady set aside the proffered treats and rose to her feet. "But might I please have a moment to freshen up? As you said, travel is quite fatiguing, and I look a fright."

"Of course, my dearest girl. Polly can show you to your room," said Mother, calling to the maid once more.

Benjamin moved to follow, but she grabbed him by the hand and tugged him down once more.

"Not yet, young man. I want to hear all the details. David and Katherine delivered your message, but I wish to hear more," said Mother.

Casting a look at Nan, he sent her a silent question, and she waved him away. A niggling thought warned him to follow her, but he couldn't imagine why that was the case after such a warm welcome. No doubt, it was simply strange to be apart when the past two days had seen them not only together but in very close quarters.

The door closed behind his wife, and Mother said with a frown, "Now that we are alone, I want to know why you sent word through your sister, rather than telling us directly."

"I thought it better than showing up on your doorstep with my wife in tow," he replied with a laugh.

"True, but it is such a shock that you would take such a step without consulting us first. Do we mean so little to you that you do not care for our opinion on the matter? I know things have been a touch strained of late, but surely, after all we've done for you, we've earned the right to hear of your plans to marry before you do so."

A Debt of Honor

Benjamin's heart sank, his brows pulling together. "I understand, Mother, but I couldn't leave Nan there. It would've broken your heart to see her in such dire straits. She needed protection and assistance, and this was the only way forward. My conscience wouldn't allow me to abandon her."

"Of course, my dear boy," said Mother, patting his hand. "You are such a good and kind man, and understandably, your sympathies would be roused by such a pathetic situation. I would expect nothing less than the noblest of actions from such a perfect gentleman."

Benjamin shifted in his seat, forcing his smile to remain even as she slathered on more compliments. Yet he also couldn't help the slight zip of pleasure that ran down his spine—as it always did when Mother was in her element. It was hard not to be pleased when someone was so effusive in her praise. Just as it was so easy to slip into idleness and frivolousness with his parents always encouraging such behavior.

Taking him by the cheeks, she pulled him close and bussed him on each one.

"You will adore her, Mother," he said, pulling back. "She is so very kind and intelligent. I am certain she'll be a great blessing to the family."

Mother's brows rose. "But I thought you didn't know the girl."

"I don't. Not much, at any rate," he replied with a shrug. "It's just a feeling. The more I come to know her, the more I admire her. No doubt, she has her flaws, but I've yet to see one. I truly feel as though this marriage will be a boon to us all."

"That is high praise indeed," murmured Mother with a speculative look. "How happy that you are content with being forced into this situation. Any other man might feel resentful of his new bride."

Benjamin frowned at the odd quality in her tone, but whatever it was evaporated as she began to ply him with cakes and biscuits. Yet as much as he enjoyed Cook's wares, the dust of the journey still clung to him, and Benjamin longed to change his clothes. And though he didn't care to be trussed up in a carriage again, the walls of Whitley Court pressed in as though the air had a weight to it; now that spring was well and truly here with summer coming quickly on its heels, he preferred to be out of doors.

"My thanks, Mother, but I think I will see if Nan wishes to explore her new home. The grounds, perhaps, or we might even venture into town," said Benjamin.

"You cannot think to take her out this very minute," said Mother with a horrified gape. "It has been raining for days, and she is already at risk of catching a chill. She is such a fragile creature, and she was worn to a thread. Do not risk her health. There is no rush."

The wisdom in those words rested heavily on his shoulders, though his mother's attentiveness lightened his heart in equal measure.

"Of course, you are right, Mother. Thank you for speaking up on Nan's behalf. I fear I am eager to show her everything and am liable to run her ragged."

"I know precisely what you mean, my dear boy," she said with a nod. "I mentioned your marriage to a few people, and word has gotten around. All of Greater Edgerton is clamoring to meet your wife, and I'm afraid I've filled her social calendar for the next several weeks."

Benjamin's brows rose at that. He was quite familiar with morning calls and the like, but being a son, he was free to set his diary as he pleased and had never been at the mercy of his mother's whims. Katherine and Prudence hadn't cared for the great number of visits their mother forced them on, but then, Rosanna and Francis had been quite pleased with all the attention, and he wondered where Nan would fall along that spectrum.

"And lest you forget," Mother added with a frown, "you have Mr. Garrison's card party tonight. You'll need to leave before long if you wish to arrive on time."

Holding in a groan, Benjamin winced at himself, recalling only this minute that with all the hubbub leading to his trip to Birmingham, he'd forgotten to make note of the party in his notebook. Fool that he was.

"I had entirely forgotten that I accepted his invitation." Rising to his feet with an absent wave, he strode toward the door. "They will understand the sudden shift in my circumstances, so I will send my apologies. I don't wish to leave my wife alone on her first evening at home."

"But the Garrisons are important people," said Mother with a frown. "You left without warning and returned with a bride. People are already whispering about the suddenness behind your marriage, and it would do you both some good if you went out and were seen. She is too exhausted to attend, the poor dear, but more to the point, she wasn't invited."

With a frown, Benjamin considered that. To leave Nan alone seemed heartless, yet to reject an invitation from the Garrisons could do much harm, even if his reason for doing so was sound. Society was a fickle creature, and with their hasty marriage already drawing attention, they'd best tread carefully and follow Mother's advice. Heaven knew she had her flaws, but the lady understood such things far better than he, and she could be counted on to do what was best to further their family's standing in society.

"As I wasn't invited, the two of us can remain here. It will give me the chance to get to know her better, mother to daughter, and I shall do so better without you hovering at our elbows," said Mother with a sweet smile. "Please, allow me time alone with the girl."

"If you think it best—"

"I do," she said, popping to her feet. "Now, you go enjoy yourself and do what you can to secure your wife's position whilst I enjoy some time alone with her. You'd best hurry if you wish to make it on time. You leave Nan to me."

Benjamin nodded and strode toward the door. "Have you moved my things into a new room? As much as I love my bedchamber, it's a touch small for us."

"'Us'?" asked Mother with raised brows. "Surely you didn't think to share a bedchamber with the girl."

Pausing at the threshold, Benjamin turned in place and stared at his mother. A delicate subject, indeed. Though he didn't condemn his parents for sleeping apart, he'd always anticipated that he and his wife would occupy the same bedchamber; having seen his sisters' happy marriages, Benjamin didn't think it boded well when people couldn't bear to share sleeping quarters.

"I had thought it best—" he began.

But Mother shook her head, her eyes wide. "You are not thinking at all, my boy. You may be happy with this sudden shift in your life, but it is frightening for any young lady to bind herself in matrimony to anyone, let alone to a stranger."

Lowering her voice, she drew nearer. "Please do not say you insisted on...after knowing her for such a short time...you didn't...?"

The significance in her tone was enough to color Benjamin's cheeks, and he shifted in place. "Of course not."

Mother let out a sigh, pressing a hand to her stomach. Then, with a beaming grin, she patted his cheek with her other hand. "Of course you didn't, my good boy. Not many men would be so understanding of a lady's sensibilities, but you are such a dear. So thoughtful."

She continued to praise his thinking, though Benjamin couldn't help but recall the night they'd spent wrapped in each other's arms and just how enjoyable that had been. And Nan hadn't seemed discomforted by the intimate arrangement. Yet she hadn't wished to disrobe in front of him. Not that he could blame her. Just the thought set Benjamin's cheeks blazing once more.

Saints above, it was burning hot in the parlor.

"Give her time, Benjamin," said Mother with another pat on his cheek. "Her world has been so upended of late. Allow her privacy for now, and with time, she will acclimate. If you rush her, she may never feel comfortable around you. And then where would you be?"

Benjamin's shoulders drooped. "That is sensible, Mother. My thanks. I fear I would've blundered in and made a mess of everything."

"You are a good boy, eager to do his duty. That is not a terrible thing, but you needn't rush matters." Then, with a bright smile, Mother straightened and added, "Oh, and I had thought that we might throw a dinner party to welcome her into the family in a fortnight. Rosanna should be in town by then—"

"She will?" asked Benjamin.

"We wrote to her immediately, and she is eager to meet your bride, so they're coming for the summer. I thought it would be nice to celebrate this blessed event together."

"That is so very kind of you, Mother, and I am certain Nan will be pleased. She's very eager to meet the family," he replied with a grin as the last of his worries eased from his heart. Father hadn't made an appearance yet, but he was just as likely to ignore the whole situation. But if Mother was pleased with his marriage, then there was no need to fret any longer.

Patting his cheek one final time, Mother nudged him toward the door. "Leave your wife to me, my dearest boy. I will manage everything."

Chapter 13

Travel ought not to be exhausting. After all, it was mostly sitting. The past few months had afforded Nan so little rest that two days in a carriage ought to be the height of luxury. Of course, one's chair didn't normally rock and bob hard enough to toss one out. Nor did one get chilled to the bone whilst lounging in a library.

For all that Nan had employed that excuse to free herself of Mrs. Leigh, the truth of her exhaustion settled into her bones as she sank onto the bed. Her trunk sat on the far side of the room, warning her not to get too comfortable. There was work to be done, and Nan didn't trust herself to remain conscious if her head touched the pillow. They'd gotten swept up in conversation last night, and though she couldn't say for certain when they'd finally drifted into sleep, she knew it had been far later than was good for them.

Then time jumped.

This time she wasn't met with grogginess; the moment her eyes opened again, Nan knew where she was and that she must have fallen asleep. No sunlight filtered through the window, but sounds of movement in the distance attested that it wasn't so very late. Perhaps not yet dinnertime. However, it was some time since she'd stepped into her new bedchamber.

Rising to her feet, Nan stretched and patted at her hair, though there was little point in that ineffectual movement. There was no dressing table or looking glass in the room, so she couldn't say for certain that she looked a fright, but Mrs. Leigh's emphasis on that word was testament enough.

Puffing out her cheeks with a sigh, Nan shifted to the edge of the mattress as her shoulders drooped. Benjamin had expounded at length about his sisters, yet his parents were a subject she knew little about, which revealed more than he realized. Now, having met her, Nan knew her chances of peaceable living with her mother-in-law were low.

Nan Price hadn't mixed often with young ladies, but she knew enough to recognize when their talons were drawn, and Mrs. Leigh had sharpened hers quickly on Nan's pride. In a few short sentences, she'd condemned Nan's appearance and labeled her mercenary by implying she had landed herself a fine husband through manipulation—all while making the words sound as sweet as honey.

To say nothing of the fact that not once had the lady ever referred to Nan by her name. "My dear" may have been her favorite appellation, but the subtle way in which she spoke it was anything but genuine. Shudders ran down Nan's spine.

Gracious, she was in for a rough go of it, if her first five minutes at Whitley Court were any indication.

Rising to her feet, Nan cast aside such thoughts. It was natural for a mother to be disturbed at the thought of her son forced into a marriage of convenience; Nan certainly hadn't wished it upon Benjamin and had even fought against it. Yet the deed was done, and the only thing she could do was hope Mrs. Leigh warmed to her.

Unlike every other lady Nan had ever met.

Striding to her trunk, she opened the lid and found Benjamin's things nestled on top. The sight brought a smile to her lips. There was something comforting about seeing their clothes mixed. Perhaps that was a silly thing to note, but like so many other little things since their wedding, Nan appreciated the sign that she was no longer alone.

Plucking out the waistcoats and jacket, she strode to the wardrobe and opened it to find nothing inside. Nan stared at the emptiness. Then, turning her gaze about the room, she realized just how bare it seemed. As this was his home, she had expected to see signs of Benjamin in his chambers, yet there was nothing remotely personal in the decorations. The shelves and drawers were all bare.

A knock at the door jolted Nan out of those thoughts, and the young maid quickly entered with a tray of food.

"My mistress thought you might require something to eat," she said with a bob, placing the offering down on the mattress.

Perhaps it was purely a kindness and not a subtle jab, but after Mrs. Leigh's pointed comment about her weight, Nan had ample reason to think the latter more probable. Brushing her hands down her rumpled skirts, Nan tried not to shift in place at the memory of the lady's words. Nan knew well enough that she was too tall and thin by fashion's standards. Mrs. Leigh wasn't the first to comment on such things, yet those condemnations couldn't help but prick at her.

"Where are Master Benjamin's things?" asked Nan, turning her attention toward more important matters. "I wish to unpack, but I do not see them anywhere."

Polly turned away from her work and gave another quick bob. "I beg your pardon, madam, but his things are in his bedchamber. The mistress said Master Benjamin preferred you to settle in a guest chamber."

Nan managed to hide her disappointment, though she couldn't stop her heart from sinking at that thought. That choice was entirely logical, as they hardly knew one another, yet she couldn't help but feel deflated at the thought of returning to a solitary bed. Despite having had only one night together, the feel of his arms around her, cradling her as she slept, was so comforting and warm.

Being an only child, Nan hadn't ever shared a bed, and the prospect had always seemed unappealing, as she couldn't imagine being squashed together in such a manner. And though Benjamin's movement had jostled her awake more than a few times, having another so close to stave off the cold was well worth that price. To say nothing of the peace that accompanied having another so near. Never waking in the night alone in the dark. The sound of her husband's breath (though it rattled at times) breaking the silence.

Drawing in a sharp breath, Nan straightened and nodded to the maid. "My thanks. Please tell Master Benjamin that I wish to unpack, but I will be down later."

"He left whilst you were asleep, madam. He didn't wish to disturb you; he asked me to give you his apologies, but he had a prior engagement. The mistress welcomes you to join her downstairs if you feel up to it."

Nan held back another shudder at that thought, and with a word of dismissal, she sent Polly back to work and returned to her task. There was no point in dwelling on her disappointment. But knowing that didn't stop the flush of heat warming Nan's skin. Benjamin had abandoned her on her first night. He had an engagement, which was entirely understandable, and he'd already done so very much for her that it was ungrateful to demand more, yet she couldn't help the prickle running across her skin as she wished he'd been a little less solicitous and awoken her.

Giving a sharp sigh, Nan lifted her things from the trunk, spreading her gowns out to hang. They were a shabby set. Though well maintained by her fastidious needle, she couldn't help but frown at the sad picture they made. Perhaps she might buy a few lengths of ribbon to liven them up; yet even as she thought that, she dismissed it.

No amount of frills and decoration would alter the silhouettes, which were becoming more and more obsolete as skirts and sleeves continued to puff outward. Then there was the issue of the sloped necklines, which were a far cry from the square and round ones before her. These gowns had been the height of fashion when Mama had worn them some fifteen years ago, but the columnar styles of that era were gone, and Nan's skill with a needle could do nothing to add yardage to the fabric, which the new styles demanded.

Brushing them down, she hung them in the wardrobe. Once the wrinkles were gone, they would look presentable at the very least, which was far more than she could say about her current frock. With quick movements, she changed into one of her day dresses, for they had fared better than the single evening gown she owned, which was damp and wrinkled.

As Nan had little to her name, it took minimal effort to settle into the room, her little touches transforming the impersonal space from a guest room to hers. Setting a small vase on the shelf, she wondered if she might convince Benjamin to show her the grounds tomorrow so she might find some wildflowers to fill it.

"Enter," she called at the sound of a knock. And when she turned, expecting to see Polly or perhaps Mrs. Leigh, Nan found a gentleman standing at the threshold.

Despite having never met him before, Nan knew in an instant that this was her new father-in-law. His clothes were too fine for a servant, and though he shared little resemblance to Benjamin, they had the same coloring, though Mr. Leigh's dark hair was speckled with streaks of gray.

"You must be Nan," he said, striding forward with a smile, and that shift in his expression instantly released the tension in her shoulders, for the easy grin matched Benjamin's, and she couldn't help but return it in kind.

"And you must be Mr. Leigh," she said, extending a hand toward him. Her muscles tightened at that faux pas, and though Mr. Leigh stared at it for a heartbeat, he shook it heartily before she had the chance to shift to a curtsy.

"I apologize for not greeting you upon your arrival, but I fear I got lost in a particularly intriguing book," he said with a wince. "I know it's abominably rude of me, but I fear I couldn't help myself."

"What was the book?" asked Nan as it was the only thing she could think to say.

"Is your forgiveness dependent on the worthiness of the tome?" he asked with a laugh.

And though Nan hadn't meant it that way, she grinned. "Not all books deserve such attention. It would be natural to be excessively offended if you decided a treatise on gray squirrels was more captivating than meeting your son's bride."

Mr. Leigh considered that with a spark of laughter in his gaze. "It was the first volume of *The Principles of Geology* by Charles Lyell."

"Then you are forgiven, sir. I have heard much about that book, and I have been interested in reading it myself, though I haven't gotten my hands on a copy."

"Ah, then you are a scholar, as well? " he asked with a raise of his brows. "It is good to have another scientific mind in the family. Though I suppose that is natural with your father's profession." Pausing, he added with a frown, "I was sad to hear of his passing. I am very sorry for your loss."

As lighthearted as she'd felt mere seconds before, Nan's stomach soured at the mention of her father. She was bound to hear much of the same over the coming weeks, and she needed to shore up her defenses. It was natural for them to assume that a daughter felt something at the loss. But then, most daughters knew their fathers. Or shared something more than a nodding acquaintance with them.

With a strained smile, she nodded, "My thanks, Mr. Leigh."

Holding up a staying hand, he began to speak but paused. Only when she prodded him to continue did he do so.

"I suppose it's presumptuous of me to ask it, but you are welcome to call me Father if you feel so inclined. I know I cannot replace that great man, but I do hope you will think of me in such a light." Mr. Leigh stopped and shook his head. "That sounds ridiculous. You hardly know me, but you are my daughter now, regardless of the circumstances that brought you into our lives."

Despite his words echoing the same sentiment Mrs. Leigh had spouted not long ago, Mr. Leigh's petition held none of the duplicity of his wife. Benjamin was not here to witness it, after all, and the gentleman had no reason to feign such compassion and caring unless he truly meant it.

"That is kind of you," said Nan. "It may take some time to acclimate to the idea, but I do welcome the sentiment. I hope to be truly happy as a Leigh."

The gentleman smiled broadly and gave a sharp nod before taking a seat in the empty armchair in the corner.

"Good. Now, tell me about yourself. My daughter and her husband relayed a little information, but only what my son sent them."

Clutching a pelisse in her hands, Nan stared at him. "I do not know where to begin, and I fear there is not much to say."

"Nonsense," he said, smacking a hand against the chair arm. "Now, I demand you tell me everything."

Nan shifted in place, but she couldn't help the smile that stretched across her lips as Mr. Leigh sat there, waiting for her to comply as though the answer was of greatest importance to him. Did he truly care to hear about the little nothings of her days? Many might claim a false modesty in saying there was little of interest in their life, but Nan had truly meant it.

Yet Mr. Leigh refused to let her demure, prodding her into conversation as she continued to organize her room.

Chapter 14

Despite being able to read in Latin, French, and Spanish, Nan didn't speak or read Italian. Eventually, she would rectify that lapse in her education, but in the meantime, she'd contented herself with exploring the Italian greats in English, and having read Dante Alighieri's "The Divine Comedy," Nan was quite familiar with Signor Alighieri's interpretation of the afterlife and his nine rings of hell. In each, the sins of man were put on display, along with their creative punishments. Despite its being an insightful piece, the fact that vanity hadn't been highlighted was a significant oversight on Signore Alighieri's part.

But then, the gentleman had likely never arranged a party.

"Not there!" Mrs. Leigh gave a heaving sigh as though only the greatest of imbeciles would've placed the oblong platter where Nan had chosen. "The blancmange needs to be in the center with the four smaller dishes around it. Otherwise, the smaller plates might be hidden, and Mrs. James's work will be for naught. Is that what you wish?"

As the question had been more of an accusation than an earnest desire to know Nan's opinion, she remained silent as Mrs. Leigh shuffled the dishes around the empty tabletop.

"I find it helpful to see them on the table," said Mrs. Leigh for what must've been the seventh time. "When Cook is ready to fill them, the servants can take them down to the kitchen and replace them exactly where I wish them. As a whole, they are incompetent and just as liable to array the dishes poorly."

Though the lady showed enough restraint not to tack on "like you" at the end of her statement, the meaning was rife in her tone and the narrowed look she gave her daughter-in-law.

Had their carriage crashed on the way to Greater Edgerton, leaving Nan trapped in her own personal circle of hell? Forever harangued about invitations, menus, and flower arrangements?

"Where are the placecards?" asked Mrs. Leigh, holding out a hand.

Drawing in a deep breath, Nan took the slips of cardstock and handed them over, fully knowing precisely what the resultant reaction would be. And her mother-in-law did not disappoint.

"Saints above, my dear girl. What atrocious handwriting!" she cried with all the horror of one having just discovered a loved one had been murdered. "I can hardly make out a single letter."

Nan drew in a silent breath and held it, tucking her hands behind her as she waited for the hysterics to clear. She had warned Mrs. Leigh about her penmanship, but clearly, the lady cared for no opinion other than her own. All in all, Nan thought the cards neat enough considering this was a family gathering, where assigned seating was unwarranted.

But then, she'd believed the layout of the dishes was entirely appropriate before Mrs. Leigh's histrionics. And then there were the flower arrangements she'd bungled.

Plenty of gentlemen prized neat handwriting, and Nan knew Father's school had emphasized proper penmanship, for he'd complained heartily of the time wasted on such shallow pursuits. A student was better served delving into meaningful subjects than beautifying one's writing. Just as one was better served reading about the world than engaging with it.

"Honestly, what good is that fancy education of yours if you cannot even write discernible English?" she said with a huff. "The future mistress of Whitley Court cannot comport herself as a proper lady."

Mrs. Leigh needn't go any further, for Nan knew quite well what she was thinking. What good was she? Having heard variations of it whenever she'd had the misfortune to venture into society (what little a scholar's daughter might do), there was nothing new to her mother-in-law's complaints.

And after a fortnight of being heaped with similar criticisms, Nan was unsurprised by any of it. No, she was surprised that Mrs. Leigh continued to ask her to assist with such things. But then, how else was she to show her daughter-in-law that she lacked in every discernible quality befitting a proper lady?

"Thankfully, I prepared a set myself," added her mother-in-law before retrieving an immaculate set of cards at the ready. With a wave of her hand, Mrs. Leigh shooed her away. "Go dress yourself. You will need all the time you can manage to make yourself presentable."

Drawing in a deep breath, Nan held it for a count of ten before turning on her heel and striding toward her bedchamber.

...

Despite being a gentleman of some means, Benjamin preferred dressing himself. His parents despaired over that peculiarity, but having learned to do so at school, he found he rather enjoyed the freedom of doing as he pleased, when he pleased. Especially as the fashion for extravagant cravats had faded into simplistic designs that were easily mimicked and jackets weren't cut so tightly that one required a second pair of hands to take it on and off.

With a brush of his hand, he straightened the cream silk waistcoat and tucked his dark blue tailcoat firmly about him as he strode from his bedchamber. The corridor was quiet, though he caught the distant sound of his mother's ministrations, and when he passed the study, it was clear Father was still ensconced inside with whatever book held his fancy at present.

The pair had been married several decades, yet still, Father refused to ready himself any sooner or put extra effort into his appearance, and Mother would inevitably harp at the decision, seeming surprised though she ought to have known not to expect different. Best to be clear of the battlefield before the first shots were fired.

Yet Benjamin paused at Nan's door. No doubt she was preoccupied with dressing for the dinner and wouldn't wish for an interruption; no matter how much his sisters adored him, they certainly hadn't welcomed it when primping. But he lingered in the corridor.

Heaps of fretting over Mother and Father's reaction to Nan, and it had all been for naught. All was well in the Leigh household. Or as well as it could ever be. Seeing Nan embraced by his mother and her circle of friends was a treat, yet Benjamin couldn't help feeling a little slighted that her attention was so fully theirs.

Which was ludicrous. Finding her footing in Greater Edgerton was necessary, and every bride spent countless hours greeting her new neighbors, but every time he hoped to catch Nan alone, she was immediately swept away by some social call or they were interrupted by visitors wishing to welcome the newest Leigh.

A fortnight gone, and they'd hardly spent more than ten minutes in each other's company. Hardly what a groom expected married life to be.

Benjamin's heart lightened at the clear sign of acceptance of his wife, but selfish creature that he was, he missed the time they'd had together on the journey home. Which just proved mankind's fickleness. Nan was receiving the sort of reception he'd hoped for (but hadn't dared to expect), and now, he resented his good fortune simply because (like all things), it came at a price.

Habit made him fidget as he awaited her answer to his knock, but he remained firm. But no answer.

Benjamin sighed. As much as he wanted to open the door and check that Nan was, in fact, not there, he couldn't bring himself to invade her sanctuary—and the sound of Mother's bedchamber door opening was enough to spur him to action. Turning on his heel, he fled whilst praying that Nan hadn't simply ignored his knock.

Hurrying down the stairs, he dodged between maids as they scurried about their work, putting the final touches on the house before the guests arrived. His eyes swept the corridors and rooms as he passed, and when he stepped through the threshold into the parlor, a smile stretched across his face as he spied his bride at the window.

Hands grasping the edges of the curtains, she stared out at the growing night. Candles and the fireplace blazed around her, catching the golden hues of her light hair. And though he knew it must only be a coincidence, Benjamin couldn't help the happy flutter inside at the sight of her gown, which matched the blue of his jacket to perfection. Faint stripes broke up the swath of color, lending her frame even more height and elegance and offsetting the gold ribbon that wound around the bottom, neck, and sleeves.

With four sisters, one might think him well-versed in female fashions, but being educated at boarding school from a young age and having most of his sisters married before his return had left him with little knowledge on that front. So, he was no expert on clothes, and no doubt there were special terms for the various accents and fabrics adorning Nan, but none of it mattered in the slightest because the result was magnificent.

"You look fetching, *Mr. Leigh*," he said.

Nan jerked, her eyes blinking as she turned to stare at Benjamin. Despite her facing him, recognition didn't seem to dawn for a long heartbeat. And even then, she gave only a vague nod of her head.

"My thanks. It was my mother's gown," she murmured.

"As I said, it looks fetching on you." Benjamin studied her, his brows pulling together. "Have you done something different with your hair?"

Nan shifted in place, her hands reflexively moving toward it, though she paused before she touched the coiffure. "Not really. No."

Yet there was something different. Benjamin couldn't say what it was, but the manner in which her hair swept back from her face felt new. And a wayward curl that had fallen free of its pins draped down her neck a touch, drawing his eye along that bare skin.

"Well, I stand by my assessment. Entirely fetching," he said with a smile, but she did not match it. "Is something amiss?"

Nan's blue eyes lightened a touch, though there was a strained quality to her smile that did little to assure him. "I have been run off my feet. That is all."

"I should say so. Mother has been keeping you so busy that I've seen neither hide nor hair of you since we returned home. That must be taxing." Motioning her over to the sofa, he guided her down and took the seat beside her. "I am happy to see you so embraced by Mother and the town, but I must say I am jealous. I've missed our time together."

Those light eyes met his, boring into him in silence and without a shred of a hint of her thoughts in her expression, though it was clear that beneath the quiet a torrent brewed.

"What is it?" he asked.

"I am surprised, that is all," she replied. "Except for sleep, you've hardly been home for a quarter of an hour at a time."

Benjamin shifted in his seat and forced himself not to fidget at that. "I apologize if I've abandoned you too often. My schedule rarely keeps me at home for long, and since Mother is enamored with showing you off, I thought it best if I leave her to it. Things will settle soon once your novelty wanes."

Nan gave a vague sound of agreement, though the stiffness in her expression remained, and Benjamin's stomach soured as he scratched at his forearm, though it did little good with the layers of fabric encasing it. While his excuses were genuine, he couldn't help but recognize the discomfort that accompanied a partial truth.

Yes, he was pleased that Mother adored Nan, and the pair were extraordinarily busy, but habit kept him abroad as often as possible, and he hadn't considered whether or not Nan would wish to join him as he whiled away his hours. Even the thought of being trapped at Whitley Court with his parents fawning and fluttering over him had him searching for some excuse to leave, yet Nan seemed to enjoy it, else she wouldn't keep accepting Mother's invitations.

And as if to emphasize the discomfort at home, the distant sound of arguing carried to them; Mother was in the midst of her usual tirade, whilst Father was doing his best to match her level of annoyance. Whether or not Nan enjoyed the social whirl, he couldn't imagine she enjoyed being around that all day long.

"I have missed our conversations," said Benjamin. "Perhaps we might put Mother off tomorrow and do something just the two of us."

Nan perked at that, her gaze brightening with genuine interest. "You wish to?"

"Of course," he replied with a frown, though he couldn't imagine why she would question that. He might spend most of his time away from home, but as he explained, that had nothing to do with her.

"That sounds delightful," she said. "Perhaps we might go on a drive. Your mother has taken me out a little, but only to pay calls. I would like to see more."

Patting at his pockets, Benjamin searched for his notebook, though it was a lost cause, for evening jackets weren't designed with pocket space enough for such things. Instead, he made a mental note of their appointment and settled back into the sofa.

"That is just the thing. Then I can show off my driving skills. I am quite adept at handling horses, you know," he said.

Nan chuckled. "You seem the sort to believe yourself skilled at anything that crosses your path."

"Are you saying I am arrogant?" he asked with a mock scowl.

"Those are your words, not mine," she replied with an innocent grin.

"You wound me, lady. You wound me!" The pair reclined into the sofa (or as much as they could given their evening wear), and Benjamin took her hand in his. "Now, you must tell me everything you've been up to. As we haven't seen each other much, I would like to hear—"

"There you are." Like a whirlwind, Mother swept into the parlor with all the drama of a stage actress. "You will not believe how pigheaded your father is!"

"I can believe it," murmured Benjamin whilst sending Nan an apologetic look; they would simply have to settle for a private chat tomorrow.

"You look handsome," said Mother as he rose to his feet. "You could teach your father a thing or two about being presentable. He is only just changing this very moment."

"He will be ready. He always is," replied Benjamin.

"Do not defend that libertine! He is always vexing me." Then she turned her gaze to Nan, and Mother's eyes swept down her gown. "My, you do look the thing tonight."

"Doesn't she?" asked Benjamin with a grin. "Quite fetching."

Taking Nan by the hand, Mother beamed. "I am in awe of you, my dear. I wish I were more courageous with my choices, but I am forever afraid of what others might think. You dress to suit yourself, and that is commendable, my dear."

Nan's cheeks heated, and Benjamin offered his arm to her, which she quickly took and held fast to.

When Mother's attention shifted from them for a moment, he leaned closer and whispered, "You'll get used to her compliments. She is often too effusive, but that is just her way."

Eyes wide, Nan stared at him, though Benjamin couldn't fathom what her expression meant. However, when a new set of guests appeared, the attention was quickly drawn away.

"Katherine," said Benjamin with a broad smile, and though Nan held tighter to his arm, he drew her over to his sister and his brother-in-law. The trio exchanged greetings, and then he nudged his wife forward. "And this is Nan."

As much as he adored his sister, Benjamin couldn't help but wince at the expression on Katherine's face as she examined Nan, her hard eyes sweeping over the other. Though his sister had softened much since her marriage, Katherine still had a knack for appearing more cold and unyielding, belying the warm heart he knew beat in her chest.

With a nudge, Katherine shifted her spectacles up her nose. "So, you are the young lady we've heard so much about."

"Are you trying to greet her or terrify her?" asked David.

"Hush," she said, keeping her attention trained on Nan. If Benjamin didn't know his sister better, he might've been afraid for his wife, but though Katherine barked aplenty, she never bit. "I am sorry to hear about your father. It must've been an awful shock."

"Yes," replied Nan, though she made no effort to speak further.

And unfortunately, Mother quickly moved to fill the silence. With a hard scowl, she huffed and shook her head at her daughter. "My dear Katherine, could you not have put a touch more effort into your toilette tonight? We are here to honor your brother's bride, and you look like you've just risen from bed. It is mortifying."

"Katherine looks splendid," said David in a tone that Benjamin knew all too well. Though his friend had displayed ample patience with the Leigh family matriarch before entering their flock, the seven months that had passed since their wedding had seen that trait wearing thin.

"And in truth, I rose from bed not long ago," replied Katherine in a dry tone. "I have been feeling awful of late."

"I am sorry for that," said Benjamin with a frown. "You needn't remain if you feel poorly."

Katherine huffed, placing a hand on her abdomen. "If this little one had his way, I would remain abed until my confinement."

"That is why it is important to have a properly trained maid on hand," said Mother, a sneer on her lips. "She could manage your coiffure so that it doesn't look as though you've been rolling in the stables. It is quite shocking, Katherine."

"I—" began David in a sharp tone, but with the arrival of another set of guests, Katherine distracted him, tugging him away from Mother whilst Benjamin flanked his other side, the four of them moving to the other side of the room as Mother greeted Mrs. Seward.

"She is unbelievable," muttered David.

"Peace," replied Katherine, patting his arm. "We aren't here for her."

But before the conversation could take root, the rest of the guests joined them in a steady trickle, filling out their numbers. Father eventually deigned to make an appearance, but only after dinner had been called—though thankfully, before Mother was required to hunt him down. Together, the pair led the other couples into dinner, walking hand in hand with all the warmth and affection of a Yorkshire moor on a windy winter night.

Delightful.

Chapter 15

If planning a party was akin to one of Dante's rings of hell, attending said celebration was the very center. But instead of Satan trapped there, feasting on the most treacherous of souls, Mrs. Leigh feasted upon Nan's dignity and peace of mind.

Having helped to prepare the table, she'd known she wouldn't be seated near Benjamin, which was no great surprise as Mrs. Leigh had taken great delight in keeping them apart over the past fortnight. Unfortunately, the lady in question had switched the cards after Nan had left to dress, leaving her wedged between Mr. Seward and Mr. Davis. The latter wasn't unappealing, except that he was seated beside Miss Meeks, who was far more interesting to a young bachelor than a married lady. And Mr. Seward was far too like his wife for Nan's liking, who (in turn) was far too like her dearest friend, Mrs. Leigh, for anyone's liking.

The food was divine, and the rich dishes filled the room with a heavenly aroma, igniting her tastebuds with their delectable flavors. The variety and presentation gave her something upon which to focus, but that couldn't keep the evening from being a misery. Had she been allowed to simply drift off into her thoughts, Nan wouldn't have minded it. But as the guest of honor, she was put on display again and again, forced into conversations around her.

It was a terrible size for a gathering, for it was neither large nor small. In the former, one was more able to find a kindred spirit with whom to pass the evening, and if that were impossible, one could simply fade into obscurity and spend the time contemplating one's thoughts. In the latter, the more intimate setting allowed for conversation that included everyone in the gathering; it didn't require one to hunt down companions, and the varied personalities guaranteed a constant flow of subjects.

With twenty guests in total, there were too many for all to share in a single conversation, yet without providing a varied enough group for her to disappear. And Benjamin threw himself into the middle of it, seeking attention like a moth to the flame. After spending the past fortnight being passed around Mrs. Leigh's friends, Nan found herself exhausted simply from watching him as he waded into the thick of things.

And as much as she preferred to be with him, Nan couldn't help but feel relieved when the ladies finally rose and retired to the drawing room. As Whitley Court was not large enough to boast a space set aside for that sole purpose, the parlor and sitting room had been transformed by the servants whilst the guests partook of the feast. The door standing between the two spaces was thrown open, allowing everyone to flow from one room to the other.

Before Nan could think of where to sit, Miss Meeks came up beside her with a smile. "It is good to see you again, Mrs. Leigh."

A fortnight was not long enough to acclimate to her new name, and Nan couldn't help but flinch whenever she heard it, for it reminded her more of her mother-in-law than herself.

"You, too." Though Nan couldn't recall the moment, she was certain it was true. She had been inundated with new faces and names, and they'd become one great blur to her.

"And how do you like your new home?" asked Miss Meeks. "It must be a bit of a shock to have one's life uprooted so thoroughly."

Nan didn't know what to say to that, especially as this young lady was the daughter of a dear friend of Mrs. Leigh. Honesty was well and good, but there was a vast difference between opinion and incontrovertible truth, and though honesty was a good policy (the best, in fact), trouble only followed when one was too apt to forget the difference between expressing truth and opinion.

"It has been an adjustment, to be certain," said Nan.

"Mother said your husband found you toiling away in a charity school," she said with a touch more glee than such a subject warranted. Before Nan could think what to say, she added with a sigh, "How exciting! To be at the mercy of the world and have a gallant gentleman swoop in and rescue you, giving you a new life and comfortable home."

"You make my life sound like a Gothic novel."

"Oh, wouldn't that be divine," replied Miss Meeks with a sigh. "The dark and brooding villains willing to burn the world to the ground in order to save you. To be honest, I cannot understand the appeal of the heroes in such circumstances. The villains sound far more appealing."

"I beg to disagree," murmured Nan.

Miss Meeks laughed and shook her head. "I don't truly wish my husband to be wicked, but Mama is determined to marry me off to a banker or a barrister or something equally insipid. Imagine spending the rest of one's days bound to someone so uninteresting. I long to find a man with a dark streak. Imagine having someone love you so much that he gives up his rakish ways. How romantic is that?"

"Romance is well and good, but what seems thrilling in a courtship may not make a marriage so appealing," replied Nan with a frown. "The redeemed villains rarely remain redeemed when they change for the sake of love."

"You do not understand," said Miss Meeks with a shake of her head. "To be tied to someone so dull would be wretched!"

"Believe me when I say that when one's future is dependent on another, you are far better served with bland righteousness than exciting wickedness. I'd rather have a tedious life with a good and steady husband than be left to the whims of a man who might gamble or drink our finances away—or run off when he grows bored of being married to someone who is as unremarkable as those bankers and barristers you disdain."

At those words, warmth settled into Nan's heart, for there was truth rife in every syllable. The past few months had been so precarious, and managing Mrs. Leigh was but a small price to pay to have a husband who prized honor and duty above even his own desires.

But Nan knew there was no way to convince Miss Meeks of her folly. The young ladies of her parish had often spouted such ridiculous notions, and though Nan enjoyed a good Gothic tale, it was clear why so many parents despaired of them. Ideas were a powerful thing, and spending their days steeped in unrealistic romantic notions was bound to end with the young ladies miserable in their married lives, unable to recognize the blessings they'd had in their boring bankers—which far outweighed those that came from catching the eye of a temporarily redeemed rake.

A lady came to stand at Nan's elbow, and when she glanced in that direction, she found herself face-to-face with Benjamin's sister, Mrs. Rosanna Tate.

Holding up her hands to forestall them, the lady smiled at the pair. "I didn't mean to interrupt. I was merely hoping to get a few moments with my sister-in-law when she is free, and unlike my children, who immediately demand attention, I am quite happy to wait until you have finished."

"You are not interrupting at all, Mrs. Tate," said Miss Meeks with a shake of her head, though Nan rather wished her companion wasn't so eager to include the newcomer.

Rosanna Tate was a stunning lady. Nan didn't think herself so vain as to be unnerved by those prettier than her (otherwise she would be in a perpetual state of agitation), but there were some ladies of such remarkable beauty that one couldn't help but feel like a gangly scarecrow beside them.

Despite being nearly twice Nan's age, Mrs. Tate looked a mere decade older with only the slightest of wrinkles beginning to show. Though her coloring was more akin to Nan's than the rest of the Leighs', Mrs. Tate's hair was golden, her complexion was alabaster, and where Nan looked faded, that lady was the quintessential English rose. More than that, Mrs. Tate maneuvered about the room with the grace and elegance of one comfortable with society and her place as a central figure within it.

All in all, she was just the sort of lady who found Nan's manners uncouth and alarming. If Mrs. Leigh thought her useless, she could only imagine what a paragon of femininity would think. And she was Benjamin's dear sister—which was why Nan had done her best to avoid the lady thus far. Clearly, she wasn't going to win over his mother, and she preferred to limit the number of family members who found her an annoyance and undeserving of their dearest boy.

Miss Meeks, the traitorous chit, said something about her mother requiring her and departed, leaving Nan to stare at her sister-in-law.

"It is so good to meet you," said Mrs. Tate. "When I received word about the marriage, I knew we must cut our time in London short and visit you as soon as possible. I only wish we could've arrived sooner. I have been very anxious to make your acquaintance."

There was nothing in her delivery that made Nan think the words were duplicitous, but the lady's mother had proven herself adept at comments that smelled as sweet as roses but hid thorns beneath the velvety petals. Even when Mrs. Leigh insulted Nan to her face, Benjamin seemed to believe the critique of her gown was a genuine compliment. And Nan didn't know what to make of the women that woman had raised.

"I am glad you could join us." That seemed polite enough, but Nan couldn't think of anything else to say. Not with her disastrous attempt at conversation with Miss Meeks still pulsing in her memory. "I hope your journey was good."

"I understand you had quite the adventure from Birmingham to Greater Edgerton," said Mrs. Tate with a laugh. "It is a wonder you put up with my brother's bungling."

"He didn't bungle anything," replied Nan with a frown, directed both at Mrs. Tate's assertion and her own unintentionally sharp tone.

Mrs. Tate held up her hands in placation. "I meant nothing by it. He told us of the trip when he visited this afternoon, and it is not surprising that a bachelor hadn't the slightest notion how to handle travel arrangements for a lady."

"He did everything he could to see to my comfort throughout the journey, caring more for my well-being and happiness than his own. That is far more than most gentlemen do. He was a godsend."

"Yes, of course," said Mrs. Tate in a careful tone. "I am pleased to know he was so good to you. He's done the family proud. I cannot imagine how difficult it must have been for you. Losing your father and your home must've been agonizing. I am so sorry for your loss."

Mrs. Tate paused as though weighing her words, and Nan steeled herself for more condolences. It felt as though her life of late was naught but a string of such sentiments. The one blessing of having lost her home so quickly on the heels of her father was that at Queensbury, people had been unaware of her situation unless she told them (which she didn't). With this marriage, there was no hiding the past, and everyone felt free to comment on it, telling her constantly how she must feel about the situation without knowing a thing about her or her father.

"I imagine it has been a rather confusing time," added Mrs. Tate, her words coming carefully. "Such a mixture of emotions."

Nan's brows pulled together as she tried to parse the meaning beneath, but whether it was her inability to communicate properly with the fairer sex or her exhaustion, she couldn't discern what Mrs. Tate intended to say.

"Oh my dear girls," said Mrs. Leigh, and everything seemed to clench inside Nan as the lady took her arm—down to her very toes, which curled in her slippers. On her mother-in-law's heels followed the eldest Leigh daughter, and though Prudence Humphreys was far less striking than her younger sister, the lady had the bearing of a queen.

"Mama," cautioned Mrs. Humphreys, but her mother waved it away.

"When I see two of my girls in conversation, I simply must see what they are up to," laughed Mrs. Leigh, and Nan couldn't help but feel as though that was simply a euphemism for, "*I wish to stick my nose into everything, whether or not it is my business.*"

"As the point of this evening was to introduce Nan to the family and closest friends, I am attempting to get to know her better," replied Mrs. Tate with a slight smirk, as though she found the intrusion more amusing than irritating.

"Oh, yes. Our dear girl. Such a blessed addition to our family." That Mrs. Leigh managed to say that all without gagging was a testament to the lady's acting ability, and Nan made note never to take her at her word. "And how lucky for her to have such a kindhearted benefactor in Benjamin. It must be a comfort to know that your father's final thoughts were of you and that his last actions in this world were to see to your welfare."

The lady looked at Nan, drawing with it the attention of her daughters, and Nan didn't know what to say. Somehow, saying that she would've preferred he gave her more attention during his life than waiting until his deathbed didn't seem the proper thing to say. Nor would it do to point out that his actions simply confirmed how little he cared for his daughter, for asking others to care for her was the least amount of effort he could expend on her part. It was something, but hardly worth noting.

So, Nan nodded in return. Let them make of it what they would. She may not be adept at finding her place amongst the womenfolk, but that didn't mean she was a complete dunce.

"Mother," began Mrs. Humphreys, but Mrs. Leigh spoke over her.

"Quite the man I raised. Benjamin is such a good boy. The perfect gentleman."

Nan shifted in place and held her tongue, casting her thoughts to the book she'd abandoned upstairs. A few nods at the right time, and little else was required of her as Mrs. Leigh continued to heap praises on her son, and by extension, herself.

"Mother, Mrs. Meeks is trying to catch your attention," said Mrs. Humphreys with a brittle smile. As Mrs. Leigh's back was to the lady, she couldn't see the lie for what it was.

Whilst the lady was occupied with that distraction, glancing about to locate her friend, Mrs. Tate leaned forward and whispered, "We shall talk again later just the two of us."

Mrs. Humphreys said not a word but gave Nan a sly wink, which had her straightening, and in quick order, the pair had their mother thoroughly distracted and herded away from Nan.

Chapter 16

No doubt the menfolk would arrive soon to invade the ladies' sanctuary, sweeping them up in the card games Mrs. Leigh had planned. Meaning, Nan would be caught in more awkward conversations as she lost again and again to people with far more practice and skill.

Inching backward, she crept toward the border between the parlor and the sitting room. Though the partitions that served as the divider were pulled back, there was still a good foot of wall blocked off on either side, giving an adequate hiding place. Especially as Nan had tucked a chair there before the evening commenced. If anyone were to walk into the sitting room, they would see her easily enough, but as most of the activity would take place in the parlor, she would be granted a modicum of peace.

Nan would've preferred a more comfortable seat, but beggars could not be choosers (or shouldn't be, at any rate), and she took refuge in the hardback chair, tucking her skirts back so that they wouldn't be seen by casual observers in the parlor.

Just a few moments of peace would do a world of good. Rubbing at her face, Nan sighed, letting out all the pent-up frustration of her situation. But more than that, it helped to recall the words she'd said to Mrs. Tate and Miss Meeks.

Whatever the price she had to pay now to be Benjamin's wife, her life was still improved compared to where he'd found her. No cold toes at night. No pokey tick mattresses upon which to sleep. And whatever exhaustion she felt now, it was nothing compared to having spent all day shepherding children through their lessons and then all night scrubbing floors, cooking, and preparing for the next day to do it all again.

To say nothing of the fears for her future. Positions would not last forever, and what would've happened to her then?

As much as she'd adored teaching, the constant exhaustion and fear were gone now, and Nan couldn't help but feel her life had improved leaps and bounds. Benjamin was a good man who treated her well. Her mother-in-law was wretched, but her father-in-law was a gem. Her newfound sisters seemed a strange bunch but not openly hostile. And Benjamin was correct in believing this turmoil would settle eventually. They were man and wife, and there was no undoing it; Mrs. Leigh would have to accept that fact eventually. Wouldn't she?

And no matter how frustrating the Leighs may be, Nan knew what it was like to be alone in the world, and that was infinitely more difficult to bear.

The only reason her situation was arduous was because Benjamin had given her hope that their life could be more. Nan scoffed at herself, for the sentiment was ludicrous. Traveling to Greater Edgerton had taken only two days, and she'd allowed those tendernesses to fill her head with all sorts of wild fancies. Benjamin was a good man and treated her fairly, but had she expected the quiet devotion he'd displayed to be a daily occurrence? Or that her world would be devoid of hardships because of his thoughtfulness?

Yes, his kindness might've allowed what otherwise would've been two horrendous days to become something genuinely beautiful, but was she entitled enough to expect the world to suddenly blossom with roses and be forever filled with sunshine? Roses required rain and cold at times, and they couldn't bloom forever if there was naught but light and warmth.

Peace settled into her heart, allowing her muscles to relax as she considered the great blessings to be found in her life. Surely Mrs. Leigh was not so wretched as to outweigh all the other blessings.

But then, the lady was determined to test that resolve. Despite having known her only a fortnight, Nan knew Mrs. Leigh's voice all too well, especially when she was passing along gossip, and those less than dulcet tones drifted to her from the other side of the room partition.

"Of course it was surprising. I never imagined my dear boy would appear on our doorstep, married—without even consulting us on the matter!" said Mrs. Leigh.

"That must've given you palpitations," said her companion, whom Nan couldn't identify. Not that it mattered, for that was not the point of the conversation. No, Mrs. Leigh wished to be overheard. Her friends all knew what had happened, and there was no need to rehash it in such a blatant fashion in the only place Nan was guaranteed to overhear.

"I had to retire to my bed for an entire day. You cannot imagine, Sybil," said Mrs. Leigh with a sigh as though the greatest of all burdens had been laid upon her shoulders. "My heart breaks for him. Benjamin was so enamored with that lovely Miss Rothschild. Now, she is lost to him—all because some old schoolmaster preyed upon his goodness."

Nan straightened, her heart dropping. Despite having met a veritable hoard of people in the past two weeks, she was fairly certain she hadn't heard the name Rothschild before, but then, she couldn't imagine the family would wish to make her acquaintance if Mrs. Leigh's assertion was true.

Had Benjamin loved another?

"She is so pretty and sweet and accomplished," the lady continued. "Miss Rothschild would make any man a wonderful bride. And he is trapped in a marriage to someone hardly worthy of being called a woman."

Mrs. Leigh went on to list all of Nan's deficiencies as a woman, all of which she was already quite keenly aware of, but try as she might, she couldn't help but feel prickles of pain upon hearing all her faults listed in such a succinct manner. But none of it compared to Mrs. Leigh's final condemnation.

"For goodness' sake, she's tall and gangly like a man and a good two years older than him. And her coloring!" Mrs. Leigh hissed with something of a gasp. "I've read of albinos, and I wonder if she might have a touch of that about her. She's so pale and colorless. It is little wonder he wishes to sleep apart. He even calls her 'Mr. Leigh' when he thinks there is no one around to hear."

Silly or not, the words pained her, painting the sweet pet name in dark colors. Benjamin didn't mean it in that fashion, for it was born of a jest between them, yet Nan couldn't help but feel the rejection steeped in the fact that he so often preferred anything over her company. But then, would it be any wonder if his heart belonged to another?

"A lady cannot help her plainness," replied her companion.

"Yes, but a lady can help her toilette. She continues to parade about in ghastly gowns without considering at all how her poor appearance reflects on the family. I considered having her replace them, but clearly, she doesn't have the taste or sense to appreciate such things, so why waste the funds? I would rather buy another for myself."

"Besides, it would be attempting to make a silk purse from a sow's ear."

Mrs. Leigh laughed. "Too true. She hasn't the figure for the new styles. Her shoulders are atrocious."

Nan didn't know shoulders could be anything but shoulders, but she supposed that only proved her mother-in-law's assertions that she hadn't taste or sense.

"And I could forgive all that if she wasn't so entirely useless as well," replied Mrs. Leigh with a sigh. "Heaven knows my eldest daughter has never been lovely, but Prudence is a useful sort. She was managing the household from a young age and did so with such skill. That 'Mr. Leigh' cannot even organize a menu without my assistance. Even Katherine can manage that..."

Nan knew better than to trust Mrs. Leigh, yet hearing validations of innate fears was hardly comforting—however logical it was to dismiss the words.

The voices dropped away, and Nan let go of the breath she'd been holding.

Had Benjamin a sweetheart? Or rather, had he *had* a sweetheart? Nan couldn't imagine him nursing a tendre when he was married. Then again, gentlemen were known to do so, yet Nan couldn't erase what she knew of the fellow. The only reason he'd married her was because of honor and duty, and it was difficult to imagine such a man dismissing his marriage vows carelessly.

Rubbing at her forehead, Nan tried to dispel the megrim threatening to take hold, but as much as she tried to turn aside from such unhelpful thoughts, they plagued her. To believe or not to believe? To trust logic or sentiment?

A head popped around the edge of the wall, and Mrs. Katherine Archer's dark gaze fell immediately to Nan. "I thought I might find you there. That was my chosen hiding place until I made the mistake of marrying a gentleman who insisted on dragging me out of the shadows."

Mrs. Archer's delivery was sharp, making it seem a condemnation of her husband. However, having seen the pair together, Nan knew the sentiment was as false as Mrs. Leigh's warmth.

"I fear you've made the same mistake," added Mrs. Archer as she dragged an empty seat to Nan's side. "Benjamin is too like Rosanna to be content with solitude. Unfortunately, you've married into a family that prizes social ability as the greatest of skills. Even Prudence, who is generally more content to be at the outskirts of a gathering, is often found side by side with Rosanna, in the heart of every conversation."

Dropping onto the chair with a sigh, Mrs. Archer studied Nan with her keen eyes, and Nan forced herself not to squirm beneath that direct regard.

"I must admit I had no idea how taxing being a lady of leisure can be," replied Nan with a wry smile. "I hadn't dreamt that sitting on sofas and traveling from parlor to parlor would be so demanding."

A faint smile graced Mrs. Archer's lips. "That is the curse of the quiet folk. Where others gain strength from being in the thick of things, I always find myself tired at the conclusion, regardless of how slothful the activity."

Nan laughed at that. "Precisely."

For all that the lady's demeanor had an edge of ice to it, Nan couldn't help but like Mrs. Archer and wonder if they weren't more alike than different.

But then the lady dared to tread down unwelcome paths.

"How are you faring?"

Such a succinct question. So commonplace. The opening to every conversation between the dearest of friends and passing strangers. Tossed about with little true meaning, despite the incredibly personal nature of its inquiry. Yet the manner in which Mrs. Archer posed it did not feel cheap, which made it all the more difficult to answer.

Considered as a whole, Nan was faring quite well. She had a comfortable home, an honorable (if absent) husband, and though she wished her mother-in-law to purgatory, surely that one blight on her life wasn't bad enough to blacken the whole of her blessings.

To say nothing of the fact that the blight in question was also this lady's mother. Given how Mrs. Leigh greeted her daughter, Nan didn't think there was much affection between the pair, yet people were strange when it came to family. They might abuse and belittle each other, but heaven help the outsider who attempted the same.

All these considerations swept through her mind in an instant, and Nan gave Mrs. Archer a faint smile. "I am well."

But the hum in response spoke of disbelief as Mrs. Archer continued to study her. "You mustn't listen to Mama. I saw her and Mrs. Davis talking, and I can only imagine what conversation you 'accidentally' overheard."

"I thank you for your concern, but I promise I am well," replied Nan. For all that she prized plain speaking, it surprised her how quickly she dipped into falsehood. But the likelihood of her honesty meeting with disaster was too high to risk it. With things strained between her and Mrs. Leigh, Nan didn't need to add another enemy to her list.

And it wasn't as though there was any evidence to be given to support Nan's claims. When in front of others, Mrs. Leigh's barbs were subtle enough to be viewed as the compliments Benjamin believed them to be, and Nan could easily imagine just how petty it would sound if she attempted to explain the turmoil brewing between her and her mother-in-law. Battles fought against such sneaky opponents couldn't be won with a direct attack, and Nan was more likely to look vindictive and unfeeling than Mrs. Leigh.

Yet Mrs. Archer watched her for a long moment, and Nan couldn't help but wonder if she might find an ally in the lady seated beside her.

"I understand you are a great reader," said Mrs. Archer, shifting the subject as she nudged her spectacles into place. "Benjamin has spoken of it often. Quite the scholar."

"As I never attended formal schooling, I had to develop a love of reading if I wished to learn anything." Nan paused as she considered the hardness of her words, which were far more curt than she'd intended. "But I also have it from Benjamin that you are quite the musician. I fear I haven't any musical talent whatsoever, but I would love to hear you play."

Mrs. Archer broke into a broad smile that reminded Nan so very much of Benjamin's. It erased all the hard lines in her features, softening them into something entirely new.

"Now you have done it, Nan. That is one subject on which I can speak incessantly, much to the dismay of my parents. You are trapped now, and I will not release you."

Chapter 17

Whitley Court was not a large house. Though comfortably appointed and with lands enough to provide amply for the family inside, it wasn't in the same league as Overbeck Hall, Leaden Court, or Boxwood Manor. A perfectly splendid home for the Leighs, though it did not boast vast wings with countless rooms. It certainly wasn't large enough to lose a person within.

Yet Benjamin couldn't deny that was precisely what he'd done.

Though equally small, the party last night had been lively enough that Nan had drifted from his side and disappeared to some quiet corner with Katherine. Every time he'd sought her company, someone had demanded his attention until he'd discovered that she'd retired for the evening without saying goodnight.

And now, Nan was nowhere to be seen. Scouring the public rooms, Benjamin finally forced himself to climb the stairs up to the family's private chambers. Despite their marital status, it always felt strange to seek her out in that sanctuary; every time he crossed that threshold he felt like an interloper.

With a gentle knock on the door, Benjamin heard the blessed answer and slipped through the door to find the lady in question seated atop her bed.

"Good morning, dear wife of mine," he said with a smile.

Nan looked up from her book with raised brows. "Morning?"

"Do not tell me that I married an early riser. Banish the thought."

"When the hour is in the double digits, I hardly think one can consider it 'early,'" she said in a wry tone as she shifted to sit higher against the headboard.

"It is when you are up until it is in the single digits," he replied.

"Then you enjoyed yourself last night?" she asked, her gaze dropping to the book. The tone was off-handed, yet Benjamin couldn't help but notice the lack of enthusiasm. Not disinterest per se, but he couldn't put a finger on the precise sentiment.

"Did you not?" With how Nan kept company with Mother and her friends, the question seemed silly, for his wife clearly adored society and all its offerings. However, Benjamin couldn't help but ask.

"I like Katherine," said Nan, a genuine smile peeking out. "I can see why you adore her so."

Tucking his hands in his pockets, Benjamin beamed. "Yes, she is a good sort. A bit odd but good, nonetheless."

Nan shifted the book in her hands, holding it close. She fiddled with the edge, her eyes studying the letters.

Without looking at him, she asked, "What are your plans for the day?" Then raising her gaze to his, she added in a wry tone, "Now that you've bothered to stir yourself, that is."

"Why am I to be made the subject of mockery, madam? You cannot expect me to forgo my beauty sleep," he said with a proud tilt of his chin. "This handsome perfection does not come from fatiguing oneself by rising in the early hours."

"Would you dare risk your complexion by wandering out of doors this afternoon?" she asked with mock concern. "If you are not careful, you might find yourself plagued with..." Leaning in, Nan added in a *sotto voce* whisper, as though it were the worst thing in the world and ought not to be spoken aloud, "...freckles."

Benjamin clutched his chest. "One cannot be too careful."

They shared a little laugh, and he drew nearer to sit on the edge of her bed.

"So, what mischief are you getting into today?" she asked with raised brows.

Having entirely forgotten what had sparked this bit of teasing, Benjamin took a moment to recall her earlier question. "Riding with Mr. Standish and a few friends. The wretched weather has pushed back those plans for several days, and now that the weather is fine for the first time in ages, we mean to make the most of it."

Holding fast to her book, Nan nodded. "That does sound amusing."

"No doubt Mother has your day packed full," he replied with a smile. "Today is her at home day, if I am not mistaken."

Another reason why the ride with Mr. Standish was so very appealing. Even if the weather were foul, Benjamin would've insisted on going. Mother's ability to pet and praise grew tenfold when her friends were about, and his discomfort increased exponentially with each additional witness. And as the steward didn't require any assistance today, Benjamin's time was his own today.

Quiet fell, and he glanced at Nan, though she did not look at him in return.

"If you wish to spend your time reading, do you not care for a proper seat?" he asked with a cocked brow as he patted the mattress. "I assure you the house is full of them."

"I am comfortable where I am," came the short reply as she turned her attention back to her book.

The bedchamber door burst open, and Mother swept in like a ruffled whirlwind. "I thought I heard your voice, my dear boy. Are you pestering our dear girl?"

Clutching her book tighter, the lady in question did not smile at the jest, and Benjamin held back a frown as he considered the downward turn of her lips.

"Isn't it a husband's job to pester his wife?" he asked, hoping to see a twitch of a smile on her face once more. When Nan did not, he leaned closer and whispered, "Have you been sleeping well? You do not seem yourself."

Brows rose at that, and Nan peered back at him with an exasperated look, though he didn't know what he'd done to earn it. Surely expressing concern wasn't a frustrating thing.

"Have I done something to vex you?" he asked.

But Mother swept around the bed to stand beside them, "What are you two whispering about?"

"Nothing," he answered, sending Nan a secret smile she did not return.

"Why are you hiding away?" asked Mother. "Surely we would be more comfortable in the parlor. I can have the maids prepare a tea tray."

Rising to his feet, Benjamin held out a hand to Nan, and though she took it, she did not look in his direction as they were herded out of the bedchamber and down the stairs. He studied Nan's expression, though it was hard to tell what was amiss from only her profile. Of course, it was difficult to tell anything, for they'd known each other such a short time. Yet Benjamin couldn't shake the thought that she was upset.

Had the party been too much for her? Perhaps he ought to have insisted that Mother wait another fortnight. With Nan traipsing about Greater Edgerton society so often, Benjamin wouldn't blame her for being worn to a thread, and one could both enjoy parties and social calls whilst finding them exhausting, after all.

Benjamin supposed Katherine might've said something, as she was known to be brusque at times (which was rather off-putting to those who did not know her—and even, at times, to those who did), but Nan had admitted to liking his sister. Perhaps someone else had vexed her. He certainly hadn't done anything.

In short order, Mother had them situated in the parlor. Benjamin moved to sit beside Nan, but he was shooed off once more by his mother, who sat at her daughter-in-law's side. Though he would rather have pressed the issue, he couldn't bear to cause offense when the lady was demanding more time with Nan. It did him good to see it—even if Benjamin wished he might have a touch more of it, himself.

"My, you do look handsome today," said Mother with a beaming smile as he took his seat across from them. "That color is so flattering, though you look fetching in anything."

"Mother, please. Nan already thinks I am puffed up; slathering me in compliments isn't helping matters," said Benjamin as he shifted in his seat.

"Nonsense. Pride is only when you think better of yourself than you are, and you, my dearest boy, are the best of men. Surely acknowledging it is no great sin," she replied with a shake of her head. "I have yet to meet a gentleman more striking, witty, or kind than you. I do not know what I did to be blessed with such a son as you."

How did one stem such tides of praise? Benjamin's cheeks heated, and when Mother attempted to foist some cakes and tea on him, he held up his hands.

"My thanks, but I fear I cannot remain. I am expected at the Standishes' before long," said Benjamin. "A group of us are going to go riding this afternoon, and I ought to be on my way. I would hate to disappoint them."

Nan's brows shot upward, almost as if in challenge, and Benjamin frowned. What had he said to garner such a reaction? Did she wish him to throw over his engagement? That seemed odd, yet he couldn't fathom the source of her expression. Then, like a sudden downpour appearing on an otherwise sunny day, dawning dripped into his consciousness as their conversation from the previous night came to light once more.

He'd promised to take Nan on a drive this afternoon.

Wincing, Benjamin shook his head. "I must apologize. I only just recalled the plans we made last night. I had meant to write it down in my diary, as I didn't have it on me last night, but it slipped my mind."

"Plans?" asked Mother, peering back and forth between them. "What plans?"

"To go on a drive. I fear I have been neglecting her," said Benjamin.

"What stuff and nonsense!" said Mother with a dismissive wave. Fixing her attention on Nan, she asked with a piteous frown, "Am I not companion enough? Benjamin has done so much for you already; would you require him to forgo time with his friends as well?" She paused, her eyes growing suspiciously bright. "I apologize if my company is so unbearable, my dear. I thought you enjoyed meeting your new neighbors and friends. I didn't mean to overstep."

Nan's cheeks blazed, spurring Benjamin to respond. "Of course, she doesn't mean any insult by it, but I've hardly been around since she arrived—"

"Stuff and nonsense," replied Mother. "You've been more at home the past fortnight than the month before it. You are a busy man—and rightly so."

"Mother, please," he said. "Might I speak with Nan for a moment?"

Stilling, the lady gazed at him with wide eyes, that glimmer of tears reappearing. "Am I to be banished from my own parlor?"

"Of course not, Mother—"

"Have I been an unkind hostess? Is that why you wish to speak where I cannot overhear? I do not understand what I've done to deserve such treatment." With a shake of her head, Mother pulled a handkerchief free of some hidden pocket. Benjamin never knew where they were kept, simply that they appeared like magic at her beck and call. Dabbing at her eyes, she continued her watery self-flagellation.

"Mother, please," said Benjamin, holding up his hands. "I do not mean to upset you."

"I know you do not, my dearest boy," she said, blotting her damp cheeks. "You are so kind and loving to your old mother. I apologize for being so ridiculous, but I cannot help but feel as though you do not trust me, and I am at a loss to know what I have done to deserve such cruel treatment."

"Not a thing. I simply wanted to prostrate myself before Nan, and I prefer to do so in private," he said with a hint of humor.

Straightening, Mother stared at him with a furrowed brow. "Prostrate yourself? For what, pray tell? Are you wicked for planning a casual outing when a previous engagement slipped your mind? That is no great sin requiring penance."

Turning to Nan, Mother reached out and patted the young lady's hand. "Do say you are not so missish as to be put out over a little mistake."

"Of course not. It is just a little mistake," murmured Nan. For all that her words might ease his conscience, she sat there, stiff and unmoving. Enough so that Benjamin's mild concern grew into something greater. Was she truly put out about it?

A smile tipped the corners of Mother's mouth, and she gave Nan's hands another pat. And the handkerchief had disappeared. "Too right, my dear girl. Nothing to get worked up over."

For all that the lady's words were kind, Benjamin couldn't help the chill that stole across his skin as he contemplated Nan.

"Do you wish me to throw them over?" he asked.

"Don't be ridiculous," said Mother with a shake of her head. "What sort of wife would demand her husband forgo a commitment simply to be at her beck and call? It is not as though she's lonely, for I am always on hand to cheer her up. Surely a mother is more adept at raising one's spirits than a husband."

Nan fiddled with her skirts, smoothing them out, and Benjamin rather wished Mother would give them just a few minutes to speak, for he would very much like to know what was going through her thoughts. If she would tell him, that was.

"Perhaps you could come with us?" asked Benjamin. "It will be a surprise to the others, but I've never heard them complain about having a pretty lady in their company."

Light eyes darted from her lap to stare into his. A slight movement made it look as though she was about to speak.

But Mother did so first.

"Don't be ridiculous, Benjamin. She cannot go with you. Even if she could ride, which I doubt she does, what sort of lady would wish to go gallivanting about the countryside with a bunch of men?" The insinuation in her tone made it clear just what sort would, but before Benjamin could respond she added, "Besides, we have a full calendar, and unless she wishes to slough off her responsibilities to our guests, Nan cannot leave."

Rising to her feet, Mother drew Benjamin up as well, his gentlemanly instincts demanding the action, and she shooed him toward the door.

"Now, you'd best be on your way if you are going to make your appointment."

For all that the lady was quite right in that assessment, Benjamin couldn't help but glance at Nan from over his shoulder. Stepping around Mother, he moved to his wife's side, crouching before her.

In a low voice that couldn't carry to Mother's ears (unless she decided to crouch down alongside him), Benjamin asked, "Do you want me to stay? I can postpone my ride if you wish."

Nan studied him, silent and inscrutable, for a long moment before she whispered in return, "Do as you see fit, Benjamin."

Despite that assurance, something in her tone gave him pause, though Benjamin couldn't name the reason why. Nan had just given him permission to go, after all.

Rising again, he nodded in farewell and strode toward the door, but paused at the threshold. "I do apologize for ducking out on you. I hadn't intended to do so. But perhaps we can spend the evening at home tonight—"

But before he could finish that thought, he pulled himself up short before he committed the same offense once more. With a wince, he amended, "Lancaster invited me to a card party, but you are welcome to join us."

"No, thank you," said Nan, hurrying out the words before Mother could answer for her. "I fear I am still recuperating from last night's festivities, and I'd prefer an evening at home."

"Understandable," he replied with a nod. "Perhaps the day after that."

"Perhaps," was the only reply he received. Benjamin smiled at Nan, hoping to elicit some warmer response, but she only motioned toward the door. "If you wish to leave, you'd best be on your way. You wouldn't want to be late."

But as Benjamin moved to do as he was bidden, Mother stopped him with a hand to his arm. Leaning close, she said in a low whisper, "The girl is happier here, and I am happy to watch over her. Do not give her a second thought."

"Thank you for all you've done for us both."

"It is my pleasure, my dear boy," she said, giving his cheek that familiar pat. "Go, enjoy yourself."

That warmed his heart, and Benjamin strode down the corridor, his step growing ever lighter as he left the confines of Whitley Court.

Chapter 18

Mother and son held a whispered conversation, and Nan could only watch, her heart panging as Mrs. Leigh wove a spell over Benjamin. For all that she couldn't believe he was so easily deceived, it was clear to see that for some inconceivable reason, he trusted his mother. But she supposed that was not surprising. However biting and bitter Mrs. Leigh could be, her dearest son received naught but sugar and honey.

Rising to her feet, Nan strode to the window. The view was hardly endearing, for it faced the street, and though tufts of grass edged the drive, the gravel path leading to the walled gate drew the most attention. It was the same wretched view Nan had from her bedchamber; as guest bedchambers were less frequently used, they did not require the finest views. She couldn't help but wonder if Benjamin's bedchamber boasted that finer vantage. No doubt it did.

Yet grim though it may be, it afforded Nan a view of her husband as he strode out the front door. Walking past the window, he made his way to the stables, sparing only a passing glance in her direction. Granted, he did bestow a wink and that flirtatious smirk with which he teased her so often, but even that lovely sight was not enough to raise her spirits.

Benjamin had abandoned her.

For all that they jested about gentlemen chasing young ladies, he seemed to prefer the company of his friends to his wife. Day after day, those parties and outings stole him away from her side, and the only time they'd attempted to make plans, his friends took precedence over her (helped along by his mother, of course). Despite all the many times he referred to her as his wife, she couldn't help but wonder if he recalled that he was married.

Nan's heart fell as she considered that. After all he'd done for her, how much more would she demand from him? That he forgo his pleasures to keep her company? With a flick of the quill, her father had stolen away Benjamin's future choice of bride, and Nan was determined to commandeer his time.

No doubt, he would've stayed had she spoken that desire aloud, for Benjamin had certainly shown himself keen to see to her comfort and happiness, but was it wrong of her to wish to hear him say that he wanted to stay with her? To have him express an interest in her company of his own volition and not some sense of duty?

"Mind your posture," snapped Mrs. Leigh. "You are a Leigh, not some destitute schoolmistress, and you needn't go slumping about."

Squaring her shoulders, Nan did as told (though her posture required little correction), and when she turned to see her mother-in-law, there was such a gleam of triumph in her gaze that Nan's stomach churned. She didn't know what schemes the lady was enacting, but it was clear to see Mrs. Leigh was celebrating a victory.

Nan strode to the doorway, and Mrs. Leigh called out, "We have guests arriving in an hour. I expect you to be here and on your best behavior."

Keeping her jaw squeezed tight, Nan marched away without responding, for she did not trust herself to do so civilly. A very large part of her longed to unleash her anger at the treatment. However, a small but strong portion of her heart couldn't be entirely angry with Mrs. Leigh: what mother would be pleased with the young lady her son had felt forced to marry?

Nan drew in a deep breath and held fast to that thought. With time, things would calm—as long as she did not exacerbate their present troubles by turning this quiet skirmish into an all-out war.

Patience. Placation. Pacification... Though Nan attempted to distract herself by listing off more synonyms that followed that alliteration, the list wasn't long enough to do much good. Propitiation! There was another, and one that Nan was certain she'd never used in her life. Though the meaning veered more toward forgiveness than appeasing. Bother. Shifting to foreign languages, she translated the list. *Patientia. Placation. Pacificatio.* Latin was hardly different from English, and the same could be said of the other Romance languages, but Greek provided more of a challenge.

Climbing the stairs, she focused on all those things to distract herself from her husband and his mother. And when she reached the landing, the sight of her father-in-law's study door standing ajar was enough to lighten her spirits further.

When closed, it felt too intrusive to knock, but the opening seemed like an invitation. Gently rapping against the wood, she peeked inside, but Mr. Leigh did not sit in his usual chair beside the fire. Though his space featured a desk like so many other studies, it looked rather forlorn and abandoned, for there was nothing atop it, and she doubted its master used it often. In contrast, the armchair was worn and the seat cushion sagged almost alarmingly in the middle. The footstool had scuffs from the heels of his shoes, and a stack of books sat atop the table at its side; a single book lay open across the arm as though Mr. Leigh had walked away in the midst of his reading.

Calling out once more, just in case he'd disappeared into some nook, Nan wandered deeper into the room. Shelves lined the walls, covering the plaster with paper that was far more interesting than any print Mrs. Leigh might've chosen. Each book was well-loved with pages pristinely cut and spines showing enough wear to have been thoroughly read without suffering fatal damage.

And what a selection it was. Science, philosophy, mathematics, and literature, the vast breadth of knowledge was represented here, though Nan was slightly disappointed to see only a scant number of novels in the midst. Sliding one of the books from its place, she flipped through the pages, though she did not recognize the author, and Nan wished Mr. Leigh was about to describe the contents, for it was impossible to say what the plot may be.

Her current book was nearly complete, and Nan longed to have another on hand. As she was about to finish something of a more scientific bent, she thought something more fanciful might be just the trick. She'd long ago found that following a captivating book with a similar work only ever led to comparisons that rarely reflected well on the second; far too often, she was left disappointed, only to come back after some time had passed and discover the book was far better than she remembered it. Better to have a literary palate cleanser between genres.

"What are you doing?"

The sharpness of Mr. Leigh's voice had Nan jerking around to face him, the book in her hand snapping shut.

"I—"

"Do you know how expensive these are?" he said, snatching it from her hand. "No one is allowed in my study. No one! These are *my* books."

"I apologize..." Nan held up placating hands and inched toward the door.

Her strength ebbed with every angry syllable, and though she thought herself stronger, the world blurred as tears gathered. With Mrs. Leigh's terrible treatment and Benjamin's indifference (to say nothing of the weeks of forced socialization),

Nan's reserves were drained utterly and completely. Her chin trembled, and Mr. Leigh straightened at the sight.

With a sigh, he scrubbed at his face. "No, it is I who should apologize. I didn't mean to be short with you, but I fear my family is not always so kind with my things, and it has left me a little testy when anyone invades my sanctuary."

Nan let out a breath and nodded, the tightness in her chest easing ever so slightly. "I feel the same about my bedchamber. It is difficult to see it disturbed when you have only one place you view as solely yours. There is no need to apologize."

"Yes, there is, my dear. And I do hope you will accept my humblest apologies," he said with a courtly bow. "I ought not to have raised my voice. The only excuse I can give is that I have been out of sorts today."

"I am sorry to hear that," she said with a frown. "Is there anything I might do?"

But he waved it aside. "I do not wish to trouble you with my financial woes. I will manage them."

Yet that did nothing to comfort her as she considered just what that might mean. Having no control over the household, Nan had no concept of the family's income or expenses, and knowing that there might be trouble was enough to restore so many fears that had fled the moment Benjamin had proposed.

Yet Mr. Leigh did not invite further discussion. Motioning toward a seat, he said, "I am more interested in how you are faring."

"I am well enough," said Nan, inching toward the door, but her father-in-law herded her in his intended direction and took the seat opposite.

His dark eyes studied her, considering her with careful shrewdness. "How is my wife treating you?"

Nan's brows shot upward, though she managed a calm, "She has been very attentive."

"That is not an answer," he said with a slight smile as he set his feet on his footstool and rested his clasped hands atop his middle.

"It is the only one I have to give."

"I highly doubt that. I am well aware that my wife is a shrew of the highest order—only content when she is making everyone around her miserable."

Though Nan had no inclination to divulge anything future, Mr. Leigh watched her with such quiet concern brimming in his gaze that she couldn't help but clutch onto the only person in this household who seemed to notice her drowning and bothered to throw her a lifeline.

"It has been difficult, Mr. Leigh."

His brows drew together. "Though I do not wish to force the issue, I do hope you will call me Father one day."

"I apologize, it is difficult to recall—"

"There is no need to apologize, Nan," he replied, holding up staying hands. "It wasn't a condemnation. Merely a reminder. Do so, if you wish to." Then, turning back to the subject at hand, Mr. Leigh added, "I am sorry to hear it has been difficult. Having been married to my wife, I can well imagine how difficult it must be for you to be thrust into this household. Though I do hope Benjamin is not part of your troubles."

Nan paused as she considered that. Yes, he had added to her burdens in a way, yet she couldn't bring herself to admit that. The balance of the good he'd done outweighed the bad, after all. And it wasn't purposefully malicious, which made a world of difference.

"Benjamin has treated me very well."

"I am glad to hear it," said Mr. Leigh with a nod. "He is a good boy, and I do hope he will prove to be a man of integrity and honor."

"He is," replied Nan, fully meaning it.

But Mr. Leigh studied her again. "And my wife?"

Nan gave a faint smile that was more regretful than happy. "I do not think she likes me at all, and that is difficult to bear."

"I can well imagine," he murmured as his brow furrowed. Pursing his lips, Mr. Leigh stared off as his thoughts roamed, and when his gaze snapped back to her, he straightened in his chair and leaned toward her. "This is my study—my sanctuary. No one is allowed inside it without my express invitation. Benjamin is hardly around to do so, but my wife knows not to cross that threshold."

As she wasn't certain what the point of that declaration was, Nan merely waited until Mr. Leigh continued his thought.

"I want you to use it whenever you wish," he said with a smile. "Whether I am at home or abroad, you have free rein to use it as you please. The books are at your disposal as well. Make this your sanctuary, too, for I can well imagine there is nowhere else where you can find any peace from her."

Nan's bedchamber was the closest thing to that, and Mrs. Leigh had proven time and again that she did not honor that boundary. Mr. Leigh's offer settled into her heart, making it flush hot and sending a wave of heat through her as she considered the generosity rife in that offer.

"You do not mind it?" she asked with a frown.

"Mind it?" he replied with a tender smile. "I would be honored. There is little I can do to rein in my wife. She is too strong-willed for me to control her. However, I have learned to corral her in a sense, and I am quite happy to offer up a bit of peace to my dear daughter-in-law."

Tears threatened anew, but Nan wouldn't let them fall. With a broad smile, she nodded.

"Thank you..." She paused as she was about to say his name. Considering everything that had just happened and the joy coursing through her heart, she knew there was no other way to finish her statement than, "Father."

The gentleman held a hand to his heart as though that was the dearest thing to him. "And thank you, my daughter."

Chapter 19

Faces blurred into a kaleidoscope as Benjamin hurried along the streets of Greater Edgerton, his feet navigating the uneven cobbles with more instinct than finesse as the persistent thrum of commerce surrounded him. Though this portion of town was far less busy than the more industrial parts, people were forever about.

Thankfully, it was quiet enough that Benjamin could move without thinking, for his thoughts were entirely occupied by the missive in his pocket. His pulse quickened, driving his feet faster as he hurried down the streets deeper into the town.

Why had Katherine settled so blasted far from Whitley Court?

Fear spiked through him as he scurried up the front steps of Stratsfield House. Hardly waiting for the maid to answer the door, he swept through the threshold, pausing only long enough to ask directions to his sister. And when he burst into the parlor, Benjamin found Katherine and David seated on the sofa, looking quite cozily situated, though their gazes (and those of the rest of the Archers) all darted toward him.

And he stood there, staring back at them.

"What is the matter?" asked David, his voice conveying all the concern Benjamin felt pumping through his veins. "You do look like the devil is at your heels."

"What do you mean, 'What is the matter?'" Holding up a crumpled paper, he glanced at his sister. "Katherine sent for me."

"I asked you to pay a call," she said with a frown. "I didn't say you needed to come this very minute."

"My sister—who is in a delicate condition—sent me a note, asking me to visit—something she has never done before—and did so right as I was leaving for the evening—an odd time of day to do so. What else was I to assume but that something was amiss?"

The corners of David's lips quirked up. "And you believed that if something were amiss with her 'delicate condition' we would immediately send for you?"

"Do not mock me," he said with a scowl. And despite it being clear that all was well, Benjamin's heart refused to calm, the rapid beat pumping that anxiety through him. Matters weren't helped by the fact that his sister and her husband—the man who was supposed to be Benjamin's friend—were both looking at him with a mixture of pity and amusement.

"What were you thinking, Katherine?" asked Benjamin.

Movement from behind him had him turning to see David's mother rising from her seat as she beckoned to her daughters.

"Come, girls, let us give them some privacy."

They did as bidden, but Clarissa glanced back at the trio, looking quite eager to listen in, and only once the door was closed did Katherine lean forward with a wince and a shake of her head.

"I apologize. I truly didn't think you would interpret my note in that manner, else I would've been more careful in my wording." She patted the empty seat at her side, and as much as Benjamin hated the thought of letting go of his frustration, the relief at finding her healthy and hale swept through him, stealing away the strength his fear had granted him.

But Benjamin refused to sit beside her, choosing the armchair across from them instead. He knew it made him look like a petulant child, but his logic had fled him the minute he'd read Katherine's note and feared the worst.

"Ever since you two married, I've hardly spent any time in your company, and then I receive a missive sending for me like a queen summons her subject," murmured Benjamin, not bothering to hide the bitterness coloring his tone. Even if he'd been able to curb his tongue after the fright he'd received, he couldn't help the pang of irritation that had been building of late.

David's expression pinched. "I am a husband now and will be a father in short order. To say nothing of the fact that I still have my family's business to manage—despite my father's efforts to bankrupt it. And even though another of my sisters is happily married off, I am still responsible for the other two, and my mother's well-being. So, you will forgive me if you are not a priority at present, Benjamin."

"If that is meant to mollify me, you have failed," he grumbled.

"It is meant to be the truth," replied David in a monotone. "You know you are one of my dearest friends and more than merely a brother-in-law. I am sorry if you feel neglected, but I will not apologize for having my priorities in proper order. Even if you do not."

Benjamin straightened. "And what does that mean?"

Casting a look at his wife, David raised their joined hands and placed a kiss on hers. He murmured something to Katherine, and though Benjamin couldn't hear it, her resultant blush spoke volumes. Clearing his throat, he drew their attention back to the matter at hand. But when Katherine's gaze swung his way once more, Benjamin wished he hadn't, for her dark eyes narrowed on him.

"What are you thinking, leaving poor Nan alone with Mama all the time?" she asked. "She is your wife, yet you hardly spend any time with her."

With a sigh, Benjamin settled more comfortably into his seat. "That is why you dragged me here?"

"Watch your tone," said David with a challenging look.

Benjamin drew in a sharp breath, his eyes narrowing.

"Calm yourself," said Katherine, giving both men a dismissive wave. "I didn't drag you anywhere, and though your tone is flippant, I assure you my concern is not a little thing. You know what Mama is like, yet you've abandoned your wife to her care."

"I haven't abandoned her. Mother adores my wife. Dotes on her, in fact." Benjamin didn't go so far as to scoff at his sister, though it was a close thing. Clearly, David was not of a mind to endure even a hint of disrespect, and Benjamin was not of a mind to poke the bear, so to speak. Katherine had no such qualms, for her sigh was steeped in the sort of long-suffering that only an older and far wiser sister could feel when facing a much younger and simpler brother.

"You cannot be serious, Benjamin."

"And why not? She is always complimenting and praising Nan. I could almost believe Mother enjoys her better than me. It's not as though the woman is a demure wallflower, unwilling to show her displeasure. You know as well as any person alive how quickly Mother offers up criticisms, yet I've never heard her offer up a cross word to or about my wife."

"I do not know what that woman is up to, but I assure you she is not 'doting' on Nan," said Katherine with a frown. "I have tried to invite her for a visit so she might have time away from Whitley Court, but Mama keeps refusing the invitation on Nan's behalf—"

"You speak as though Mother is holding her hostage," replied Benjamin with a laugh. "Nan is a grown woman and free to go where she pleases. She is no prisoner, and she chooses to host gatherings with Mother and pay calls on others. Not long ago, you lived under her roof, and though she made some demands on your time, you were free to do as you please."

"And I paid dearly for it." With another scoff, Katherine threw her arms wide, as though pleading for the heavens to intervene. "You do not understand how manipulative and cruel that woman can be. You've never faced her wrath—"

As his sister felt free to be petulant, Benjamin followed suit, his gaze narrowing. "You forget that I just went toe to toe with 'that woman' a few weeks ago. I have spent my life with the expectation that I *must* break the entail, and I was terrified about what would happen. Yet when the time came, both she and Father accepted my answer and let things lie—"

"If you think for one moment that either of them has accepted it, then you are a fool!"

"Katherine," murmured David, his hand squeezing hers.

A flash of heat swept over Benjamin's cheeks, and despite the brief flash of knowledge that warned that a hasty response was unwise, he let it loose. "I am sorry Mother treats you poorly, Katherine. I do not understand it and will not excuse it in any fashion. But just because she is cruel to you doesn't mean she feels the same about the rest of us."

Katherine jerked back, and David's eyes narrowed on Benjamin.

"Don't you dare speak to her that way," he said in a low voice. "I will not allow that. And though I do not agree with the blunt manner in which she spoke to you, I agree with the sentiment. You are being a fool."

Benjamin threw up his hands. "You are my friend—"

"She is my wife, and that trumps all else," said David. "And as my friend, you need to treat my wife with respect. And as her brother, that is doubly true."

Those words were like dumping a bucket of ice water on the growing heat building in Benjamin's chest. For all that he did consider David a friend of the highest order, there was a truth he didn't wish to acknowledge to the gentleman. Despite being different in appearance, there was something of Mr. Price in David's advice and companionship. Being five years older, David had always felt as much like an older brother as a friend, and his advice frequently mirrored that which Mr. Price so often offered.

And hearing those hard words and seeing the disappointment dimming David's gaze, Benjamin felt that more keenly now. Especially when the subject regarded Mr. Price's daughter.

Scratching at the back of his head, Benjamin shifted forward in his seat. "I apologize, Katherine. I didn't mean to be short with you. However, not only did you give me quite a fright tonight, but you make it sound as though I have neglected my responsibility. I married Nan, after all. Surely that is proof enough that I care deeply about doing right by her."

Katherine opened her mouth to respond, but Benjamin held up a staying hand.

"I assure you if Nan gave any indication that she was miserable, I would do my utmost to resolve it. I wish for nothing more than to make her happy."

"Do you think she would speak her mind so readily?" said Katherine with a tone that clearly said she knew the answer. "You only just know each other, and this concerns your mother. Surely you can see how difficult it would be for her to speak out. Even having known David for years and trusting him more than just about anyone, it took quite some time before I allowed myself to be vulnerable to be entirely honest with him."

David huffed, slanting his wife a look. "Even keeping quiet until the vows were spoken, and it was too late for me to flee."

Straightening, Katherine pulled her brows together, her gaze filling with that very vulnerability she'd spoken of. Despite having known her his entire life, Benjamin was still amazed to see such fragility in his sister. The lady had always seemed so indomitable, yet she cast a look steeped in sorrow at her husband, and Benjamin felt like echoing David's earlier words, warning him to tread carefully.

But before he could do or say anything, the gentleman lifted their joined hands and pressed his lips to her knuckles, murmuring a quiet word that erased those dark sentiments and replaced them with something far warmer. Only their hands touched, and though they said little, Benjamin shifted in his seat, turning his eyes from the private moment.

And cleared his throat.

"I concede that you may be correct," said Benjamin, though it was more to appease his sister than it was truthful, "but Nan is not as finicky as most ladies, and I doubt she is afraid of anything. I wish you could've seen her working away in that hovel of a school, determined to make her way in the world."

The memory was both inspiring and haunting at the same moment, for Benjamin couldn't help but imagine what might've happened had he accepted her initial dismissals and left her alone.

Shaking free of that thought, he added, "And from the very first, Nan has been unfailingly honest. The nature of our marriage forced the issue, in fact, for we had to discuss things that most would find intolerably uncomfortable between strangers. She speaks her mind, yet she has said not a single word to indicate that she is anything but happy at Whitley Court."

When he glanced back at Katherine and his friend, he found them staring at him—the first with amusement and the second with disbelief. Yet Benjamin couldn't help but feel the rightness of his words. Katherine was a dear to concern herself about Nan's happiness, but the two ladies were not the same, which was immediately evident within minutes of speaking with them.

Benjamin had come to appreciate his sister. Adore her, in fact. Yet he couldn't ignore the fact that until recently, he'd despaired of ever liking her. Katherine Leigh, now Katherine Archer, was brusque and difficult at times. Their two elder sisters had managed to find happy footing with Gertrude Leigh, even if the relationship was complicated at times; Rosanna often enjoyed Mother, in fact. Nan was infinitely more intelligent, sweet, and endearing than any of the Leigh girls, so it was no mystery that she'd earned Mother's approval.

But shrugging those thoughts away, he returned to the subject at hand. "Besides, it is not as though I am avoiding Nan. Once you decamped, I only ever returned home to sleep, after all, and I am there far more often now. Not that it would do any good, for Nan is so occupied with Mother that she is never about."

Katherine stared at him as though he was speaking gibberish, and Benjamin refused to squirm beneath her steely regard.

"So, because Mother is forever putting her nose into Nan's business and commandeering all her time, you think she is happy about your marrying a lady who is your inferior?" asked Katherine with an arched brow.

"Nan isn't my inferior," Benjamin shot back with a frown.

"In every way that matters to Mother, she is. Nan has no family connections or money. She is older than you, quite tall, and plain, to boot—"

"Katherine!" said Benjamin.

But the lady merely held up placating hands. "I am plain—"

"Ridiculous," added David with a scowl. "Utter nonsense."

Taking hold of his hand once more, Katherine gave him a sweet little smile that looked utterly strange on her face, for Benjamin was certain she'd never given such an expression before winning David's heart.

Turning her attention back to her brother, Katherine amended, "To everyone but my exceptionally blind but dear husband, I am plain—not to mention far older than him—so I am not condemning the match. Merely explaining how Mother views it."

"Every man would do well to find himself an older bride," said David with a self-satisfied grin, drawing his wife's gaze to him. The pair sat there in silence for a moment, and checking for an escape, Benjamin readied himself for a retreat if she began giggling.

"Katherine?" prodded Benjamin.

She jerked her gaze from her husband, as though only just recalling that her brother was sitting there. "Yes?"

Benjamin raised a brow, and she pressed her free hand to her cheek as though to cool it.

"Uh...Mama. Yes." Giving herself a little mental shake, Katherine returned to the subject at hand. "I do not know what game Mama is playing, but I will never believe that she is happy you married Nan. You weren't there to see the torrent of tears she unleashed when we told her. She was so overcome that she took to her bed. More likely, she is doing everything she can to force a wedge between you two."

"But to what purpose?" asked Benjamin with a shrug. "We are married. There is no undoing it now, even if Nan and I wished to."

"If I could comprehend our mother's logic, then I wouldn't constantly be in her black books."

Benjamin gave her a faint smirk. "I would wager large amounts that you understand Mother quite fine. You just do not wish to play her games."

But that didn't stymie Katherine, for she immediately countered with, "Then you ought to listen to me when I say that Mama is up to something, and I fear your Nan is bearing the brunt of those machinations."

"You make it sound as though Mother is torturing her," replied Benjamin with a laugh. "I know she has treated you horribly, and I will not deny that your warning gives me pause, but I again reply by saying that though your experience with Mother is wretched business indeed, that doesn't mean she is treating Nan that way."

Katherine opened her mouth (no doubt to argue), but Benjamin hurried to add, "We all believed Mother and Father would rain hellfire down upon my head if I refused to break the entail, and other than an uncomfortable conversation, they've shown no inclination to do anything more in the two months since. You fret about Mother's treatment of Nan, but I assure you I have seen nothing but kindness, and even you haven't any solid evidence, else you would've given it. Yes, you've received terrible treatment at their hands, but can you not see that she doesn't treat everyone in that manner?"

Letting out a heavy breath, Katherine gestured at Benjamin and said to her husband, "You speak to him. I cannot bear his pigheadedness for another minute."

Benjamin straightened once more, his pulse quickening at Katherine's frustrated words and tone, but before he could give his temper free rein, David hurried to ask a question that gave Benjamin pause.

"Do you dislike Nan?"

Chapter 20

The words settled like ice in his veins, and his forehead creased as Benjamin stared at his brother-in-law. "How could you ask such a thing? I know this marriage wasn't planned, but that doesn't presuppose that I am bound to dislike her. This situation was not of her making. My work with the estate and my social obligations keep me from home—not her."

"And you think she understands that distinction?" asked David with a knowing look that held more than a touch of judgment.

Crossing his arms, Benjamin frowned. "I would hope so. But why do you both assume that the issue lies wholly with me? Her time is occupied as often as mine is. And might I point out that at the dinner party last week, she never sought me out."

Benjamin nodded at Katherine. "I know you do not care for parties, yet you spent much of it at David's side. Nan hardly ever looked in my direction. Clearly, she is content with our arrangement, and I have only ever wished to ensure that happiness. Beyond the issues with our journey home, I have done my utmost to ensure she is cared for and comfortable. Isn't that the sign of a good and attentive husband?"

For all that he did view David as a sort of advisor and confidant, Benjamin was rather eager to belt the fellow in his smug face, for he gave such a knowing look, as though he were the font of all wisdom. Arrogant twit.

"As someone who has an equally poor example of what it means to be a father and a husband, I can say it is understandable that you would be ignorant of what it truly means to be a good one. And as someone who has come to see it for the incredible joy it is, I will tell you that being a husband is more than providing for your wife."

David's tone softened, turning from a lecture to more of a secret shared amongst friends. "So often, we speak of it as a responsibility, and while that is true, being a husband is so much more than that. It's about yoking yourself to her."

His hand tightened around Katherine's, and she leaned into him as he spoke. "She isn't a duty to oversee but a priority that ought to be placed first because she is the one person who will be at your side throughout this life. Friends come and go. Children leave home. Your wife is there for all of it. Whether or not your mother is taking care of her, it is your right and privilege to do so yourself. Stop leaving it to someone who doesn't know the meaning of kindness."

Drawing in a deep breath, David shifted in his seat, and Benjamin readied himself for more; he knew the signs, for he was quite familiar with David Archer's lectures, and interrupting him did no good.

"You've done right by Nan in many ways—done more for her than many might've done, to be true. But when you arrived home, you slipped back into your previous life. From what I've seen and heard, you swan about town as though nothing has changed, and I am left wondering if you want to be married. And if so, do you want a marriage like our parents'? Or something better?"

For all that Benjamin wished to dismiss the meddling as just that, truth rang through the words, leaving him with one question echoing in his thoughts. Did he wish for a marriage like his parents'? The answer to that was easy enough to supply, for he didn't think anyone in his right mind would wish such a thing.

Though David sat there as though waiting for an answer, Benjamin wasn't ready to give it to him. Besides, it was no one else's business except his and Nan's.

"Are we finished?" mumbled Benjamin, folding his arms.

"You wish to leave and lick your wounds?" asked Katherine with far too much astuteness for his comfort.

"You've given me much to consider," he replied, rising to his feet. Moving toward the door, he paused when his sister called out to him.

"One more thing, Benjamin."

When he paused and met her gaze, there was far more sweetness and empathy than he would've ever expected from Katherine had this been a year ago. But the more he came to know her better, the more Benjamin wondered how anyone was fooled by the hard exterior she employed to hide her tender heart.

"Yes, Katherine?" he prodded.

"If you are so unhappy being at Whitley Court, how much more difficult do you think it is for Nan? That isn't her home. Those aren't her parents. She was uprooted from everything she knows and loves."

Benjamin straightened, those words sinking deep into his heart as he nodded in acknowledgment before turning on his heel and fleeing.

...

Shadows darkened the bedchamber, fought off by a lone candle and the banked embers of the fire. Had Father seen Nan in such a position, he would've reprimanded her for reading in such poor light, but as Mrs. Leigh controlled how many candlesticks were given to each room, asking for more would've been a pointless endeavor.

Nan had grown too comfortable in her father-in-law's study. There, he had lights aplenty. Here, she had blankets and pillows. A trade-off, to be certain.

Not that it mattered, for though her eyes tracked the words on the page, they left little impression; her hands moved on instinct, turning the pages once she'd glanced at each line. Forcing herself back, she tried to read it again, though she had as little luck as before.

In truth, she was too tired to read, but if she put the book down, Nan was certain to fall asleep—something she did not wish to do. Not yet. Time away from Mrs. Leigh was precious, and she couldn't bear to part with a single moment. Even for sleep.

A knock at the door had her attention darting up from the page; her fingers tightened around the book, and she forced her voice to remain even as she called out to the person. Mrs. Leigh was abed, after all. It was doubtful that the lady would rise from her slumber just to harp at her daughter-in-law. Or so Nan hoped.

But when the door opened, Nan was faced with someone she certainly did not expect to see. Benjamin poked his head inside as though checking that no one was about, and he slipped into the room, shutting the door behind him. And stood there.

"Do you require something?" she asked.

Benjamin tugged on the edge of his dressing gown. "No. I simply wished to see how you are faring."

"Well enough," she replied, which was a truth she ought not to forget. So many people struggled in this world, and it did no good to hope for more than that when she was already so blessed.

His slippers scuffed against the floor as he shifted from foot to foot. "That is good."

Perhaps she ought to welcome him into her bedchamber, invite him to sit, or give at least a passing nod at politeness, but with her fortitude so depleted, Nan could hardly muster the thought that she ought to do so, never mind acting upon it.

So, she returned to her book as Benjamin seemed determined to stand there, mute. Of course, it was even more difficult to pay attention to her story now, for Nan was aware of every flutter of his nightclothes and creak of the floorboards as he fidgeted. And then his footsteps moved across the room, and though she did not look up, she spied him in her periphery as he came to the bedside.

"Nan?" Benjamin's question held such uncertainty and timidness that she couldn't help but turn her full attention on him.

"Yes?"

With a faint smile, he shifted in place. "Can I join you here tonight?"

Nan's brows rose at that, her thoughts quickly sifting through his meaning, but before she could settle on an interpretation or his motives behind it, Benjamin hurried to explain.

Scratching at the back of his head, he shrugged. "We may have shared a bed only one night, but I have to admit I prefer it to sleeping apart. You are very good at heating the blankets."

Perhaps not the sentiment a lady hoped to hear, but Nan couldn't help but smile all the same. "Is that so?"

"I've found myself missing that old inn." Benjamin's grin quirked to the side. But then it vanished as he hurried to add, "Not that I wish you to feel obligated. I agreed to keep my bedchamber because I wanted you to have privacy, should you wish it, and I do not wish to press the issue."

Nan's brows pinched together, though she smoothed her sharp edge of surprise. Certainly, it ought not to be startling to discover that Benjamin's reasons for sleeping apart were more than what Mrs. Leigh or the staff had given her. Yet she couldn't help the pang that pained her at yet another bit of evidence of her mother-in-law's disdain.

Shutting her book, Nan held it to her chest. "And you want to sleep here because you're cold at night?"

With a huff of laughter, Benjamin seemed to scoff at his poor excuse, but when he spoke, that hint of uncertainty returned to his tone, calling to the tender corners of Nan's heart.

"In truth, we've hardly had the opportunity to speak since we arrived home, and as both our schedules are keeping us apart, I thought the only solution would be to carve out some time. With you." Silence followed that before Benjamin added in a quiet voice, "Please."

Nan studied him as he stood there, awaiting her response, and for all that she was quite ready to throw back the covers for him, she couldn't help but pause and consider what he was asking. "Do you wish to?"

Benjamin cocked his head to the side, his brows pulling low. "Why wouldn't I?"

As much as she wanted to remain silent on the matter, Nan couldn't help the response that sprang forth at his question. "You've done your utmost to avoid me."

Any levity fled from his expression as he winced at her statement. Clearing his throat, Benjamin shifted in place, tugging at the edges of his dressing gown, and Nan couldn't help but feel her cheeks heat as she considered what she was saying.

"I did not mean for that to sound like an accusation," she hurried to add. "You've sacrificed so much for me already, and you are free to use your time as you please—"

"Do not speak like that." Benjamin paused, softening his tone as he continued, "You have said similar things before, and I think it is in both our interests to not label our marriage a 'sacrifice' for me, as though I am the only one whom this affected."

Nan sighed, but before she could let forth the words she wished to say, he went on.

"Not only is it supremely unhelpful to think about it in such terms, but you are not the only one whom this marriage benefits, nor am I the only one who had to give up something when we exchanged vows. You surrendered the opportunity to find a spouse you love as much as I did."

"We both know that my marriage prospects were hardly favorable, Benjamin."

"I know nothing of the sort."

The words, so firmly spoken, gave Nan pause as she studied him, but for all his jesting at times, it was clear that Benjamin meant what he said.

Holding up a staying hand, he went on, "I do not view this as a sacrifice, Nan, so please do not speak as though you are some great burden to me."

Yet Nan couldn't help but consider all the many hours he'd spent avoiding Whitley Court since their return. Though she wanted to believe him, it was impossible not to feel as though this was a slight against her. And though she knew doubly that Mrs. Leigh couldn't be counted on to speak a lick of truth, Nan couldn't help but wonder if there wasn't a particle of truth concerning Miss Rothschild.

"What is that expression?" asked Benjamin, his eyes narrowing.

Nan opened her mouth with a ready answer, but he frowned.

"Tell me the truth, Nan."

And as much as she wanted to retreat, her feelings were too close to the surface to hide—especially as Benjamin watched her with the determination of a bloodhound scenting a fox. So, Nan spoke those hidden thoughts aloud as he stood at her bedside, though she touched on only the barest points concerning Miss Rothschild; he may wish for honesty, but Mrs. Leigh was still his mother, and he didn't need to know just how much she needled Nan.

The lady was angry at this turn of events that had dropped an unwanted daughter-in-law in her lap. No good would come from antagonizing Mrs. Leigh further.

Chapter 21

Benjamin placed his hands on his hips with a shake of his head. Then, nodding toward the bed, he said, "I hate to rush matters, but is it possible that I can slip under the blankets while we discuss this? It was a weak excuse to pester you, but I am nearly chilled to the bone now. My toes are turning to icicles."

Nodding, Nan set her book on her bedside table as he threw open the covers and climbed inside. A slight shiver took hold as the blast of cold air seeped into her warm cocoon, but the next moment, Benjamin was tucked up tight and the pair leaned up against the headboard as they stared off at the fireplace opposite.

"Firstly, I was never serious about Miss Rothschild. I flirted with her a bit, and though I liked her well enough, it wasn't anything of consequence. We were friendly, and I had a passing interest in her for a time, but that ended months before I met you."

Though that admission didn't surprise her entirely, it did lift a weight from her chest that Nan hadn't realized was there until it pulled free.

"Secondly, my absences from Whitley Court have nothing

to do with you, Nan."

She clutched the bedclothes, her gaze drifting from him. "It is your home—"

"A home is more than a house," he said, drawing her eyes back to him. A frown marred his expression, and Benjamin's gaze met hers. "I love Whitley Court in many ways. It is my family's legacy, and my childhood home, but I do not like the person I am inside it."

Picking at the bedcover, Benjamin pinched his brows together as he studied the swirls of the flowers stretching across the fabric. With quiet words, he described his upbringing. The praising and pampering he received, even at his sisters' expense, and how pivotal his time at school had been to change his view of the world.

For all that Nan didn't think Benjamin spoiled, she recognized how easy it would've been for him to follow that path. In truth, it would be difficult for anyone to keep a healthy level of pride in the face of such adoration. And when he finally finished, the silence that followed his confession testified to how greatly this weighed on him.

"Would it help if I tell you when you are being an insufferable fool?" asked Nan with a hint of a smile.

And though she'd hoped to coax a laugh from him, the air around him grew heavier as Benjamin answered in a firm voice, "Yes, it would. I'm terrified I will become that person. David and my sisters are decent consciences when I require them, but they are all too occupied with their own lives to give me as much assistance as I require."

Nan's brows rose at that, but she didn't know what to say to such an admission.

"I know it may seem like quite the undertaking," he added with a hint of the humor she'd hoped to see earlier. "However, David was just reminding me that marriage is a way of yoking people together. I know myself well enough to recognize that if left to my own devices I will become everything I fear. I require someone at my side to help me see when I am veering into 'insufferable' territory. What do you think, *Mr. Leigh*? Are you up for the challenge?"

For all that his pet name ought to bring a smile to her lips, Nan couldn't help the frown that took hold.

Benjamin straightened. "What is the matter?"

Settling into the bed, Nan pulled the covers close, her head resting heavily against her pillow. "I'm being silly. That is all."

"Must I drag out all your secrets?" he asked with a raised eyebrow that was both teasing and challenging at the same time.

Nan drew the covers closer, snuggling into the bedding as her cheeks began to heat. For all that she felt herself to be a mature lady, far wiser and stronger than in her younger years, there were times when she felt utterly juvenile. Surely a lady past her majority, who had been forced to make her way in the world, ought to be more reserved than this.

"Out with it," he said, following suit and settling into his side of the bed.

"I am being silly," she replied with a sigh. "However, I cannot help but feel a bit sensitive about my femininity at times."

Turning onto his side, he stared at her, and though the dark room cast shadows across his features, it was easy to see his concern. "You mean the nickname? I do not mean anything by that—"

"I know. That is why I am being silly. I like hearing you say it because of the memories attached to it. However, I cannot help but recall that I am far from the feminine ideal. I am tall and older than you, after all."

"Not by much."

"By enough."

Benjamin huffed. "What does two years difference make? And I like that you are tall. Makes you easier to spot when you're chatting with the other ladies after church. Every other gentleman has to hunt down his wife, searching through the crowds. But not me."

Tucking the edge of the bedclothes under her chin, Nan hardly dared to meet his gaze; she felt like a little child peeking out to see if the monsters were still in the shadows. Yet for all that his response was a little teasing, it warmed her through.

"Is that so?" she asked.

But Benjamin merely watched her, his head resting on his pillow as his brows drew tight together. "This truly bothers you?"

Nan shook her head with a sigh. "As I said, I know I am being silly. I know well enough not to listen to hurtful comments—"

Sitting up, Benjamin stared down at her. "Has someone said something to you?"

Oh, such dangerous ground. Though part of her considered a full confession, Nan knew better. With time, perhaps, but in the fledgling days of her marriage, it seemed far more foolhardy than wise to disparage her husband's kin.

Besides, Benjamin might not believe her; he didn't see his mother's behavior for what it was, and instinct warned her that no good would come from attempting to convince him otherwise. After all, Benjamin still held her father at the ideal to live up to—despite the times she'd shared his shortcomings—and it was likely to be doubly difficult to convince him he was wrong when it concerned his own family.

"I will simply say that there are those who find the pairing...odd." Though she couldn't bring herself to give him the whole truth, Nan gave him enough of it to set her conscience at ease. "Laughable, in fact. Which is not entirely out of bounds. Gentlemen do not marry a lady like me unless she possesses a covetable dowry."

And when he looked ready to contest that idea, Nan held up a staying hand.

"I am not speaking to belittle myself, Benjamin. But to ignore the truth of the matter is pointless as well. When was the last time you saw such a disparate pairing?"

Crossing his arms, Benjamin frowned. "My sister and her

husband. Katherine is a good five years older than David, far plainer than he, and almost as poor as you since Father put aside a pittance for her dowry."

"Don't be silly—"

"I am not. It is the truth."

Nan stilled, though her thoughts whirled as she considered the pair she'd met not long ago. "Katherine doesn't look older than David."

"And he would say it's because she's a lovely creature and he's aged poorly, but it doesn't alter the fact that they are perfectly happy despite their outward differences. So, no, I do not see any reason to think it strange that my wife isn't some narrow definition of 'perfect.'"

Heat stole across her face, and Nan forced herself to relax once more. "I think we've drifted far from the topic."

"I don't believe we have," he replied, shifting once more to his side so he could face her. "Does my calling you *Mr. Leigh* bother you because of the tart comments of bitter ladies?"

Matching his position, Nan curled onto her side, her hands tucking the blankets beneath her jaw. "I said I was being silly, Benjamin. I know better than to listen to their words."

"Clearly not, else you wouldn't have mentioned it," he said with an arched brow. "If you do not care for the nickname, I shan't use it again. But I like it, Nan Leigh, because it makes me smile. Teasing is only fun when it is ridiculous, and thinking of you as 'manly' is so very far from the truth that I cannot help but laugh."

Once more, she echoed his expression, matching his arched brows with her own, questioning that assertion without words.

"Others may claim a lady ought to be shorter than her husband, but I think your extra inches are elegant. And though you despair of your looks, your coloring is so very fair that it brings to mind the fairy princesses from the stories my grandmother and sisters used to read to me."

Nan stared at him, her nose wrinkling as she considered that. "Now, that is definitely teasing."

"Is not, and though your mouth objects, your nose tells a different story," he said, pulling a hand free of the blankets to point at the offending appendage. "It scrunches up whenever you think something is adorable or sweet."

Now it was her forehead that was furrowing instead of her nose. "No, it doesn't."

"Yes, it does," he said, poking the tip of it. "I saw it several times during our trip home."

A smile threatened to spring forth, revealing just how her heart warmed at that. Perhaps it was a silly thing to enjoy so much, but Nan couldn't help it. Benjamin had noticed it.

"Ah, there it is again," he said with a triumphant grin, and Nan's hands broke free of the blankets to cup her nose, which was most certainly scrunching. Having never noticed that habit before, it sent another flush of heat through her in a combination of embarrassment and pleasure.

"Do not hide it," he said, his hand reaching to pull hers free. "I like it."

Nan's brows rose. "You do?"

"I have already admitted that I have too much pride for my good, and seeing such a clear sign of approval does wonders to inflate it to untenable levels," he replied with a faint laugh.

With a scoff, she pushed his hands away, but Benjamin caught hold of them. Nan couldn't say how or when, for the world shifted far too quickly for her to register even that faint touch, but then he was simply holding her hands, his thumbs brushing gentle touches along her skin.

"All jests aside, I like you as you are, *Mr. Leigh*."

All other connotations with that pet name died a quick death, for Benjamin spoke it in a manner that couldn't be construed as anything but approving. Not a quarter of an hour ago, Nan had halfway believed he didn't care for her as anything more than a responsibility, yet the feel of her hand in his and the tender way he spoke denoted the antithesis. Could his feelings be bending toward something more?

Good heavens, she hoped so.

Chapter 22

Nan's pulse quickened, for that thought popped into her mind without bidding, and she couldn't help but think it must be true. She couldn't say where her feelings lay, but the desire for something grander than companionship was certainly there. What woman wished to settle for a marriage of obligation when a better possibility sat just beyond the horizon?

But it was so much more than that. Despite knowing so little of him, Nan felt as though she knew Benjamin better than anyone else. His humor and sweetness of temper were like little rays of sunshine when she was feeling blue.

Then his free fingers were brushing her nose once more, drawing her attention back to the little movement that gave away her heart far more than she realized.

And Benjamin was drawing close. Nan's breath froze in her lungs. Did he mean to kiss her? Did she wish him to? Despite the obviousness of the answers to both those questions, she couldn't help but ask them all the same. But then, she'd already admitted to being a very silly woman.

Thank heavens Benjamin was holding her hands, for they started to tremble in a way she couldn't control any more than the ridiculous nose on her face, all while a swarm of butterflies spilled into her middle, urging her closer and warning her away at the very same time. They were man and wife, so it seemed natural to touch her husband, yet Nan's hands grew clammy at the thought.

Then his lips touched hers, and though Benjamin's eyes closed, Nan stared at him.

How had all this happened? A month ago, she'd been teaching in Birmingham, certain in her circumstances (or as much as any lady could be). Now, she was married, living in a new home, and her husband was kissing her. His hand released hers and rested upon her cheek, his thumb brushing along the apple, and Nan's eyes closed. All thought stopped, leaving her immersed in the feel of his touch.

It was so perfect. She couldn't think of anything else to call it, for her thoughts seized, leaving her awash in Benjamin's kiss.

For a time, at least.

That moment of calm enveloped her, wrapping her in more warmth and joy than she had ever thought to feel. But Nan's mind was too powerful a thing to ever be silenced completely, and it quickly began to wonder what this meant, what was to come, and if her untutored attempts to return the token were successful.

Nan tried to silence those questions and wade back into the moment, but her ridiculous mind refused to quiet, and soon, it was joined by the pounding of her heart, which thumped a frantic beat against her chest. Though it was pleasant in some respects, she couldn't clear her thoughts of a question that pulsed through her in time with her heartbeat.

What did this kiss mean?

For all that Benjamin Leigh had the appearance of a man of the world, spending much of his youth in a boys' school with little interaction with young ladies hadn't given him much education on the fairer sex; Weathersby College prided itself on teaching its students the utmost of gentlemanly decorum, and

Mr. Price, in particular, was a stickler for behaving in a gentlemanly manner toward all women.

In the past two years, many of his friends had attempted to broaden his knowledge and understanding, and whilst it had afforded Benjamin more opportunities to mix with young ladies, the lessons of his youth were impossible to ignore when it came to the more flirtatious behaviors so many young men adopted. Greater Edgerton boasted a larger population than many towns, but society was still limited enough that stealing kisses from young ladies was bound to be remarked upon, and no man of honor dared to damage another's reputation.

So, Benjamin's knowledge was minimal compared to many young men of his age. With four sisters, he was familiar with the behavior of ladies—but only from a brotherly standpoint, which was vastly different than that of a beau. Or husband, rather.

Had he known just how thrilling it was to kiss a lady, Benjamin's hard-earned morals would've evaporated in a trice. He couldn't say why he'd decided to kiss her, only that it had felt like the right thing. And he couldn't deny just how much he enjoyed the feel of Nan in his embrace, holding her close as their lips explored one another.

His fingertips brushed the edge of her velvet cheek, and her scent filled his nose; not some perfumed miasma that choked the senses, but the unique and indescribable fragrance that belonged solely to her. It had lingered in his greatcoat for several days after their journey together, and Benjamin hadn't realized how much he'd missed it until this moment.

So strange to feel a connection to someone he couldn't truly claim to know. Their days alone in Birmingham and the coach had allowed Benjamin a glimpse into her heart, and with each peek, he couldn't help but long for more. So much more.

But before he could consider that, a slight tremor in Nan's touch ripped Benjamin from his haze and forced his eyes open. A lovely pink tinged her cheeks, and the slight smile to her lips urged him to return to their previous activity, but though Nan's gaze flickered with interest, there was a hint of fear there that forced Benjamin to take notice—a small, even fleeting, expression that others might easily brush aside, but his instincts refused to be ignored. Whether or not she welcomed his advances, some part of Nan was unnerved by the kiss, and he couldn't dismiss it. No matter how much he longed to take her into his arms once more.

Settling back into the pillow, Benjamin smirked, sending her a waggle of his brows. "I see I've rendered you speechless with my kiss."

Nan scoffed, the noise waving away the last of the charged air surrounding them. "If it is my responsibility to keep your pride from puffing up, it seems that my position as your wife is going to be far more arduous than that of a schoolmistress. At least I had the evenings to myself with the occasional holiday off."

Benjamin laughed, though he forced himself to stifle it, as it would do no one any good if he woke the rest of the household. "You ought to have inquired more about your duties and responsibilities before you married me."

"Indeed. A great oversight on my part," she said whilst wriggling into a more comfortable position. With careful movements, Benjamin tested the waters by placing an arm out, resting it across the top of her pillow, and though Nan paused for a heartbeat, she leaned into the crook, settling once more with the blankets pulled up against the night chill. Her head rested against his chest, followed quickly by her hand, and Benjamin smiled to himself as he enjoyed the small victory they'd gained tonight.

"I am sorry if you've felt abandoned of late," he said, sneaking a kiss to her crown.

"No need to fret over it. What's done is done."

Yet there was something to her tone that belied that easy dismissal, and Benjamin sent out a silent prayer of gratitude that his meddling sister had meddled so thoroughly. Clearly, it mattered to Nan, and though Benjamin couldn't entirely explain why it was, he'd quickly discovered that there was joy to be found in looking after his wife.

"I think we ought to take a drive tomorrow."

Silence met that statement, enough so that he wondered if Nan had fallen asleep.

"I would enjoy that," she finally murmured.

"But?" he prodded.

"But?"

"There was a clear 'but' that belonged at the end of that statement."

Nan drew in a deep breath and sighed. "But the last time we discussed going on a drive, you forgot and went riding with your friends."

"Have I mentioned I am a fool of the highest order?" he asked.

"Not often enough," she replied, and though Benjamin couldn't glimpse her expression, a smile was laced through her tone, allowing his guilt to ease—but only a touch.

"So, not only was I a bounder for making plans with you when I wasn't available, but I have yet to rectify the mistake and give you the promised outing." Casting his thoughts to his schedule, he considered how to move things about. Without his notebook on hand, Benjamin couldn't be certain he wasn't forgetting something, but there were far more pressing matters to attend to. "I have time tomorrow."

There was a long pause before she replied, "You needn't feel obligated to clear your afternoon."

"I would think a husband is obligated to introduce his wife to her new home, but that is not my motivation, Nan." With a quiet sigh, he stared at the ceiling as the flickers of the candle from the side table cast dancing light across the plaster. "In truth, I want to spend time with you, and I've been missing our time together. I simply cannot bear to be locked away in Whitley Court. Perhaps we could make it a habit to go out together when your schedule permits it."

Another long silence followed that, and Benjamin's breath stilled as he awaited her answer.

"If you wish to, I would enjoy that." One more pause before she tacked on, "Quite a lot."

Smiling at the ceiling, Benjamin felt his muscles relax as air filled his lungs once more. "I would, as well."

And never had such a statement been truer, for hearing the lightness in Nan's tone infused him with far more pleasure than he'd thought possible to feel over something so small. A drive out was hardly momentous, but clearly, it meant much to her, and being the one to grant her that joy was quite thrilling. Far better than riding, playing cards, or any of the other insipid pastimes with which his friends filled his days.

Do not be a ninny! Nan tried to be firm with her heart, but it was filled to bursting as Benjamin described all that they might do tomorrow. The list was far longer than they had hours in the day, but his excitement at the prospect whispered to her that perhaps—just perhaps—he might wish to spend time with her, and this wasn't an isolated event.

Benjamin wanted to be with her.

That knowledge deep inside her, allowing Nan to relax into her husband's hold, despite the rapid beat of her heart at their cozy position. But then, this wasn't so very different than the hours they'd spent cuddled together against the rain and cold on the carriage. Breathing deeply, Nan reveled in the scent of his soap and the barest hint of his cologne. That touch of spice that, though faded, lingered on his clothes throughout the day.

She couldn't help but feel the frisson of excitement at the prospect of time alone with her husband—away from Whitley Court and the prying eyes of her mother-in-law. Especially as Benjamin painted grand images of all that they could do. The sights he wanted to show her. It was impossible not to be swept up in his excitement.

Soon, the conversation drifted along, sweeping them both up in its comfortable current. Nan didn't know why it was the case, but despite feeling out of place in genteel society, Benjamin felt like an old friend. But she supposed that was just part of his magic. His way with people was a gift she could never mimic, no matter how much she might wish to.

Perhaps that was one of the great benefits of marriage, for she needn't be talented in that area if her husband was bountifully blessed. Nan couldn't imagine him being discomforted in a gathering.

Their voices filled the night, lingering long after the candle sputtered and died, and for the first time since arriving at Whitley Court, Nan slept soundly, certain that tomorrow would be far better than today.

Chapter 23

Knowing her new home was an industrial town had given Nan some preconceived notions before she ever clapped eyes on it. The first being that she had rather anticipated it looking rather like her old one. Yet rather than stretching far and wide as Birmingham did, petering out slowly until one couldn't tell what was city or country, Greater Edgerton felt as though it had been dropped amid a green expanse. Once one stepped beyond the border, one was surrounded by the vast countryside.

Fields stretched outward, seemingly into eternity, only broken by winding stone walls that cut up the landscape like the lead seams of a quarry glass window. If not for the verdant colors and the occasional grand tree sprouting toward the heavens, it might've seemed a desolate place with nary another creature about. But with the bright colors, it was breathtaking.

And no matter how many times they drove down this patch of road, Nan was awed by it.

"Yet again, I would like to draw your attention to the utter perfection that is my skill with the reins," said Benjamin, giving her that impish grin whilst waggling his brows like the rascal he was. "I've brought some smelling salts, should you find yourself desperately lightheaded and liable to swoon at my prowess."

Turning her bright smile toward the passing greenery, Nan replied in an even tone, "As I've hardly ever been in a carriage of any sort, I am hardly the judge of such things."

Despite having few comparisons, Nan slanted a glance toward the man at her side and couldn't help but think he looked especially striking with the ribbons threaded through his fingers, his hands deftly turning the horse this way and that as they bumped along the country road.

"And I know I am not as familiar with the roads as you, but we've taken this route a few times over the past sennight, and I do believe you just drove us past our turn," she quickly added, pointing toward the fork in the road they ought to have taken, which was quickly disappearing behind them.

Giving her a playful scowl, he shook his head. "It is a wife's duty to gaze adoringly at her husband and praise his every action, not point out his missteps."

"Did you or did you not ask me to keep your arrogance in check?" she quipped.

"I am merely stating a fact. I am an excellent driver. It is not arrogant when it is true."

"Except when you insist that I inflate your vanity by gazing adoringly whilst I praise your every action—though I will admit that you did an exceedingly excellent job at taking us down the wrong road. Quite expert."

With a heavy sigh, he shook his head. "You are too good for me, *Mr. Leigh*."

"Too right," she teased, slipping her arm through his whilst being careful not to jostle him too much.

Nan held fast to him and wished (not for the first time) that she was a touch more petite; this would be the perfect moment to lean her head against his shoulder. Unfortunately, being similarly sized made it ungainly to affect such a cozy position. It was so much easier when they were abed, and over the past sennight, Nan had discovered her favorite pillow was her husband's chest as his breaths rocked her in slow, even movements.

"Thank you, Benjamin. This has been a perfect day."

"You say that every time I take you out, and I cannot help but feel that I am a poor excuse for a husband if my wife feels the need to profusely thank me for quiet outings," he replied.

"Stating my thanks is hardly profuse."

"It is when you say it with that tone," he replied, peeking at her from the corner of his eye.

And there was truth in that, for Nan couldn't express her gratitude often enough at having some time away from her mother-in-law. The lady always did her utmost to dissuade Benjamin from stealing her away, but he held firm in his determination, which was a small miracle and a victory wrapped into one.

Straightening, she ran a hand down her skirts and said in a prim voice, "I had been wondering if you were ever going to bestow me with vast chests of jewels, as husbands ought to do, but I suppose I will settle for being squired about."

A slight smile curled the edges of his lips, and Nan dropped her teasing to add, "This has been a wonderful afternoon, Benjamin. Truly. I couldn't ask for more."

Except for more time. The accidental detour home allowed them a few more minutes together, but even that was drawing to a quick close, and she held fast to Benjamin's arm. For all that these hours together were a godsend that filled her with joy and contentment, Nan's heart sank all the more as the drive to Whitley Court came into view.

Benjamin led the horses toward the stables and tossed the reins to the groom before leaping down and hurrying round to her side. His hand was there before she could even consider alighting, and Nan couldn't help the grin as he helped her down. The gig was high, to be true, but certainly navigable on her own.

Though she could easily brush the action aside as a bit of gentlemanly decorum, Benjamin looked so genuinely pleased to be of service that Nan felt an echo of that joy in her own heart.

His helping her brought him pleasure, which in turn brought her pleasure. A never-ending cycle of bliss.

But despite being safely delivered to the ground, Benjamin did not relinquish his hold of Nan's hand. The groom led the gig away, leaving them standing on the gravel drive, hand in hand.

"Are you certain you do not wish to join me tonight?" he asked.

There were two certainties surrounding Benjamin's offer: Nan longed to accept, and she couldn't. Even if she could ignore the discomfort that came from intruding, she wasn't presentable. Her single evening gown had been worn to death over the past month. The poor thing had seen better days before her marriage and was now liable to fall apart at the seams.

And wouldn't that make them a laughingstock?

Once more, she wondered if she mightn't use a bit of her savings to purchase one. Nan's funds were meager, to be certain, but she had enough to acquire a simple gown. Unfortunately, that led her down the same path it always did, for it wasn't so much a matter of means as it was opportunity. Nan didn't know the first thing about purchasing a gown here, and she shuddered to think of what Mrs. Leigh might do if she asked for assistance.

Nan hated that her vanity forced her to remain firm in her conviction, but each foray into society only highlighted how she lacked both the skills to fulfill the role of mistress and a proper wardrobe to play the part. There was so little she could do for Benjamin, and if sitting at home with his mother whilst he passed the evening with his friends was her sacrifice, Nan would make it.

"That is gratuitous of you, Benjamin, but I wouldn't wish to impose—"

"It isn't an imposition," he replied.

But Nan met that with a challenging raise of her brows. "And how many other wives are intruding on your evening with the gentlemen?"

Benjamin didn't need to answer the question, for he was the only one in that group with a wife.

With a smile, she straightened the edge of his cravat. "Besides, I have a novel I am desperate to finish, and a quiet night at home is the perfect time to do so."

"And Mother is going to be at hand to keep you company."

It was something of a miracle that her expression remained impassive at that statement, but Benjamin looked so pleased with the prospect that she couldn't bear to give even a hint of her disappointment.

Besides, what did she have to complain about? The past sennight had been so much happier than her first weeks at Whitley Court. Even a few hours away with Benjamin was enough to lighten her spirits for the day, and when things grew truly unbearable, Nan escaped to her father-in-law's study (something she was doing with more and more frequency).

Yet her heart grew heavy at the thought of the coming evening. Mrs. Leigh would insist they sit in the parlor together, though Nan couldn't fathom why; the lady only grew nastier with each passing day.

"I suppose you ought to dress if you plan on going out tonight," she said with a genuine smile—not because of the words, but because she managed to speak them without a hint of disappointment.

"I suppose you are correct." But Benjamin didn't move from his place.

As he held her gaze, something shifted in his own. Nan couldn't say precisely what it was, but there was a spark in his eyes and a ghost of a smile (though not his usual one). It was the expression that graced his face just before he was about to do some mischief, as though he was laughing about the idea before taking action.

Before she knew what he was about, he snatched her up in a kiss. Just a quick thing, to be certain, but with the sun blazing above them and in full view of anyone who might wish to see. Nan's cheeks instantly flamed, heating her through with a mixture of embarrassment at being caught in such a tender moment and disappointment that said moment ended so quickly. Benjamin tipped his hat with a wink and a satisfied grin that warned her that he knew she wanted more; then, turning on his heel, he hurried away as though fleeing from a scolding.

Holding a hand to her lips, Nan watched him go. With the sun shining above, she couldn't help but wish for a few more minutes out of doors. One must enjoy fair weather when one could, especially when storm clouds loomed on the horizon. And when her mother-in-law watched from the window.

Mrs. Leigh's narrowed gaze fixed upon Nan with a scalding heat, and she could well hear the caustic words flitting through the lady's mind. She rarely moderated them when it was only the two of them about, and Mrs. Leigh's eyes spoke volumes. The world dimmed a touch, the lightness in her heart sinking. But Nan jutted out her chin, meeting that glare without flinching. Then, dismissing the lady from her thoughts, she drifted around the gardens, turning her thoughts back to Benjamin.

A tune echoed around her, and it took a moment before Nan recognized the song she was humming. It was one of those sweet country melodies the girls had often sung as they worked, and though she couldn't recall the words, she knew the notes and the meaning behind the sweet little ballad—a milkmaid and her sweetheart's silly attempts at courtship before finally finding themselves wed.

The sun dipped low, driving Nan toward the front door, but the song followed her as she made her way up the stairs to her bedchamber.

"Nan?" called her father-in-law as she passed his study. When she appeared at the doorway, he smiled and motioned for her to come in. "I thought that was you."

Shutting the door behind her, she took the armchair beside him. The window was open, allowing the fragrance of the garden to fill the space and mingle with the scent of paper, leather, and ink. Quite possibly the most perfect perfume she'd ever smelled.

"Am I to assume things are going well between you and my son?" he asked with a knowing grin that reminded her all too much of Benjamin.

Nan's cheeks pinked again, but she couldn't hide her smile if she wished to. "You may, Father."

Though it was still a touch strange to employ that appellation, with each passing week, it was growing familiar, and that sweet sentiment was made all the more joyous when the gentleman in question beamed every time she called him by that important title.

"That makes me very happy, my dear girl. Both for your sake and Benjamin's. He needs a steady young lady like yourself to keep him from making mistakes." The edge of his expression strained, his bright gaze dimming a touch when he added, almost as an afterthought, "He needs good people to look out for his best interests."

Nan's shoulders tightened. "What do you mean?"

Father echoed her stiff posture before shaking his head. "Ignore me. Just an old fool mumbling nonsense."

"Is something the matter?"

But he met that with a dismissive wave, though the kindness in his gaze gentled the harshness of the movement. "As I said, ignore me. You needn't concern yourself about such matters."

"Benjamin is my husband, and this is my family," said Nan with a frown. "Surely I ought to concern myself with 'such matters,' whatever they may be."

Leaning forward, he took her hand in his, giving it a fatherly pat. "Finances are my obligation to manage, and as such, I cannot burden you—"

"Nonsense, Father. I am not so fragile that I will fall to pieces if you share your load with me," she said, clinging to his hand. Her brows drew closer together, and Nan begged him with her gaze. "I wish to be of service to my family."

Her throat tightened as memories came roaring into her thoughts, filling her head with what ifs and if onlys, darkening her present with how the future might mirror the past. Father shook his head, but Nan tightened her grip, forcing her lips to speak the words she didn't wish to say.

"You've hinted at troubles several times over the past weeks, and keeping it to yourself helps nothing. My father refused to speak of finances and money, leaving me entirely blind to what was to come. Then, I was left with nothing in this world, and I cannot help but be angry with him for hiding something so important from me. I might be able to help." Pausing and forcing herself to speak evenly, she added, "Please, Father."

Letting out a deep sigh and patting her hand, the gentleman shook his head. "You are such a good, kind daughter, my girl. Far better than I deserve." With only a brief pause, he asked, "What has Benjamin told you of the estate and the entail?"

Straightening, Nan frowned. "Nothing. Though you and your wife have hinted at troubles, I've never seen anything to indicate any financial strain on the household."

Father shifted in his seat, releasing her hand as he settled once more. "My father was a stubborn fool who didn't trust me in the slightest. Was forever convinced I would ruin Whitley Court, and even once said he'd rather give it to the blacksmith's son than me."

The gentleman's fingers curled against the arm of his chair, and Nan couldn't help but take hold of his hand again.

With a faint smile, Father shook his head. "Don't fret over me, Nan. That is over and done, and in the end, his threats were empty: estates always go to the eldest son."

"Not always."

"True. Inheritances are not required by the courts to go to the eldest son, so there are always exceptions, but common practice and society's expectations are as good as law. Few forge their own paths. However, that didn't stop him from placing an entail on the property, which then makes my inheritance a legal matter."

"I cannot say that I know much of the matter, but after suffering a bout of curiosity concerning the law, I spent some time learning about various aspects, and I am familiar with the concept," she said with a frown. "The heir has power over the income from the estate but cannot sell it off, so I'm afraid I do not understand the trouble. Isn't Whitley Court's income enough?"

Father's brow furrowed as he drummed his fingers rapidly against the arm of the chair. "Things are changing so quickly in the world. Modernizations and mechanizations are now required to keep abreast with farming practices, and though we have money enough to meet our needs, the cost of the improvements is too dear. However, the entail keeps me from mortgaging the property as well. To do so would require intervention from the Court of Chancery, which is nigh on impossible and far too costly a gamble."

"You would need to break the entail," she murmured.

"Precisely." Father's tone was so entirely pleased that she'd guessed the direction he was heading that a jolt of joy skittered along her spine. "You are such an intelligent young lady. Quite remarkable."

Nan fought against a grin, for she already felt like a puppy eagerly nipping at her master's heels. But she couldn't help the brightness in her gaze or the delightful flutters in her stomach.

"Benjamin is a good lad. Unfortunately, that goodness is going to be the undoing of our family," said Father with a heavy sigh. "Before my mother passed, she extracted a promise that he wouldn't break the entail, and honorable man that he is, Benjamin is holding firm to that vow—despite being only nine years of age when he made it. What sort of grandmother would speak to a boy about such matters in the first place, let alone bully him into such an agreement when he couldn't have possibly understood the implications?"

Gaping, Nan tried to picture such a thing, but it was impossible. Her students had been about that age, and there was so much of the world they did not understand; though life caused them to mature faster than genteel children, most still couldn't see beyond the here and now.

"That is horrible," she whispered.

"My point exactly," said Father with a nod. "I adored my mother—as much as any son could—but when Benjamin confessed what she'd done, I was sickened by her manipulations. The poor lad is twisted up inside, fully believing that holding firm to the entail is his duty. He will not see reason."

Leaning forward, he took hold of her hand once more and patted it. "The moment I met you, I knew you were a gift from God. He sent you here to help me and my family. To help my son see the error of his ways. Such a special young lady here to bless our lives. I know if you speak to Benjamin, he will soften and keep our family from falling into ruin."

Brows pinched together, Nan stared at him. "Is our situation truly so terrible? Couldn't we economize? Surely a mortgage should be a last resort—"

"Believe me, my girl, I have considered every possibility. But with four daughters all married, I am at a loss. We were lucky enough that their husbands were content to receive stipends instead of a lump sum dowry, but they are costing me as much as they ever have. And now, our household has expanded and will continue to do so."

Nan's gaze fell to her lap as she considered all those implications. Though they were still sorting out their marriage, she and Benjamin would eventually live as proper man and wife, and children were bound to follow, each of which would increase the family's budget and not their income.

"I see your predicament," she murmured, all while considering her own.

For all that Benjamin was gregarious, her husband had never let it slip that troubles were on their horizon. No mention of an entail or mortgages. She hadn't the slightest notion as to Whitley Court's income.

How would she broach such a thing with Benjamin? Even if she did, would he listen? Did she wish him to? Father's request seemed rational enough, but Nan's stomach churned at the thought of debts. Living within one's means was a basic tenet of good living. Yet some purchases required assistance, and if the Leighs were so restrained in their ability, surely she should do something about it if she could.

Yet her ribs contracted as she considered the path forward, uncertain what to do or how to do it.

"Oh, my dear Nan, I didn't mean to make you uncomfortable," said Father, patting her hand again. "Ignore me. I am an old fool."

"Not at all," she said with a shake of her head. "I am grateful you mentioned it, and I would like to be of service, but I do not know what I might do."

Father gave her a kind smile, yet there was a tightness to the expression that caused her insides to churn all the more. Rising to his feet, he placed a kiss on Nan's cheek, echoing his assurances that all would be well, but they rang hollow as he wandered out of his study, leaving her alone.

Chapter 24

"Behave!" For all that Nan's chiding had an edge to it, the faint laugh in her whisper stole away any edge to the word. And Benjamin couldn't help but fidget some more.

Mr. Hasket was a pleasant fellow and just the sort of gentleman one expected to choose the church as his profession. Eloquent and of a pensive mentality, their vicar possessed a talent for public speaking that made Sundays less of a bore. However, every sermon revolved around the same principles, varying little since his childhood.

Granted, there were plenty amongst the congregation who weren't listening, and they were all far from having perfected those virtues and commandments, making repetition necessary. But the sermons needn't be delivered in the same manner or with the same shallow discourse. In this modern day and age, never had there been more writings to draw upon, more ideas to expand the mind. Yet Mr. Hasket revisited the same passages again and again.

Which was why Benjamin was entertaining himself by seeing how much he could pester his wife without causing a stir.

Carefully, he shifted toward her, poking her thigh as she held her hands clasped primly in her lap. From the corner of his eye, he watched her as he nudged her, tapping out a rhythm. Her lips flattened, though there was a spark of laughter in her gaze.

"Benjamin," she whispered in warning, and he gave her an innocent look in return. Nan's stern expression strained, fighting to hold back a chuckle, which only pushed him to further mischief. Leaning closer, he invaded her space, and though she tried to distance herself, there was only so far she could go as she was firmly wedged between him and the arm of the pew.

Thankfully for Nan's sanity, Mr. Hasket came to a close, and the final words and prayers were spoken, releasing the congregation back into the world of men. Despite glimpsing the gloomy skies through the windows, Benjamin found himself ushering Nan quickly toward the church doors.

"A little anxious to leave, are we?" she teased as he bundled her through.

"I enjoy learning and books, but good heavens, I do grow tired of the repetition that comes with education, be that secular or spiritual." With a smile, he drew in a lungful, the faint promise of rain permeating the air. "Your father was forever despairing over my ability to focus."

"I can well imagine. I learned at a very young age never to fidget when he was about," replied Nan, though her lightheartedness dimmed a touch, and Benjamin huffed at himself for having spoken so carelessly. He'd avoided the subject for the most part, but her loss was still so fresh that any reminder of her father was bound to pain her.

"Come now," he said, offering his arm. "Let us escape while we still have the opportunity."

A genuine smile graced Nan's lips, and she took the proffered limb as they hurried down the church steps. The rest of the congregation were already forming small pockets of conversations throughout the churchyard, and Benjamin quickly navigated around them as the church gate drew closer.

Only to pull up short when Mrs. Paddock stepped in front of him, forming a formidable wall with her bell skirt and puffed sleeves expanding out in front of them.

"Why, Mrs. Leigh, you are not leaving so soon, are you?" asked the old matron. "I would think your mother-in-law would wish to show you off some more. There are still so many in the parish you haven't met."

Nan's expression hardly faltered, though Benjamin noticed the strain at the edges of her smile.

"We were hoping to steal some time away," he interjected, drawing the lady's attention, and though he'd meant it innocently enough, Mrs. Paddock gave him a knowing smile.

"No doubt you newlyweds do wish for more time alone," she said with far more insinuation in her tone than Benjamin cared to hear from a lady his mother's age. "It's little wonder, what with your mother keeping your bride so busy."

Stepping aside, Mrs. Paddock motioned toward the gate. "Make your escape. And as I haven't had the opportunity to say it before, congratulations on your marriage."

"Many thanks, my dear lady."

Then, reaching over to give Nan a pat on her arm, Mrs. Paddock added, "Before you go—I have long wished to tell you just how much I admire your gowns. I don't care much for these new fashions. The old styles were far more practical, and I applaud ladies with enough sense to dress as they wish, rather than bending to whatever is *à la mode*."

Mrs. Paddock gave a bright laugh, bestowed another smile, and wandered away. Nan stood rigid at his side, and Benjamin slanted a look at her, but her gaze was downturned.

"Is something the matter?" he asked.

With a sigh and a shake of her head, Nan seemed to return to herself. "Never mind. Mrs. Paddock meant well."

Benjamin frowned and glanced over at the lady as she inserted herself into another conversation. No matter what Nan said, he felt something was amiss. Was she distressed about her gown? Mrs. Paddock had complimented her, and it had been genuine and kindly meant. Benjamin couldn't help but agree with the sentiment, for he adored the fact that she dressed to please herself.

And it wasn't as though her style was entirely out of place. The shift in styles between that of his youth and the modern appearance was quite drastic, making the difference between the two obvious (even to his eye), but many ladies still chose the older silhouettes. Just a glance around, and Benjamin spied Miss Thomas and Mrs. Dillard both dressed similarly to Nan.

Except his wife wore the style far better than either of those ladies, which was no surprise as those ladies had at least two decades over his wife.

Benjamin paused as an inkling of something wriggled in the back of his thoughts, fighting to make itself known. Glancing back over the crowd, he turned his gaze to each of the ladies who eschewed the latest fashions. There was not an unwrinkled face among them. Except for Miss Porter.

Odd that.

Turning back to their escape, he stepped toward the gate, but hands wedged between him and Nan, forcing them apart as Mother stepped between them, taking each by the arm.

"Here you are," she said, glancing at her son. "Were you trying to sneak our dear girl away before I have the opportunity to introduce her around?"

"In the past month, you've introduced her to all and sundry. Is there anyone left in town she doesn't know?" asked Benjamin.

"Don't be silly," said Mother with a tisk. "Besides, you will never guess who I stumbled across."

Turning the pair around, she beamed as she revealed Miss Rothschild standing behind them. Benjamin kept from gawking—but only just. In the time he'd spent pursuing the young lady (however frivolous that flirtation had been), Mother had treated her like a byword. Seeing the lady so warmly received by the Leigh matriarch was something akin to a sign of the Last Days.

But then, Benjamin supposed the danger of his marrying Miss Rothschild had passed now, giving his mother no more reason to behave so.

Glancing between the lady he'd married and one he'd admired, Benjamin was struck by the strangeness of the situation, and Katherine's assertion rose to his thoughts once more, forcing him to consider it. Mother's main objection to Miss Rothschild had been her inferiority of connections and income. Being the daughter of a mill owner was hardly fitting for her "dear boy." Yet Nan's station was far below that.

Benjamin couldn't help but feel a niggling that something was not right in the situation. Why would Mother embrace Nan when she'd never failed to make her disappointment with Miss Rothschild known?

But he supposed the answer was clear enough: Mother enjoyed Nan. How could she not? His wife was witty, kind, generous, patient, and possessed all sorts of lovely qualities. Whatever "deficiencies" society might identify, they could never outnumber the goodness to be found in his Nan.

Besides, there was no undoing the marriage once forged. No doubt Mother's reaction would've been far different had he presented Nan as only a sweetheart and not his wife.

And so, Benjamin's surprise ebbed, and he met Miss Rothschild with a smile. "Good afternoon."

Before she could respond in kind, Mother released his arm and gave him a casual wave. "I have some people Nan needs to meet. Could you please keep him entertained in the meantime, Miss Rothschild?"

As his wife shared his height and Benjamin was taller than Mother, it was easy for Nan to send him a questioning look over the lady's head, her eyes wide and brows raised. The expression confused him for a heartbeat until he recalled the conversation they'd shared concerning Miss Rothschild, and Benjamin gave Nan a wink in response, which never failed to pull a smile from her lips.

Except now.

But Mother was leading her away before he could think what to do or say to reassure Nan that there was no need to fear Miss Rothschild. Perhaps she was simply feeling out of sorts after their conversation with Mrs. Paddock.

Wading through the meanings behind ladies' words was a difficult endeavor. Benjamin didn't understand why they couldn't simply say what they meant. His sisters were forever saying nothing was amiss when they meant that everything was, and the menfolk in their lives were left to decipher the thoughts buried beneath their evasions.

Benjamin had thought Nan was more clear in her communication, but had he been wrong? And if something was amiss, what could he do to right that wrong?

"I apologize, Mr. Leigh. Your mother was very persistent. Fairly dragging me over."

Despite standing before her, Benjamin had utterly forgotten Miss Rothschild. Turning his gaze away from his wife, he met the young lady with a smile. "Then it is my turn to apologize if she made you uncomfortable. I do not know why she felt the need, but none of the blame lies on you."

A smile graced her lips, and though Benjamin recognized the beauty that had once entranced him, he couldn't help but compare it to Nan's unrestrained grin. He preferred the latter.

"As I haven't said so before, congratulations on your nuptials," said Miss Rothschild. "Marriage seems to suit you."

"I think it does," he replied with a nod. "And I've heard rumor that you and Mr. Kipling are courting. Congratulations."

Miss Rothschild's eyes glimmered despite the overcast day, her grin growing brighter. "It has only been a few weeks, but I think we are well suited."

"I am so very happy for you."

"And I, you."

Now that Benjamin was married and Miss Rothschild would soon follow suit (to some lucky gentleman, if not Mr. Kipling), it was unlikely their paths would cross much in the future. Though they'd shared a friendship once upon a time, it had run its course, leading them in different directions, and their tones reflected that, ringing with a sense of finality.

As they'd shared nothing so formal as a courtship, there had been no true ending between them. They'd merely drifted apart. Standing there, Benjamin felt and saw the contentment they'd both found in their respective paths, and he couldn't help but wish them both luck.

With a bob and a bow, the two turned away from one another, but just as Miss Rothschild moved to leave, a thought caught hold of Benjamin.

"How does one go about purchasing a gown?"

The young lady's head cocked to the side, her brows pulling together. "Much in the same way one purchases a suit, I suppose."

As Nan was uncomfortable about Miss Rothschild, he didn't wish to tarry at her side, but once the thought had caught hold of him, he couldn't help but press the issue. Mrs. Paddock's comment clearly disturbed Nan, and if she was unhappy with her dress, she ought to have a new one.

"I know it is an odd question, but despite having sisters, I haven't the slightest notion what is involved with the process, except to know that it is vastly more complicated than a gentleman's wardrobe," he explained. "My sisters and mother simply go 'shopping' and buy what they wish. I can speak with them about it, but as you are here, I thought I would ask. Do you know a good shop?"

Miss Rothschild's brows rose. "I know several, but do you want a modiste, seamstress, draper, or haberdashery?"

"Isn't there a single place?"

"Where you go depends on whether you wish for bespoke, ready-made, or to fashion your own. And many ladies employ a combination based on how much they wish to be part of the process and what they can afford."

With a huff of laughter, the lady looked at him with sympathy. "Mr. Leigh, you are out of your depth. If you are asking for the reason I believe you are asking, my suggestion would be to give your wife a generous allowance and allow her to choose for herself."

Chapter 25

A chill stole down Benjamin's spine, and he managed a quiet, "Thank you, Miss Rothschild," before the young lady drifted off in search of her friends.

Standing like the dense chunk of rock that occupied the space in his skull, Benjamin blinked off at nothing as the very air pressed in on him. Awareness struck like a pickaxe, chipping away at his thoughts as he realized the enormity of the mistake he'd made.

The ladies in the congregation who wore those aged styles were all either old and set in their ways or too poor to afford a new wardrobe. Nan had often said her dresses were her mother's, so perhaps she kept them for sentimentality's sake, but as Mr. Price hadn't been able to provide savings or a dowry for his daughter, it was equally likely that he hadn't been able to afford to purchase his daughter new fashions.

A husband's primary duty was to provide for his wife and children. Before marriage, the vast majority of young men spoke with the lady's father, and whether by formal contract or a gentleman's agreement, allowances and dowers were decided upon. A lady's financial future was set during that meeting, and as Mr. Price hadn't been able to insist upon the discussion, Benjamin hadn't considered that aspect of their marriage.

In his experience, the ladies of his household simply placed whatever they wished for on account, to be paid by Father when the bill came due, but did Nan feel free to do so? No doubt she had some funds left from the sale of her father's things and her teaching (assuming they'd paid her, which many employers wouldn't bother with for such a short stint), but otherwise, she had no ready cash to purchase what she needed, and they'd never discussed pin money.

Confound it! He was turning out to be a poor excuse for a husband. The most basic of requirements, and he was falling short. Once again.

Someone raised a hand in greeting, and Benjamin echoed the movement but forced his feet to move in a different direction. Whatever shock was running through his thoughts at present, it wouldn't do to be standing about like a lump or someone was bound to intrude. And he needed to think.

Here he'd imagined himself being thoughtful enough to purchase Nan a gown, and in fact, Benjamin Leigh was a bounder who'd left his wife without the means of purchasing one if she required it.

But then, how was he to provide those funds for her?

Whitley Court provided room and board, and most everything else simply needed to be requested of the housekeeper, so Benjamin rarely gave ready funds a second thought. Every quarter day, his father handed him a stipend to spend as he wished for all those things the estate couldn't provide. The money simply appeared in his bedchamber, eager to see to his needs, and though it was generous, Benjamin didn't think it would cover both his expenses and those of his wife.

There was only one answer. Turning his feet toward the far end of the churchyard, Benjamin sought out his father's hiding place. Whether the vicar had placed the bench there for him or Father had chosen the spot because of it, that quiet corner had always been known as Osmond Leigh's for as long as Benjamin could recall.

With his legs crossed and a book balanced atop his knee, Father's entire attention was fixed on the words. Though he faithfully attended every Sunday, it was rare that the fellow bothered to look up from whatever tome he secreted into his pocket, and the moment the church doors opened, he fought through the crowd to plant himself there until his wife deigned to leave.

Years of habit had Benjamin fidgeting as he approached, yet for all that he didn't wish to intrude, the question needed asking, and this was the best time. Once home, Father sequestered himself in his study and rarely emerged until meals.

Benjamin cleared his throat. When Father didn't stir, he hesitated to speak.

"Father?"

The gentleman hummed in response, his attention never straying from the page.

"I need to speak with you," he pressed.

It took several more attempts before Father sighed and glanced up. "What is it?"

"I have been considering the situation with Nan, and we need to discuss the finances."

Brows rose. "Is that so? What of it?"

Benjamin shifted in place, tucking his hands behind him. "She is my wife and thus has a right to some pin money. As of now, she has no way to purchase the incidentals she requires."

"We haven't the funds," said Father, turning his attention back to his book.

"With the girls married, surely there is money enough. You could give her a fraction of what you allowed your daughters, and I am certain she would be pleased. Nan isn't an extravagant lady."

"As you've seen fit to hobble our finances, I don't see why you think you have the right to request anything," said Father, not bothering to glance up. "You've shown how little you care for your mother and me, but now, you wish us to sacrifice our few comforts for yours?"

"With economy—"

"You speak of economy whilst standing there, asking us to spend more?" Glancing up from his book, Father arched a brow at that.

Benjamin's mouth dried, making it hard to speak. "I just wish to provide for my wife, Father. She is my responsibility."

"She is, and I am pleased to see you are taking that duty seriously. Nan is such a dear girl, and it pleases me to see you so happily situated together. However, I made several investments and financial decisions several months ago that were contingent on my belief that the entail would be broken by now. We have no excess funds available at this time. I wish I could be of assistance, but my hands are tied."

Father didn't demand. He didn't need to. The request hung in the air between them, making it as clear as if he'd spoken the words. Break the entail, and Father would give the money. Otherwise, Benjamin was left to his own devices.

"It grieves me that I cannot do as you wish," Father continued. "But at present, I must see to the good of the estate."

Again, the unspoken words rang in Benjamin's thoughts, tacking on the silent, "*since you refuse to do so.*"

Despite knowing Father's motivations did not hinge on the good of the family, Benjamin couldn't help but feel the weight of the accusation. Having known his purpose since he was a small boy, the entail had occupied so much of his life. Yet despite knowing that breaking it would likely see the end of Whitley Court, Benjamin couldn't help but question his decision.

If it were only he who were to suffer by refusing his parents, the price would be easily paid. But what about Nan?

Giving a sharp bow of the head, Benjamin turned on his heel and wandered around the church, avoiding the vast majority of people as he tried to exorcise the frustrations building in him, but that question nipped at his heels.

What to do? What could he do?

Only a few short weeks ago, Nan had brushed aside the thought of marriage because binding herself to a poor young man would do nothing to improve her situation. Yet Benjamin had convinced her that being a Leigh would provide better than teaching. Stability and protection had been the main points in his favor, so what good was he if he couldn't even clothe the lady? He'd plucked her from the proverbial frying pan only to drop her amidst a blazing fire.

Nan's fair head peeked out above the other ladies, making it easy to spy her in the thick of things, and Benjamin hoped Mother would keep her occupied for some time, for he couldn't bear to face her whilst these concerns clogged his thoughts.

Unfortunately, the visual she presented made his mistakes even clearer, for now that thoughts of gowns filled his head, Benjamin couldn't help but notice the stark contrast between her dress and those around her. And the image of her pinched expression at Mrs. Paddock's comment flashed in his mind, enhancing the revelation pulsing in his thoughts.

Forcing his feet to move casually, he avoided the majority of the people speaking and stared at the ground so as not to make eye contact and invite conversation. Whether Nan wished to dress fashionably or like a beggar woman, she ought to have the choice, and once more, Benjamin puzzled over the question of money.

Scrubbing his face, he considered his conundrum. His wife needed an allowance. Father controlled the finances in the household, and he wouldn't budge unless Benjamin broke the entail. But to do so would see the ruination of Whitley Court.

The first possibility to pop into his head was that of credit. Many bills did not require immediate payment, and Benjamin could sort out how to manage the money somehow. But the moment that thought entered, it was quickly followed by Mr. Price's stern frown.

"Bad choice, my boy."

To Benjamin's sorrow, that sentence had been uttered so often by his schoolmaster that the words were indelibly written in his memory. But in many ways, Benjamin was grateful for it, for that phrase had proven to be his conscience on many an occasion.

Credit was the fool's way out. Mr. Price had been emphatic on that point, and as much as Benjamin wished to ignore that sage advice, he couldn't embrace a life of debt collectors nipping at his heels. One ought never to spend what one could not afford. It would be a poor show if he refused to break the entail because of his parents' reckless spending, only to run up debts himself.

But he did have money to cover such debts. In theory. As Benjamin's allowances always exceeded his needs, David had assisted him in investing the excess, which had grown to a tidy sum. Unfortunately, as his friend had pointed out when the issue of traveling to Birmingham had arisen, there was a world of difference between income and ready cash.

And though his speculations weren't wild or liable to fail, as so many were, it was best not to borrow against them until one was certain of a healthy payout.

Which left him with one possibility: find a profession. If Mother and Father couldn't be counted on to assist his family financially, then Benjamin needed to secure an income. Unfortunately, he was left with the same conundrum he'd been considering in the years leading to his twenty-first birthday.

A son's ability to settle into a profession relied heavily on his father's assistance. Every option required money for an education or training and family connections to find a proper situation, and Father wouldn't aid him in that endeavor. No doubt, his brothers-in-law would offer assistance, but that didn't negate the fact that most young men were already firmly established in their profession by now, leaving Benjamin years behind his peers.

Then there was the issue of his wife. Gentlemen didn't marry young because they couldn't afford it. Years of unpaid clerkships and apprenticeships led to more meager years (even decades) before one's profession was established enough to afford a wife and family. Benjamin knew plenty of gentlemen in their thirties and older who remained unwed not because of desire but financial difficulties.

And then there was the trouble with his choice of profession. The army and navy required no education, but both paid more in prestige than income. The church appealed to Benjamin, but that required an extensive university education and significant connections to secure a living (neither of which he possessed). The law was the most likely solution, but to spend one's life dedicated to legal tomes was to surrender to a lifetime of monotony.

Benjamin was back at the same stalemate with few options, none of which were both feasible and appealing.

Having been born and trained to be the master of an estate, he couldn't imagine taking on another profession. Benjamin enjoyed puzzling out the investments and improvements to be made, shifting resources to maximize efficiency and profitability. Ledgers were fascinating; seeing one's successes and failures in such a tangible way was so satisfying. And though he had no interest in farming himself, the relationships he'd developed with the tenants over the past few months were far more enjoyable than arguing before the court.

Benjamin Leigh was a master through and through, and he couldn't pursue a new profession and continue his work on the estate; the steward did a fine job, but Benjamin couldn't bear to relinquish his role after spending so many months carving it out for himself.

And for what? To give Nan a few gowns?

Getting her properly attired was important, and Benjamin was determined to see her purchase a whole new wardrobe if she wished, but to overturn his life for that alone seemed too much. After all, most of their expenses were handled by the household; an allowance was necessary, but surely he could find another solution to supplement it.

Tucking his hands behind him, he paused at the edge of the gathering, glancing out at the people milling about. With children nudging the families to leave, the congregation was finally beginning to trickle out the church gate. Though far enough away that he couldn't meet Nan's eyes, he saw her glance in his direction, and he raised a hand.

No doubt, it was time to be on their way, and Benjamin drew in a deep breath. He would get her a whole host of new dresses if she wished, but there had to be another way.

Chapter 26

"And where are we going today?" asked Nan as they walked, arm in arm, along the streets of Greater Edgerton. But like all the other times she'd posed that question, Benjamin gave her only that rascally—but silent—grin. With a huff of feigned annoyance, she scoured the streets ahead to see if she could guess before they arrived at their mystery destination. With the clouds overhead looking a touch concerning, she could only hope they arrived soon.

Despite being an industrial town, Greater Edgerton was sectioned off in a manner so unlike her old home. In Birmingham, it wasn't uncommon to have manufacturing settled next to housing, with dollops of commerce and residential spread around the city in a haphazard fashion. But here, there was a distinct divide between the mills and warehouses that drove so much of the town's economics and the houses and shops.

River Dennick cut a line between the two, the great commercial enterprises rising along one riverbank like a jagged brown cliff face, whilst the majority of houses, cottages, and shops expanded out the other. It seemed such an odd yet practical arrangement, allowing the town to be a unique blend of urban and rural with the Olde and New Towne serving different needs.

Those names always made Nan smile, for some people were very insistent on the antiquated spellings, although her research showed that the terms were only some fifteen or twenty years old, having been adopted when a riot and subsequent fire had devastated many of the mills and warehouses along one side of the river (which led to the unique development of the current town). But society adored pretension.

Unfortunately, her knowledge of Greater Edgerton's layout was still in its infancy, and it was impossible to discern their destination from their path as he led her along the riverfront. Her eyes scoured ahead as Benjamin turned them deeper into New Towne, past the shops and terraced houses.

"Might I have a hint?" she prodded, but Benjamin shook his head and remained silent.

Twisting and turning through the streets, Nan was so thoroughly turned about that she wasn't certain she could find her way back to Whitley Court if she tried. And when Benjamin paused on the pavement with a flourish of his hand, she was at a loss to understand the surprise. The shingle named it Massey's Boutique, but otherwise, there was no hint as to what the shop sold; though windows lined the face of the old timber building, no examples stood there to demonstrate the wares inside.

Pulling from his pocket a hefty purse, Benjamin dropped it into Nan's hands with another flourish.

"What is this?" she asked. "And where are we?"

Tucking his hands behind him and rocking on his heels, Benjamin scuffed the pavers with the toe of his shoe and began to babble about blindness, righting some wrong, duty, and some other nonsense that Nan couldn't comprehend.

"To be honest," he continued, "I think you look lovely regardless, but it has been made abundantly clear that I have been neglecting you once more—something I swore not to do again, yet it seems I am forever bound to do. But truly, I think you fetching regardless—"

"I am certain you mean to be eloquent and clear, but I fear I cannot follow you," said Nan. "Speak plainly. What are we doing here? And where is 'here,' precisely?"

Benjamin drew in a deep breath. "My sisters assure me this is the best dress shop in town, and we are here to purchase you a new wardrobe."

The purse in her hand felt all the heavier, almost threatening to drop to the ground. "Pardon?"

"I can finally see how uncomfortable you are concerning your gowns, and I—fool that I was—didn't consider the fact that I never provided you with funds enough to replace them," he said with a frown.

But Nan shook her head, shoving the purse back. "I do not require a new wardrobe. My dresses are serviceable enough for my needs."

"Don't be ridiculous," he replied, forcing it into her hands once more. "You ought to have funds to buy such things—"

"It is too much!"

"No, it isn't."

The purse danced back and forth between them, and Nan's thoughts filled with Father's words about their finances. Even if it was filled with only sixpences and shillings, it was still far more than she wished to spend. But when Benjamin grabbed hold of her hands and forced them around the purse, Nan stopped fighting and met his gaze.

"Please, Nan. Let me do this for you."

"You've done so much already," she said, "whilst I've done nothing—"

"Let us not bring that up again," he said with a sigh. "We are husband and wife, and I never want to see you embarrassed over something so simple as a dress—"

"We cannot spend so much simply because of a little embarrassment," she countered. "I can manage just fine without it."

With their hands wrapped around the purse, he drew her closer, his eyes so full of concern and determination that it cut short the objections she was already formulating.

"Please, Nan. Allow me this."

Despite the worries and shock of the moment, Nan's nose betrayed her with a scrunch. There was no other thing for her to do when Benjamin was being so sweetly domineering about something so insignificant.

Having felt embarrassed often enough, she was immune to so many of the titters and stares, yet she couldn't help but admit that this silly little matter had caused her heartache many times over the past months. In her father's home, she rarely ventured into society, making her wardrobe unimportant. But now, she was a gentleman's wife, and the future mistress of an estate, and her shabbiness did not go unnoticed.

Benjamin's eyes lit at the sight of her wrinkled nose, and despite Nan erasing it quickly, he'd seen it, and they both knew what her heart thought. Yet she couldn't dismiss Father's words so readily. The family was struggling financially, and surely there was a better use of the funds than her vanity.

"That is so kind of you, Benjamin, but this is too much money," she murmured, her voice lowering so no passersby might overhear. Plenty of people were about, though none paid them any heed, but Nan didn't wish to add to their troubles by being indiscreet. "A wardrobe for me is an unnecessary drain on the family's income—"

"My parents have always granted me more allowance than is good or necessary. The quarter day just passed, giving me another infusion—"

"And you ought to spend it on yourself—"

"I have few expenses, and none of them are as important as getting you properly turned out," said Benjamin. "I will find a way to manage until the next quarter, but for now, I wish to spend my money on what will make me happiest—and that means purchasing you new dresses. Please, Nan."

Her nose wrinkled, for hearing him say such a thing couldn't help but make it crinkle once more, and Benjamin raised a brow in triumph, daring her to deny that she wished to take the money as much as he wished to give it. If this was his allowance, then surely it wasn't going to be such a great burden to the family to purchase a gown or two.

And she had her meager savings to replace a small portion if need be.

Benjamin put an arm around her, guiding her toward the shop as though the battle was won, and despite knowing she ought not to give in so easily, Nan couldn't help but clutch the purse to her chest and allow herself to be led into the shop.

"And as an added surprise, I called upon a few special shopping assistants to be of service today," he whispered into her ear as they stepped through the door.

The shock of this moment was great enough that Nan hardly heard Benjamin's words; they registered far too late for her to brace herself as she came face to face with Mrs. Rosanna Tate.

"There you are." The lady's perfect features stretched into a broad smile, and she swept across the shop with the grace of a swan, enfolding Nan with a buss in greeting before she knew what the lady was about. "I saw you two outside, and I feared he wouldn't convince you to come in."

Despite being nearly twenty years her senior, Mrs. Tate had a glow about her that defied age, stripping away the subtle signs that time had stamped upon her face and leaving her looking as fresh as a spring blossom. More than that, there was an ease about her as she shepherded Nan deeper into the store that had the very opposite effect on her; Mrs. Tate was a lady of the highest order, and Nan felt all the more ungainly around her.

Benjamin looked so pleased that she couldn't help but feign a smile, but ladies like Mrs. Tate rarely embraced an awkward hoyden, and Nan had managed to avoid the lady enough to keep her sister-in-law from discovering that fact. Managing Mrs.

Leigh was trouble enough without adding to her list of familial antagonists.

And it would be impossible to hide her unsuitability to be a gentleman's wife whilst shopping.

"My sisters are here to ensure that you spend the whole of the purse," said Benjamin with a teasing laugh, clearly anticipating Nan's reticence—hardly realizing that she was more discomforted by being surrounded by her superior sisters-in-law than the money.

Nan could only hope Katherine would join them as well. She seemed a good sort who would not expect her to be a fashion plate. But that was dashed when Benjamin inquired after the others.

"Prudence should be here by now," said Mrs. Tate with a frown, glancing at the door. "But I am certain she will be here soon. Katherine sends her apologies. She is feeling poorly this morning and cannot join us."

And just like that, Nan's toes curled inside her shoes, tightening into claws. An afternoon alone with Mrs. Tate and Mrs. Humphreys whilst putting on display all her ignorance concerning fashions, fabrics, trims, and the like.

"Rosanna will deliver you home when you are done," said Benjamin, and though Nan recognized the words as a farewell, she couldn't entirely comprehend it whilst the whole of her world seemed determined to turn itself on its head. Little Miss Nan Price was standing in a dress shop with an obscene amount of money whilst her husband begged her to spend every last farthing. Despite knowing every twist and turn that had brought her to this point, she couldn't comprehend how her life had become so topsy-turvy.

Before she knew it, Benjamin strode out the door, leaving her alone with Mrs. Rosanna Tate in a shop that was as foreign to her as a street market in India. Bolts of fabric filled the shelves, forming what might be an orderly display, but the variation of colors, patterns, and textures made the rolls look haphazard in their placement. Then the piles of ribbons, lace, and trim added to the visual cacophony, as glaring as the scent of lavender hanging heavily in the air.

Mrs. Tate turned Nan about, facing her toward Mrs. Massey with hardly a word of greeting. With a twirl of her finger, the former motioned for Nan to spin, and despite the feeling of being a specimen on display, she did as told.

"Yes, she is rather tall and thin," said Mrs. Massey with a frown, crossing her arms. "But the line of her neck is so long and lovely. Quite elegant."

"Precisely what I was thinking," replied Mrs. Tate. Then, with a gentle hand, she paused Nan before the ladies. "And look at her coloring."

Nan's muscles tightened, though she forced her expression to remain slack, and she watched as the two circled about her.

"Heavenly," said Mrs. Massey. "Absolutely striking. I've never seen a woman her age with such pale locks."

Eyes darting between the two, Nan's brows furrowed.

"Just the sort of complexion that goes with practically any color," said Mrs. Tate with a smile, though it faded as she took in Nan's current gown. With a faint frown, the lady met her gaze, and Nan braced herself for whatever was to come. "This gown wasn't made for you, was it?"

The pressure in her chest eased a touch, and Nan gave a slight shake of the head. "It was my mother's."

"Gorgeous fabric," said Mrs. Tate, brushing a hand against the blue muslin.

"Your mother had a fine eye, and it looks as though you two were of a similar size, which was quite lucky," said Mrs. Massey, her eyes roving the gown.

Her lungs deflated, and Nan stared at the women, though they continued their assessment with far more compliments than criticisms. Did Mrs. Tate truly think her coloring was lovely? That might've been Mrs. Massey's description, but her sister-in-law accepted it without caveat. And when Mrs. Tate gazed into Nan's eyes, the lady seemed aglow with praise.

Neither went so far as to say Nan was a beauty, for that would be too outlandish, but every examination brought with it a few kindly meant critiques followed with a heaping dose of compliments. She couldn't blame them for the first, for there was no good in denying the fact that she was too tall and thin to be deemed gorgeous by society's fickle standards, but it was so rare to hear her odd coloring praised; it was one thing to be pale, but it was another altogether to be nearly colorless.

Then the door burst open, bringing with it a gust of summer breeze, causing the fabrics to flutter.

"I apologize," said the eldest Leigh sister, sweeping in with the wind and blowing through to buss her sister and greet the dressmaker. "I took the children to play with their cousins, which was an ordeal in and of itself, but when I arrived, Lydia had the most wonderful announcement, and I couldn't leave without celebrating: she is expecting."

Mrs. Tate gaped before wrapping her sister in another embrace. "Oh, what blessed news. You must give them my congratulations when you fetch the children."

"I nearly didn't leave them there," said Mrs. Humphreys with a grimace. "Even with the nursery maid, she's going to be run off her feet by my little terrors, especially in her delicate condition."

Mrs. Humphreys turned to face Nan whilst tugging off her bonnet and tossing aside her cloak. "Now, tell me the truth. Is my sister plaguing you?"

Chapter 27

The arrival and deluge of information was so great that Nan couldn't help but stare at the lady, her lagging wits struggling to formulate a response.

"She's been very kind."

That earned her a broad smile. "Ah, so very politic of you. But I know Rosanna well enough to guess that she has been scrutinizing you with the eye of a housekeeper inspecting the greengrocer's deliveries."

What to make of such a question? And such a lady. Both of the Leigh sisters sent Nan's pulse spiking, for though they possessed very different talents, they were forces to be reckoned with, and she couldn't think how to answer Mrs. Humphreys' inquest. So, she stood there, mute.

"What an accusation, Prudence," said Mrs. Tate with a scoff that noted her affront.

"She is still wearing her bonnet, jacket, and gloves, and despite Mrs. Massey keeping a fine selection of cakes and tea on hand, she is going without," replied Mrs. Humphreys. Then, drawing closer, she helped Nan with her things. "We might as well make ourselves comfortable."

A large table sat in the middle of the room with a vast selection of ladies' magazines spread across the top along with several bolts of fabric. Mrs. Massey held up one roll of dusty rose silk, draping the edge over Nan's shoulder with a smile.

"Isn't that perfect," said Mrs. Tate, rubbing the fabric between her fingers. "That is gorgeous on you. Perfection."

Turning Nan toward the mirror set up on the far side of the room, the ladies began layering various colors and patterns on her shoulders, prattling on about the hues and how they complemented her complexion whilst Nan felt drowned in a rainbow. Mrs. Humphreys riffled through the fashion plates, speaking what must be English, though it was utterly incomprehensible to Nan's ears.

Between them and the dressmaker, she felt as though she'd been swallowed up in a snowstorm, with the women tossing a flurry of fabrics, frills, and ribbons.

"Gigot sleeves are divine," said Mrs. Tate. "I think it would suit you perfectly."

"But it's impractical," said Mrs. Humphreys with a shake of her head. "It might suit a ballgown, but I think a bishop's sleeve achieves much of the same effect, but without the size."

"What say you?" asked the former, and both ladies turned their gaze to Nan. And waited.

Blinking back at them, she didn't know what to say, for she didn't know the slightest thing about sleeve shapes or the lace or the fabric types or neckline styles. Her cheeks heated as she fumbled for something to say that wouldn't make her out to be the ignoramus she was and turn a lovely (though overwhelming) afternoon sour.

"They are both nice," she said, her gaze turning down to the table, hoping that one of the drawings might give some hint so she could give a proper opinion. Abandoning that course, Nan spoke the motto of the flustered and overtaxed: "Whatever you think is best."

Mrs. Tate's brows rose at that, and her gaze turned to her sister, which did nothing to calm the flutter in Nan's stomach.

For her part, Mrs. Humphreys pushed aside the magazines she'd been examining and waved away Mrs. Massey and her avalanche of fabrics.

"This can be a touch daunting," said Mrs. Humphreys with a warm smile. "Perhaps we should begin with a list of the dresses you require."

"Yes, that is just the thing," echoed Mrs. Tate, setting down the ribbons and leading the pair over to the chairs along the edge of the room. Waving her assistant forward, Mrs. Massey presented them with a tray of treats and tea, and the ladies settled into the chairs as the seamstress stood at the ready with a notebook and pencil in hand.

Nan tried to enjoy the goodies, but it was difficult when her insides were doing acrobatics. Doubly so when Mrs. Tate turned that attention back to her.

"What sort of dresses do you require?" asked Mrs. Tate in a gentle tone, as though she were guiding a spooked horse over a jump rather than a flustered lady through a shopping excursion.

"Something for the evening," said Nan, running her free hand down her skirts. She may not know much about fashions themselves, but that much was clear. "And some day dresses, as well. Three, I think. That has suited me well."

Mrs. Tate's eyes bulged. "Only three?"

But Mrs. Humphreys cleared her throat, and her sister seemed to recall herself with a shake of her head. With a dry tone, Mrs. Humphreys added, "Ignore my sister. She thinks having anything less than a dozen is a travesty."

"A dozen?" echoed Nan in the same astonishment Mrs. Tate had displayed. "That is too much for me. I know Benjamin wishes me to purchase a new wardrobe, but I cannot bear to spend so much."

A smile crept across Mrs. Humphreys' face. "To think that Whitley Court will have a mistress who is fiscally responsible. What a novel idea."

"He made us promise that we wouldn't allow you to leave this shop until you had sorted your entire wardrobe out," said Mrs. Tate with a challenging raise of the brows. And with a hint of humor, she added, "You wouldn't wish to make us break our word, would you?"

Nan frowned, knowing she was truly caught. "You—and most especially my husband—are too manipulative for my good sometimes."

"He wishes you to be properly outfitted," said Mrs. Humphreys with a kind grin. "And if it does bother you so much, we can purchase a few gowns and then the fabric and trims for the rest."

There was no way around this confession. Though Nan preferred to remain silent, she knew she must admit the whole of her inexperience. If they thought her as useless as so many other ladies had, then there was nothing to be done about it. Nan wouldn't spend the money on fabric she couldn't use.

"I fear I do not know how to make a gown," she said, forcing herself not to wilt at the admission. "I can mend as well as anyone, and I understand the basics, but I have no experience with dressmaking, and as fabric is so expensive, I didn't wish to attempt it on my own. As a schoolmistress, I would've had to sort it out in time, but at present, I only have the barest understanding of how to go about it."

"Would you still care to learn?" asked Mrs. Humphreys, which drew a nod from Mrs. Tate.

"Oh, yes. Prudence can teach you. I never cared to construct an entire thing myself, as I preferred embellishing it more, but she makes her own."

Of all possible reactions, Nan hadn't expected that from either lady. She blinked at the pair, her brows pulling together.

"I would love that," said Nan, for it was the only answer she could give to such generosity, though she couldn't help but look for some sign of Mrs. Leigh's duplicity. That lady feigned sweetness with such ease that it was impossible not to doubt the kindness her daughters offered so freely.

Yet as they waded once more into the discussion, the two ladies guided Nan through each step with unending patience, explaining in turn the benefits of various fabrics and styles. Though they offered their own opinions on the matter, the two left Nan to make the final decision and praised the choices she made, and she was left feeling even more overwhelmed by the consideration and compassion of the two ladies as they led her through the mire.

Nan had often wondered what it would be like to have siblings, but her experience with womenfolk hadn't recommended the idea.

"What is that expression?" asked Mrs. Humphreys in a manner that was so like her brother that Nan felt all the more overcome. Between the awareness and concern, her heart was quite ready to do something entirely silly like grow teary.

Mrs. Humphreys cast a furtive glance toward her sister, and Mrs. Tate drew Mrs. Massey's attention, pulling her and the woman's assistant away enough so they could not overhear. The whole thing was done so quickly and easily, and Nan felt that sweetness anew.

"I am not much of a shopper, myself, and I understand how overwhelming it can all be," said the lady, her gaze so full of concern. "We can rest for a few minutes if you wish. Rosanna secured the shop for the entire afternoon, and we have free run of the place. We shan't be bothered if we take the rest of the day."

Nan's throat tightened at that confession. "Don't mind me. I am being silly. That is all."

But Mrs. Humphreys looked unappeased by that confession, so Nan offered more; she and her sister had been too generous with their time and attention to be granted anything less.

"I am a touch overwhelmed—but more from your generosity than the shopping. In my experience, my unrefined tastes, education, and manners are unsavory in ladies' opinions, and it is unusual for me to find such kinship in their midst."

"I can well imagine," replied Mrs. Humphreys with a huff. Nodding toward Mrs. Tate, she added, "As you well know, my younger sister is a favorite of society, and if not for her, I would've been a miserable wallflower. So, when I see a way to assist another awkward sister-in-arms, I cannot turn away."

Then, leaning closer, Mrs. Humphreys added in a low voice, "And I do not think ignorance of fashion is a great crime. I do not know the sort of ladies you have associated with, but I know plenty who care about it only so much as they wish to look their best. I imagine being raised by a widower was hardly conducive to a feminine education."

Nan huffed a laugh. "If it wasn't about dead languages, philosophy, history, or mathematics, Father didn't see the use for it. I can recite any number of epic poems in foreign tongues, but ask me the difference between a gigot and a bishop's sleeve, and I am a dunce."

"I can well imagine," replied Mrs. Humphreys with a half-smile. "As children educated at home, we are at the mercy of our parents' knowledge, which left me and my sisters at a loss—"

"I have fended off Mrs. Massey as long as I can," called Mrs. Tate, bustling back to her seat. "But I fear we must start getting measurements. There is so much work to be done, and that is foremost on the list."

Before Nan knew what they were about, she was ushered behind a privacy screen, where she was summarily stripped of her outer clothes, leaving her in a chemise as Mrs. Massey began to document every inch of her. Mrs. Massey positioned Nan's arms outstretched, and she stared at the screen as though she could see her sisters-in-law behind it, though there was no hint of their shapes.

"Please don't move," said Mrs. Massey, giving Nan a warning look.

"My apologies."

"Go easy on the girl, Mrs. Massey," called Mrs. Tate from beyond.

"Allow me to do my job, madam," came the sharp retort, though that bit of disrespect was met with a laugh.

"I understand from Katherine that you are a great reader," said Mrs. Humphreys. It was odd to hear the disembodied voice whilst she was dishabille, but Mrs. Massey moved methodically, and somehow that impartiality allowed Nan to ignore the vulnerable state she was in and turn her attention to the question.

"Is it any wonder with a father such as mine?" replied Nan. "Your father may be a great reader, but mine made a living off books."

There was a pause, and with a tone that held a touch of pity to it, Mrs. Humphreys said, "I haven't had the opportunity to say so before, but I was very sorry to hear about your father. That must've been very difficult."

Holding her breath for a count of three, Nan forced herself to speak kindly in return, for the sentiment was kindly meant. "Having one's world so upended is difficult for anyone, I imagine. I simply remind myself that he is with Mother now."

Nothing but the truth crossed her lips, but she couldn't help the twist of her heart as she considered it. What sort of daughter felt nothing for the loss of her father? Or rather, what she did feel was hardly filial. Surely, after months of hearing such sympathies, it ought to be easier to slough them away, yet they dug into her like burrs.

"I am certain you miss your father," said Mrs. Humphreys, her tone so full of careful neutrality that Nan's ears couldn't help but prick up. "However, I was speaking of the difficulties of finding yourself at the mercy of the world, without help or the means to provide for oneself. That is a daunting prospect."

Something in her tone rang true, as though this lady truly understood. Nan didn't know what to say to that, but Mrs. Massey broke through the moment with another sharp command.

"Arms, Mrs. Leigh."

Chapter 28

Despite being what most considered "a man of the world," Benjamin had never been one to focus on his appearance beyond a general sense of good or bad. He was no dandy to primp or fret about his cravat, nor was he forever chasing the latest fashions. He wore quality vestments but nothing overdone or eye-catching. So, he'd never considered a shopping excursion as something to celebrate, yet as he strode from Mrs. Massey's dress shop, his steps were decidedly jauntier.

Giving Nan his allowance didn't solve the problem, but it lightened his conscience.

So much of his life had been spent entertaining himself, and yet how much happier he was spending that time assisting the tenants or contemplating ways to enliven his wife's spirits. And so, though Benjamin felt no personal inclination to join Nan in the shopping flurry, he felt an immense swell of joy filling his chest at having given her that experience.

He moved quickly down the streets, winding his way back to Whitley Court, the lightness of his steps driving him fast along and weeding out any trepidation he felt at the forthcoming discussion. Any other day, intruding on his father's sanctuary might be a daunting notion, but with Nan's scrunched nose spurring him on, he entered the front door without hesitation and climbed the steps, sweeping into Father's study before he could truly consider just what he was doing.

"We need to discuss the allowance."

But for all that his statement had been clear and direct, Father didn't even look up from his book.

Benjamin frowned. "Father?"

It took several more calls before the gentleman's gaze turned up from the page, his eyes blinking like an owl.

"You know better than to come in here without an invitation, Son," said Father with a frown of his own.

"I need to speak to you, and as you rarely emerge from your study, I have no choice but to invade it."

Father didn't bother to close his book; he peered at his son from over his reading spectacles and seemed to give a silent sigh. "And what is so very important?"

"I won't allow Nan to be neglected," said Benjamin.

"It is not my actions that are leading to her neglect." And with that, Father turned his attention back to his book.

"I know we discussed this last week, but I thought we might examine the ledgers together and consider where we might find some funds—"

Father scoffed. "You, my boy, presume to tell me my business? I have been master of this estate for longer than you've been alive."

Holding up placating hands, Benjamin shook his head. "By no means, Father. But I have a good head for sums and economics, and a new perspective might be just the thing. I spoke with Mr. Turley, and with some maneuvering, we can easily set aside some money for her."

"I've told you precisely what we require from you, and you refuse to do it," came the sharp answer.

Dropping onto the seat before his desk, Benjamin held back the huff he wanted to let loose. "And I have told you why I cannot break the entail. Surely there must be another solution other than selling off property or mortgaging the house. It is too risky."

"And I assure you there isn't," said Father, turning his gaze back to his book.

"What harm can it do to go through the expenditures again?" asked Benjamin, forcing the man's attention back to the subject before he was lost in another novel. "Even the best of men can overlook something that fresh eyes can see."

"Do you trust me so little?" But without waiting for his son to answer, the gentleman supplied his own. "Of course not. Why ask such a question? You've made that clear by refusing to break the entail. Just as you've made it clear that you care only about your future, and not that of your parents. This is my birthright, yet I am forced to beg my son to assist me, despite having given him so much."

With a shake of his head, Father gave a dramatic sigh. "Oh, no. My dear son only cares that he keeps his birthright intact and untouched by his foolhardy father. Holding firm to tradition and an ill-gotten promise, rather than filial duty and affection. He's content to let us flounder about, only willing to stir himself now that his wife is inconvenienced."

At that, Father shut the book with his finger tucked in as his bookmark. "But as you've forced your way in here, demanding your wife's allowance, I think it's high time we discuss yours."

Benjamin leaned back, his brows pinching together. "Meaning?"

"As you refuse to treat us with the respect and dignity parents ought to be afforded, I think it only fair that we return the favor," said Father, his expression growing as cold as Benjamin had ever seen it. "You've lived off our beneficence for some time, and I had hoped you would come to your senses, but it seems you are stubbornly sticking to your decision. As you claim to do this for the good of the estate, then it'd be better if we invested those funds into your inheritance instead."

Benjamin stilled as he spoke, his blood running as cold as the snow runoff in spring. "Surely you cannot be serious. You would cut me off?"

"You have cut yourself off, Son," said Father with a sad shake of his head. "I had hoped you would see reason, but I fear I've failed you as a father. You are so blessed, Benjamin, that you do not comprehend how difficult the world is, and it's time I stop coddling you. Perhaps a touch of financial hardship will help you come to your senses."

Mouth agape, he stared at his father. Benjamin knew he looked a fool, but he couldn't help the expression. "But what about Nan?"

"Precisely," replied Father. "What about your wife? She is such a dear young lady, and she has suffered so much already. Would you add to her burdens? To rescue her from poverty, only to place her right back in it?"

Pausing, the gentleman considered that and amended the statement. "You would worsen it, in fact, for she had an income in Birmingham. And your expenses will quickly outstrip your income when the children arrive, which they are bound to do in due course. A maid would be out of the question, so your wife would be forced to act the part—scrubbing floors, cooking meals, managing the laundry—on top of caring for your children. No funds for physicians or medicines when they grow ill. Likely not enough to keep them fed and clothed. And all because you will not break the entail."

Throat tight and dry, Benjamin struggled to form the words. "You speak as though you are evicting us from Whitley Court."

"I do not want to, but if you will not see reason, it may be my only course of action to teach you responsibility. If I've failed to do so before, it is my duty to do so now, however hard that lesson may be," said Father. "Please, do not make me do it.

Your wife has suffered enough. Do what is best for her and this family."

With a heavy sigh, he added, "You needn't decide this very moment, but I must know soon."

And just like that, Father returned to his book, seemingly deaf and blind to his son seated before him. Benjamin rose on weak legs and left, his feet dragging him through the house he both loved and loathed.

...

Despite the dressmaker's assistant's best efforts, the shop was a mess, with bolts of fabric slung to and fro and buttons, ribbons, lace, and braiding all scattered about the worktable. Nan couldn't help but grin at the prospect of all these new dresses.

What ought she to do with her old gowns? Fabric was too expensive to waste, but there was not enough yardage to remake them. Perhaps she could sell them to a secondhand store and make back some of the funds her sisters-in-law were spending so cavalierly.

Mrs. Massey swept into the back rooms to gather some other trims, leaving the three to look at the arrangements they'd chosen so far.

"Are you happy?" said Mrs. Tate.

"Very much so," replied Nan with a beaming smile.

The lady's eyes sparked in return, but she nodded toward the selection of fabric and trims. "I meant the dress."

"I did as well, but thank you for coming today as well. It has been so kind of you to give up your afternoon."

Mrs. Tate waved that away. "Nonsense. I've wanted an excuse to spend some time with the lady desperate enough to marry my brother."

"Your brother is a very good man," retorted Nan with a frown. "I am lucky to have him."

"Ignore her," added Mrs. Humphreys. "She likes to tease too much."

"As far as I can tell, all Leigh siblings treat teasing like a pastime," said Nan, earning a laugh from both ladies.

"Too true," said Mrs. Tate. "It doesn't help matters that so many of us have married men who bring that out in us."

Mrs. Humphreys huffed and turned the conversation back to the subject at hand. "We were both eager to accept when Benjamin asked us to join you today. I've wanted to pay a call before, but I fear my children and household keep me very occupied, and whenever I've had the opportunity, you have been out. Mama seems to be commandeering all your time."

There was something heavy in her tone, and it took no great leap of imagination to infer Mrs. Humphreys' curiosity and concern. And that realization left Nan feeling pinched and clammy all over again.

"Yes, she has been quite attentive," said Nan.

Mrs. Tate gave a knowing hum that was full of disbelief, and she watched her new sister-in-law with far more intensity than Nan wished to have pointed in her direction.

"How are things at home?" Though Mrs. Humphreys tiptoed around an outright declaration, Nan felt it in the subtext, and she struggled to know what to say. The tightness in her chest redoubled, and she considered speaking the truth—but though a kinship was growing between her and her sisters-in-law, they were still related to the lady in question, and family bonds were a tricky business.

"It has been an adjustment, to be certain, but I am sure you felt the same way when you married your husbands," replied Nan.

The sisters shared a glance, though she couldn't decipher the meaning, except that something significant passed between them.

"We do hope you are happy at Whitley Court," said Mrs. Tate.

"We know how difficult it can be at times," added Mrs. Humphreys.

A long pause followed those statements, and Nan struggled with what she wished to say and that which she ought to say. As much as the past hour had proven the ladies were far more ingratiating and less terrifying than Nan had believed them to be, they were still strangers. And the difficulties in her life at present took the form of their mother.

"I am happy," said Nan, though she wished her words were as confident as they'd been before.

Comparing the past fortnight to the weeks before it, there was a stark difference in her life, with the present being much more bright and cheery than she'd expected it to be. Benjamin was proving himself an excellent husband and growing to be a dear friend. Her sisters-in-law seemed more and more the sort of ladies with whom Nan could form a bond. Her father-in-law doted upon her.

Besides concerns about the money and her mother-in-law, Nan's life was full of sunshine. Would she allow a few clouds to spoil it?

"I am happy," she echoed, feeling the words more than before, and the ladies nodded, though there was a hint of uncertainty in Mrs. Humphreys' gaze. But before either of them could address the subject again, Mrs. Massey returned from the back rooms with yet more options for them to pick over. And once more, they were drawn into the task at hand.

Chapter 29

The immediate grounds around Whitley Court weren't as intricate as the finer estates in the area. Mother cared little about gardens beyond the impression they made to guests, which was why their grounds weren't as modern as others. Adjacent to the back was a small paved square, which had been installed by Benjamin's great-grandfather when the fashions had both women and men in heels, requiring hard surfaces to promenade. Grandmother had installed planting beds, trees, and shrubs around it, giving a passing nod at the shifting fashions as shoes became more manageable out in nature.

Beyond that was the quintessential green space, of which Benjamin was making good use. He didn't dare venture too far from the house, for the clouds above looked bleak, and he didn't wish to get caught in a downpour. Catching a cold would hardly improve his situation. So, his feet followed familiar paths and deposited him beneath his favorite oak tree.

For all that the open air and scent of growing things ought to have filled him with contentment, Benjamin's thoughts were far too chaotic to enjoy the beauty around him. Even with the dull sky, his home was beautiful. The green of the grass was aglow with vitality, and though many compared the color to sparkling emeralds, the comparison was too cold for his liking. The shade wasn't some lifeless stone but a living, breathing thing, brimming with energy and spirit.

Drawing in a deep breath, Benjamin tried to calm his pulse, but it was as frantic as his thoughts. What was he to do?

He wanted to believe Father wouldn't be so cruel—if not for a similar threat the gentleman had leveled at Katherine last year. In that same apologetic tone, their father had outlined the steps he'd take toward his daughter if Benjamin didn't do as bidden, and he'd believed it enough to push Katherine into David's path. His meddling in their courtship had won them a happy life and granted Benjamin the peace of mind that if anyone were to suffer at his parents' hands, it would be him and him alone.

But he'd never truly believed that Father would turn that ire toward his beloved son. How had he been so blind? How had he forgotten Father's cruelty toward his own daughter so easily? Though he didn't boast a close relationship with the gentleman, Father had always been generous and warm. Now, Nan was in the same situation as Katherine had been, and it was Benjamin's doing that had landed her in such dire straits.

Society wasn't content with simply maintaining the course; with each generation, wealth was added to or diminished, and rarely did it do so in even turns. Benjamin had known boys at school who hailed from distinguished family lines, who now were little more than the disappointing twigs on a decaying family tree. If one lived within one's means, it was easy enough to establish an estate that could survive for generations without fail.

However, no family chain was without its weak links, and their poor decisions destroyed everything their ancestors had built. And for what? A larger library? More dresses and parties? Whitley Court was more than comfortable if his parents would simply be content with what they had.

But was his determination to maintain that legacy more important than his family? Not the one his father claimed, for Benjamin felt little guilt in denying them. His parents could reap the consequences of their actions.

If he owed any of his family anything, it was his sisters, for they had so often been neglected in favor of himself. But they were comfortably and mostly happily settled. Benjamin couldn't swear to Francis's being the latter, as that sister had left Greater Edgerton to marry and hardly contacted anyone in the family except Mother. But Prudence, Rosanna, and Katherine were most certainly blessed with both.

And now, there was Nan.

Could he subject her to a life of drudgery? Would Nan have accepted his proposal if she'd known it would end with her acting the part of maid-of-all-work? The lady hadn't wished to marry him in the first place, and Benjamin was all too aware of how much effort it had taken to convince her to do so.

And their children? To break the entail would give his sons and daughters a lesser portion, whether through inheritances or dowries when they were grown. There were young heirs aplenty whose futures were defunct and derelict, receiving an estate that took more than it gave, binding them to mortgages and debts they couldn't hope to repay. The children might know luxury now, only to be forced into penury when they were grown.

Yet to maintain the entail would make that penury an immediate thing with the hope of something greater only when their father inherited. Either decision was bound to cause the rising generation turmoil. Hardships now or later. There was no avoiding tribulation in his future, but now, it wasn't only himself who would be made to suffer.

Which burden was greater for his children to bear?

Scrubbing at his face, Benjamin let out a low sigh, and his head fell against the tree trunk as he considered it all once more. How had he come to this? Why had he been so foolhardy in marrying Nan? He'd arrived in Birmingham expecting to find some way around the duty he was called to bear, and somehow it had ended with him begging Nan to marry him. Benjamin had thought himself her savior, come to rescue her from toil—only to drop her into other troubles.

Had he ruined Nan's future, coercing her into a marriage that no longer served its original purpose? Dragging her farther into financial troubles rather than lifting her out of them?

With several sharp thuds, he hit his head against the trunk, and resting it there, he stared at the gray skies above. There were no answers. No happy ones, at least.

The distant sound of wheels and hooves against gravel drew his attention to the drive as Rosanna's carriage rounded to the front of the house.

Without bidding, he rose to his feet and was moving across the yard. A maid hurried from the house and began hefting packages inside whilst Nan climbed down, speaking animatedly to the ladies still inside. Leaning into the window, Prudence waved at him, and the others followed suit. Benjamin's steps came faster as Nan's beaming grin drew him in.

A twinge set his stomach roiling as he considered whether or not they'd just spent the majority of their funds, but the eagerness with which she greeted him helped to ease away some of those darker thoughts as the carriage rolled away.

What was done was done.

"Thank you so much," said Nan, throwing her arms around Benjamin's neck. "This has been a wonderful day. Simply perfect. I adore your sisters and my new wardrobe."

Before he knew what she was about, he found himself dragged to her bedchamber, where she unwrapped the many packages to show him all her treasures. Nan touched the edges of the fabric with a reverence that wiped away the residual worries plaguing him; foolhardy or not to spend the funds, they were spent, but Nan was the happier for it. If they were to struggle in the future, at least she'd have this moment.

With little prodding, she cast aside her old gown and donned a new one. It was a simple afternoon dress, but it wrought a mighty change in her. The rich pink brought a rose to her cheek, and the bell skirt added a fullness to her figure far better than the older fashions. Then there was the neckline, which sloped toward her shoulders, giving a peek of skin that filled Benjamin with an urge to place a kiss there.

"I thought I ought to have a proper afternoon dress, so I chose a gown Mrs. Massey had on hand whilst she prepares the others. Rosanna insisted on an evening dress and two other afternoon dresses, for though Prudence said she will teach me to sew my own, it will take some time." Nan sifted through the packages and pulled back a bit of brown paper. "Isn't that pattern lovely? The moment I saw it, I knew I wanted it."

And so she went through her purchases, and though Benjamin had not the slightest interest in trims and fabrics, he couldn't help but smile as Nan detailed all the effort made with each purchase. His amusement grew when her cheeks pinked as she stuffed away a package holding her new undergarments.

Yet Father's threat lurked in the back of his thoughts, dimming the beauty of the moment.

"Prudence made certain we paid fair prices for everything, and though you wished me to, I couldn't bring myself to spend everything you gave me," she said, slipping the purse from her reticule and handing it to him. "I have so much, and I do not need another farthing. Rosanna wished me to spend it all, but I held firm. Truly, I only purchased what I required—" Her babbling halted, and Nan's brows drew together. "What is the matter?"

Benjamin forced his features to soften, though he wasn't sure what aspect of his expression gave his worry away. "Nothing. What else did you purchase?"

But Nan clutched one of the brown paper packages to her chest and stared at him.

A fleeting thought had him wondering if he ought to tell her all that was happening, but as quickly as that came into his mind, he banished it. Nan had married him for stability and security. The jest about his being a shag-bag of a man and their marriage being a rum deal for her was proving prophetic, but surely, he would find a resolution before she discovered it for herself.

His role as husband was to protect; admitting the troubles behind the entail ran contrary to that directive. Besides, what good would it do beyond making them both fret and worry when only he needed to be concerned at present? Did he wish to ruin her happy moment with that darkness? Best not.

If they were to be tossed into the street, surely the least he could do was keep her from that troubling knowledge for as long as he could.

Rising from his seat in the corner, he strode toward her and draped his arms around her waist. Nan's eyes widened, her muscles stiffening only a touch before she relaxed into his hold.

"How can anything be amiss when you are so happy?" he asked in a low voice.

Nan's brows inched upward. "Is that so?"

Benjamin nodded, and then turned her in place, pointing her toward the dressing table mirror. It was a tad small to see her properly, but standing away as they were, they were both visible enough to admire the picture she made. Giving in to the impulse, Benjamin placed a kiss on the sliver of bare shoulder, and Nan jerked, her head swinging from the mirror to look at him with wide eyes.

Heavens, she looked so fetching. Doubly so when her nose gave away her thoughts at the moment, wrinkling as her cheeks pinked.

"I do love a tall woman," he said. "I don't have to crane my neck to kiss you."

Nan's brows rose in challenge, a hint of humor coloring her eyes as they narrowed. "And you have ample enough experience kissing shorter women to know the difference, do you?"

He didn't offer an answer, merely giving her a wicked grin that never failed to make her smile and huff, and Benjamin wasn't disappointed as she did precisely that.

"You look beautiful," he whispered, his arms pulling her closer.

"I do?" she answered in kind, her voice far more timid and uncertain than he liked to hear.

"Quite."

One of his arms remained wrapped around her waist, holding her tight to him, and his other rose to her cheek, brushing a gentle touch across it. Shifting, Nan turned to face him, their lips so close that he felt them brush, and she trembled before melting into his embrace.

When the bedchamber door burst open.

"I thought I heard you two up here," said Mother as she swept inside.

Chapter 30

Nan jerked out of his hold (despite Benjamin's best efforts to keep her put), and the frustration bubbling in his heart colored his tone as he turned his attention to his mother.

"This is Nan's room. You ought to respect her privacy," said Benjamin with a scowl.

Mother held up placating hands. "I mean no disrespect, my dear boy. I simply wish to see what all the fuss was about. I overheard Polly speaking of Nan's purchases. Besides, what are you doing here? This is Nan's bedchamber. Not yours."

For all that Benjamin knew children ought to respect their parents, never had he felt more inclined to toss his mother out on her ear.

"She is showing me her new gowns," he said, pointing a jerky finger toward the packages as he tried to clear his thoughts, though he longed to shove her back out the door. Expectation still hung heavy in the air, and he longed to recapture the spoiled moment.

But Mother wouldn't be deterred.

"Oh, you must show me," she said, taking Nan by the hand and dragging her to the bed. "I understand my daughters took pity on you and helped you to purchase an entire new wardrobe."

Drawing in a deep breath, Benjamin rubbed his face, forced his pulse to calm, and accepted defeat. For now.

With a cleansing breath, Nan unclenched her jaw and held onto that happy moment before her mother-in-law had appeared. She refused to allow that woman to ruin what was quickly turning into one of the best days of her life.

"Doesn't Nan look lovely?" said Benjamin with a bright smile that helped to erase the last of Nan's irritation.

Of course, Mrs. Leigh had an uncanny knack for undoing even the most soothing of balms, and Nan found herself on edge once more when the lady said, "It is certainly an improvement, my dear."

The words were so serenely spoken that Nan couldn't muster any irritation toward Benjamin, who took the statement at its surface meaning, even if she felt the truth beneath it. The current gown was an improvement, but to Mrs. Leigh's thinking, it was only because the previous gowns were disasters.

No, she would not allow that wretched woman power over her. Miserable people liked making others miserable, and Nan refused to allow herself to give in to another of that woman's barbs.

"What fun for you and the girls. Had I known you were taking a shopping excursion, I would've cleared my diary. But no one mentioned a word of it to me," said Mrs. Leigh with just enough of a put-upon sigh that Nan felt like scoffing—and all the more because Benjamin looked truly aggrieved.

"I am sorry about that oversight," he said. "But I knew you were otherwise occupied, and I didn't want to throw over your plans."

The lady patted her son's cheek in that manner of hers that never failed to raise Nan's hackles, for it feigned sweetness when the lady had little in her heart. And there was an odd sort of possessiveness that had Nan longing to smack that hand away, whether or not it was his mother.

"I do not blame you, my dear boy. You are such a good, thoughtful son." Then, turning to Nan, Mrs. Leigh added, "But you really should change, my dear. It would be such a shame to ruin your dress so soon after purchasing it, and we are only sitting about the house."

Nan's thoughts filled with possibilities. Surely Benjamin was amenable to a drive, and that would be reason enough to keep the gown on. Yet it still looked like rain, and the dust from the horses would dirty it terribly. And as much as Nan wished to brush aside Mrs. Leigh's logic, her practical side wouldn't cast away good advice when given.

Even if she wished the giver of said advice to Hades.

A small fortune had been spent today, and she wouldn't allow her pride to get the better of her. Most of the gowns were still planned, and it would take time before her wardrobe filled out to its proper size. In the meantime, it wouldn't do to waste new dresses whilst simply lazing about the house.

"Shoo!" said Mrs. Leigh to Benjamin, brushing him toward the door. "I will help her change. You find something better to do with yourself than lurking around our dear girl's bedchamber."

As Nan had gotten the dress on without assistance, she didn't require Mrs. Leigh to remove it, but the lady was as determined as ever, ushering Benjamin downstairs before either of them could mount a decent protest.

Coming back to Nan, Mrs. Leigh's smile grew cold. "Now, we'd best get this off before you ruin it. That would be such a waste."

Though Nan felt the attack in the words, they didn't harm as the lady intended. It wasn't Mrs. Leigh's unabashed disappointment that plagued her at present.

Once Benjamin drifted away and the haze from their interrupted embrace cleared from her foggy brain, Nan realized that something was amiss with her husband. Father's warning rang in her thoughts, and though Benjamin had done a fair job of distracting her, the memory of his concerned expression rose again to her thoughts, stoking those concerns like a billow. Whatever his assurances, Nan knew something was amiss with her husband, and with Father's concern about money, it wasn't difficult to connect the two.

And here she was standing amidst a veritable fortune of clothes and notions.

"Are you well?" asked Mrs. Leigh with far more concern than Nan had credited her to feel.

Feigning a smile, she waved the question away. "Yes. Perfectly well."

Mrs. Leigh shifted to stand before her, and despite her best efforts to avoid them, the lady's hands clasped Nan's. Brows pulled tight together, she gazed into her daughter-in-law's eyes as Nan shifted in place. They remained there far too long to be comfortable, but though she tried to free herself from Mrs. Leigh's grasp, the lady's hands were like a vise.

And so, Nan waited for her to get to whatever point she was about to make.

"Are you happy here, my dear?" she asked.

Nan managed not to scoff. But only just. Then she offered as much truth as she wished to share with Mrs. Leigh. "I am very blessed to be at Whitley Court."

Mrs. Leigh nodded, though her brows remained pinched. "I know how difficult it can be to adjust to a new life, and no one would fault you if you decided you'd made a mistake."

"Mistake or not, I am married," replied Nan in a dry tone.

"That is precisely what I mean, my dear," said Mrs. Leigh. With a kindly arm around her shoulders, the lady shepherded her toward the bed and sat her down there. Nan would be more inclined to believe the motherly facade if she hadn't seen the truth lurking beneath the surface, but in the meantime, she waited for Mrs. Leigh to arrive at her point.

Though Nan longed to shoo her out of her bedchamber and call Benjamin back in.

"I simply wish to make you aware of your options, my dear. I am thinking only of your future and what is best for you." It was a wonder the lady didn't choke on the words, for there was nary a truth in them. "You two may be married in a sense, but—do forgive me for being crass—you are still man and wife in name only, as you two have not..."

The lady paused with a significant tone that brought a blush to Nan's cheeks before continuing, "Though I am not certain of the entire process, I have looked into annulments, and I believe it is possible to undo this hasty marriage."

Straightening, Nan stared at her, and Mrs. Leigh held up placating hands.

"I mean no offense, of course. But my dear boy can be so shortsighted at times. It is well and good that he wished to do his duty to your father, but surely you can see that his asking Benjamin to sacrifice his future is hardly honorable. It was your father's responsibility to provide for you, and it is monstrous that he would slough that onto my son."

Nan refused to let her emotions show, but the words were far too familiar to ones she'd thought herself to dismiss them off-hand.

"Surely you are not so selfish that you would wish to keep Benjamin trapped in a marriage he doesn't want simply to secure financial stability. You are both miserable, and it is only right that you set him free."

There was no denying the pain those words caused, for Nan's heart ached beneath the load of worries and guilt that had arisen the moment Benjamin crossed her path. And for the briefest moment, she couldn't help but be swept up in Mrs. Leigh's vision.

To allow Benjamin to go free would be the kind thing to do. And it was selfish of her to keep him locked in this arrangement.

Yet Nan's heart pulsed with a certainty, which helped to clear away the fog Mrs. Leigh's arguments produced, helping her to see the world as it was, not as she feared it to be. And the truth was that Benjamin had demanded the marriage. It hadn't been Nan's proposition, and she'd agreed to it only after much effort on his part. Whether Benjamin had been a fool to propose in the first place was his business, but this marriage was not due to her selfishness.

That peace ushered in the memory of Benjamin's eyes as he held her in a manner that was hardly duty-bound. All the nights they'd spent wrapped up together, their words filling the darkness as they spoke of everything and nothing. This marriage may have started as an arrangement, but Nan felt it transforming into something more. Her heart stirred at the very thought of Benjamin and the time she stole away with him. And though she couldn't comprehend it, she saw a similar yearning in him when he gazed into her eyes.

And his kisses...

Nan fought the smile that threatened to burst free as she considered those little tendernesses that were becoming commonplace between them. Her nose crinkled, and she raised a hand to hide it from her mother-in-law; Mrs. Leigh wouldn't recognize it for what it was, but Nan refused to share even that sign with her.

No, she refused to believe Mrs. Leigh's tactics. They would not touch her.

Besides, the only reason either she or Benjamin were dissatisfied with their marriage was the woman standing before her, and though an annulment would free Nan from that blight, he would Mrs. Leigh would still be his mother.

"You must see reason," said Mrs. Leigh. "Benjamin could marry a proper wife, and Mr. Leigh and I will ensure you find a comfortable situation somewhere far from here. Birmingham, if you like. We have connections—"

And once more, her bedchamber door swung open, ushering in an intruder. But in this instance, Nan was quite pleased, for Father swept inside and scowled at his wife.

"What are you doing here, Gertrude?" demanded Father. "Are you pestering our dear Nan?"

"Nothing of the sort—" she began, but her husband cut her short.

"Leave her be, you sour-faced crone," said Father with a frown. Mrs. Leigh straightened, but before she could offer a word of argument, he pointed to the door and said, "Now!"

Mrs. Leigh raised her chin, staring down her husband for a long, silent moment. Then she turned and swept out of the bedchamber with the same determined steps with which she'd entered.

With a sigh and shake of his head, Father turned to Nan. "I heard her voice and thought you might not want her inside your sanctuary."

Brushing hands down her skirts, she tried to shake off that interlude. "Your study is more of a sanctuary than my bedchamber."

"I can speak with her if you wish," said Father, frowning. "You ought not to be pestered in your own home."

"That is kind of you, but I think it's best to leave things be."

But the gentleman did not look pleased by that answer. His brows pulled tight together, and he studied her for a long moment before his attention snapped to her gown.

"You look a picture, Nan," he said with a broad smile. "Of course, you were lovely before, but the dress suits you perfectly. You have quite the eye for fashion, my girl. You make your father proud."

"Rosanna and Prudence had a hand in it," replied Nan, for it was the only thing she could think to say. His effusive praise made her heart flutter and her skin prickle, as she wished both to lap up each morsel and to flee from it. Such a strange dichotomy, but she couldn't deny that she adored the attention and felt extremely flustered by it in the same breath.

The sweetness pouring from him helped to ease away the last of Mrs. Leigh's poison, and Nan felt like smiling anew as she turned for her audience, showing all the little details of her gown.

"You deserve a treat, my girl." Father crossed his arms, his smile faltering a touch. "If hard times are to come, we'd best enjoy the present while we can."

Chapter 31

Nan turned from the mirror, her hands falling to her sides. Father did not meet her gaze, and his smile dimmed further.

"Are things truly that dire?" she asked.

Drawing in a sharp breath, Father straightened, his expression lightening as though the darkness had never been there. "Do not listen to me, my dear girl. I am an old fool, apt to blather on if I am not careful."

"Do not brush it aside, Father. Clearly, it is worrying you, and I wish to do what I can to help," said Nan, moving to his side and taking hold of his hand.

"I hate to mention it again, for I do not wish to put you in a difficult position, but I fear the only thing to do is convince Benjamin to break the entail," said Father.

Nan stiffened, her brows pulling together as she considered that. "Benjamin doesn't speak of money to me. All he ever says is that all is well and I needn't worry."

A hint of his smile returned, and Father let out a soft sigh. "No doubt he doesn't wish to frighten you. Heaven knows I do not wish to, either, but as you are already aware of the trouble looming on the horizon, I see no reason to keep the truth from you. He likely gave you the last of his allowance, and by Michaelmas, you may need to quit Whitley Court altogether—unless we break the entail."

"Retrench?" Nan's pulse stilled, and her lungs struggled to draw in breath. "I hadn't thought it as bad as all that—"

"Benjamin has spoken to me of seeking out employment, but I fear it won't do any good." Father pinched his nose and winced. "Even if we were able to find him a profession, at this late stage, it would be some time before his income could sustain the two of you."

"Surely Rosanna would come to the rescue," said Nan. "She has money enough to aid the family, and I doubt she'd wish to see her parents and brother come to ruin."

"True. My daughter is a kind and generous person who would likely wish to do so," said Father with a nod of agreement. "However, we have the means of saving the family from ruin ourselves—if Benjamin will simply be reasonable. I know you can convince him. Would you please try?"

Everything inside Nan stilled as she considered it. Benjamin refused to speak to her about such an important thing, yet Father wished her to broach the subject? How would that play out? Benjamin had proven himself a good husband and friend in many ways, but the silence on this subject spoke volumes. If he desired her opinion, he would ask her.

Patting her on the shoulder, Father held her gaze. "You can do this, Nan. You are so capable and intelligent. I know you can help Benjamin make the right choice. You simply need to be bold."

"But—"

"For me?" Father's gaze bore into hers with such begging that Nan's heart couldn't help but melt a touch. "I have done my utmost to treat you as one of my own. Surely you can do this little thing in return."

Nan couldn't deny the truth in that statement, yet something inside her twisted, writhing like overeager earthworms, leaving her unsettled, though she couldn't say why that was.

Everything he said was true. She owed him so very much. He'd been so very kind to her. Surely a conversation was the least she could do in return.

"You are part of this family now, Nan, and Leighs help one another." Father's tone was so pleading that Nan nodded, though her stomach sank as she considered the position in which she found herself.

"My good girl," he said with a broad grin before turning away and striding from the bedchamber as Nan frowned at the door shutting behind him.

The walls pressed in on her, yet Nan couldn't bear the thought of joining Benjamin downstairs. Turning toward the window, she spied the first sprinkles speckling the pane; they were merely a warning, for in the distance a wall of rain drifted toward her, carried along in a thick expanse of clouds. In moments, the world was engulfed in it.

Father's request was a little one. Surely she ought to honor it. Yet she couldn't quite believe things were so dire that they ought to risk the future of Whitley Court by breaking the entail. Mortgages and selling off property weren't guaranteed to lead to its downfall, but she had read enough about such things to know entails were not placed willy-nilly on properties.

And then there was the issue of Benjamin himself.

Nan stared out at the world, listening to the clatter of the rain. There was something so soothing about that sound, but even its gentle touch couldn't calm her twisting insides.

Something wasn't right at Whitley Court, and she couldn't decide where the trouble lay.

Instincts prodded at her, leaving her uneasy as she moved through the last few hours of the day, unaware of anything but her thoughts, none of which led her to any clarity on the subject. What a miserable end to a wonderful day.

Even as she spent its final moments rearranging her purchases, Nan couldn't help but wonder if she'd been foolhardy to trust Benjamin's generosity. Had they just spent themselves into the poorhouse? Nothing in his character suggested he was a spendthrift, eager to cast about the last of his funds.

To believe her father-in-law or her husband? Both could not be correct, yet both were honorable and good men who cared about her.

But Benjamin wasn't being honest with her. Nan felt it to her core. He'd erected a barrier, and as he slipped into her bedchamber that night, she couldn't help but feel it standing between them. Her thoughts circled back to the awkward moment that afternoon; Benjamin had assured her nothing was amiss, but something had been. She knew it.

What was happening with her husband?

And it was at that time that her mind decided to dredge up another point with which to torture her. Though Nan had dismissed it, Mrs. Leigh's talk of annulment leapt into her thoughts, and like adding a bucket of pitch to the fire, it poured that fear straight into the churning mix of emotions roiling about in her heart.

Could Benjamin be thinking of annulment? Nan didn't think it possible, for the reasons with which she dismissed that possibility remained sound. He'd been the one to push for marriage, after all. Yet plenty of people were determined in their course of action at the moment, only to find themselves regretting the impulse as time wore on.

Nan moved without thought, climbing into bed, and despite all those questions and frustrations ruining what was usually her favorite part of the day, they didn't stop her from resting her head on his chest; the position was already too familiar and comforting for her to choose another. And it allowed her to speak to him without meeting his gaze.

"Thank you for such a wonderful afternoon," she said, for though she'd said the words before and though the day had ended on a far different note, the sentiment was true and ought to be acknowledged again.

Nan felt him place a kiss on her head, and some of that anxiety settled.

"It was my pleasure. And if you require anything in the future, do not hesitate to tell me."

That seemed as good a beginning as she could ask for, and Nan sifted through the words, struggling to formulate a question that might get to the heart of the matter without ruffling feathers.

"When are you and Prudence going to start on the other dresses?" he asked, interrupting her internal dialogue.

"On Tuesday. We thought to make a day of it and ask Rosanna and Katherine to come and work on their sewing if they wish."

"Are you going to invite Mother?" asked Benjamin, and Nan was grateful he couldn't see her expression, for her eyes opened wide, her brows scrunching at that bizarre question. Silence followed it as she tried to think how to answer that oddity, and he went on to add, "Katherine won't appreciate my asking it, but Mother seemed so saddened that she was excluded from your shopping excursion, and she enjoys your company so very much."

Nan managed to stifle her scoff and thanked the heavens once more that her face was unseen by Benjamin, for she couldn't disguise the frown that pulled at her lips.

Forcing her tone into neutrality, she said, "You know how full her diary is, and I do not believe she cares for sewing."

"True, but it would be nice to ask her."

Nan could imagine the lady accepting the invitation simply to be a bother. Closing her eyes briefly, she sent a silent prayer heavenward that Rosanna and Prudence wouldn't think to extend an invitation. There'd been no mention of it, but Nan couldn't think of a more thorough way to ruin what could be a potentially delightful day than including Mrs. Leigh. She could well imagine how many underhanded things she'd say about the choice in fabrics, styles, and trims, weaving her bitterness into every inch of Nan's beloved gowns.

Better not to make them than to be reminded of Mrs. Leigh every time she wore them.

"Is something the matter?" asked Benjamin.

She lifted her head to look at him. "Why would you ask that?"

His brows lifted knowingly. "You were conspicuously silent."

"Is there such a thing?"

"With you, certainly," he replied.

Shifting her head back to rest on his chest, Nan listened to the thump of his heartbeat, allowing the rise and fall of his lungs to calm her disquiet.

"Do you not want to invite her to the sewing party?" asked Benjamin, erasing all good her cozy position granted her. Nan forced herself not to stiffen, for he would certainly feel that.

"I do not think she'll enjoy it," she said, offering up a truth— a partial one, at least. Mrs. Leigh would likely enjoy it immensely, for it would grant her an afternoon of feasting upon Nan's pride. "But I will consider it."

If she thought about it for the length of a heartbeat before dismissing it, that was "considering," wasn't it?

Benjamin gave an uncertain hum, and it buzzed in Nan's ears. She hoped he would leave it at that, for she knew no good would come from telling him that his mother was a harpy of the highest order. Or a "sour-faced crone," as Father put it. Her kindness toward him blinded him to all but the most obvious barbs, and with so many things unsteady in their lives at present, the last thing she needed to do was force another wedge.

They had a large enough one causing trouble at present.

Ought she to demand an answer from Benjamin? Armed with Father's confidences, it was easy enough to confront him. In theory. But perhaps a bit of subtlety mightn't go awry. So, Nan seized the opportunity and turned the conversation in a different direction.

"I suppose I am a little anxious. This afternoon was perfect. Simply lovely. And I am so grateful for your generosity, but I fear I spent too much."

Benjamin's arms came around her, his hands rubbing along her back, and with a smile in his tone, he replied, "You didn't even spend the whole amount."

"I spent more than I ought to." Then, carefully, she added, "We could've put that money toward Whitley Court. Do something to improve matters at home."

"Is that your concern?" he asked with a slight huff of laughter. "I assure you, Whitley Court is secure. It doesn't need my allowance to thrive."

As much as she wanted to hold onto that assurance, Nan's heart chilled. Was he telling her the truth?

Benjamin pressed another kiss to her head. "Your concern does you credit, Nan, but do not worry. I have it in hand."

Nan couldn't claim to know her husband as well as one ought to know the man to whom she was bound for life. Yet with each day, many aspects of his personality became clearer, giving her a greater understanding of his tones and expressions. And Nan didn't need to see his face to know Benjamin wasn't telling her the whole truth; she heard it in his voice. Something so small, she wasn't certain how she felt the lie—just that she did.

Could Father have been right? Were they to lose their home soon? Michaelmas was not so very far away, and she felt the cold fingers of dread wrap around her heart. But as much as she wanted to ask about the entail, she couldn't speak the words.

Benjamin was lying to her.

Chapter 32

Drumming his fingers against the arm of the chair, Benjamin's gaze flitted over the study, which served as Parker's office and herb garret, and pointedly did not look at the man in question. The room was stifling, and despite the large windows letting in sunlight, the room was as gloomy as a tomb. Benjamin didn't know how Parker worked here. But then, he wasn't certain how his brother-in-law could stomach medicine.

To be a physician was one thing, for they dealt solely with illnesses—checking the odd pulse and prescribing a powder, pill, or poultice before going on their merry way. But as Parker often skirted the line between physician and surgeon, he dealt with injuries and operations in all their bloody glory. Benjamin shuddered at the thought and forced his attention away from that messy business.

Thick bundles of plants hung from the ceiling as they dried, and shelves covered every spare inch of the walls, which contained a myriad of jars and boxes, each neatly labeled, though Benjamin couldn't read them from his seat. A mighty selection of books were housed next to the thick table sitting below the window, which looked more at home at a butcher's shop than a study. But as Benjamin considered that, he wondered if it hadn't been used for more grim purposes than simply holding aloft his brother-in-law's materials.

Leaning forward, Benjamin reached to scrub at his face, but his jacket restricted his arms, so he rose to his feet and cast the thing off, tossing it across the back of his armchair and nearly knocking over several bottles as the fabric bumped the glass. Parker Humphreys' brows rose at the movement, watching as his brother-in-law settled once more.

Unfortunately, releasing himself from the tight article did nothing to relieve the tautness in Benjamin's shoulders.

"You can sit there all day, but it doesn't alter the truth staring you in the face," said Parker in a dry tone.

"Surely there is something else I can do. I require an income, but to subject myself to such menial work..." Benjamin's words drifted off, and he hung his head, his shoulders drooping.

"David hasn't anything suitable at present, and even if you had the inclination to apprentice with me, you haven't the education to pursue medicine. Malcolm has many opportunities, but you'd have to leave Greater Edgerton, and we all agree that you'd do better being near family—"

"You three have discussed my situation?" Benjamin's head rose again, his brows following suit.

"Of course we have," said Parker, folding his arms. "We all knew this business with the entail would likely end with you requiring assistance."

"It isn't to that point yet..." But as much as he wanted to cling to that belief, Father's words echoed in his thoughts, warning him that if things weren't to that point, they would be soon. Of course, Parker merely sat there with his brows ticked upward as though waiting for him to concede the point.

"Has anyone ever told you how extremely irritating you can be?" muttered Benjamin with a frown.

"My wife, on many occasions," replied Parker, taking up the mortar and pestle he'd abandoned when Benjamin had interrupted his work. "If your wife hasn't, give it time."

"Nan is nicer than Prudence."

Parker scoffed. "Even if that were true, your stubbornness is bound to earn your wife's ire before long."

Crossing his arms, Benjamin studied his brother-in-law. "Correct me if I am wrong—for I was very young at the time—but I do recall someone mentioning that your courtship was stymied by your blindness. Something about you being too enamored with our sister Rosanna to even notice Prudence."

Then, straightening, Benjamin added, "In fact, except for Francis's entirely unexceptional courtship, am I not right in saying that all of my brothers-in-law have struggled with being stubborn, blind, and ridiculous in their own ways? It's a miracle any of you managed to convince my sisters to marry you, so I do not think you have any right to lecture me about being stubborn or irritating. My marriage might've begun unconventionally, but otherwise, it has been entirely ordinary."

But rather than his brother-in-law being cowed, Parker's lips twitched ever so slightly up, those mocking brows holding firm as he held Benjamin's gaze.

Why did he come here? He ought to have waited until David was free to discuss the issue. Granted, even his old friend found too much pleasure in teasing the youngest Leigh. To say nothing of Katherine, who was always at her husband's side and enjoyed twitting him even more than David and Parker combined.

Leaning back in his seat, Benjamin shoved his feet out and crossed his ankles, though the movement bumped the leg of Parker's desk, causing the array of apothecary jars atop it to tinkle. The wretched office was far too cramped and cluttered for a man to move. Benjamin was almost afraid to breathe lest he upend something fragile.

"I appreciate your frustrations concerning a profession, but I fear your options are limited," said Parker, dumping the paste from his mortar into his hand and sectioning it off into balls. Grabbing one, he rolled it along a wooden paddle sitting on his desk, forming it into a long snake. Benjamin couldn't help but watch the physician at work, especially as Parker's hands moved without thinking.

"Malcolm may be able to find you something more palatable," continued Parker, "but if you left Greater Edgerton, you would be on your own. Here, you have family to assist you in crises. To say nothing of the fact that we do not wish you and Nan to leave."

"Nor do I wish to. She adores the girls, and I do not want to take her from that. Nan has no family but us," said Benjamin.

"Which leads us back to your best possibility at present." With a quick movement, Parker placed a second paddle atop the mass and dragged the paste snake over a section of the board that had metal grooves, which sliced the round log into pills. "My brother-in-law, Robert, has been very gracious and offered to take you on as a clerk, even offering to waive the usual fees attached to such a position and train you gratis."

For all that those words ought to lighten his heart, Benjamin's sank. A solicitor's clerk. Considering a profession was difficult enough, but that was such a large step down in the world. Clerking for a barrister would be just as wretched, but at least he'd be in a gentleman's profession. There was the law and *the law*, after all. Benjamin had no interest in debating cases before the courts, but solicitors were akin to tradesmen.

"That is very generous of Mr. Bradshaw," said Benjamin, for that was true enough. "But Mother and Father would be beside themselves if I began working for a solicitor."

"True," said Parker with a nod as he rolled out another paste rope. "But would it matter if you angered them?"

Benjamin's arms tightened, and his gaze drifted from Parker as he considered that. Mother and Father were difficult, but to cause a possible fracture between them? Something that might never be healed? Wasn't that the very reason he'd used his promise to Grandmother to avoid telling his parents that he had no intention of breaking the entail of his own accord?

"I know that expression," said Parker with a sad smile. "I've seen it on Prudence's face far too often when the subject of your parents arises. Though Katherine and Francis both seem to know where they stand concerning their feelings, the rest of you straddle the line between love and loathe, never knowing precisely how to respond to that dichotomy. And I suspect it will never be an easy answer."

"They are my parents," murmured Benjamin with a frown. "Flawed and selfish, yes, but..."

"You cannot help but hope that things will get better," finished Parker with an understanding lift of his brows. "But in my experience, little pleases your parents, and when they realize you cannot be threatened or bullied into breaking the entail, they will be beside themselves, regardless."

Setting aside his implements, Parker leaned forward, resting his elbows against his desk. "The truth is, some of your friends will cut ties because they will view it as beneath themselves to associate with a mere solicitor's clerk—something I've learned again and again as I flirt with the line between being a respectable physician and a disdainful surgeon. However, most gentlemanly professions blur the lines at times because the more 'acceptable' types of work aren't as lucrative or plentiful."

"Another truth," sighed Benjamin. With a regretful smile, he added, "However, if I am to make such a drastic change in my life, I had hoped it would be for something better than law books. I cannot imagine anything more monotonous than clerking for a lawyer."

Parker tapped his fingers against his desk and arched his brow once more at Benjamin. "Adoring one's profession is a luxury afforded to men who do not require an income, as most sons are never given the option and must go where their father sends them. The lucky ones do not bother with resenting their path, and the luckier ones find joy in it."

Reaching to the far side of the table, Parker fetched a circular metal sieve and placed the pills along the flat bottom. "In truth, I think you will like it more than you think. While you will spend the first bit of your training knee-deep in those law books you despise, Robert does a lot of work as a land agent, serving as the intermediary between owners and tenants, which isn't much different than the work you've been doing at Whitley Court. He's a steward of sorts, and training at his side could be beneficial to you after you inherit."

"That is intriguing." Benjamin's brows rose, but with a sigh, he shifted in his seat. "However, it would be some time before I would be allowed to assist him in such matters and even longer before I have a proper income. My savings are tied up in investments, and though I can liquidate those funds in time, it isn't enough to allow us to live for years whilst I am being trained. At best, it is a supplement to an income."

"Which is why we think you should remain in Greater Edgerton," said Parker, rising from his seat to place the sieve on a high shelf, far from the window. "Though neither David nor I can do much to assist you financially, we've been searching for affordable lodgings, and Malcolm is quite willing to pay the rent. Between all our assistance, you and your wife could live while you establish yourself as a land agent."

Coming around to the front of his desk, Parker sat on the edge, crossing his arms. "I know it isn't ideal, but I do think it will work."

Benjamin forced a smile. "You are all very generous and kind to help."

"You are family. We cannot let you starve while your parents are being so…difficult."

"That is a kind description for them."

Parker huffed. "I will always tread carefully when it comes to disparaging my wife's family."

"But you just said we are family," replied Benjamin.

"True, but you Leighs share a bond I do not, and I learned long ago to be circumspect in my criticisms. No matter how 'difficult' your parents may be, there is some affection on all your parts that I cannot feel. I will always appreciate that they gave life to the woman I love, but I will never tolerate them as well as you do."

There was a quality to his tone that made Benjamin wonder if "tolerate" was a far kinder word than Parker wished to choose, but that was neither here nor there, for it had nothing to do with the subject at hand.

Remaining perched on the desk as he was, Parker studied his brother-in-law, and Benjamin forced himself not to squirm.

"My thanks to you and all the meddling brothers-in-law, but forgive me for slipping away. I need to return home for an appointment with the steward," said Benjamin, rising to his feet and putting on his jacket.

Following suit, Parker extended a hand. "Do you wish to speak to Robert directly? Or I can arrange a meeting if you'd prefer."

"I need to give it some consideration first."

Parker gave him a nod before shaking Benjamin's hand. "Good. Best to discuss it with Nan, for this decision impacts her as well, and you both need to agree upon it before accepting."

Benjamin feigned a smile and allowed his brother-in-law's inference to stand. Leveling this burden on his wife was not at all what he ought to do, but if it allowed him time to consider his options, he was content to let Parker believe what he wished.

"Say goodbye to Prudence and the children before you leave," said Parker as he led Benjamin to the office door. When it opened, the sound of laughter echoed from down in the parlor as little feet scrambled about. "They'll want to see their Uncle Benjamin."

Nodding, he took the stairs down, but though Benjamin did wish to see his nieces and nephews, he hadn't the heart for another interlude with his family. No doubt Prudence knew the subject of their conversation and would wish to give her opinion on the matter, and Benjamin was in no mood to hear a lecture from his sister.

Quietly, he slipped down the hall and snatched his hat and gloves from the side table before sneaking out the front door. Rain poured from the heavens, and he stuffed his hat on his head; the rim was broad enough to keep rivulets from slipping down his neck, but that was of little comfort, for the rest of him was quickly soaked through. Flipping up his lapels, he burrowed into his jacket, though it did little good.

Not bothering to avoid the puddles (for there was little point), Benjamin trudged along the road, allowing his feet to drag him wherever they wished. But no matter how quickly he moved, he couldn't outpace his thoughts.

Being a small industrial town full of self-made men, Greater Edgerton society was far less stringent in what they deemed acceptable professions. Low-born men like Robert Bradshaw and millowners like David skirted the line of respectability in other corners of the country, but as their incomes and prestige were equal to and often greater than the true gentry, society's rigid rules slackened. A touch.

Thus, taking this drastic step wouldn't automatically label Benjamin a pariah; his true friends would remain loyal, but that wouldn't keep some from disdaining him and his wife.

And for what? A profession? The thought was difficult enough to embrace when one considered the decades of toiling with work one disliked, but to subject himself to years of unpaid labor in the hopes that one day he might secure a tenth of the income Whitley Court produced?

Ought he to take such a step? It may be a logical course of action, but as Shakespeare once wrote, "The better part of valor is discretion." And the rash Romeo was cautioned, "Wisely and slow. They stumble that run fast." Several other quotes echoed after them, all emphasizing the importance of caution. It was as though Mr. Price had resurrected and was at his elbow, whispering those pearls of wisdom.

What if Father was merely testing his resolve? A threat was only a threat, after all. It may signify nothing in the end. And if Benjamin acted hastily, he would be trapped in an unnecessary and menial position. Pausing on the pavement, he straightened and blinked: in truth, becoming a clerk might push Father to act, even if the gentleman had no true intention of doing so.

When pride was involved, it was best to tread carefully, or else he could lose everything for a position he didn't want.

Besides, Father wouldn't toss them out. Cutting his allowance was certainly possible. Probable, even. But to evict his son and heir from Whitley Court was far too public a thing. It would be much talked about, and Father wouldn't wish to invite such a megrim—especially as Mother was bound to fall to pieces if she became the source of such gossip. Osmond Leigh cared for his peace and quiet more than anything else, and a fretful wife was bound to disrupt that.

So, at worst, they only needed enough to pay for the incidentals of life. Room and board were the greatest of expenses, and did he truly wish to subject himself to such monotony simply to buy his wife a few baubles when a few pounds here and there from Malcolm would solve matters?

Forcing his feet forward, he considered all that Parker had said. Malcolm was wealthy, after all. No doubt, his income could provide for the Tates and the Leighs. Not that Benjamin wished to live off his brother-in-law's generosity, but it wasn't as though they required a full income. Surely caution was the better course.

Yet something inside him refused to settle at the thought. Mr. Bradshaw's offer was extremely generous, and it could easily disappear if he waited too long to accept. But how could he, if he didn't know if it was necessary? It may be prudent to wait, but accepting would be prudent in another fashion.

Which left Benjamin lost once more.

Stopping in place, he didn't know which direction to go—metaphorically and literally. Benjamin needed to get out of the rain, but his usual haunts were not available. David was occupied, and various other gentlemen with warm fires who were willing to take him in were off on other pursuits. And Whitley Court was hardly appealing.

Yet Nan was there.

Benjamin's brows rose at that. A distraction was precisely what he needed.

Chapter 33

"Enter." The word was spoken softly and with such disinterest that Nan almost missed it, and she remained in place, staring at the door. Was it too late to sneak away? Surely she could speak to him later.

"Stop hovering and come in, blast it," barked Father.

Nan jerked, pushing open the study door and peeking inside. "I didn't mean to disturb you."

The gentleman gazed up from his book, his reading glasses perched on the end of his nose. "Yet you are."

Shrinking back, Nan forced a smile. "I apologize. It is nothing—"

"No," he said, setting the book aside and motioning for her to join him. And though she wanted to feel reassured by that, the heavy sigh in his tone kept Nan in place. Father's expression softened, and with a more genuine show, he nodded toward the chair. "Please, come in, Nan."

Doing as bidden, she sat, perched on the edge of the cushion, her hands clasped together. This was a mistake. Even without the inauspicious beginning, Nan didn't know why her senses had deserted her before taking this course.

"What is it, my dear girl?" he asked.

"I was hoping to speak to you about Benjamin—"

"You've spoken to him about the entail?"

Nan's shoulders stiffened. "Not yet. I am concerned about him, and I was hoping for advice."

Heat suffused her cheeks, and her toes curled in her slippers. Benjamin refused to speak about his troubles, so it was only logical to seek guidance from those who knew him better, and though she was very fond of her sisters-in-law, she didn't know them enough to speak so openly. Father was the best choice, yet she couldn't shake the discomfort souring her stomach.

"I understand the entail is a delicate matter, Nan, but I am depending on you to convince him," said Father with a frown. "You cannot do that if you do not bring it up."

"True, but he never speaks to me about such things. He refuses to acknowledge there is an issue—"

"You must make him understand, my girl. That is the entire trouble we are facing. I have tried to make him see the truth of things, and he insists all will be well."

"Yes, but I do not know how to—"

"You are an intelligent girl," he said with a warm smile. "I am certain you can sort it out. There are many ways a wife can persuade a husband to her way of thinking."

Heat engulfed her, making Nan's head so light she was certain it was warping her thoughts, for it seemed as though Father was suggesting something far too personal for such a flippant remark. Yet there was such insinuation in his tone that it felt as though spiders skittered across her skin.

"Time is running out for us, my dear," added Father. "If you do not take strides soon, it will be too late. I am counting on you."

"I know, Father, but I am trying to tell you I am concerned about Benjamin—"

"As you should be. This entail is serious business." Father rose from his seat and came to her side to pat her stiffly on the shoulder. "You are a good girl. You will sort it out, but you need to make haste. I am relying on you."

She turned her eyes to gaze up at him, her tongue tying into knots. Was he hearing her at all? She tried to think of what to say to convey the questions she wished to discuss, but every answer pointed back to the entail. The flush of her skin grew hotter, and that wretched little part of her that had timidly knocked on the study door now roared up to laugh at her for making such a horrid mistake (despite its many warnings).

"Now, is there anything else?" he asked. "I would like to return to my book."

Nan's muscles were tight, but she forced herself to shake her head and rise to her feet. "I apologize for taking your time."

"Think nothing of it, my girl. I understand your fears. Once we sort out the entail, everything will be better. Just do your part."

Her head jerked, giving as much of a nod as she could manage.

"You are such a dear," he said, putting his arm around her shoulders as he guided her out of the study. "As I said, I knew you would be the perfect addition to our family. Such a boon. I count myself lucky to be your father."

Yet Nan hardly heard those praises above the sound of the door shutting behind her. Despite the afternoon sun blazing somewhere in the heavens, little light made its way through the canopy of clouds and even less brightened the corridor, and she stood there in silent darkness.

A clock chimed somewhere inside the house, snapping her from her haze, and she turned away from the solid door standing between her and the man she called Father. As it was nearly time to leave, Nan moved toward her bedchamber, drifting through the hallway like an apparition.

Questions and feelings buzzed beneath her skin, wishing to be spoken, but there was no one to hear them as she sank onto her bed.

...

"Benjamin? Is that you?" Mother's voice rang from the parlor, and he froze on the stairs. Holding his breath, Benjamin didn't even blink as he stood at the bottom. Several long moments passed before he hazarded to climb up, moving carefully to avoid the creaks. Thankfully, he knew each one very well and managed to get to the landing without drawing the lady's attention once more.

The last thing he wished to do at this moment was speak to her.

In truth, he ought to return to his bedchamber and change his sopping clothing, but with thoughts of Parker and professions still tumbling about his thoughts, Benjamin wanted nothing more than to pass an hour with his wife. Moving stealthily through the corridor, he crept into her chamber, but rather than being curled up with a book (as she was so often apt to do), Nan was packing her sewing things. Despite his being in her line of sight, she didn't look up from her work, and she moved about, tucking in the fabric, notions, and whatnot into a small portmanteau.

Goodness, what strange twists and turns life took. Despite having been married for two months, Benjamin still could not believe how vastly different his world was now. And how lucky a turn it had taken. Even now, he recalled the weeks he'd spent dragging his feet, refusing to answer Mr. Price's call for assistance, and he couldn't believe what a fool he'd been. Thankfully, even fools received great blessings from time to time.

Even if it did make his current troubles more difficult, she was well worth it. Somehow, he would sort out the money, entail, and all that rubbish. Nan was such an excellent woman, and she was his wife.

Benjamin snuck over and slipped his arms around her waist. Gasping, Nan dropped her fabric to the ground, and seizing the opportunity, he swept her into an embrace, placing a kiss on her lips. But when he leaned back, she stared at him with wide eyes.

"Good afternoon, dear wife of mine," he said before stepping away. "I am sorry for getting you wet, but I couldn't bear to go another minute without kissing you."

But that garnered little response. Nan stood before him, her pale eyes holding his with a furrowed brow.

"What is troubling you?" she asked.

Benjamin stiffened and wondered what it was about his expression that warranted such a blunt question. Slipping her a smile, he laughed. "Nothing is the matter. Why do you ask?"

"I can tell something is amiss." Stepping closer, Nan brushed a finger across the skin between his brows. "Whenever you are especially pensive, it wrinkles just there."

Benjamin forced the muscles to loosen, and he gave her a half-smile with a half-truth. "I was thinking about your father. At times, the loss strikes me, and I feel it anew. He was so insightful and offered the best advice, and I find that I miss that the most."

"You can always speak to me. I may not be as insightful, but I may have guidance when you require it," she said, her brows rising in invitation.

"I will hold you to that."

But Nan didn't smile. "What is bothering you so much that you've been tromping through the rain?"

Scratching at the back of his head, Benjamin offered her an easy grin. "Just a bit of nonsense."

"Yet it is troubling you," she said with a frown. "That is not nonsense."

Benjamin's thoughts whirled, providing possible avenues of escape from the mess he'd stepped into. "I wasn't saying I am troubled at this very moment—more that I was feeling the loss of my best confidant. In a general manner. I went to your father for everything, after all."

The damp from his clothes settled into his skin, bringing with it a shiver, and he moved toward the wardrobe. Though he still stored most of his things in his bedchamber, a few articles had made their way to Nan's, and he pulled out a fresh jacket.

"You were lucky to have a father like that," he said, slipping off the wet article. The shirt and waistcoat were equally soaked, and he cast off the latter. Thankfully, the former was thin enough that it was bound to dry quickly, but even wet, placing the dry jacket atop it helped some. "Even when he feigns interest, my father is only ever put out when I approach him. Mr. Price always welcomed a chat."

"Are you forgetting that he forced you into a marriage not of your choosing to make his life easier?" asked Nan in a dry tone.

Tugging at the cuffs, Benjamin shifted the jacket into place and slanted her a scoffing smile. "That isn't how I would describe it—"

"My father ignored his responsibility and simply handed it off to you." Nan crossed her arms and looked at him through hooded eyes. "That is precisely what happened."

"He did his best."

"No, he didn't," she snapped, a scowl marring her face. "You sit there, condemning your father, who isn't perfect by any means, but he has shown me more affection and care than the man you hold up as the example by which all others should live."

Benjamin leaned back, studying her. "What is the matter? You've been testy of late."

Nan scoffed and turned to her work, snatching the fallen bit of fabric and stuffing it into her bag.

"Something is bothering you. What aren't you telling me?"

No sooner had he spoken the words than Nan smacked her armful of sewing things onto the bed. "Oh, that is a laugh."

"What does that mean?"

With sharp movements, she shoved them haphazardly into her bag. "You know what it means."

"No, I truly do not." Had she been speaking Latin, he might've understood better, but the string of words made not

A Debt of Honor

the slightest impression on him. What was so laughable about asking her what was raising her dander?

Benjamin stared at his bride, watching her temper rise as she snapped the portmanteau shut. Jerking it from the bed, she stormed to the door, sweeping past him.

"Nan—"

"I'm going to be late for the sewing party with your sisters," she said, not sparing a backward glance, and leaving Benjamin staring at the door as it swung shut behind her. Throwing out his hands, as though pleading for answers, he stood there mute and blinking.

Despite having many reasons to be angry, Nan had never lost her temper before, and the oddest thing was that Benjamin still could not comprehend what it was they were arguing about. He'd kissed his wife and gotten an earful instead of a smile.

The only thing he could parse was that mentioning her father had sparked the outburst, but Benjamin couldn't see why she would be so angry. Little mentions here and there made it clear their relationship had been strained to a degree, but the venom with which she blackened her father's memory left him dumbfounded.

How could she say that about him? Mr. Price was a man, flawed like any other, but she spoke as though he were a wretch. And to find his father the better of the two was downright flabbergasting.

The door opened, and Benjamin quickly gathered words to throw out, but he reined them in when Mother peeked her head through the door.

"Oh, my. Were you two arguing?" she asked with a pained frown.

"A disagreement. That is all," said Benjamin, moving past her. He couldn't think until he got these blasted wet things off.

But Mother followed at his heels. "It sounded a touch more than that. And the way she stormed out the front door…"

"Tempers will cool, and all will be fine," he grumbled as he strode toward his bedchamber, but he stopped short of his wardrobe when she grabbed his wrist.

"But I am concerned." Mother released him and plucked another of her hidden handkerchiefs. Her fingers worried the lace, her brows knitting together. "I have tried my best to make her welcome, but that girl seems forever short with me. I worry she is unhappy at Whitley Court."

"She has been out of sorts of late—"

"Not only of late, Benjamin," she said, clutching the bit of linen to her chest. "She is such a dear, but I am worried for her. Do you think she might leave?"

Benjamin flinched, and his pulse spiked, coursing through him with such force that all thoughts of their conversation burned away, leaving him mute and gaping as he stared at his mother.

"Oh, I do not mean to upset you, my dear boy," she said, drawing him into her arms and patting his back. "She is such a sweet thing, I am certain she just needs time to settle. I will do my best to help her all I can."

Leaning into that hold, Benjamin accepted the bit of comfort, though he couldn't find the strength to speak yet. Surely things were not so bad as all that. He'd thought they were on a good path, but Mother saw her more throughout the day. Perhaps there was something she'd witnessed that he'd missed. Nan's mood had seemed especially stormy the last fortnight or so.

"Thank you, Mother."

Leaning back, she patted him on the cheek. "You are very welcome. I want the best for you, my boy, and I will do whatever I can to help you."

Benjamin couldn't muster much of a smile, but he gave what he could to her, and she left him alone once more to change. But his feet dragged him to the window instead, where Nan's carriage was just pulling down the drive.

All would be well. It had to be.

Chapter 34

Stabbing the needle through the folds of muslin, Nan forced the seam together, her movements jerky and far too haphazard for the work. She paused and filled her lungs, hoping that a deep breath might help to calm her hands. And while that usually helped, her stitches remained as violent as before.

All she could do was be thankful Prudence was handling the delicate fabrics and trims, for Nan was bound to massacre them. At least this was a simple, straight seam. But unfortunately, that simplicity allowed her mind to dwell on things she'd rather forget at present.

Ridiculous man! Or rather men, for more than one Leigh was setting her thoughts in a dither. Nan drew air in deeply through her nose, and she scowled at the fabric in her lap, but it did nothing to ease the pressure in her chest. Her temper had gotten the better of her earlier, and she wasn't going to let it cause her more trouble this afternoon.

This was supposed to be entertaining. A lovely way to pass the afternoon. Yet all Nan could think of was Father's strange mood in the study and Benjamin's infuriating behavior in their bedchamber. She couldn't comprehend either gentleman, though her thoughts wouldn't let the subject be until she discovered the answer.

Her heart ached as she considered both situations. She didn't know what to do about either, what with Father's behavior growing more erratic and her husband's constant lying. And then Benjamin had the gall to ask her what was amiss? Demanding answers when he refused to give any?

To say nothing of the fact that once more Benjamin had extolled the vast virtues of Mr. Irving Price. That god among men, who never stepped a toe out of line. That pattern book for all gentlemen. That paragon. That man who ignored his most basic of responsibilities and left his daughter to fend for herself. But no, Benjamin refused to see that: dear Mr. Price had provided for her by preying upon his student's gratitude to his favorite schoolmaster and manipulating him into marrying her.

Nan forced her jaw open, relaxing the muscles before they cracked her teeth. Turning her gaze from her work, she tried to herd her thoughts toward the conversation around her. Circled together in Rosanna's parlor, the other ladies laughed and chatted, their hands easily moving through their stitches as they embroidered and mended. Katherine merely picked at her work, preferring to avail herself of the tea and cakes the maids had provided whilst reclining on the chaise.

"What happy news for Mr. and Mrs. Bradshaw," said Rosanna, tying off the end of her stitch. Turning her gaze to Nan, she added, "Have you met them?"

"Not that I recall."

Rosanna slanted a look at her sister, and Prudence said, "He is a solicitor, and before the current Mrs. Bradshaw, he was married to my husband's sister, though she passed away before Parker and I married."

Nan gave a hum of acknowledgment, though she had nothing to say to that, so she tried to focus on her stitches.

"Yes, he is quite talented," added Rosanna. "The best solicitor in town, if my husband is to be believed."

Prudence nodded. "I may be biased, but I would certainly say so. He always has a steady line of young men wishing to secure a clerkship with him. Quite a coveted position."

Katherine merely munched on her cake, her half-lidded gaze drifting between her sisters.

"Has Benjamin mentioned Mr. Bradshaw?" asked Prudence.

The question was quite pointed, and Nan looked up from her work. "Not that I can recall."

Though that seemed a simple enough answer, the other ladies stared back at her whilst attempting to cover their odd behavior by turning their attention back to their work (and cakes).

"Is there a reason he would?" asked Nan.

"The Bradshaws are old friends of my family. That is all," said Prudence.

Something was afoot, though she wasn't certain what great mysteries surrounded Mr. Bradshaw. But then, they'd mentioned pointedly that he was a solicitor. Had this something to do with the entail? Wills and inheritances were their purview, and if Benjamin was fretting over such things, it was logical that he might counsel with his sister's dear friends—and that his wife would be aware of such things. If her husband wasn't such a pig-headed fool, that is.

Nan didn't know if they were seeking out details or wishing to give their input, but either way, she had nothing to say on the subject because her irritating husband hadn't bothered to mention a word of it to her. Infuriating man! Why couldn't he simply tell her what was troubling him? Why hide the truth of the situation behind false assurances that "all was well"?

Prudence cleared her throat and added, "And Mrs. Bradshaw owns a superb school in town. My daughters love their lessons there."

"Oh, yes," said Rosanna. "My girls prefer it to their tutors in Kent."

Katherine drew in a deep breath and popped a biscuit into her mouth with a turn of her eyes heavenward, and despite the frustrated burbling in Nan's heart, that managed to make her smile, though she didn't know what had earned their younger sister's sign of annoyance.

"She keeps a school?" asked Nan.

"Mrs. Bradshaw established it before she married Mr. Bradshaw, and though she no longer teaches, it's a prime establishment," said Rosanna. "Mrs. Bradshaw's first husband was a baronet, you know, and she moved in very high circles before her widowhood and removal to Greater Edgerton."

"True. When I met her, I was certain I was bound to disappoint, but she has no pretensions," said Prudence with a laugh. "But her first husband left her penniless, so she opened a girls' school that focuses on dancing, etiquette, entertaining, and all the refinement required of a lady."

Nan huffed. "Does she accept adult pupils?"

With her nerves so frayed, the comment came out louder than intended, allowing the others to hear what she'd meant only for herself. And as much as she had meant it to be a jest, there was a touch too much self-pity in her tone to make it merely self-deprecating.

All three ladies looked at her with varying degrees of surprise and concern.

"Do you wish to learn more?" asked Rosanna with raised brows. "If so, we would all be eager to help you in any way you wish."

Nan straightened. "Would you want to?"

Prudence nodded whilst Rosanna replied, "I wouldn't offer if I didn't mean it."

"Though I am not nearly as talented as my sisters, I would be pleased to do what I can," added Katherine. Then, with a slight wince, she amended, "Though I would suggest looking to them for advice. I am only just beginning to establish my own household, and I rely daily on my mother-in-law for guidance."

A helpful mother-in-law? What a thought—one that Nan was pleased had remained in her head, rather than being spoken aloud.

The others echoed those offers, speaking with such genuine interest and eagerness that Nan's heart couldn't help but stutter. Such kindness and generosity. After a difficult day, such sweetness overwhelmed her, as though suppressing the pains and disappointments of the past few hours had stripped the last of her reserves, making their affection all the more potent.

"Heaven knows your father wasn't likely to teach you much about such things, and it can be difficult to manage it all on your own," said Rosanna.

"And we all know how critical people can be when one does not meet expectations," continued Katherine with a grimace as she availed herself of another biscuit.

Setting down her work, Prudence scoffed and adopted a mocking tone. "'You are too bookish and utterly lack sophistication.'"

Nodding in agreement, Katherine nudged her spectacles up her nose and arched a brow. "When David and I announced our engagement, do you know what I heard most?"

The tone had Nan bracing herself as the lady answered her own question.

"It wasn't a congratulation of any sort. Outside of our dearest friends and loved ones, most people answered the announcement with 'Truly?' or 'Her?' or some other shocked outburst." Katherine scoffed. "They couldn't believe the eligible Mr. David Archer would pursue the Leigh spinster."

Leaning forward, she added in a stage whisper to Nan, "'Did you know she wears *spectacles*? And she discusses mill business with her beau?'"

Both Rosanna and Prudence gazed at their sister with sympathy, though Katherine waved it away. "The fact of the matter is that 'society' isn't kind. It is about appearance and hierarchy, and heaven help those who are ignorant or dismissive of their rules. Society will feast upon their dignity until there is not a scrap left."

Nan's gaze fell to her work, and she attempted to focus on it, but it was difficult when Mrs. Leigh entered her thoughts.

How many times had that lady badgered and belittled her? The question was ridiculous to ask, for it was impossible to count. An easier one to answer would be: how many times had she been kind and gracious, showing even a particle of the warmth and goodwill her daughters displayed?

When Nan lifted her head once more, she found all three sets of eyes watching her, their work abandoned as they scrutinized her. Something significant was passing between the sisters, though she didn't know what it was.

Rosanna began first. "We know certain expectations can be very…difficult to manage at times."

"Yes," said Prudence with a nod. "Especially when one is constantly surrounded by it."

"Day and night," added Rosanna.

Nan felt a significance to their tones. Perhaps she was inferring it, but she couldn't help but think of Mrs. Leigh as they spoke, their pointed statements attempting to imply that which they did not say explicitly.

Katherine had a difficult relationship with her mother, but Nan had seen the lady with her eldest daughters. Certainly, she was critical, as far too many mothers could be when the world didn't match their ideal, but Mrs. Leigh doted on Rosanna's beauty and grace and admired Prudence's intelligence and capability. Surely they had little reason to disparage their mother.

"That can be very difficult," said Nan with a nod, turning back to her work.

The conversation halted, a heavy silence following her vague statement, and then Katherine set down her teacup with a clink of china.

"For goodness' sake! Is there a need to be so delicate in our conversation? Mama isn't here, so there's no reason we cannot be direct. We are getting nowhere." Turning her attention to Nan, Katherine quickly added, "We are concerned about you because our mother is a beastly creature who takes great pleasure in sharpening her tongue on anyone she doesn't like, and it is clear she detests you."

"Katherine!" hissed Rosanna, scowling at her sister. "A little tact would not go amiss."

"We've attempted subtlety, and it has gained us nothing. A direct approach is required."

"But—"

"Ladies," said Prudence, cutting Rosanna's argument (whatever it may have been) short. "The topic has been broached. It is done. Sniping at each other isn't helpful, and certainly isn't going to gain Nan's trust."

Rosanna's lips pinched for a moment before her expression slackened. "I suppose you're right. I apologize, Katherine."

Another heavy sigh before Katherine replied, "And I apologize for being more curt than I intended. I am eager to have a child, but I am not enjoying the process of bringing her into the world. I feel wretched, and I fear that leaves me with little tact—and I've never possessed much."

But then the attention was turned back to Nan, and she couldn't help but squirm beneath their regard.

"We are concerned, Nan," said Katherine. "We know how difficult Mama can be, and we've wished to broach the subject, but you are so reluctant to discuss her."

Nan's brows rose. "Is it any wonder? She is your mother—the lady who gave you life and raised you."

"Believe me when I say she didn't raise us," said Prudence with a huff. "Other than Rosanna and Benjamin, she hardly spent time with any of us as children, leaving us entirely to the nursemaids and siblings."

Rosanna's cheeks pinked, and Prudence reached over to squeeze her sister's hand, adding, "It wasn't your fault that she loved you best, and I can hardly fault her, for you are quite loveable, dearest."

"But to the subject at hand," said Katherine, drawing them back, "we know how difficult she is. You've heard how she speaks to me and know I can do nothing right in her eyes."

And for all her blunt speaking, the lady's eyes grew misty, and she turned her gaze to the window, as though studying the gloomy clouds. Though she lacked the grace and polish of her elder sisters, the vulnerability in that movement assured Nan far more than any of her sisters' assurances.

Could she tell them the whole of her pain?

The thought of revealing the truth was so appealing that Nan wasn't certain she could hold her tongue if she wished. Silence weighed heavy on her heart, leaving her so alone, and she couldn't bear it anymore.

"We know her," murmured Prudence. "And we know what high hopes she had for Benjamin's marriage. Mama was bound to despise you, regardless of how wonderful you are, and for that fact alone, I know she treats you poorly."

Nan let out a sharp scoff, her brows pulling low. "You can see that without having spent much time with the pair of us, yet Benjamin—who lives under the same roof as her—cannot see anything but her sweetness, accepting every duplicitous compliment as truth."

"Of course, he doesn't," said Katherine with a scoff, turning her gaze back to the group with no sign of her previous weakness showing. "He is the favorite. Her 'dear boy.' The only reason my sisters and I exist is because our parents wanted a son. Had Prudence been male, they wouldn't have bothered with the rest. He can do no wrong, just as I can do no right."

With a heavy sigh, Prudence nodded. "It is a miracle he isn't thoroughly spoiled."

"But Mama wouldn't risk antagonizing him by being openly rude to you," added Rosanna. "And as he's never experienced her subtle cruelty before, he wouldn't recognize it for what it is."

Nan's thoughts sped back to that first conversation they'd had at Whitley Court. Cuddled in bed, Benjamin had admitted the reasons he disliked being at home. Not one of them had anything to do with the viciousness and nastiness that were synonymous with Mrs. Leigh. No, he didn't care for how they spoiled him.

"So, Nan," said Katherine with a knowing look. "How are you faring at Whitley Court?"

Chapter 35

Drawing in a deep breath, Nan steeled herself against the longing pulsing in her heart, begging her to divulge all that very minute, for it wouldn't do to act hastily; so many quotes and proverbs reiterated that wisdom. The reasons she'd remained silent on the subject of her mother-in-law remained, yet the more she came to know these ladies, the less logical it seemed to remain mum.

Sorting through her words, Nan let out a breath and murmured, "It has been wretched. I can do no right in her eyes, and she is forever finding fault with me, but even that wouldn't be so very terrible if it weren't for how duplicitous she is, feigning as though we are the best of friends whenever Benjamin is about."

Or rather, it wouldn't be so terrible if he saw through the lie.

"Things have gotten better now that he spends more time with me, and I am not trapped with her alone all the day long—and your father has been unfailingly kind to me," she added, for though their last interlude was distressing, she couldn't erase all the other kindnesses he'd bestowed. Father was mercurial, to be certain, but he wouldn't spend so many hours with her if he found her as repugnant as his wife did.

"Father is kind to you?" asked Prudence with raised brows.

Nan's expression matched hers. "Is that so shocking? I know he doesn't allow many people in his study, but he was very insistent I should have a refuge from your mother—"

Katherine's teacup clattered, and all three ladies looked like deer scenting a predator.

"He allows you into his study?" asked Rosanna.

"'Insistent' was the word she used," mumbled Katherine.

Cold settled into her heart, and prickles ran down her spine, though Nan couldn't explain why she felt such dread. Father had been odd at times, but he had been kind. More so than most. Yet the phantom of her earlier sentiments hovered in the back of her heart, and it was all the more difficult the bat aside the discomfort flitting through her when his daughters all stared at her with varying degrees of concern and disbelief.

Prudence cleared her throat, and her words came out carefully. "Nan, I am very glad to hear that, but I believe I know him better than any of our siblings. Before my marriage, I managed the household. He prized my good sense and work ethic, and though I do love him in many complicated ways, I can say without hesitation that he is selfish through and through."

Lips trembling, Prudence blew out a sharp breath and waited to compose herself before she spoke again. "Mother is more obvious in her cruelty, but Father is just as bad. Worse in some ways, for he is more manipulative. Quick to compliment and praise perhaps, but only to get his way—"

"I have only seen kindness from him," said Nan, though her heart shivered, reminding her of those small, lingering doubts.

"And I could say the same," said Prudence with a sad smile. "Until I chose to marry a man he deemed unworthy of me. Papa has little patience for people. He would rather spend his time in a book—"

"Amen," murmured Katherine.

That drew a sharp laugh from Prudence, and she sent her sister a wry smile. "I will admit there are plenty of times that I would rather deal with fictional people than the real sort, but the truth is that he cares only about his comfort. Papa would be quite content if the world outside his study disappeared altogether. Even his children are mostly a burden, and when I left him to manage things on his own, he was angry and bitter. He didn't understand why I would 'take such a step down in the world.' As though being with the man I loved and building a family with him was an annoyance."

Shaking that away, Prudence straightened and gave Nan a sad smile. "He is cordial enough when our paths cross, but now that I am not at his beck and call, he treats me with the same indifference as everyone else."

Silence met that, and Nan felt as though the ground was sinking beneath her, and though she was seated, she felt unsteady.

"He threatened to turn me out of the house to coerce Benjamin into breaking the entail," said Katherine, picking a bit of lint from her skirts, and both Prudence and Rosanna gaped as readily as Nan did when she made that stark announcement.

"What?" whispered Prudence.

"Why didn't you tell us?" added Rosanna, but Katherine waved it away.

"I married before it became an issue, so I didn't think it mattered," she replied, but as indifferent as her tone was, Nan felt the darkness and ache beneath her words as Katherine detailed the threats he'd leveled against Benjamin and her. Though Nan was happy to know that it ended far better with her blissfully wed to her dear David, she couldn't help but wonder at the similarities between their situations.

Could Father be doing so again? If so, why treat her kindly? Her father-in-law hadn't ingratiated himself with Katherine, so surely this must be different. Yet there was a common thread between so many of their conversations. One that arose again and again with such frequency that no matter how Nan wished to ignore it, she couldn't deny the commonality.

"He wants me to convince Benjamin to break the entail," whispered Nan, her gaze fixed on her lap as her fingers twisted in the fabric, her needle and sewing notions abandoned to the side. Her throat tightened, her words sticking to her tongue, but she forced them out. "He has spoken of little else. Brings it up in every conversation."

Sucking in a deep breath, she forced her tremors to calm as she turned her gaze to Prudence. "Are Whitley Court's finances truly so bad that it will crumble if he doesn't break it? Benjamin refuses to tell me, and I am not certain I can trust your father's word anymore."

Prudence's expression pinched, and her eyes filled with sorrow, making her answer clear before she spoke the words. "Whitley Court is profitable enough. Thriving, in fact. The land is good and their tenants are hardworking, providing a steady income that many families envy, but Mama and Papa desire more. Their tastes are too fine for their income, and they live to the edge of their means, unable to set aside much in the way of savings or dowries. If they showed a little self-restraint, there would be no discussions of selling off bits of the property or mortgaging."

"The only ones who wish to break the entail are them," added Katherine, her gaze lowering to her lap. "Grandfather placed it to protect Whitley Court from his spendthrift son, and Father will be the end of our family's legacy if Benjamin gives in."

Nan's breath shuddered, and she tried to hold onto her composure, forcing herself to calm, but after weeks of suffering Mrs. Leigh's tender care and fretting over Benjamin's silence, discovering Father's duplicity was one trial too many. Her chin trembled, her breaths jerking as she tried to seize control once more, but there was no stopping it.

The walls pressed in on her as memories flooded her mind, bringing forth every compliment and kindness he'd bestowed.

"*...my daughter...*"

How quickly he'd adopted that term, wishing her to view him as her father. And how quickly she'd lapped up every crumb of affection he'd bestowed. No matter how she tried to justify his actions or erase the doubts in her heart, Nan couldn't deny the truth she felt in their words.

That man had lied to her. Used her. Manipulated her.

A sob broke free, and Nan's cheeks blazed red, but she couldn't stop the tears from pouring any more than she could stop her heart from fracturing. How blind had she been? So eager to find a father who loved her that she ignored the signs of his duplicity and embraced the man.

Father. Had a word ever tasted so bitter? Caused so much pain?

Nan's vision blurred, and she was lost to the world, engulfed in the pain that followed this awakening. Arms folded around her, and through the mess of tears, she saw Rosanna and Prudence on either side, holding her fast as she sobbed whilst Katherine sat on the edge of her seat, looking eager to do something to comfort her, though there was no saving her from her blindness.

Mr. Leigh had recognized her weakness and exploited it. Had made her feel loved. Had made her love him in return. The father she'd always desired.

Fighting through the words, Nan unfolded the whole of her woes, detailing all that Mr. and Mrs. Leigh had done since her arrival, and though she wished to keep back her concerns about Benjamin, they were too wrapped up in her present agony to be overlooked. It all tumbled forth, broken by tears and stuttering breaths.

Nan had no clock on hand to tell her how long it took, for she circled back and forth between various thoughts, returning to previous ones to repeat them before moving on to others. With her heart and mind such a muddled mess, it was a miracle she managed anything coherent, but it was some time before she finished.

"Oh, you poor dear," whispered Rosanna, holding fast to Nan's hand, which was tucked in Rosanna's lap. Prudence added nothing, her arm simply banded around Nan's shoulders as though holding the young lady together.

"Have you spoken to Benjamin about this?" asked Katherine.

Nan sniffed, her eyes cast down. "He is oblivious. Your mother paints criticisms as praise, and he doesn't question it. She lies and tells him how much she adores me, and he believes her. And your father…"

That word broke, and Nan struggled to speak. Instead, she offered, "They are your parents, and though they frustrate him, he is rather blind when it comes to them. If I were to tell him everything, he might simply dismiss it. Or not speak about it at all. He refuses to acknowledge anything is the matter, though I know he is struggling with the whole entail business. He doesn't even know that I know about it—"

A hiccup drew her up short, and Nan raised her eyes to the ceiling as though that might provide answers. "And he has done so much for me. Should I burden him further by placing a wedge between him and his parents?"

"Oh, Nan, do you think your marriage will survive with our mother placing a wedge between you and Benjamin?" said Katherine with a sigh. "You cannot have a marriage if you do not trust one another. As my husband told Benjamin recently, it is a yoke that binds man and woman together for the duration of this life, and you cannot thrive or even survive if you refuse to pull together. You cannot hope to have a successful and happy marriage if you do not tell him what is troubling you."

Nan opened her mouth to argue, but she stopped when Katherine held up a staying hand.

"I know Benjamin is keeping secrets as well, but if you want him to trust you, you have to trust him. If you both hold back, waiting for the other to move first, you will go nowhere—and I say this from the perspective of one who held onto far too many secrets during my courtship. I realize now that I couldn't fully love and cherish David if I didn't trust him to love me in return," she said, her dark eyes blazing with such certainty that though Nan shuddered at the thought, she couldn't help but feel the truth of those words.

"Why must you speak sense?" murmured Nan. "I had hoped for a simpler solution."

"You could always leave him. You are intelligent and capable, and no doubt, you could find a way to provide for yourself. You did so before Benjamin arrived, after all," replied Katherine with a gimlet eye.

The shock of those words pierced the teary haze surrounding her. The thought made everything inside Nan tense, her heart rejecting that possibility without consideration.

"I thought so," added Katherine, a faint smile curling her lips. "Honesty is the better course, frightening though it may be."

"But know that we are here for you," said Prudence, giving Nan's shoulder another squeeze.

Rosanna nodded. "Anything you need, simply say it."

"Given what you've gone through, it may sound hollow," added Katherine, "but you are a Leigh now. You are our sister, for better or worse. We are doing our best to help Benjamin, and we hope to do the same for you."

Nan nodded, her heart warming at the thought, though the remnant marks Mr. Leigh had left made it difficult to fully embrace that truth at present. However, it didn't stop her from accepting the possibility.

Her sisters.

Chapter 36

Pacing the length of his bedchamber, Benjamin turned on his heel and returned to his starting point, making a small path through the space. Pausing, he let out a huff and turned toward the door. Staying here wasn't doing any good. Granted, he didn't know where else to go, but surely there were other possibilities.

Yet when Benjamin opened his door, he halted at the sight of Father's study door standing open. Raised voices echoed from inside, which made the startling moment all the stranger, for Mother and Father rarely bothered with conversation of any sort. But a lifetime of experience had him closing his ears to anything he might overhear between the pair; it was never good.

However, his escape route would take him directly past that door, and it was bound to draw attention, which was just as terrible as listening in to anything the pair were "discussing." Backing up, he tried to close the door quietly, but Father's voice called out.

"Benjamin, is that you?"

Closing his eyes, he stilled, hoping to once more throw his parents off the scent.

"I know you're out there. Come here," said Father.

With a sigh, Benjamin did as bidden, closing the bedchamber door behind him. Feeling like a man facing the gallows, he forced himself not to show weakness, his feet striding forward without hesitation as he entered that most holy of sanctuaries. Mother stood before the desk, her hands on her hips and a frown on her lips, whilst Father sat at his desk, a book in his hands, peering over his reading spectacles.

"You wished to see me?" asked Benjamin.

"Have you come to your senses? It's been a fortnight since our last discussion, and I am done being patient."

Drawing in a breath, Benjamin tried to hold onto his strength, but today had already been so wretched, and his spirits hadn't the fortitude to manage another battle.

"Are you ready to do your duty to your family and your wife?" prodded Father. "If you care for her, my boy, there's no need to hesitate. I can send for the lawyer, and we'll have the whole agreement signed and formalized in a trice."

"I appreciate your patience, but—"

"Would you deny your bride?" asked Father, his spectacles dipping lower down his nose as he stared at Benjamin over the top. "Do you truly care so little about her?"

"I care deeply for her," said Benjamin with a huff. "Of course I do. Nan is brilliant, and I am lucky to have her, but I cannot break the entail—"

"Then you ought to let her go, my dear boy," said Mother, her frown growing more pronounced as she glanced between her husband and son. "If you do not wish to provide for her or break the entail, annulment is the only solution."

Both men stared back at her.

"Are you mad?" asked Father, and Benjamin couldn't think of anything more fitting to say.

Mother held up placating hands. "Consider it, my dear boy. She is so very unhappy, and it would be selfish to hold her here if she wishes to go. I've spoken to the girl, and she is amenable to the idea."

"What?" Benjamin gaped, his blood running cold as it froze

him through. "She wants an annulment?"

"Gertrude—" said Father with a scowl.

"Hear me out," she said. "If you refuse to consider breaking the entail, then the least you can do is annul your marriage and find an heiress or a lady with a large dowry. That would bring the necessary capital into the family. You could remarry someone who is less of a burden—"

"Nan isn't a burden!" spat Benjamin. "Do not call her that. Not ever."

Mother jerked back, her hands rising even higher. "I mean no disrespect, my dear boy, but she never wanted the marriage in the first place. Do you want to hold her here if she is so unhappy? Surely I haven't failed so greatly as a mother that I raised a son to be so selfish."

Father watched the pair, his brows rising, but he remained silent as Benjamin struggled with that accusation. Was he being selfish? Their marriage was intended to be a boon to them both, and he knew Nan had often thought herself more selfish in having accepted it, but had her feelings shifted? The Nan he'd spoken to that afternoon certainly wasn't content with her situation.

Benjamin's jaw clenched, his muscles straining as he fought to remain in place, though his feet wished to leave. "Nan is happy."

With brows raised, Mother moved to stand before him, her hand rising to his cheek in that familiar way of hers, but she used the movement to draw his attention to her.

"Are you certain of that?" she asked, the words low and gentle—and with far too much pity for Benjamin to bear. "She has grown paler and more wan the past few weeks. Perhaps she accepted your proposal out of fear or obligation, but what if she has grown to resent her situation? If security was her only consideration, we can provide for her in other manners. It isn't too late to correct this mistake."

Benjamin jerked from her touch and glanced between his parents. "Is there anything else you wish to discuss?"

Father's brow arched, and he waved a hand in dismissal. "That will be all."

Needing no further prodding, Benjamin turned on his heel and fled. Yet he knew not where to go. Standing in the corridor, he glanced left and right. Whilst one path led back to his bedchamber, the other offered the out-of-doors. Yet the world was too drenched to wander about, and his usual escapes were unavailable, leaving him with the same conundrum that had led him to his bedchamber in the first place.

Benjamin had nowhere to go. The walls squeezed in on him, and he longed to quit the place, but the closest thing to solitude he could find in this world was in his bedchamber. Giving in to the inevitable, he returned and cast off his jacket, slinging it across the armchair in the corner before he fell onto the bed.

Annulment. The word sent chills skittering through him, and they settled in his stomach, making it churn as he considered Nan's coldness this afternoon. But surely, marriage to him was preferred over living as a poor schoolmistress. Nan had been pleased about the dresses he'd purchased her, after all. There was no denying her joy when she'd eagerly shown her bounty.

His muscles slackened, and Benjamin lay limply, staring at the canopy overhead without seeing the boards stretching above him. Did he truly think bribes would keep Nan happy? The lady's heart was so full of sweetness and love, and her ready wit never failed to make him laugh. To say nothing of her ethereal beauty. And Nan was well-read and far more studious than Benjamin could ever hope to be.

Did he truly think tossing a few dresses at her would be enough to secure her affection?

Memories of their nights spent together surfaced, softening the edges of that recrimination. They may be silly little moments, but Benjamin couldn't help but think that she adored his company as much as he enjoyed hers. That soft laughter in the darkness. The feel of her head resting against his chest. Her fingers brushing unconscious touches along his ribs.

In the silence, he lay there as his thoughts stormed about, tossing possibilities and probabilities at him remorselessly. The rain beating against the window slowed as the clouds cleared, and the sun dipped lower along the horizon, but he hardly noticed it or the time ticking away.

Surely Nan wasn't so very unhappy that she would wish to quit him as readily as she'd quit Whitley Court that afternoon. If her time here had soured, there must be something he could do to restore that good humor once more. Benjamin didn't know what he was going to do, but surely he could make Nan happy just as she made him. There wasn't another person who could entice him to spend so much time trapped in Whitley Court.

That meant something, didn't it?

Footsteps in the corridor had Benjamin's ears pricking. No doubt it was just a servant scurrying about their business, but he couldn't help but listen. When the footsteps paused before his door, he jerked upright, staring at it, and when a quiet knock followed, he pushed off the bed and flung the door open.

With wide eyes, Nan stared at him, her hand still poised to knock, and she lowered it. "So, you are home. Your mother said you were out."

Stepping out of the doorway, Benjamin motioned for her to enter. He tried to think of something to say, but his mind supplied nothing useful.

"I am happy to find you here." Nan clasped her hands before her. He motioned for her to sit on the bed, but she remained standing, though Benjamin wasn't certain she had noticed his invitation. Her gaze was distant, and her fingers twisted as she shifted from foot to foot. "I need to speak with you."

He stiffened, his brows rising, and as much as he wished to sit down, only the habit of a lifetime kept him from doing so whilst the lady remained standing.

"Are you unhappy?" he asked, somehow finding the words he didn't wish to speak.

Nan's throat contracted, and she did not meet his gaze, making Benjamin's whole body feel all the heavier, as though gravity itself was pulling on him harder than before.

"I am finding it difficult to be happy at Whitley Court," she said.

"Are you going to leave me?" he blurted.

Nan's eyes widened, her gaze snapping to his. "I said nothing about leaving."

"But you are unhappy—"

"I am, but I said nothing about leaving," she replied, her muscles stiffening as she stared at him. "But clearly, it is on your mind."

Benjamin let out a sharp breath. "I can think of nothing else."

"I see…" Nan's voice was so quiet he could hardly hear her, but her eyes fell to the ground once more. "Do you wish to be free of me?"

Jerking back, Benjamin scowled, his brows and lips pulling sharp lines. "Of course not. But I do not wish you to be miserable and force you to stay if you are miserable with me—"

"I never said I was miserable with you!" Once more her eyes met his, her gaze filled with such confusion. "I am unhappy at Whitley Court, but it has nothing to do with you. Your parents have done their utmost to drive me from this house, and I cannot bear it another day."

Benjamin's muscles slackened, and a new weight settled in his middle as he tried to grasp her meaning.

Nan turned away from him, her hands gesturing as she attempted to pace, but there was hardly enough space with one of them, let alone two, so she surrendered and dropped onto the bed as words spilled forth, dredging up all the misery Mother and Father had inflicted on her.

And Benjamin couldn't help but stare at her as tears gathered in her eyes.

Having even a brief affirmation that leaving wasn't foremost in her thoughts was enough to calm his racing pulse and clear his thoughts. But the hole they left behind was quickly filled with a new concern. For weeks—months, really—Nan had been tormented and never spoken a word of it. Suffering in silence and pretending all was well.

All while Benjamin had thought her greatest concern was her wardrobe.

"I couldn't bring myself to tell you because they are your parents, and I didn't want to cause you more trouble, but I cannot remain silent any longer—"

"You should've told me, Nan," he said with a frown. "I know they are my parents, but you are my wife. How could you lie to me and pretend nothing was amiss?"

From the moment she'd confessed to her sisters-in-law, Nan had known this conversation was coming, and she certainly hadn't wanted to draw out the suspense by letting it linger, unspoken. Yet in that short time since the decision had been made, she had already spent much time thinking about how it would go. A sharp word perhaps, though mostly because it would take some convincing for him to believe her accusations. Certainly a heaping portion of excuses to explain away the simple miscommunications that must have caused the rift between his wife and his parents.

Yet he stood there, glaring at her not because he thought his parents were incapable of such behavior but because she hadn't told him.

"Pardon?" she asked, her spine stiffening. Nan tried to moderate her tone, just as she tried to keep her temper in check, but now that the dam had been opened in front of his sisters, it felt as though the floodgate was unable to shut once more. Despite recognizing the trouble afoot, Nan couldn't grasp hold of enough self-control to exercise empathy and patience in the face of Benjamin's ill-placed frustrations.

"I have done my utmost to see to your comfort and happiness, Nan, and though I know I've fallen short at times, I cannot believe you'd assume I would knowingly abandon you to such vitriol. How could you keep this from me? What have I done to earn your distrust?"

"Do not speak of secrets and trust, Benjamin Leigh!" Rising to her feet, she leveled a finger at him. "You wish me to be open with my troubles, but you refuse to speak to me of yours. I know about the money. I know about the entail. I know you are struggling with your own demons, and you refuse to share them with me, yet you expect me to share with you?"

"I was protecting you, Nan," he replied with a huff. "I am your husband, and my duty is to take care of you. To provide for you. I've done a wretched job of it so far, but the least I could do was shield you from that—"

"From what? From my life? My future?"

"Your father—"

Nan groaned, her hands clenching. "My father! Must you bring him into every conversation—"

A creak of the floorboards in the corridor stopped her short, and she glared at the door. Servants were certainly known to eavesdrop, but in the pit of her stomach—in the very darkness of her furious heart—Nan knew who was standing outside the door, eagerly lapping up every angry morsel.

"Why shouldn't I?" continued Benjamin, though Nan was no longer listening to him. Striding to the door, she ripped it open, and Mrs. Leigh stood on the other side, her eyes wide. The lady stood there for only a moment, gaping at Nan before affecting a concerned frown.

"Oh, dear. I heard raised voices," she said, glancing around Nan to her son with that same look of feigned innocence that had blinded Benjamin so many times before. "Not arguing, are we?"

Chapter 37

Nan didn't think she had any restraint left in her, but the fact that she stepped around Mrs. Leigh, rather than bowling through her, ought to make Nan worthy of sainthood. Benjamin called after her, but Nan ignored him and stomped down the hall, making haste down the stairs and to the front door.

A gray world greeted her, and though the last vestiges of her good sense knew the weather was too fickle to venture out at present, Nan couldn't remain in this house another moment. Drawing in a deep breath, she reveled in the moisture-laden air that was free of the scents and sounds of Whitley Court. That cleanness helped to wash away a bit of the gloom in her heart, though anger and frustration quickly expanded to fill in those gaps.

She couldn't bear it anymore. Mrs. Leigh's interference. Mr. Leigh's duplicity. The weight of expectations and entitlement that pressed down on her the moment she ventured into society. It all lifted as Nan stepped onto the sodden gravel, and without plan or purpose, she gave her feet free rein as she hurried across the drive and onto the lawn.

"Nan!" Benjamin moved after her, but Mother stepped in his path, holding a hand between them. He tried to move around her, but she adjusted, keeping him trapped.

"Don't you think it's time to let her go, my dear boy? Can't you see her misery?" Then, with that familiar movement, Mother patted his cheek and said, "Let her go."

Jerking out of her hold, Benjamin scowled at her. "It is none of your business. Get out of my way."

Mother gaped at him. "You would speak to your mother in such a manner? How dare you be so disrespectful!"

Glaring at the lady, Benjamin had to remind himself that she was both a lady and his mother, and whether or not she deserved it, he needed to treat her with respect. But with Nan's confession still burning in his brain, he did not soften his tone when he spoke.

"Out of my way, Mother. Now," and rather than waiting for her to do as bidden, he forced his way past her. Moving as quickly as Nan was, Benjamin took the stairs two at a time, catching sight of her through the parlor window as he passed the doorway.

"Nan!" he called as he threw open the front door and hurried after her. The only sign she gave that she heard him was a quickening of her steps, and Benjamin put on an extra burst of speed. "Please, Nan."

Grabbing for her hand, he tried to stop her, but she yanked free of his hold and didn't slow. With fists at her side and a hard scowl pointed into the distance, Nan marched forward. Benjamin planted himself in front of her, and when she tried to dodge around him, her foot slipped on the wet grass. Putting a hand on her elbow, he steadied her before she tumbled to the ground.

Nan pulled free once more, but before she could continue, Benjamin leapt in front of her and blurted, "Please don't leave me. I know I've been a fool, but surely we can find a way to live together. Surely we needn't resort to an annulment—"

"Why do you keep mentioning that?" she asked with a scowl. "I am not going to cut ties with you. We are married!"

Benjamin straightened, and he stood there silent as he forced his pulse to slow. "You aren't leaving."

Setting her hands on his hips, Nan drew in a deep breath and turned her face to the heavens. After a moment, she relaxed and faced him once more, though her scowl hadn't eased.

"I am angry with you. Furious, in fact. I long to scream and rail at you and all the frustrations I've had to bear of late. I cannot bear another moment in that wretched house at present, and if I am forced to speak with your mother, I shan't be responsible for what I will do or say to her. However, none of that means our marriage is over, Benjamin."

Though that statement did help to ease the strain as his ribs squeezed his heart, the world had shifted one too many times in too short a time for Benjamin to fully understand and accept that assurance.

Letting out a low sigh, some of the tension eased from Nan's shoulders. "And it is a moot point, Benjamin Leigh. Despite what your mother says, an annulment isn't so easy to obtain. I've been reading about it—"

"You have?" Whatever calm he'd managed disappeared at that moment, and Benjamin stared at his wife as his heart threatened to pound straight through his ribs.

Giving a guttural groan, Nan turned her face to the skies again, her hands planted on her hips. A moment later, she faced him again.

"I did so because I was afraid you might want one, you fool. Your *dear* mother planted the idea in my head, and though I know better than to trust a single word that comes from her lips, I was afraid she might manipulate you to leave me. I wanted to ensure you couldn't—regardless of her meddling."

Nan's posture softened, and she crossed her arms, looking at him from the corner of her eye. "We spoke those vows without coercion or deceit, and short of an act of Parliament, we are husband and wife forevermore, regardless of whether or not we've shared the intimacies your mother has been so desperate for us to avoid. Unless you have more connections and money than I am aware of, I doubt either of us has the means to attempt it, even if we wished it."

Benjamin blinked at her. "And you don't wish it?"

"Do you?" she shot back, her arms tightening around her chest.

"Not in the slightest."

Those arms loosened, though Nan remained rigid as she met his gaze. "Neither do I."

Brows drawing tight together, Benjamin asked, "So we are arguing over an annulment neither of us desires? Not that we could obtain it, even if we did."

Nan stared at him, her expression still cold and impassive. "We are arguing because your parents are wretched, and when I told you just how awful they were, you were more concerned that I hadn't told you than you were with their behavior. You accused me of lying to you."

Knowing that his marriage was still secure (legally, that was), Benjamin's emotions ebbed, easing away with each heartbeat.

This afternoon had been too convoluted for him to recall the details of even a few minutes ago, for he had spoken without thinking, but a vague recollection of those very words swept into his thoughts. Of course, Nan had returned his temper tit for tat, but some semblance of rational thought was returning once more, and it warned him that admitting such was a most terrible idea.

"Might we take a moment?" he said, nodding to the tree in the distance.

As Benjamin hadn't told her about it, Nan couldn't have known she'd been headed to his favorite thinking spot, and this discussion certainly required such a special place. He offered his arm to her, and his breath stilled as he waited to see if she would take it. Nan didn't fully look at it, her own still crossed before her. Then, with another deep breath, she lowered hers and slid one through his.

Benjamin tried to gather his thoughts during the short trip to the oak tree. He truly did. But the best he could do was steady his pulse and allow himself a moment to gather his composure. When they reached the trunk, he helped her down, and it was only when she was settled against it that he recalled Nan was wearing one of her new dresses—which she seemed to remember at the same time, for her eyes widened a fraction.

With a huff, Nan seemed to shake the concern away and settled against the wood, and Benjamin was thrilled to find it was wide enough for him to seat himself beside her. She took hold of him once more, her arm twining with his as she leaned into him. Benjamin rested his head back against the trunk, and they sat in silence for a long moment.

Nan sniffled, and Benjamin looked over, but she turned away.

"Perhaps we can attempt to discuss this again?" he asked.

"Assuming your mother doesn't conveniently interrupt again." Nan's words had a watery quality to them, but she spoke evenly enough to testify she wasn't crying, which allowed him a touch of peace. "Some part of me was afraid you wouldn't follow, and that she would finally convince you to leave me."

Benjamin sighed. "Impossible. I want you as my wife. I was only afraid you regretted our marriage."

Nan turned red eyes to him, her brows knitted together, and though they were in an awkward position, he lifted his free hand to her cheek and brushed away a little tear that had escaped.

"Tell me what they've been doing to you, Nan. I want to hear it all, now that my wits aren't rattled. I fear I was so discomposed that I heard only one word in three."

With them snuggled together beneath the branches of the massive oak that had been there longer than Whitley Court, he heard the details anew. Nan spoke evenly this time, her words measured but firm as she recounted everything from the first moments she arrived to the present, and though Benjamin's

A Debt of Honor

grip on her hand tightened, he said nothing, allowing her to unburden herself as he took on one of his own.

"I am sorry, Nan," he murmured. "I ought to have seen what was happening, but I didn't. The only excuse I can offer in my defense is that Mother is usually more direct in her criticisms. She doesn't demure in showing her displeasure with Katherine or my other sisters, and she truly seemed to enjoy your company so very much."

Benjamin paused, wondering how to proceed when the previous attempt to broach the subject had gone so awry. "However—"

Nan stiffened, her eyes swinging to his as they narrowed on him. "However?"

Clearing his throat, he added, "I do wish you had said something to me sooner. I do not know why you didn't tell me what was happening."

Relaxing once more, Nan sighed. "I didn't realize what your father was doing until today, so there was nothing I could've done on that front. However, I hardly knew you when your mother began her campaign to rid the family of me. How was I to know you would believe me? You didn't even understand her insults when she spoke them in front of you."

"Touché," murmured Benjamin with a frown.

"And..." Nan paused and drew in a deep breath, letting it and the words out in a rush, "...once I began to wonder if I ought to, it was clear you were keeping secrets, and I may have been a touch hurt that you wouldn't confide in me. Then your father told me about the entail..."

With a grimace, Benjamin added, "And tried to convince you to use your 'womanly ways' to win my agreement."

Nan shuddered and leaned in closer, so Benjamin shifted his arm, bringing it around her shoulders to draw her closer.

"That is a memory I can do without," she mumbled.

Pressing a kiss to her head, Benjamin sighed. "I apologize for not telling you everything, but it is my job to provide for you and protect you. Admitting that my father is threatening to cast us out is hardly fulfilling either role."

"I am not your pet, Benjamin. I am your wife. I wish to be of assistance, but I cannot if I do not know what is troubling you. I know I have gotten the better end of this marriage—"

"Pardon?" Benjamin leaned away, turning enough so he didn't have to crane his neck to see her.

"Do not pretend that this has been a marriage of equals," she said with a frown. "It is impossible not to feel like a burden when I brought no dowry, I have none of the skills of a lady, and—"

"And nothing. This isn't some exchange of goods, Nan. I love you. Even if you brought nothing else into this marriage, I would count myself lucky."

Chapter 38

Brows shooting upward, Nan stared at him. "You what?" But Benjamin didn't seem to hear her. "I have so little purpose in this world. I was created to break this entail. If I don't do it, what do I have left?"

"You have purpose, Benjamin," she whispered, squeezing his hand.

"I am the heir to an estate, but what of it? My father is still alive, and I haven't inherited yet. I do what I can to aid our steward, but I spend far too much of my time pursuing amusements. Then you came along, and what you call a burden, I call a purpose. Meaning. Something to care about beyond entails and contracts."

Meeting her eyes, he smiled. "I have been happier the last two months whilst caring for this 'burden' than I have been in years before it. I love to be of service to you. I love making you happy. I love you."

There were those words again, and Nan felt her eyes prickle, but she forced herself not to give in to the sentiment. And for once, she had control enough over that traitorous nose to keep from showing just how much that confession meant to her.

"How can you say you love me and keep me at arm's length?" she asked.

"You've done the same. For months, you've been miserable and have hidden it away. I know you had your reasons, but so did I. Your father entrusted you to my care, and I have fallen short of that expectation again and again—"

Nan put her free hand over his mouth, forcing him to stop. "I need you to understand something important, Benjamin. I have tried to talk to you about this so many times, and you haven't listened, but I need you to now."

His forehead furrowed, his eyes looking none too pleased at the thought (though she couldn't say if it was his not having listened before or her silencing him), but he didn't speak when Nan released him.

"Again and again, you've placed my father on a pedestal, and though I know you think him a saint among men, I assure you he was not. You say he cared for me, but he left me without money, connections, or even the skills to survive. To be honest, I am surprised he bothered to write to you, for he gave little consideration to my future before his death. He had decades before that moment to provide for me, yet I was only given a letter, hastily written at the last possible moment."

Holding fast to Benjamin's hand, she gazed into his eyes, hoping he would hear and understand. "You've done more for me than he ever did. He spent his time and money on *his* pursuits and *his* students, whilst I was left alone in old, ill-fitting clothes, reading whatever books he deigned to bring home."

Gaze falling to her lap, Nan swallowed, but it did nothing to ease the lump in her throat. "Perhaps he was too broken after Mother passed or perhaps he was simply ill-equipped to manage a daughter on his own, but I do not recall him ever showing an interest in me beyond academic pursuits. I longed for any sign of affection and attention, and to this day, I don't know if he felt anything for me. He certainly didn't show it in any meaningful manner."

Each word felt like a stone, piling atop Benjamin, and their combined weight threatened to crush him. His heart crumpled beneath her admission, leaving his chest hollow and empty as he tried to grasp onto some explanation that might align her words with the world as he knew it. Surely there was a mistake. Some way to reconcile Nan's description of her father with the man who had done so much for him. Yet even as he flinched away from it, longing to find some mistake in her confession, he knew this dear lady well enough that he couldn't believe she would say this lightly.

The more she spoke, the more he saw his father reflected in the words—someone selfish enough to always place his desires before those of the children he created. Benjamin's pain shifted, taking new shape as he recognized an echo of his heartbreak in Nan. The love of a rejected child. Yes, his parents had doted on him. Spoiled him, even. But Benjamin had needed a father who stirred himself to do more than simply toss money and treats at him, or give a few glowing words and a pat on the head.

Especially as the affection heaped on him had nothing to do with Benjamin Leigh as a person. Just as the heir who could break their hateful entail.

"I thought your father was a good man," he whispered, pulling the words free like a tooth-puller with rusty pliers.

Nan stiffened and looked at him. "I didn't say he wasn't, Benjamin. I think he truly adored you boys. He loved that school, and he believed in being a good man—honorable and upright. But a person can believe things while still falling short of that ideology."

Settling into his embrace once more, she added, "And though it doesn't give me much comfort to know he wrote to you on his deathbed, it does help a little to know Father did not wish for me to be left alone. In the end, he was concerned for me—if only a little."

Did he need more evidence that Nan was a superior woman? Her heart was far more taxed and broken than his, but she defended his idealized vision of his hero, giving him hope.

Yet no matter how worthy the lessons Mr. Price had taught him, Benjamin's memory of the man dimmed and darkened.

How could he ever adore someone who had overlooked and ignored his Nan?

The pair sat there, entwined beneath the oak tree with only the sound of the occasional raindrop striking the leaves overhead to break the silence. Wet seeped into her backside, and the bark was hard against her back, but Nan couldn't think of a more comfortable situation. Benjamin's arms were wrapped around her, his body so close, and despite all the pain that had preceded this moment, she felt as though something had clicked into place. Where before, they'd attempted to fit two pieces of a puzzle in the wrong way, now they were turned the right way around, snapping perfectly together.

And that had her thoughts turning back to something important that had been overlooked during their argument. Seated side by side so snugly, it wasn't easy to meet Benjamin's gaze, but this question most certainly warranted seeing the whole of his expression. As Nan felt certain about the answer, she couldn't help but ask for confirmation. Nor could she help a slight shiver at the thought that, like many things said in the heat of the moment, it might not have been the whole truth.

"Did you mean it?" she asked, and when that was met with a puzzled look in return, Nan realized only then that Benjamin did not have a window into her thoughts and could not understand the context of her question. "You said you loved me. Do you?"

Benjamin's brow crinkled, and he gazed at her as though she were speaking gibberish. "Of course I do. I liked you from the very first. Loving you was inevitable."

Nan tried to duck away from him, but his finger was faster, coming up to tap her wrinkled nose.

"Hello there, my friend," he teased.

Despite having heard his confession, it still felt strange and petrifying to admit her feelings, but Nan couldn't leave it unsaid. "I love you, too, Benjamin."

And despite the self-assured manner in which he'd expressed himself, her husband's eyes opened as though fully astonished that she might feel the same.

"It was inevitable," she whispered.

Before Nan knew what he was about, Benjamin's lips were on hers, his arms tightening as he drew her even closer. Though her eyes remained open at first, when the suddenness of his action faded, she closed them and sank into his embrace, meeting his urgency with her own.

They hadn't shared enough kisses for them to be passé or unexceptional, but the others had been sweet or exploratory. Joyful even. This was almost desperate, as though releasing the last of the anxiety and frustration of the day in this blissful moment, and Nan matched his eagerness. There was no fear. No uncertainty. Though their situation had been technically settled for some time, this moment sealed them together, husband and wife. Bound heart to heart as much as they were before the eyes of the law.

And when it slowed, Benjamin's heated gaze met hers, and Nan couldn't catch her breath at the sight of his longing burning there.

"I love you, *Mr. Leigh*," he whispered.

Nan huffed, her nose wrinkling at the sweetness infused in that endearment. No one hearing it could think Benjamin meant it as anything but a declaration straight from his heart.

"I think I need to give you a pet name as well," she replied.

"'Handsome' would do just fine."

Nan narrowed her eyes. "'Rascal' would be a better fit. Or perhaps 'Peacock.'"

Benjamin waggled his eyebrows at her, and she laughed, settling back into his side once more as she realized there was still one question left unanswered.

"So, are you going to share your secrets?" she asked, giving him a poke in the ribs.

"It sounds as though you know the whole of them." But he paused and added, "Assuming you listen to my sisters on the subject, and not Father. The estate is healthy. The entail needs to remain. He may well evict us, but I am not certain he will. As long as there is hope that I will break it, he will attempt to get on my good side."

Nan gave a hum, though even she did not know if it was a good or bad one—simply a noise that said she'd heard him. Having been so thoroughly deceived by Mr. Leigh, she didn't trust her understanding of the gentleman to say one way or another.

"What are we going to do?" she asked with a heavy sigh.

"What do you wish to do?"

Benjamin's hand settled on her arm, his fingers brushing along the skin, and for all that the question was an important one, Nan found it difficult to concentrate. Her throat tightened as she considered the possibilities, and there were too many unknowns to say anything for certain—except one.

"I do not wish to live at Whitley Court. I cannot bear to be there anymore. Not with them turning us on one another. What marriage can survive such torment?"

Nan tried her best to speak evenly—Benjamin heard it in the careful manner in which she expressed herself—but the slight quiver at the beginning gave away her feelings, despite the calmness with which she delivered it. It was not some whim or general desire; his wife was desperate to leave his parents' home. He placed another kiss on her head.

"I apologize for not seeing your pain sooner, Nan."

"And I apologize for not speaking up sooner," she said in return. "Let us agree to be honest from now on."

"Certainly," he whispered.

For all that she wanted no more secrets, some needed to remain. Just as she still tried to hide how much his father's betrayal hurt her to lessen his guilt, Benjamin couldn't let her know how much his regret weighed down his heart; for the past two months, his parents had tormented his Nan, and even her understanding and forgiveness couldn't erase his shame so easily. Time would heal those pains and bind those wounds, so he let her have her secrets, and he kept his. Neither did any harm.

But there was one he needed to reveal.

Chapter 39

Despite having spoken with Parker today, so much had happened in the interim that Benjamin had nearly forgotten Mr. Bradshaw's offer. And despite having dismissed the possibility, he knew he'd been a fool. For all that he touted taking on the responsibilities of a husband, what had he truly done to fulfill them beyond sacrificing a little time and part of his allowance?

Even if Father didn't evict them, their lives would forever revolve around his parents if they remained at Whitley Court. How much longer would he allow his inactivity to cause his wife pain? Would he be no better than their fathers, choosing their comfort over Nan's?

"If you do not wish to remain at Whitley Court, we do have an alternative." Drawing in a deep breath, Benjamin described the discussion with Parker, leaving nothing out nor softening the truth of what choosing the clerkship would mean for them. "In time, we might find stability—though that is no guarantee—and in the interim, we would be poor. If we survive the next few years, it would be due to my siblings' charity, and it could be years before we could afford anything resembling comfort—let alone luxuries."

"We do not need luxuries, Benjamin," she said, holding fast to him.

"It will be difficult—"

"But not impossible," she replied. Lifting her head just enough to meet his gaze, Nan added with a faint smile, "And I think your idea of 'poor' is far different than mine. We would have a roof over our heads, clothes on our backs, and food in our bellies."

Benjamin sighed. "Our lodgings would be tiny, and we won't be able to afford even a maid-of-all-work."

"Our lodgings would be cozy, and I know how to cook and clean far better than I know how to word invitations or set a table. Need I remind you that I did such work before you appeared in my life?"

Yet her answers didn't settle the uneasiness in his heart; the prickling frustration had plagued him from the first moment he'd landed her in a rainstorm atop a stagecoach. And though he wished to keep it hidden, for speaking such things often gave them new life, he knew he couldn't.

"Nan, this isn't going to be easy—"

Straightening, she pulled away from him and turned, tucking her legs to the side as she studied him. "I know that, and if you do not wish to follow this course, then we will have to decide upon another, but what is truly troubling you? You speak as though you are concerned for me, but I think this change will be far more difficult on you, darling."

The endearment rolled off her tongue easily, though Nan had never said such a thing to him before, and Benjamin's heart burned at the simple word, holding it tight.

"What is the matter?" she asked, nudging his chin so he looked at her.

"I came to you, offering stability and comfort, and I've landed you right back in uncertainty and hardship. I've done a poor job of giving you that which I promised when I proposed, and I cannot help but wonder if it might've been better if I'd never darkened your doorstep."

Nan's expression fell, her brow furrowing as she stared at him. "How can you think that?"

"How can I not?"

"I didn't marry you for stability or comfort, Benjamin. I will admit they were enticing, but that alone wouldn't have moved me to accept." Nan took his hand in hers, and her eyes brightened as she held his gaze. "I married you so I wouldn't be alone anymore. I was home by myself most days whilst Father taught at school. I had few friends. My days were so solitary. And it was growing worse with Father's passing. I was in a new part of town without any companionship beyond my students…"

Nan sniffed and straightened. "Then you appeared, and I thought this was a chance to belong with someone. To have a friend, at the very least. A sweetheart, hopefully. But someone to keep me company—"

Her voice broke, and she scowled at herself, swiping at her cheek as she said in a mock growl, "Before I met you, I rarely cried, and now the floodgates have opened, and I'm determined to make a ninny of myself at every possible turn."

Benjamin couldn't bear having her seated apart any longer, and he drew her into his arms once more, settling her precisely where she ought to be as she snuffled into his waistcoat.

"I can handle hardships, Benjamin," she whispered. "Labor and toiling don't frighten me if you are by my side. But I cannot bear to be alone any longer."

Nan reached up her hand to grasp his from where it draped over her shoulder, and their fingers entwined, joining them together. Though there were so many unanswered questions and so much about their future that remained precarious, Benjamin couldn't help but feel at the moment that she was right.

Together, they wouldn't just survive the hardships to come. They would be happy despite them.

…

A Debt of Honor

Avoidance was such a lovely thing—especially when it involved cuddling and kissing his wife. The trouble was that reality eventually demanded attention, bringing with it an equal portion of dread and frustration. With the large canopy overhead, they were protected from rogue raindrops, but when the leaves began to shudder in earnest, even that great covering couldn't keep them dry.

"We ought to go, or we'll catch our death," mumbled Benjamin, though he made no move to leave.

Nan sighed and straightened, pulling from his embrace. "I suppose we must return to the house."

Despite the evenness of her tone, she couldn't disguise the furrows marring her brow. Nan met his gaze with a smile, but it was more brave than joyous, and his heart sank at the sight.

"Do we?" he asked.

That drew a hint of a genuine grin. "Should we make our home beneath this tree?"

"Wouldn't that surprise my parents?" Benjamin chuckled. Then, with a shake of his head, he added, "I didn't mean that. Parker made it clear that he and the rest of my brothers-in-law discussed the situation—"

"Oh, and have I mentioned that your sisters knew something was afoot with all their questions about Mr. Bradshaw yet gave me no clue?" interrupted Nan with a frown. "That is hardly sisterly."

"And no doubt, you will find some way to twit them about it, and you do so with my blessing." Taking her hand, Benjamin raised it to his lips. Lowering it once more, he continued, "But I meant that Parker made it clear that everyone is willing to help as they can. I do not wish to abuse Rosanna's generosity, but she and Malcolm have space at Boxwood Manor. If we arrived on their doorstep, I am certain they would welcome us until we can find something suitable."

Nan's brows rose at that, and Benjamin hurried to add, "It is far, but we can walk over and send for our things later. We needn't step foot back inside Whitley Court whilst my parents are there if you do not wish it."

"Surely we ought to speak to them about our decision."

"What good would that do?" he asked with a slight shrug of his shoulders. "We have discussed the issue at length, and I have been clear that I do not wish to break the entail. I may not have been forthright in all my reasons, but I have been firm, and they will not listen. If I tell them we are leaving for me to start a new profession as a solicitor's clerk, they will have much to say and none of it good—no matter how logical the path, how coveted the position, or how highly esteemed the employer."

Benjamin squeezed her hand. "I am a grown man. We are married. This choice is ours, and though I have no doubt they will wish to discuss it, I have no interest in hearing their opinions on the matter. At best, they will bribe me to stay, and we cannot remain there. At worst, they will bully and belittle us, and I will not stand to hear them speak ill of you."

"Nor I, you," she added, giving him a firm look as though challenging him to deny the ferocity of her pledge.

"We know how it will unfold. Neither they nor we have anything new to say. It will unfold the same way it has so many times before, and though we will have to speak to them at some point, need it be tonight?"

Nan's brows rose at that, but when the branch above them shuddered, dropping several bursts of water on them, Benjamin hopped to his feet and pulled her up beside him.

"What say you, Nan? If we are to begin this journey together, let us not put it off until tomorrow. To go to Whitley Court would only be an unnecessary misery. Why invite trouble?"

A smile stretched across her face, and she held up her hand to him. Taking it, Benjamin ran out from under the tree, and the rain enveloped them.

Nan's dress was drenched in a trice, and with the mud and grass likely staining her backside, she feared it was thoroughly ruined. Hardly an auspicious beginning to a modest life. But then, her old gowns were quite suited for that work, and thankfully, Nan's caution had kept her from selling them off immediately.

Turning around, Benjamin opened his mouth to speak but stopped when he spied her, no doubt looking like a wet kitten. Veering toward the stables, he snatched a greatcoat hanging on a peg inside the door and drew it about her shoulders. He straightened it, tucking it tight around her, and standing there, she couldn't help but remember a similar day not too long ago.

Pulling the greatcoat closer, Nan smiled despite the scent of horse clinging to it. "This reminds me of the first time I knew I liked you."

Benjamin paused, his hands holding the lapels tight. "Is that so?"

"You gave me your greatcoat on the stagecoach. And I knew I could feel something more for you because here was someone who cared so much for my comfort that he was willing to sacrifice his own for my sake. It was one of the kindest things anyone has ever done for me."

His hand drifted from the greatcoat and brushed her cheek, wiping away the raindrops. "It was my honor, Nan."

Her lips trembled. "I love you, Benjamin."

And with that, she drew her arms around his neck, pulling him in for a kiss. Without hesitation, his arms slid around her, taking and giving that affection back in equal measure. Despite the rain pouring from the heavens, it felt as though the sun were blazing through the clouds, warming the world and enveloping them in a golden haze. And when they parted, Nan panted, her arms still locked around his neck.

Benjamin gazed at her with that smirk she loved and loathed, especially when it was pointed at her. "As much as I would love to keep kissing you—and believe me, I hate myself for saying this—I am getting very wet, and it is a long way to Boxwood Manor."

Nan dropped her arms with a chagrined smile. "I apologize."

"Oh, there is nothing to apologize for, love. Knowing I drive you to distraction is quite worth getting drenched."

Huffing, she poked him in the side. "Peacock."

Then he tucked his arm around her, as though she required more shielding when it was he who was engulfed by the rain, and they set off down the drive, not sparing a backward glance for Whitley Court.

Epilogue

One Year Later

For all that the sun was setting, heat radiated from the stone entry, making Benjamin dab at the sweat gathering on his temples. Clearly, someone had not informed the weather that this was England, for it was doing a fine impression of Southern Italy. But at least he was out of doors. Finally.

Boxwood Manor loomed above them, the great palatial building serving as a prime example of the neoclassical style that so many estates favored in the last century. The gray stone stood out amongst the vast greenery surrounding the building, though the sodden grass of last year was now showing a tinge of brown after so many sweltering days.

Shifting in place on the doorstep, Benjamin adjusted his jacket. He'd forgotten how snugly his evening clothes fit, and though he appreciated the gleam in Nan's gaze when he strutted about in that finery, he found himself missing his regular clothing.

"What is the matter?" she asked, turning to straighten his cravat.

Nan possessed some form of magic; watching her study and straighten the bit of linen helped to quiet the last of his irritation. Thoughts of sweltering offices, thick books, and confusing ledgers faded from his thoughts at the sight of his wife's smile.

"A rather trying day, my love. That is all," he murmured, leaning forward to press a kiss to her lips. Though he'd intended it to be a brief touch, Nan seized control, holding him close as she showed her affection with such sweetness.

A throat cleared, and Nan's cheeks blazed red as she leapt away, pressing a hand to her lips as though that might hide what they'd been doing. The butler looked dignified, as though he hadn't witnessed that private moment, and for his part, Benjamin merely laughed and gave her that satisfied smile of his.

"Peacock," she hissed.

With a bow, the butler ushered them in, and Nan took her husband's arm whilst failing to give him a proper scowl. For all that she hoped the matter would be ignored, she knew her family too well to believe their interlude would remain discreet, and as they entered the party proper, she braced herself for the inevitable.

Boxwood Manor was a fine home. The finest Nan had ever visited, and despite wearing the finest of her gowns, she couldn't help but feel a touch of heat in her cheeks as she tried to hide her bare hands from view. But Benjamin took hold of them, his unclothed fingers entwining with hers. Though the touch was meant to reassure, Nan felt more at peace remembering the moment he'd appeared without them.

The wife of a clerk didn't require fancy dresses and gloves. At Rosanna's behest, Nan had kept her favorite evening gown, and Prudence had helped to adjust her day dresses to suit her simpler life at present, but formal gloves were a luxury she refused to indulge and her everyday ones were entirely wrong for such an outfit. And though Benjamin's position required such gentlemanly vestments, he'd gone without tonight so she would not be the only one ungloved.

Benjamin winked at her, and Nan's silly nose made its feelings on the matter known as they stepped into the parlor, which was stuffed to the brim with Leighs. Whilst the siblings and spouses had taken up residence in the various chairs scattered around the vast space, the children ran to and fro, bouncing between favorite uncles and aunts as they vied for attention.

The moment they spied Benjamin, the children rushed him, making it clear to anyone with eyes how popular he was among their ranks—a fact that pleased him to no end, leaving Nan to remind him it was because in their eyes he was more peer than adult.

Benjamin made a good show of it, throwing in with the little ones as each demanded a greeting. Tickles and laughter abounded, and the adults rose to greet Nan in a more dignified manner, though little Hope made her preference known when she rocked away from Aunt Prudence's hold and reached for Aunt Nan. Taking the girl in her arms, Nan availed herself of the babe's sweet neck, nibbling on the soft skin there until the child was bubbling with laughter.

Only when Benjamin's cravat and hair were well and truly mussed did he join the others, coming up behind her with a hand to the small of her back.

"I see Nan has already commandeered Hope," he said, glancing at Prudence's empty arms.

"Now that she is pulling herself up, she rarely deigns to be held," said Katherine with a smile. "So, enjoy it while you can."

"Soon, even Mama will only be allowed to kiss and cuddle for mere seconds at a time," added Prudence, glancing at her youngest, who squirmed out of reach when her mother attempted to catch Joan up.

"It is about time you two arrived," said Malcolm with a grin. "It is usually Parker who slows dinner."

"There is no rest for a physician," said the man in question, and glancing at Benjamin, he added, "Or a clerk."

"Too right," said Benjamin. "Mr. Bradshaw is a fine employer, but he demands much of us. That said, I have learned more in the past year about land acquisition, tenant law, and the like than in the one and twenty years before it."

"Robert mentioned you have a head for such things," replied Parker.

"He's agreed to focus my education on that, and by the time I finish my clerkship, I am going to be better armed than any gentleman I know. Now, if I could only convince him it is the only thing I must learn…" said Benjamin with a chuckle. "Today he had me digging through the dullest case laws about some minuscule rulings concerning contract disputes. I know it may be useful for me to know in the future, but heaven help me, I was stuck in that stifling room, subjecting myself to death by papercuts. I am lucky to have arrived at all, for I would still be there if I hadn't found the answer Mr. Bradshaw required."

The party laughed, and Nan joined in, though for reasons entirely different from theirs. Yes, her husband was amusing as he described the drudgery found in his profession (as all did from time to time), but the truth was that the work was good for Benjamin. Beyond the income and the stability that he was determined to secure for them, the joy of a job well done resonated through him.

Her Benjamin had found purpose. Not the one he'd imagined, but that didn't lessen that triumph, and Nan beamed all the more for it.

David crossed his arms, his eyes alight with a laugh. "Mr. Bradshaw's assignment might've made you late arriving home, but it didn't keep you lingering on the doorstep for so long."

Nan forced herself to show no sign that the jest had hit its mark, but matters weren't helped when Benjamin gave her a rascally grin and said, "My wife was overcome by the sight of me in my finery. What is a fellow to do?"

"Benjamin!" said Nan, her eyes widening as the others chortled, though the ladies had the decency to look chagrined before doing so.

But Rosanna's hostess instinct surged up, saving Nan from further comments as she said, "I do love that gown on you. It is beautiful."

Nan ran her hands along the deep blue folds of fabric, her smile brightening even further. "It is my favorite, and I am always happy to have an excuse to wear it."

"It suits you," said Prudence.

"Quite," added Katherine, nudging her spectacles.

Though there had been utter honesty in Rosanna's compliment, her gaze fell to Nan's bare hands; there was no judgment there, but the quick flash of a smile warned Nan that her sister-in-law would soon "tire" of a perfectly good pair of evening gloves and insist that Nan ought to make use of them. Arching her brow, she sent a warning in return, but Rosanna was not cowed. She took far too much pleasure in finding creative manners in which to gift her brother and his wife little presents as they would not live entirely off the Tates' generosity.

But before Nan could dissuade Rosanna of any such plans, Ernest and Layton collided with each other as they ran past, and their larger bodies served as lawn boules, toppling several of the younger children in the process, which drew the attention of their parents.

"Oh, those boys," said Prudence with a shake of her head as they set to work attempting to calm their antics, but the older children ran off as though unaware that they'd caused any trouble.

Straightening, Prudence returned her attention to Nan. She added with a wince, "And I fear I must warn you: Mama is threatening to visit you soon. She paid a call on me and mentioned she might do so."

For all that the others watched her and Benjamin with wary expressions, Nan slanted a look at her husband, and at the same time, Benjamin said, "Bully," whilst Nan said, "Bribe." Which earned them puzzled looks from the rest. Nan bounced Hope, shifting the child's weight to her hip as she grinned at Benjamin.

"Mother and Father ignore us for the most part," he explained. "However, about once a fortnight or so, they cross paths with one of us. They cannot help but still hope I will break the entail."

Nan gave Hope's cheek a nibble and added, "It was irritating at first, but we've made a game of it. They either beg, bribe, or bully, and we wager on which will feature in the visit."

"Oh, Nan," said Prudence, her brows pinching together as her husband drew up beside her, placing a hand at her waist. "That is horrible."

Benjamin glanced at her, but Nan sent him a stealthy wink in return, before saying, "It was at first, but unless we wish to leave Greater Edgerton, there is no choice. We love the rest of the family too much to allow them to chase us away, so we avoid them as much as we can. They still force their way into our lives from time to time, so we've decided to be amused by it."

When Hope began rocking, Nan set the child down. She was too slow and unsteady to join in the other children's fracas, so she contented herself by tugging on the ladies' hems, pulling them up over her head as she laughed.

"That hardly sounds amusing," said Katherine with a frown.

"That would depend on what you're wagering," murmured Malcolm with a smirk that set the ladies blushing and giggling as Rosanna gaped as though affronted (an expression that lost all potency when the corners of her mouth twitched upward).

Benjamin had the good sense not to answer, but heaven help her, the rascal gave his brother-in-law a knowing grin that said far more than Nan wished to admit. Thankfully, the butler rescued her from embarrassment by announcing dinner, and the men's mischief was lost in the chaos of managing the children.

The nursemaids arrived to gather the children for their dinner in the nursery, and by the time the swarm gave their farewells, Nan was afraid for the poor cook, whose food was growing steadily colder. But neither could she stop reveling in the little affections her nieces and nephews bestowed upon her.

A life lived alone for so long, and now she was a sister and aunt to a veritable horde. When little Viola's arms pulled away from her neck, Nan rose from a crouch to find Benjamin at her side. His gaze held hers, aglow with that tenderness that warmed her days and brightened her nights, and Nan couldn't help but send out a prayer of gratitude that she'd been brave enough to accept this dear man's proposal.

She had hoped for a morsel of peace and joy when she'd married him, and now, her life overflowed with that light and beauty.

Curse his siblings, for when Nan looked at him in such a manner, Benjamin couldn't help but wish to kiss her senseless. Those light eyes burned with such happiness and a hint of longing that he nearly ignored good sense and swept her into his arms.

He offered his hand and Nan took it, and Benjamin felt the calluses that had no business marring her flesh. His brows drew together, and he turned her hand to inspect that wear. Despite all the sweetness of their life, he couldn't help but wish so very often that he could do more—

As though she could hear his thoughts, Nan shifted, drawing his fingers into focus, displaying the black splotches of ink that had dyed the skin. Calluses and stains. A matching pair.

Benjamin's gaze rose to hers, and she leaned close to whisper, "I love you."

"It was inevitable, *Mr. Leigh*," he whispered in return.

Nan's sweet nose wrinkled, and Benjamin laughed, lifting her fingers to his lips.

Exclusive Offer

Join the M.A. Nichols VIP Reader Club at

www.ma-nichols.com

to receive up-to-date information about upcoming books, freebies, and VIP content!

About the Author

Born and raised in Anchorage, M.A. Nichols is a lifelong Alaskan with a love of the outdoors. As a child she despised reading but through the love and persistence of her mother was taught the error of her ways and has had a deep, abiding relationship with it ever since.

She graduated with a bachelor's degree in landscape management from Brigham Young University and a master's in landscape architecture from Utah State University, neither of which has anything to do with why she became a writer, but is a fun little tidbit none-the-less. And no, she doesn't have any idea what type of plant you should put in that shady spot out by your deck. She's not that kind of landscape architect. Stop asking.

| Website | Facebook | Instagram | BookBub |

Printed in Great Britain
by Amazon